THE HEIGHTS

Also by Parker Bilal

Crane and Drake series

THE DIVINITIES

Makana Investigations series

THE GOLDEN SCALES
DOGSTAR RISING
THE GHOST RUNNER
THE BURNING GATES
CITY OF JACKALS
DARK WATER

Writing as Jamal Mahjoub

NAVIGATION OF A RAINMAKER
WINGS OF DUST
IN THE HOUR OF SIGNS
THE CARRIER
TRAVELLING WITH DJINNS
THE DRIFT LATITUDES
NUBIAN INDIGO

(non-fiction)

A LINE IN THE RIVER:
KHARTOUM, CITY OF MEMORY

THE HEIGHTS

Parker Bilal

This first world edition published 2019
in Great Britain and 2020 in the USA by
SEVERN HOUSE PUBLISHERS LTD of
Eardley House, 4 Uxbridge Street, London W8 7SY.
Trade paperback edition first published
in Great Britain and the USA 2020 by
SEVERN HOUSE PUBLISHERS LTD.

British Library Cataloguing in Publication Data
A CIP catalogue record for this title is available from the British Library.

ISBN-13: 978-0-7278-9028-3 (cased)
ISBN-13: 978-1-4483-0370-0 (e-book) (US only)

All Severn House titles are printed on acid-free paper.

Severn House Publishers support the Forest Stewardship Council™ [FSC™],
the leading international forest certification organisation.
All our titles that are printed on FSC certified paper carry the FSC logo.

Typeset by Palimpsest Book Production Ltd.,
Falkirk, Stirlingshire, Scotland.
Printed and bound in Great Britain by
TJ International, Padstow, Cornwall.

A barrier will divide them,
And on the Heights there will be men who
recognise each one by his look.
To those in Paradise they shall say:
'Peace be upon you.'
But they shall not enter.
And when they turn their eyes towards
the inmates of the Fire they will cry:
'Lord do not cast us among those wicked people!'

– *Al Quran*, 7:46: The Heights

Apart from Heaven's Eternity,
And yet so far from Hell!

– Edgar Allan Poe, 'Al Aaraaf' ('The Heights')

1

Like an unsettled thought, the train rattled through the tunnels beneath the city. Ruby Brown was praying to get home. That was her only concern. The baby was finally asleep, thank God, cradled against her chest in the harness, but her legs ached and her breasts were leaking. The journey was pure Hell. Ruby just wanted to be off this train. She hated the Tube. She hated the noise, the smells, the screeching wheels and the endless delays. Why couldn't it just be over?

Most of all she hated the crowds. So many people. They shuffled into the carriage, pressing up to her. Closer and closer. Why couldn't they just back off? She wanted to yell and scream at them to give her space. They didn't. Instead, they pressed in around her, digging their briefcases into her back, shoving their stupid rucksacks into her face.

It was like this every day now, thanks to Marvellous Marvin, who had chosen this moment in time to lose his job. They'd lost the place they had and now he was living with his brother while Ruby was staying with her mother again. This would have been bad enough in itself, but it also meant commuting every day from Morden, back and forth to deliver her son to school in Finsbury Park and then pick him up again. Not that she minded not having Marvin around. There hadn't been anything marvellous about him for longer than she could remember.

'I'm not fucking telling you again, Tyler! Stop it!'

Ruby ignored the frowns of disapproval from the people around her. Fuck them. She was tired. The boy was driving her insane. She couldn't take any more. He just went on and on, kicking and kicking. His foot went back and forth, knocking against the knee of the old man standing over him. Ruby ignored the man's glare. It was bad enough having to deal with the boy, let alone apologise for him. What did people expect? Tyler's foot began to move in circles, ramming out right, straight into her knee, over and over. What did he want? She'd given up trying to find an answer to that one. He wanted whatever he couldn't have. That's what it felt like. Her mother said he needed help. But her mother's head was stuck back in 1984 or whatever. She thought you could still get that kind of help on the NHS for free. Nothing was free nowadays. His smart arse teacher, Mr Perfect, said he was suffering from ADHD, that he needed to be enrolled in one of those special needs schools. Marvin, being Marvin, insisted all the boy needed was a little discipline. Not that he was ever around enough to take care of that himself. And besides, when he was around Marvin tended to let the boy do whatever the hell he liked until he lost his temper and started yelling, which made all the little ones cry.

'I said, stop it!'

Ruby leaned over and jerked his arm hard.

'Aouw!' Tyler cried, making a meal of it. More looks. As if any of them would be better at parenting than her. The boy sat still for all of ten seconds.

Her legs were aching. She had thought that letting Tyler have the only seat might calm him down. Fat chance. To add insult to injury the train had come to a halt. They were just outside Clapham Common station. This was the worst. She felt trapped. The ticking over of the engine felt like a bomb way down inside her.

What was it that made him think he could just sit there and kick her? Some kind of male instinct. And the little bastard wasn't even nine years old yet. No prizes for guessing where he got that from. She closed her eyes and wished herself far away from all of it.

They were close to the doors. She was holding onto the handrail. Behind her was another mother with a pushchair the size of a fucking SUV. She kept shifting it from side to side so the wheel dug into Ruby's ankle. Her child sat staring up at Ruby, a blonde princess on a fucking throne. The mother and her friend, a couple of snooty bitches, were giving Ruby the cold stare, but she ignored them. Why did the Tube always smell so badly? She reached out to slap Tyler's arm.

'I won't tell you again.'

Tyler sulked the same way his father did. The same sorry grudge against the world. What can you do? You can't fight nature. Of all the bad choices she had made in life, Marvin was up there at the top of the list.

Miraculously Tyler had stopped kicking. Her knees would be covered in bruises. Not that anyone was going to notice that these days. Marvin had lost interest in her that way with the arrival of the baby. He had other women now. She didn't care.

'Leave that alone!'

Tyler had turned his attention to something tucked into the corner of the baggage area to his right. She was standing over it, but she hadn't noticed it when they'd got on. One of those blue nylon bags with yellow writing on the side. She had one for the laundry. He was twisting his foot round, kicking at it, nagging. She ignored him. All he wanted was more attention. The toe of his shoe eventually found the strap and pulled it. Again and again.

'I said, leave it, Tyler!'

A woman in a suit was watching her from further down the carriage. All dolled up with make-up and lipstick. The kind of woman who looked like she never had any problems. Ruby threw her a cold stare until the bitch dropped her eyes back to her phone.

The baby began to cry. Ruby felt exhaustion wash over her. Tyler took her silence as a reason to carry on. Let him, she thought. What difference does it make? Maybe it will stop him kicking my legs.

'When are we there, Mummy?' Tyler asked. 'When, Mummy, when?'

'Soon.'

Tyler had managed to hook his foot through the tape handle. He jerked the bag forward with a kick. Ignore him and he'll lose interest. Ruby jogged the baby up and down, willing it to stop crying. The train crawled along a few hundred metres and then stopped again. It was humming to itself. The baby was getting louder. No way was she going to try feeding her in here. She avoided looking in the direction of the perfect mum with the little princess who was staring at her as if she was something you might find in a zoo. Please God, just let us get into the station. Tyler was hunched forward, kicking lightly, eyes still fixed on the bag. Ruby closed her eyes again.

Kick. Kick. Kick.

Tyler's foot thumped back and forth. His foot looped round each time, trying to catch the strap. It caught again and dragged. The bag shifted. There was something heavy inside. He kicked again. Ruby began to notice the smell. Something rotten, which she had thought at first was coming from her son. Now she was sure it was from the bag.

'Leave that alone!'

Miraculously, the train began to move. Tyler was caught off balance. His legs weren't touching the floor. When he lurched forwards, he put his foot down to stop himself falling, which pulled open one side of the bag.

That's when it rolled out, under their feet, causing people to yell and jump aside. It rolled one way and then, as the train lurched again, back down the middle of the aisle. Instinctively, people stepped aside or knocked it away from them. It was wrapped in dirty cloth and what looked like newspaper. The stench coming off it was disgusting. It filled the carriage. The train swerved and it rolled to one side. Someone nudged it back towards the centre of the aisle. The bitch looked up from her phone and swore as the object touched her fancy boot. Ruby barely registered what was happening. The baby was starting up again. The woman was suddenly on her feet, eyes wide, screaming at the top of her lungs. People all around were surging away, leaping aside, as a space cleared around the object that now came to a halt back at Ruby's feet. She wasn't sure what she was looking at. It looked like somebody's head, lying on the floor, staring up at her. She didn't understand how that could be. Then she too began to scream.

2

Drake put Marco Foulkes at just north of fifty. His taste in clothes was definitely older. A rust-coloured corduroy jacket that displayed just the right combination of wear and exclusivity to make the owner appear both down on his luck but also unmistakeably wealthy. The kind of look Drake wouldn't be caught dead in any time soon. The ash-blond hair was cut boyishly, hanging down a little too long in the neck. It all added up to the impression of a man who was having trouble shaking off the fact that his youth was behind him.

Foulkes was seated on one of the chic black leather armchairs that Crane had inherited along with the office. They were designed by an architect whose name she had told Drake but which he had subsequently forgotten. Van something or other. Dutch? German?

His mind was wandering. Truth be told he was still undecided about this private lark. There was the change of pace, but there was also the fact that clients were paramount. You needed them. He was having trouble disguising the fact that he had instinctively taken an immediate dislike to Foulkes. Maybe it was because he was a writer (and what did someone like that have to write about?), or maybe it was just the paisley silk scarf slung artistically around his neck. Something about the smug way he waltzed in here expecting them to swallow his story.

The dislike was clearly mutual.

'Ever since your father moved back, my mother has been taking care of him. She's concerned, says the place is like a menagerie.'

Foulkes was addressing Crane and could barely bring himself to throw a wary glance at Drake as he went on. 'I gather you haven't seen Sir Edmund for a while. He's the one who suggested I look you up.'

Crane cleared her throat impatiently. She was behind her desk, taking notes in a big ledger with one of her fancy pens. She liked doing that, writing things out slowly in longhand. It gave her time to think, and also, in this case, to hide her annoyance. Drake guessed that this had something to do with Foulkes' overfamiliarity. One thing Drake understood: there were some areas where Crane liked to keep a certain distance. The subject of her family being one of them. That much he knew about her and Foulkes walking in here playing the old family friend was clearly rubbing her up the wrong way.

'So, Marco,' Drake smiled, taking the initiative. 'Remind me again, how did you meet this woman?'

'How did I meet her?' Foulkes carried himself like a man who did not like being taken lightly. 'I already explained that.'

'Cal is a former Detective Inspector with the Met,' Crane explained. 'It's an interview technique, to get people to repeat their stories, in order to sift out the holes.'

'I'm not a suspect,' Foulkes pointed out. 'I'm a client. Potential client,' he added for Drake's benefit.

'Sorry, Mr Foulkes,' Drake said, trying to make amends. 'Old habits die hard, but perhaps you could humour me and go back over it one more time?'

With a sigh, Foulkes began his tale over again.

'Her name is Howeida Almanara. She's from Kuwait. She's doing a postgrad at LSE. That's how we met. I was doing a reading there one evening and a few of us went for a drink afterwards.'

'Is that something that happens often?'

'Well, it depends. If there is a good vibe with an audience, and I have no other pressing engagements, then I'm happy to socialise. The personal touch can really help to gain the loyalty of readers.'

'Right.' Drake managed, just, not to roll his eyes. 'And I'm assuming that the fact that she is an attractive young woman didn't hurt.'

'Well, no, of course not.' The smile on Foulkes' face faded.

'And this was five months ago,' said Crane, following up with a glance back over at her notes.

'Six months. It was just before my birthday, which is in September.'

'Exactly. Five months, then.'

Drake could see the irritation on his face. Was that because she was a woman, or did he just not like being corrected by anyone? His manner suggested he felt a certain propriety over the girlfriend.

'Is it possible that she hasn't disappeared?'

'How do you mean?' Foulkes turned back to Drake.

'I mean, is it possible she just doesn't want to see you again?'

The half-smile wavering on Foulkes' face seemed to suggest that he wasn't sure if Cal was trying to be funny.

'I'm just stating the obvious,' Drake continued. 'You claim she's disappeared. Before we can take on this case, we need to know that you're not mistaken. You can understand that, right?'

The creak of leather broke the ensuing silence as Foulkes leaned back in his chair, his hands folded together over his slight paunch. He looked over at Crane.

'Perhaps this was a mistake.'

'All my partner is saying is that we need to examine this from every angle.'

'Which includes treating this as a joke? Dammit, I came here because I think she's in danger.'

'We appreciate that, Marco.' The use of his first name was an offering. Ray was trying to roll it back. The truth was that she too was having trouble suppressing her real feelings. She had never really liked Marco Foulkes when they were growing up. She had stayed at what was then her grandfather's family home quite often, whenever her parents were going through a bad patch, and later when she was alone with her father and he simply couldn't cope. It had been a difficult time for her, and she still felt vulnerable talking about it.

The other problem was Drake. They would have to talk. He still carried the attitude of a police officer about him: the suspicion, the sense of authority, of power. If they were to make a success of this game he was going to have to brush up his personal skills.

'You mentioned an uncle of hers.'

'I mean, I don't want to be judgemental.' Another micro glance in Drake's direction felt like a cautious feeler. A means of gauging whether he might be treading on sensitive ground. Drake was silent. 'I just have a feeling about this guy.'

'A feeling?' Drake fought the urge to laugh. 'Meaning you didn't like the cut of his jib?'

'The cut of his . . .?' echoed Foulkes.

'Do you have a name?' Crane interjected quickly. 'For the uncle?'

'No, sorry.' Foulkes shook his head. 'I only met him once. He wasn't happy for her to be around men. I got the feeling he was a little jealous. I mean, I think he wanted her for himself.'

'He said this?' said Crane.

'No, he didn't say it. But it was clear, in the subtext.'

'The subtext?' Drake exhaled slowly. 'So, what you're saying is that this nameless bearded male relative planned to throw her over his shoulder and cart her off to Arabialand?'

'Are you taking the mickey?' Foulkes was offended. 'Look, I don't have to put up with this.' He appealed to Crane. 'I actually thought I was doing you a favour coming here. You know, your father said . . .'

'Hold on.' Crane lifted a hand. 'You spoke to my father about me?'

'I came here partly because I felt sorry for him. He wasn't doing well.' Foulkes sighed as he got to his feet and headed for the door. 'Obviously, that was a mistake.'

'You seem to have trouble grasping the fact that we actually need clients,' said Crane, when Foulkes had gone.

She had walked Foulkes to the door. Drake was standing by the window watching their lost client walking towards his car. A nice little two-door Porsche, white with a racing stripe down the middle. It looked like a later version of the 911, not as stylish as the original. The kind of car that screamed insecurity. Holding open the door, Foulkes paused to look straight up at Drake. It wasn't a kind look.

'In the Met you were paid whether you solved the crime or not. Out here in the real world, it's a little different.'

'Right.' Drake leaned his weight on the window sill and folded his arms. 'What exactly is your connection to this guy?'

'We've been over this.' Crane shooed him away as she went behind her desk. 'Our families were friends, back in the days when I had family.'

Drake waited, expecting her to go on, but Crane was looking at her wristwatch.

'Oh, what the hell. Is it too early to go for a drink?'

'Not by my watch.'

3

The Moonstone was quiet at that hour. The only customers being a skinny, white-haired man in a cloth cap reading a well-creased newspaper and a postman furtively downing half a lager. Drake fetched a large white wine for Crane and a bottle of IPA for himself. They sat in the far corner.

'What happened to your hand, by the way?' she asked, indicating the bandage.

'A mishap in the kitchen. Opening a tin, if you must know. Don't let anyone tell you cooking is fun.'

'I'll try to remember that.' Crane paused as she stared into her glass. 'He'll call back.'

'What makes you so sure?'

'The air of desperation about him.'

Drake wasn't entirely convinced, but he let it go. He wasn't sure he wanted to see Foulkes again. A ray of sunshine sneaked through the window, briefly lifting the tired air.

'So, *Sir* Edmund? You kept that quiet.'

Crane swallowed two large gulps out of her glass.

'It's not the kind of thing that comes up in conversation.'

'Right, but to be clear, we are talking about Edmund Crane? The Iraq War? The fake dossier?'

Crane winced. 'No need to rub it in.'

Drake was surprised at how much the subject still angered him. It was a long time ago and Ray had nothing to do with it, but still. 'Sorry,' he managed to say, quite evenly. 'I just never saw that coming.'

'Family. What can I say?'

It was a little more than that. Three years ago, Drake had read the Chilcot report into the Iraq war. Not that he'd expected to find any answers. He'd been in the Met for long enough to have pretty low expectations when it came to bringing politicians to book. They lied and then they were forgiven, or forgotten. It was the name of the game. He never voted, for that same reason. There wasn't a single one of them that he trusted.

Drake had seen the consequences of their actions. He'd lived through it. The roadside bombs, the men, women and children covered in ash and grey dust. The bodies of mates twisted into unrecognisable corpses in a split second. At a certain point it felt as if there was no enemy, just death. The hot metal of destruction thrust through blood and bone.

He'd read the report because he wanted to know who or what had sent them to their deaths. There wasn't a day went by when he didn't think what he would like to do to the people who had engineered the war. He wanted to understand, to come to terms with what he'd seen out there. Later on he realised that he never would, not fully.

One thing he had learned was the name Edmund Crane. One of the foremost architects of the intelligence dossier that linked Saddam Hussein to WMDs. The dossier was a sham, a piece of imaginative fantasy designed to dig into the fears of the nation, offering a forty-five-minute countdown before weapons of mass destruction could be launched. If there was one person in Drake's eyes who deserved a long and slow death in the lowest depths of hell, it was Edmund Crane.

'I haven't seen him in over ten years,' Crane said, adding, 'Not after what he did to my mother.'

Drake was beginning to get a sense of how deep this ran with her. He watched her get up and walk over to the bar. He waited until she came back with two large whiskies. So far he'd barely touched his drink, but he sensed this wasn't the moment to quibble.

'When Blair decided to throw his lot in with Bush's crusade to rid the Middle East of anyone willing to stand up to America, my father was the one who constructed the fake dossier.'

'Tell me about it. I read the report.'

'Let me ask you a question.' Crane sipped her drink. 'What made you join up?'

'It seemed like a way out.' Drake sighed. 'I was trying to get away from something.'

'You didn't believe in the war?'

'I didn't believe in anything.' Drake studied the golden colour in his glass before correcting himself. 'Maybe I just needed a place to belong.'

Ray nodded. They were times when she thought she understood him, perhaps more than he realised.

'I never figured out what brought my parents together,' she said, going back into her own thoughts. Marco Foulkes had walked into the office and suddenly this. Everything she had spent so long getting away from. 'The whole thing has always been a mystery to me. Why would two people so clearly unsuited to one another get together.'

'Maybe it was just instant attraction. No logic to love.'

'Of course not. Besides, this was the seventies. They were lost in some kind of late hippiedom. They thought they could do anything.'

'I think drugs had something to do with that.'

'In his case, for sure. He was a pot head for years.'

'This would be before he went into the Secret Intelligence Services.'

'His kind aren't governed by the same rules. Privileged background, which he always denied, until he didn't. When he decided to button down and follow the family tradition, the doors opened and he was whisked all the way to the top.'

'Does this have anything to do with that guy you used to work for?'

'Stewart Mason?'

'That's the one. What did you do for him exactly?'

Crane considered the question. What did she do for Stewart? A lot of things, was the answer to that one. Most of which she was not allowed to talk about.

'Mostly I wrote assessments.'

'About?'

'Risk. Outlining possible outcomes, feasible scenarios. It's not that complicated.'

'So you say. Where does Foulkes come into the picture?'

'Like I said, I spent a lot of time at my grandparents' house.' Crane stopped herself. 'It's kind of an estate, really.'

'Fancy name for a castle, isn't it?'

'Not quite a castle, but it's big.'

'And Marco was across the street.'

'In a manner of speaking.' Crane took another belt of her whisky. 'Marco comes from that background. He downplays it on television because it's not too cool for his public image as a common or garden writer of the people.'

'So, this is all just coincidence? He goes home to visit his mother. She takes him over to see your father and he happens to mention that you are running an investigations bureau?'

Crane frowned. 'I'm not even sure how he would have known that. Like I said, I haven't spoken to my father in years.'

'So how did Foulkes find us?'

'We'll have to ask him, or rather, we could have asked him before you chased him away.'

'What happened to the air of desperation that would bring him running back?

Crane smiled. 'Are you having second thoughts?'

Drake slumped back with a sigh. 'I'm not sure I'm cut out for this private sector gig.'

'We've been over this. We both know you would never have lasted at the Met. You're not the institution type. You hate authority, having it or submitting to it. It's against your nature.'

'I thought we were talking about the case, not analysing me.'

'You don't need me to tell you all this. You'd have got yourself suspended again. It was only a matter of time.'

Drake knew she was right. It was something he had known for years.

'They scapegoated you, sacrificed you for the good of the force. You were never going to come back from that. They undermined your trust in the whole system.'

'I made a mistake.'

'We all make mistakes. You were doing your job within a corrupt institution.'

'Explain how this conversation turned around from your father to me?'

'It's what I do,' Crane said, lifting her glass in salute. 'You're not upset, are you?'

'Not really. Just so long as I don't have to go and apologise to Foulkes.'

'No, I suppose I'll have to do that.' Crane gave a long sigh. 'You shouldn't have scared him off.'

'Now you're being mean.'

'Sorry. You're right. I'm a little edgy.' Crane sat back. 'I have a date tonight.'

'Anyone I know?'

Crane threw him a wary look as she reached for her glass. Before she could speak her phone began to buzz. She glanced at the screen.

'Please don't say I told you so.'

'Wouldn't dream of it,' said Crane.

4

Clapham Common station was cordoned off, fenced in by a flurry of flashing lights stirring the grey light. Police cars and ambulances were parked up on all sides. Motorcycle officers were directing traffic that was already backed up around the common. A line of disgruntled commuters stood urgently jabbing at their phones as they waited for shuttle buses to ferry them to the next station. DS Kelly Marsh slung her identity badge lanyard around her neck as she pushed her way through the crowd choking the entrance. Milo Kowalski was inside sheltering from the rain. He filled her in as they made their way down the escalators.

'The head was wrapped in old rags and newspaper. It was placed in a blue nylon IKEA bag, the kind you buy there when you go shopping.'

'Ah, the bag of choice for psychos. That'll do wonders for their brand.'

Milo looked sceptical. 'Not sure that's going to be their first thought.'

'What is it about my humour that you never seem to get?' Kelly sighed. 'Who found it?'

'Nine-year-old Tyler. His mother Ruby Brown was with him, along with his baby sister.' As usual, Milo had already committed the salient facts to memory. The notebook he held loosely was just a prop. 'Parents split up but got back together a few months ago when Mrs Brown's mother broke up with *her* boyfriend.'

'I hear the makings of a soap opera in there somewhere.'

Milo ignored the remark. 'That's why they were on the train. They have to commute now.'

'Fair enough. I know I've said this before, but you might have missed your calling. So, we're talking about a human head, right?'

'Yeah, when it's an alien they call in the woman from *The X-Files*.'

'Cute.' Milo's attempts at humour never failed to surprise Kelly. He saw the look on her face and shrugged apologetically. 'Sorry.'

At the bottom of the escalators a collection of uniformed officers was interviewing passengers from the train. Kelly ran an eye over them all slowly, taking in the faces, the ages, the way they dressed. She was looking for oddities, elements that seemed incongruous or out of place. At this point everyone was a suspect. But looking at the tired faces she saw fear and impatience. People wanted to get out of here. Most didn't care who the dead person was. Not because they were heartless but because it wasn't their problem. Because in a city like London everyone has a problem and you can't carry all of them. It was an inconvenience. A delay to their journey. They just wanted to get home, to call their loved ones and tell their story to someone who mattered to them, not to these faceless uniforms. Maybe that was the thing about getting murdered in this town; finding someone who cared enough to do something about it. And that, Kelly surmised, was her role.

By now they were on the platform where the train was still stalled. Up ahead, the stutter of a camera flash exploded in quick succession, lighting up the interior of a carriage at the far end. The platform was crowded with London Transport officials and paramedic crews. A woman in her sixties was being treated for shock, an oxygen mask over her face, her eyes wide.

'Male, female, what are we talking about?'

'Hard to tell. First impressions say female. Caucasian. Blonde. Dyed, if you ask me. Full set of teeth. Age, anywhere between thirty-five and fifty.'

Kelly was surprised. 'You got all that from the CSO?'

'No, those are my own observations.'

Milo's confidence was daunting at the best of times. She had the sense that what awaited her inside that carriage was bigger than anything she had dealt with before.

'Tell me again why I was the last person to hear about this.'

'There was a mix-up in the list of duty officers. News of your promotion hadn't come through, apparently. They still had the chief down. When they couldn't reach him they called me. I just happened to be close by.' Milo wagged his head in a kind of apology.

'Why am I not surprised?'

Kelly was having a hard time getting used to her new rank, and not having Drake around to lean on weighed heavily. She knew she had to get past it.

'Forensics are already going over the carriage, but the clock is ticking. They have to get the line running again. It's causing all kinds of hell.'

'Welcome to London. We climb over dead people to get you to work on time.'

'Do I detect a note of cynicism there, chief?' Milo grinned.

'No, that's just my natural cheery demeanour.'

They came to a halt as they were buttonholed by an irate station manager.

'Who's in charge here?' Broad Yorkshire accent. Fifties, overweight, his shirt collar grubby and frayed, hair thinning.

'That would be Detective Sergeant Marsh.'

'Right, and where's he when he's needed?'

'You're looking at her.' Kelly enjoyed the look of confusion on his bloated face.

'Fair enough.' He took a moment to size her up. 'Do you have any idea how many people are affected by the fact that we have no service in either direction?'

'We're working as fast as we can.' Marsh didn't wait for the man to answer. Milo had to jog to keep up with her. 'Try to keep him happy,' she said without turning. 'We don't want him ringing up the chain of command.'

'Gotcha, chief.'

Kelly and Milo were struggling to recalibrate their relationship to accommodate this change in their status. References to Drake notwithstanding, on the whole it was going well. Kelly hadn't changed her style. She still dressed in dark, off-the-peg suits that provided anonymity and some degree of androgynous authority. She never wore make-up and her hair was still dyed jet black and cut in a clumsy, punkish style that recalled the sixteen-year-old anarchist she had once been.

Around the entrance to the carriage high-powered klieg lights had been set up. Cables and generators ran this way and that. Cases of equipment. Cooler boxes. High aluminium tool chests. Another burst of flash guns went off as the SOCO photographer circled, trying to cover all the angles. In the middle of this circus was a large man with greying hair held down by a blue cap that did its best to cut down the level of dandruff scattered on his shoulders. Archie Narayan was the Home Office chief pathologist. He glanced up as Marsh leaned in the doorway of the carriage.

'Nice to see you, Archie.'

'Try to restrain yourself,' muttered the pathologist. 'You know I can't stand emotion.' Archie had known Drake since he was a DC, stumbling around his first crime scene like a drunk in a glass factory. It was taking time for him to adjust to Kelly Marsh.

'Where is she, then, our Lady of the Northern Line?'

'Step this way, DS Marsh.'

From where she was standing Kelly could still not see the object in question. It was fenced in by shields and technicians.

'Give us a little room here.'

When Archie gave an order, people jumped. The forensics team generally gave him a wide berth. The pathologist was not someone you wanted to get on the wrong side of. Many of them had felt the wrath of his tongue. On the scale of PC etiquette, Archie was about as off the charts as you could hope to get.

'Not a lot to work with, eh, doc?'

Archie shot her a glance. Oddly, he found he was developing a soft spot for Marsh and so he held his tongue.

'There's enough. Dental records. Earrings. They look old, could be valuable, or second-hand. That's a diamond stud in her right ear. New. Might yield something. Traces of make-up, also shampoo. We can run DNA tests, see if that throws up a match. One thing I would lay a small wager on . . .'

'What's that, then?' Archie had a twinkle in his eye.

'Eastern European.'

'I'm impressed. How can you deduce that?'

'Pink teeth. It's the result of a type of amalgam used by dentists in the Eastern Bloc countries.'

'A veritable wiki-feast,' Marsh muttered to herself. Archie disappeared as she bent down for a better look.

Alongside the head was a portable refrigerator unit to keep it cool and try to delay the process of decomposition. The temperature inside the train was high enough for Kelly to feel sweat beads popping on her forehead. The head was lying on its left side. The eyes were half closed. The woman, and it was clearly a woman, still wore faint traces of green eyeshade. The head was distorted in shape. Marsh turned to the crime scene officer, who was bagging and tagging the pile of rags and newspaper that the head had been wrapped in.

'Anything in there that might tell us who she was?'

The CSO shook his head.

'How much longer do you need?'

'As soon as we can get things bagged, we'll get the carriage moved somewhere we can work.'

'Sounds good.'

Milo tapped her on the shoulder and jerked a thumb towards the platform. 'Chief.'

Marsh leaned out through the doors and saw Superintendent Wheeler making his way along, accompanied by an entourage that included DCI Pryce and the stationmaster.

'Christ, that's all we need! And he's brought his pet poodle with him.'

'Now, now,' chided Archie, who was just within earshot.

Wheeler took up a position outside the carriage, arms folded.

'Okay, DS Marsh, what have we got?'

'One severed head, sir. Female. IC1. Age somewhere between thirty-five and fifty. No distinguishing marks. No signs of identity.'

'Where was she?'

'In a bag, sir.' Kelly indicated the bright blue bag that was being folded by two SOCOs before being packed away in a sealed evidence envelope. 'A blue nylon IKEA bag.'

'A what?' Wheeler's face clouded.

'It's a furniture chain, sir.'

'Good grief! Does nobody care about raising the alarm? A bag left on a crowded tube?'

'You know what commuters are like, sir. Everyone's minding their own business.' Kelly glanced over at Pryce and saw the familiar cold, flat look in his eyes. She knew what he was thinking. He was trying to decide if he wanted the case for himself.

'What about witnesses?' Wheeler asked.

Milo tapped his notebook. 'A carriage full. Uniforms are processing them, but so far it's slim pickings. The person who found her was a nine-year-old boy. He and his mother are being treated for shock. I'll be going over the CCTV footage as soon as we get back.'

'I can't believe nobody thought to raise the alarm.'

'No, sir,' Marsh sympathised. There was nothing to understand. Most commuters were dead on their feet and wouldn't notice a bomb if it had cartoon wires and a Mickey Mouse clock attached.

Milo cleared his throat. 'A couple of passengers said they assumed it belonged to them, sir, to the woman with the children, I mean.'

'DC Kowalski, is it?'

'That's correct, sir.' Milo looked pleased to be noticed.

'Right, well, you know the drill. We need to identify the victim and we need to know how this thing got onto the train and where.' Wheeler turned back to Pryce. 'What's your feeling?'

'To be honest, I've got a full plate right now. I'm happy to leave it to your team for the moment. If it turns out to be too much, we'll be glad to take over.'

Kelly did her best not to smile. She had guessed that Pryce wouldn't want to saddle himself with a murder that had so little going for it the chances of getting a conviction were close to zero. Pryce was a numbers man, always thinking of his clearance rate. He wouldn't touch this with the proverbial barge pole. She became aware that Milo was tugging her sleeve. She threw him a look of impatience and returned her attention to the two senior officers, although they appeared to have forgotten about her. Wheeler and Pryce were discussing something else in low voices that she couldn't quite make out.

'Carry on, DS Marsh,' Wheeler said. 'I shall expect a report by the end of the day.'

'Yes, sir.' She turned to Milo. 'Okay, you've got my attention.'

'I think you should see this.' Glancing over his shoulder, Milo led her back towards the carriage. As they stepped inside Milo indicated for the SOCOs to step back. 'Give us a moment, would you?'

Crouching down, Milo held up the evidence bag containing the crumpled newspaper the head had been wrapped in. At first Marsh couldn't see what Milo was on about, but then she read the headline over the article.

'Shit!' she muttered.

5

Crane and Drake were issued with day passes at the reception desk by the entrance on Kingsway. The nervous young man stood wringing his hands while they were signed in before stepping forwards to lead them through the library to the lifts. As they rose through the building they were afforded a view down through the circular hoops of the staircase that wound around the central atrium.

Doctor Janet Lempel, the faculty dean, was in her forties. Slim and keenly intelligent, she shook their hands and thanked her assistant before dismissing him. They followed her to a small office with a narrow window that offered a view of the dome of St Paul's. The dean sat down and linked her fingers together on the desktop.

'I understand this is a private investigation,' she said, looking them over. 'Why isn't it being handled by the police?'

'I can't answer that,' Crane said.

'I suppose they have better things to do with their time.'

'Most missing persons cases turn out to have a perfectly simple explanation,' Drake offered. 'People disappear of their own free will and come back when they are ready.'

'Mr Drake is a former detective inspector with the Met,' explained Crane.

'Ah.' The dean nodded. 'I understand, but I'm still not sure how I can help.'

'Our starting point is Howeida's safety. It's important that we form a picture of her. What kind of person she is, what her habits are. For that we need to speak to people who know her.'

'I haven't had much contact with her. I tend to be up to my neck in administrative tasks, but I do remember meeting her and being impressed by how single-minded she was. She's doing a master's degree and we are hoping she will carry on to do a doctorate. Certainly, I got the impression she wanted to make the most of her time here.'

'At the LSE?' Crane asked.

'In London, in this country.' The dean held her hands wide as if to emphasise her point. 'Considering her background, I think it's safe to assume she values her freedom.'

The dean picked up her telephone and pressed a button. 'After your call I took the liberty of trying to round up a few of her friends. They're waiting for you.'

There were three of them. All young women in their mid twenties. They occupied a table in the café in the plaza next to the library. Drake decided to take a backseat and let Crane handle things at this stage. The conversation was dominated by the odd one out of the trio. While the other two spoke in quiet, measured tones, it was the gregarious American who set herself up as the authority. Savannah was the only white girl out of the three. Skinny, with voluminous red hair that hung down over her shoulders. She shared a flat with Howeida.

'Howie's just awesome. And I mean, super intelligent.'

'Howie, that's what you call her?' Crane glanced at the others.

'That's what I always call her. It's just easier.'

'Right.'

While Savannah rushed on, the other two nodded and murmured monosyllabic responses but said little. When Crane tried to engage them they would demurely agree, giving way to another torrent of excited chatter from their self-appointed spokesperson.

'I mean, I'm just a little old girl from Virginia, and then I meet her and she comes from this totally, like, medieval place where she can't go out without a male cousin to chaperone her and she knows so much!'

None of them had any idea of where Howeida might have gone, or why. She had simply vanished.

'One day she was there and the next, she wasn't. It's so strange.' The smaller of the other two was Adela. She had a round face framed by dark hair that made her resemble a cat.

'You were hired by Marco?' Crane detected a certain degree of suspicion in her tone.

'Do you know him too?'

Adela and the South Asian woman, Meena, exchanged looks.

Crane smiled. 'Whatever you tell us is confidential.'

'We only met him a couple of times,' said Adela, glancing at Savannah. 'He's a little older.'

'A little?' Meena blurted out, only to immediately fall silent again. Crane turned to her.

'Did that make things uncomfortable?'

'Not uncomfortable.' She was struggling to find the words. 'Just a bit awkward. I mean he was trying really hard to be nice, but too hard, you know?'

Drake noticed how Savannah had fallen silent. They talked for a while longer but it was clear the girls were eager to get away, citing classes or assignments. Drake stepped in to take their contact details while Crane handed out business cards.

'Please, if anything springs to mind, no matter how trivial, just give us a call.'

'I always wondered what went on in places like this,' said Drake once they were safely outside in the plaza behind the college.

'We need to talk to them separately.'

'Agreed. What did you make of the dean?'

'She's trying to protect herself.' Crane nodded at the building behind them. 'These places receive so much overseas sponsorship they are sensitive about bad publicity.'

'Howeida's background.'

'Exactly. Our friend the dean is motivated less out of a concern for her safety than for the dent this might put in the university's reputation. She doesn't want to scare people off.'

'Which explains her eagerness to cooperate. What did you make of the girls?'

'A lot of animosity between them. We need to break them up.'

'Agreed. You can have Miss Savannah all to yourself. Our Virginian friend.'

'Thanks a lot.' Crane looked up and down the street. 'Not a bad place to be.'

'You're thinking of what the dean said, about this being an opportunity for Howeida?'

They turned and began walking in the direction of The Strand. Students wandered by them going to and from lectures, meetings, lunch.

'I wonder if there is anything to that, the idea of new found freedoms.'

'The dean said she was smart. Would she risk throwing that away?'

'Considering her wealthy background, we have to assume that her parents are liberal enough since they allowed her to come to London alone to study.'

'So not the most traditional types. But what about this uncle Foulkes was talking about?'

'You're still not over your initial distrust of the man.'

Drake shrugged. 'It's just instinct.'

'Right, your old police sixth sense.'

'You can laugh, but I'm telling you, nine times out of ten . . .'

'Have you any idea how twentieth century you sound?'

Drake was momentarily nonplussed, but he did his best to recover. 'It's human nature. Some things don't change.'

'Fair enough,' said Crane. 'So much for evolution. Where are you headed?'

'I'm going to take a look at our favourite writer.'

'Well, don't forget that he's also our client, Cal. Never upset the customer, or whatever.'

'Whatever is right.'

6

On the radio a man with a French accent was speaking: 'Ze irony is zat ze people who were elected to parliament to defend ze best interests of ze country 'av been outvoted by zee ignorant masses. I yuze zis word with a measure of irony, yes? Zey are ignorant, and zey are proud of zis fact. Zey do not care what comes next, so long as it is defferent from what zey 'av now.'

Impatiently, Drake reached over and flicked the voice off.

It was late afternoon and he was growing restless. Across the street, he could see the subject of his surveillance through the windows of the wine bar in Fulham. Marco Foulkes was drinking with an unidentified man. They were seated at a counter that ran along the front window, which was convenient for Drake. He had followed them here from a snooker club close to Fulham Broadway station. That had posed its own challenges. Getting close had been difficult. He had cautiously followed the two men inside and then hung around the bar, keeping his back to the tables. Luckily the place was both big and dark, but after about twenty minutes he was getting leery looks from the heavies who were minding the place. He decided not to risk any kind of altercation and left, crossing the street to some kind of health food place that served fair trade coffee from the Honduran Highlands. The owner of the place, a sexagenarian with aspirations to sainthood, explained this patiently then watched over Cal as he took a sip, just to make sure of his approval. Drake took up residence at the single table outside, where he could keep an eye on the narrow doorway across the street.

Another hour went by before they emerged. Drake followed them to the wine bar, then went to fetch the car. He was lucky enough to find a parking space in a side street from where he observed them drinking something that looked like imported beer out of bottles. There was a lot to dislike about Foulkes, he decided. The silk scarf draped around his neck. The scruffy beard, carefully crafted to give him a bohemian, yachtsman type look. The tweed jacket and unkempt hair. If he hadn't been a writer he would have perfectly fitted the cliché of one as described in one of his novels.

On the seat beside him was one of Foulkes' books, *The Clandestine Countess*. He wasn't making much progress. It had something to do with a retired barber remembering the Holocaust. There was the mysterious countess of the title, a fair amount of weird sex and voyeurism, but beyond that Cal simply couldn't get into it. He didn't care what happened to the characters. What the book didn't tell him was how anyone made a living from this racket, or maybe you didn't have to worry about that when you were Marco Foulkes.

Throwing the book aside, Drake reached for the half bottle of spiced rum that sat in the door pocket next to him. He took a sip to warm himself up before screwing the top back on. He liked to think that he was drinking less these days. Getting out of the Met and on to this freelancing gig had been something of a leap of faith, but once he'd taken the decision he had experienced a feeling of relief.

'You'll die of boredom,' Kelly Marsh had said. 'Ten to one you'll be back here in three months.'

But he hadn't died, of boredom or anything else, and he hadn't gone back. True, there were moments when he missed the excitement of the old days, but they were easily outweighed by the feeling that he no longer represented an organisation he had stopped believing in years ago.

Drake was curious to know who Foulkes' friend was and what they were talking about. From what he could see the conversation seemed to be getting more animated. Drake sat up in his seat as the other man suddenly got to his feet and headed for the door. Foulkes thumped his fist on the counter to the annoyance of the couple sitting next to him.

Drake shifted his focus to the friend. He got out of the car, locked it and followed on foot, trailing the man on the opposite side of the street. The man, who was in his late forties, was slimmer and more nervous-looking than Foulkes. He had thinning hair and grey, unhealthy-looking skin. Fulham Broadway tube station loomed up ahead out of the gloom and Drake watched as the man passed the barrier and descended the stairs towards the eastbound line. There were enough people milling around to make Drake less worried about being spotted. Also, whoever the man was, he was paying no attention to the other passengers. A District Line train arrived and Drake stepped into the next carriage, positioning himself with his back to the end of the train. Through the separation doors he could see the man sitting down and taking out his phone to scroll through his messages before slumping back and turning his face upwards to close his eyes. Drake took the opportunity to have a better look at him. A long face, narrow jaw and grey eyes. He was wearing a Barbour waxed jacket over a pullover and white shirt. Alongside Foulkes he was the boring friend who could always be relied upon to have time for you.

At Earls Court, Drake followed at a distance as the man descended the stairs and then the escalators to the Piccadilly Line. The eastbound platform was crowded with people. Backpackers, tourists, battalions of teenagers jostling one another. Through the mayhem Drake managed not to lose sight of his target. Moving ahead of him, he boarded the next carriage and waited in the doorway to make sure that the man stayed onboard. The doors closed and they shuddered away.

The train took them across London to Finsbury Park, where the man changed again, this time to a southbound Victoria Line train that took him one stop to Highbury and Islington. As they changed again to board an overground train, Drake was intrigued. Although he was going to a lot of trouble to cover his tracks the man appeared to be going through the motions like a sleepwalker, paying no particular attention to his surroundings or whether or not he was being followed.

By the time they got off at Dalston Junction it was dark and the rain was coming down. People were rushing towards the station entrance with newspapers held over their heads. The man turned left and walked for about ten minutes before producing a set of keys. He unlocked the door of a darkened, glass-fronted shop entrance and disappeared inside.

Drake crossed the street to put a bit of distance between them. With his phone he took a picture of the shop front. The sign read Nathanson's Solicitors. A list of services were stencilled down the left-hand side of the window: Immigration/Nationality law, Civil litigation, Family law, Wills, Crime, Welfare benefits, Landlords and Tenants, Housing/Homelessness, Employment law.

Through the window he watched the man settle himself within an inner office cubicle separated from the front by a glass wall and a door that remained open. The other two desks in the place were empty. There appeared to be nobody else in there.

Nathanson, if that was the man's name, stayed in the office for just over an hour. An unmarked car pulled up outside and a moment later the man hurried out and got into the car. Looking up and down the street, Drake could see there was no chance he was going to be able to follow. Instead he made a note of the number plate.

When he got back to his car in Fulham an hour later, it had acquired a parking ticket. He plugged his phone in to charge and a message popped up from Kelly Marsh.

'Watch the news this evening. Then give me a call.'

Forty minutes later he was home, clicking through the channels until he found it: a woman's head had been found on a train. Drake had no idea what connection there could be to him, but he knew Kelly wouldn't have called to tell him for nothing. And that was an unsettling thought.

7

Something about the place had changed. It wasn't all that long ago that Drake could recall his first conversation with Crane in here. Just around the corner from Raven Hill police station. It used to have another name. Now it was the Coffee Cartel. Some kind of a wry joke on the drug trade. It was that kind of a place. Alternative in a palatable, hipsterish fashion. Men with wild mountain-man beards and chains hanging off their belts who wouldn't say boo to a cat.

'The latté is excellent,' declared Milo, who seemed to be coming out of his shell. Both Marsh and Drake looked at him. 'It's made with soy milk.'

'Good to hear,' said Drake, 'but I'll stick with a black coffee.'

'Americano?'

'Whatever.'

'So, how's life on the streets treating you?' Marsh tilted her head back.

'Yeah, well, you know. Civilian life. It takes a little getting used to.'

'Of course.' Milo snapped his fingers as if to a tune nobody else could hear. 'You were long time undercover, right?'

'Right,' nodded Drake. 'What am I missing here? The thing on the news, the head?'

The others exchanged looks. Marsh explained what they had found on the Tube.

'In an IKEA bag?'

'The criminal type is getting more inventive,' nodded Milo.

'Forensics are still going over it of course, but something seemed to stand out.'

Marsh fell silent as the waiter returned with their coffee. Drake's came with a note telling him the coffee beans had come from an independent farming collective somewhere in Kenya. Why go to the trouble of printing out a label like that?

Marsh was unfolding a photocopy, which she then placed on the table.

Drake didn't need to reach for it. He recognised it almost immediately. He had seen it before, countless times. For a while he had carried it tucked into his wallet. It took him back in an instant, to a much darker period in his life when everything had seemed to come crashing down and the Met had fulfilled every assertion of prejudice levelled at it.

But it was more than that.

On a personal level it was an affirmation of his failure to beat the system. For a time he had believed that hard work and dedication would allow him to punch through the ceiling. All he needed was to break one good case and that was to be Goran Malevich. Only Operation Hemlock, as it was known, turned sour. Drake's prime witness disappeared and Goran was gunned down in a car park in Brighton, leaving Drake with a problem, and a lot of explaining to do.

The papers went further than that. The headline of the article in front of him summed it all up: 'Finger of Suspicion Pointed at Rising Star of Met Police. Links to Organised Crime'. Drake didn't need to read further. He knew the article virtually by heart. Written by a certain Charlie Inwood, it had been the last nail in his coffin. For a time he had contemplated the idea that Inwood was in somebody's pocket, but he'd drawn a blank on that too.

'Where did you get this?'

'The head was wrapped in it,' said Marsh. 'Along with some rags.'

Drake glanced up. 'I assume you think this is more than just coincidence.'

'Don't you?'

'Maybe. Maybe not.'

'Come on, Cal.' Marsh leaned her elbows on the table. 'We're both thinking the same thing, right? A head turns up with a link to your name attached? What I'm asking myself is why. We have very little to go on. No scene of crime. Without a body, not even a cause of death. They're doing DNA tests now to see if there is a match, but you know how that goes.'

Drake tapped the article. 'If you're right, and this is supposed to mean something, then we already have the body.'

Milo and Kelly exchanged glances.

'Come again,' said Marsh.

'Headless torso washed up on the beach in Brighton. Four years ago now.'

'And you know this from looking at the picture?' Milo was incredulous. 'How can you be sure?'

'I'm not sure, not a hundred per cent,' said Drake. 'But if we assume this is more than coincidence, then it's got to be her. Zelda.'

'All due respect, chief,' Milo began. 'We can't go back to Superintendent Wheeler and say you recognise her. Her own mother wouldn't recognise her. She's been somewhere all this time.'

'Which raises other questions, namely where was she stored and why?'

'Deep freeze probably, is the answer to the first,' said Marsh. 'The second question is more to the point. Why would anyone do something like that?'

'Also' – Milo raised a finger – 'where were they taking her? I mean, why leave her on the train?'

'Two possibilities occur,' said Drake. 'Either someone panicked, or they wanted us to find her.'

Marsh nodded her agreement. 'Which brings us back to motive. Why store the head?' She paused to take a sip of coffee. 'So, why is someone trying to draw our attention back to your involvement in that case. Zelda was the name of your informant, the one who went missing.'

'Right.'

Marsh thought for a moment. 'Archie might already have confirmed that it's her. She was Eastern European, right?'

'Serbian Roma.'

'One of Archie's preliminary observations was that the victim had pink teeth.'

'Pink?' asked Drake.

'Apparently it's a side effect of a kind of dentistry, a type of filling found in Eastern Europe.'

'Just because she's Eastern European doesn't mean it's her,' Milo pointed out.

'But it's beginning to stack up that way,' said Drake.

'But why?' asked Milo. 'Why go to all that trouble? Someone's idea of a joke?'

'If this is a joke,' said Marsh, 'it's in pretty poor taste.'

'What else does Archie say?' Drake asked.

Marsh shrugged. 'The usual. Too early to say. Wait for the tests.'

'Maybe he has a point. We shouldn't be jumping to conclusions.'

Marsh and Milo exchanged looks.

'This is your case,' said Milo, who was having trouble not adding the word 'chief' whenever he addressed Drake. 'This is what brought you down.'

'Look, I want to put this thing to rest as much as anyone, but I have to be sure.'

'What can you tell us about this body?' Marsh asked. 'Was it identified as your informant?'

Drake's mind went back to that time.

'The headless body of a woman washed up on the shore in Brunswick Town, just west of Brighton. A DNA match was made later with items found in the room we discovered Zelda had been staying in.'

'Why did they remove her head?' Milo asked.

'They were sending a message,' Drake explained. 'This is what happens to people who talk.'

'Goran Malevich was your target so that would have made him the prime suspect,' said Kelly. 'Why wasn't he charged?'

Drake shook his head. 'Not enough evidence. Malevich was careful never to get his hands dirty.'

'But she was your witness.'

'Correct.' Drake looked at Marsh. 'Pryce used that to make a case against me. He argued that it was more than incompetence that had got our major witness killed.'

'Implying you were in Goran's pocket.'

Drake shrugged. 'I had been too secretive. I kept her to myself. Nobody else knew where she was.'

'Why?'

'Because I knew there was a leak inside our team. Too many operations had gone wrong.'

'So Pryce turned this into a way of taking you down? Does the man have no scruples?' Marsh's voice betrayed her anger. 'You think he was on the take?'

'If he was I could never prove it. Maybe he was just doing what he thought was right.'

'You don't believe that, do you?'

'No,' said Drake. 'I think there's more to it than that.'

Milo cleared his throat, eager to get back into the conversation. 'If they identified the body, why was the case shut down?'

'You'd have to ask Pryce about that. By then I was suspended from duty and facing an inquiry. Maybe we'll get the answers now, with the head showing up.'

'Don't hold your breath,' said Marsh. 'Pryce has made it clear that we don't have the resources to start digging up cold cases.'

'The cuts,' explained Milo, as if Drake didn't already know. 'We're struggling to cope as it is.'

Marsh was drawing circles on the table with her index finger.

'What is it, Kelly?'

'Just the fact of this head turning up now, and the newspaper clipping. It almost seems like someone is trying to set you up.'

'Yes,' sighed Drake. 'It does look that way, doesn't it?'

'Any ideas?'

'Take your pick. Malevich is gone, but there are plenty of others still out there from that time.'

'But storing the head like that, for so long. That's pretty sick.'

'I didn't make this world, I only live in it.'

'Well, that's basically the reason I wanted to give you a heads-up.'

'Appreciated. I mean that, both of you.' Drake nodded at Milo. 'You could get into trouble for this.'

'It's the right thing to do, chief,' said Milo.

On the way out, Drake handed him a slip of paper. 'Can I ask you a favour? Could you run that registration through the system?'

'Who is it?' asked Milo.

'A solicitor by the name of Nathanson. Barnaby Nathanson. His offices are in Kingsland Road. I think it's an Uber. Can you do that?'

'Sure, I can get into their system and check it. Kingsland Road, you said?'

'Around eight in the evening. I need to know where it took him.'

'Shouldn't be a problem.'

'Thanks, Milo. I appreciate it.'

Marsh held the door for him and then blocked his path. 'You're not using us for your private sector enterprise, are you?'

'You scratch my back . . .'

'So you're going to look into the Zelda case?'

'I'll do what I can, but, Kelly, not a word of this to anyone, not even Wheeler.'

'You're not going to turn this into some kind of personal vendetta against Pryce, are you?'

'Wouldn't dream of it,' grinned Drake. Then he was past her and out of the door before she had time to reply.

8

The flat Howeida Almanara shared with Savannah Reeves was actually just off Drury Lane. Whichever way you cut it, this was a very nice neighbourhood. The building was a neatly faced red-brick structure on a corner. Not old, but not new either. Crane was buzzed in and climbed a wide staircase that appeared to have been recently refurbished. When she reached the second floor the slim woman was waiting in the doorway, her red hair tied back now with a black ribbon.

'There is an elevator, you know,' she said, as if the idea might never have occurred to Crane.

'I have a tendency towards claustrophobia.'

'Wow, that must really suck.'

'I had a bad experience once.' Crane turned the conversation back. 'Nice place.'

'Thank you,' cooed Savannah.

The flat was untidy in the way that you might expect from two students with means. Crane surmised that they had a cleaning service which probably came in a couple of times a week to prevent things tipping over the edge into real chaos. Just two rich kids trying their best to look normal.

Crane allowed herself to be led around. Each of the girls had their own room. Savannah's bed was covered with fluffy toy animals; bunnies with big ears and so forth.

'The little girl in me that refuses to grow up,' she laughed.

Howeida's room was more austere and tidy. There were clothes in the wardrobe and dresser. A large, hard-shell suitcase big enough to pack a Shetland pony inside stood behind the door. Crane looked around quickly but saw nothing out of place.

'What a great flat.'

'Oh, we love it. We looked at a few others. But once we saw this we had to have it.'

Crane made appreciative sounds as the young woman led

her through to the kitchen, where she made a valiant attempt at producing coffee from the stainless steel machine on the marble counter. Either she was nervous or she had no practical experience of kitchen appliances. Crane guessed she didn't spend a lot of time making her own coffee.

'Why don't I?' she suggested. Savannah's eyes widened in amazement.

'Oh, would you? I'm terrible with these things. I usually run downstairs to the café.'

'Nothing to it. Why don't you sit down and tell me about Howeida. How did you meet?'

'Oh, wow!' Savannah tugged the ribbon off her hair, releasing her long red locks. She settled onto a high stool like a model waiting for a photoshoot to get started. 'I mean, like I said the other day when your partner was with you, we just hit it off. He's not working with you today?'

Crane ran an eye over the coffee machine and went to work. 'He's working on another angle.'

'Oh, right. Well, anyway, Howie and I, we just clicked right from the get-go. First day on campus, we just got to talking and we haven't stopped since.' She giggled in a self-conscious way. Crane asked what had brought her to London.

'I've just always had a romantic thing for London. Don't ask me why. I guess I read too many of those old novels as a child.'

Specifically, Savannah had come to London to do a masters in international development.

'So, what did you and she get up to?'

'Well, I mean, I'm from Virginia, I didn't know anything about London,' she gushed. 'I'd never met anyone like her before. She just knew *everything*.'

'She had a lot of contacts here? Family? Friends?'

'Her family is just, like, so international? So there are aunts and cousins everywhere. Paris, Copenhagen, all over the States. So there were people coming through all the time.'

As she went back over their time together, how they had decided to move out of collegiate rooms and find a place to share, the kind of places they went, a picture began to form in Crane's mind. Two young women, quite different in principle but connected by some kind of common transnational culture of mobility and wealth. They had grown up on opposite sides of the world, but shared the same references. They watched the same television shows and listened to the same music. They probably had more in common with one another than with people living round the corner from them, in Richmond, Virginia, or Kuwait City. London had brought them together.

'Tell me about Marco Foulkes,' said Crane, setting another frothy cappuccino on the counter.

'Wow, that looks amazing!' Savannah gushed. 'How do you do that?'

'I used to work for a living.'

That produced a blank look. Crane repeated her question about Foulkes.

'Marco. Yeah, I mean, like I said, Howie knows everybody. So she had heard about this guy. I mean, she'd read one of his books or something. So when she found out he was doing a reading she insisted we go. Afterwards she just went up to him and started talking.' She frowned and tossed her hair back again. 'I remember he invited us to this party? Really fancy, lots of earls and dukes? Really cool. And that's it. We were all friends after that. It was clear that she was the one Marco was interested in. But that's cool. I mean, he's like a lord or something.'

'Something,' muttered Crane, sitting opposite the other woman. Savannah was drawing a question mark in the air.

'Right, so he hired you, right?'

'That's right.'

'But you're like old friends or something?'

The tone in her voice gave Crane pause. She was digging for something.

'He told you that?'

Savannah nodded. 'He said you were like old friends. I mean, I think he was trying to put me at ease, you know?'

'It was a long time ago. We were kids.'

'That's great. I mean, like, he's so famous! We went to a couple of readings? In, like, bookshops? People just love him. They all wanted his autograph and stuff.'

'Sounds like you got along.'

'Well, I wasn't into being a groupie, you know?' Savannah flushed lightly. 'But he was a lord and all, right? We went out together a few times, all of us. Marco would bring along a friend sometimes to make up a foursome, but it became clear that they just wanted to be together.'

'Was it mutual?'

'I guess so.' The red hair swayed as she tilted her head. 'Howie didn't like talking about personal stuff like that. The opposite of me, really. I just talk.'

It was almost as if she were speaking about someone in the past. Crane wondered if Savannah was aware of that.

'Did you ever visit his family home?'

'Oh, yeah, the castle.' Savannah waved off the description before it was out of her mouth. 'I mean, it's not really a castle, but to a small town girl from Virginia it was pretty close.'

'I'm sure.'

'We went up there a couple of times. It was real nice and his mother is amazing. She just took such good care of us.' Savannah scrunched up her nose. 'Truth is I was always like the third wheel. You know? Staring out the window while they carried on. I got tired of it, to be honest. The last time I left a day early. I told a little lie? I said an old friend was passing through London.'

'How long ago was this?'

'Just before she went missing.'

'So you left her up there with Marco?'

'And his mother.'

'His mother, yes.' Crane had her notebook out to compare dates. 'Marco said that she went missing around the nineteenth, so this was the weekend before that? The sixteenth and seventeenth?'

'I think so, if that's when he says.'

'Didn't you notice her not being around?'

'Really, I didn't think about it.' The thin shoulders lifted and fell. 'It wasn't a big deal. I mean, missing a couple of days is no big deal.'

'You weren't worried?'

'Not really. She's a big girl.'

'Marco mentioned an uncle of hers . . .'

'Oh, god! Now he was a real piece of work.' Savannah was shaking her head as if trying to get rid of a memory. 'He just showed up out of nowhere. Said he had a message for Howie, from her folks.'

'What did she say?'

'She said he wanted to take her home.'

'You heard them talking?'

'Well, most of it was in Arabic. At least I think it was Arabic.' The thin shoulders rose and fell. 'I couldn't really understand.'

'Right, but she seemed stressed about him being here?'

'Oh, yes. I mean, I'm not even sure if he was an uncle or a cousin. I think over there it's pretty much the same thing.'

'Uh huh. What was he like? Can you describe him?'

'He must be at least ten years older than her, maybe more.'

'And how would you characterise his interest in her, from what you saw?'

'I don't know. To me there was always something a little off about him. I mean, I think that out there it's okay to marry your cousin, right? I mean, more than okay, everyone does it.'

'So you're saying that he was interested in marrying her?'

Savannah was suddenly unsure. 'Like I said, it was difficult to know what was really going on between them. And Howie didn't like talking about it.'

'But you got the impression he didn't approve of the way she was living here?'

'That's it exactly. Right from the get-go he was trying to tell us what to do. I mean, not just her, even me. He kind of assumed he had the right.'

'How did Howeida – Howie, react?'

'That's the thing.' Savannah's eyes dropped. She began picking at the cuticles around her fingernails. 'She was scared. I'd never seen her like that. She was really scared.'

'Did you get a name for this guy, the cousin or uncle?'

'Abdul hah-something. I forget.'

'Any idea where he was staying? Anything at all?'

'The thing is, when he first showed up he was really sweet. He even took us both for dinner.'

'When was this?'

'You mean, the date?' She reached for her phone. 'The seventh.'

'Where was this? I mean, do you remember where you ate?'

'Oh, just across the street, the nice Italian place? I think he wanted to make a big impression. Anyway, he wouldn't leave her alone after that. He would follow her. That was creepy.'

'Then what happened to him?'

'I don't know. He just disappeared. Weird, like I said.' Savannah fell silent for a moment. 'So, what do you think happened to her?'

'I don't know,' said Crane, getting to her feet. 'But I'm going to find out.'

9

Archie Narayan was in buoyant mood, which for him was saying something. He had the kind of jovial radiance you might associate with a newly minted grandfather, not a man who spent his days carving up cadavers.

'Just like old times, almost.'

'Steady on,' said Kelly Marsh.

Archie tilted his head at her. 'This one is beginning to grow on me.'

'And there was me thinking we had something special,' said Drake.

'Time moves on for all of us,' lamented Archie. 'I take it you're here for our Mary Stuart.'

'Mary Stuart?' queried Drake.

'She lost her head, remember?'

'A history lesson? Really?' Drake glanced over at Marsh. She seemed resigned. Maybe she and Archie Narayan had more in common than he realised.

'I warn you,' said the pathologist, 'coming here asking for miracles is never a good plan. She's fresh. Well, as fresh as can be under the circumstances. Literally just come through the door. Hardly had time to clean her off.' He squinted at Marsh. 'I understood this wasn't a priority.'

'You heard that from DCI Pryce?'

'He is still the one calling the tunes, isn't he?'

'Looks that way.'

Archie gave a theatrical sigh, a hint perhaps at a frustrated career in amateur dramatics. Nothing about Archie would surprise Drake. 'These days the blue line is so thin it's more of a blue rinse.'

This struck a chord with Marsh. 'Rising knife crime, mental-health statistics through the roof and a budget that has been slashed to ribbons. Yeah, I would say that was fairly accurate.'

'I hate to break up your love-in here, but there was a time when a severed head warranted some kind of urgency,' said Drake.

'Ah, that's precisely the point, old bean, changing times and all that.'

Marsh was in agreement. 'What we have now is the management of unmitigated disaster.'

'Sad, the lack of faith in one so young, wouldn't you say?'

'I wouldn't know,' said Drake.

They were coming down the dark stairs to the basement, which always had a dank feeling to them despite the modern fittings and the discreet lighting. Archie punched a code into the keypad and led the way to the darkened room. The smell of chemicals hit Drake's nostrils with a jolt. Familiar, in the way that the taste of last night's vindaloo can bubble to the surface like gas in a geyser. The autopsy room crackled with electric energy. Neon lights buzzed, refrigerators hummed, a gigantic extractor whirred overhead, and in the corner a centrifuge spun in regular cycles, up to who knows what mischief. Only one of the four dissection tables in the centre of the room was occupied.

With a showman's flourish, Archie pulled back the sheet to reveal the steel basin and its contents. There wasn't much left of the head. The skull had been sliced open and the brain removed.

'Meet Mary Stuart.'

'So you said. Your idea, I take it?'

Archie shrugged. 'Makes a change from Jane Doe. It seemed fitting. The realm under threat. Catholic queen challenging Elizabeth for the throne. That's what got her killed.'

As he looked down at the human remains lying on the examination table Drake was struck by a feeling of dread, as though the past was reaching out to him.

Archie stared at Drake. 'I know it's an obvious question, but why are you here actually?'

Marsh said, 'We're going off the record on this one, doc.'

'I don't know what that means.' Archie folded his arms.

'It means I'm not here, actually.' Drake was leaning over for a closer look. The head was slightly deformed in shape, as if it had been crushed, pressed to one side.

'Is it her?' Marsh was leaning over his shoulder.

'Is it who?' Archie asked.

Drake wasn't sure. The skin had a greenish sheen to it and in death people rarely resemble themselves in life.

'I think this might be Zelda,' he murmured.

'Zelda?' Archie frowned. 'Your witness from the Malevich case?'

'We had a body in at the time, found near Brighton.'

'Of course I remember. That would have been taken care of elsewhere.'

'Can you still access the body for tests?'

'Possibly. That case was unresolved.'

'So you could do a DNA match?'

Archie straightened up. 'If I had reason to. As I recall the body was matched to items from the victim's flat.'

'I could be wrong, but I think this is her.' Drake moved round the table. 'She would have had to be frozen to preserve it like this, right?'

'That's the only way to account for the relatively good shape she's in.'

'How do you explain the discolouration?' Marsh asked.

Archie glanced at her. 'The colour and the mould are indications of humidity, meaning the head wasn't perfectly sealed, wherever it was kept. If I was to guess, I would say she has been moved around for short periods, not long. Slight defrosting and refreezing.'

'Where could she have been kept?'

'Your guess is as good as mine. A large home freezer would do the trick, beside the pork chops.'

'Charming,' muttered Marsh.

'A commercial freezer can produce temperatures as low as minus forty degrees centigrade. Once out of that environment thawing would commence, and with that deterioration, which explains the pallor. This suggests that she had been left for periods of time exposed to room temperature, then possibly re-frozen, which would suggest she was moved. The worst of it occurred on the train, where the elevated heat would have accelerated the process. Also, the person doing the transporting didn't know, or think, about moisture. She was in a plastic bag that didn't allow for ventilation.'

'Kelly mentioned something about pink teeth? Did you manage to confirm it?'

'Ah, yes.' Archie moved around, reaching for a pair of clamps. He pressed the jaw open. Drake recoiled as the smell hit him again, the chemical sting starting to tangle with the contents of his stomach.

'What exactly are we talking about?'

'It's a side effect of arsenic trioxide. It was used to kill the nerves.'

'So that would at least confirm she's from Eastern Europe.'

'Which would tie into your theory that it's her, wouldn't it?' Archie withdrew his hand holding the clamps. The head's jaw remained at an awkward angle. Drake stared at the open mouth. He had to remind himself that this had once been a living person.

'What else can you tell us at this stage?'

'I would say that she was frozen relatively quickly.'

'And how long between coming out of the freezer and landing on the Tube?'

'A matter of hours. Hard to say.'

Drake rested one hand on the steel table. The cold ran up his arm.

Sensing that he needed a moment, Marsh stepped in. 'What else can you tell us?'

'The skin shows traces of cleaning fluid, some kind of disinfectant. That would remove any excess blood and dirt. Neat, methodical, not frenzied. This man knew what he was doing. The spinal chord: the bone has been chipped in places and pulverised in others. Evidence, I would say, of the use of a mechanical device.'

'What, like a wood saw?'

Archie looked at her and shrugged. 'A narrow blade, straight saw would be my guess. We've taken enhanced microscopic pictures to compare and work out exactly what kind of blade he used.' Archie stepped back to survey the head. 'Looks like our killer went to a lot of trouble to keep her.'

'Anything at all about who she was, where she came from?'

'Well, what can I tell you?' Archie looked at Marsh. 'She was a Capricorn, with a fondness for Cocker Spaniels and a weakness for the good life; Dom Perignon champagne and Beluga caviar from the Caspian Sea. She summered in the Riviera and skiied on the Italian side of the French Alps.' Archie gave a dismissive shrug. 'Sorry, couldn't help it. All that Sherlock nonsense really gets on my wick.'

'Very droll,' said Marsh.

Archie's eyes met Drake's over the table. 'We'll know more when we do a DNA test.'

'But it could be her?'

'It could be.'

Drake felt his head spinning. He stared at the lump of rotting flesh and found himself fighting the urge to throw up. He realised that, irrational though it was, he had always believed she could still be alive somewhere. The DNA tests on the washed-up corpse could have been bungled. It wouldn't be the first time. But now he was looking right at her. He knew in his heart it was her.

'People look different in life than in death,' Archie said gently. 'I don't need to tell you that. But rest assured I'll do everything I can.'

'I know you will.'

'You were close,' said Archie.

Drake stared down at her. 'She was a witness. Nothing more.' Archie and Kelly exchanged glances, but neither of them said anything. Then Archie cleared his throat.

'One thing I would stress, regarding the freezing. It had to happen quickly, after the head was removed. Literally within hours.'

'But you're saying she was moved.'

Archie shrugged. 'Could have been a refrigerated van, say, or a cooler box of some kind. Whoever did this took great care not to allow decomposition to occur. It's almost . . .' Archie broke off.

'Almost?' repeated Marsh.

'Almost as if they cared, I was going to say.'

'Caring killers,' muttered Drake. 'Now there's a novelty.'

10

They left the coroner's office and walked down Black Prince Road, under the railway arch to a café on a corner with a striped green awning and a vaguely Mediterranean look about it. Marsh set a mug of coffee in front of Drake as she sat down.

'You were looking a little pale back there.'

'Yeah, sorry about that. Must be out of practice.'

Marsh sipped her coffee thoughtfully. 'You really cared about her.'

'You ever done any undercover work?'

Marsh shook her head. 'Not very good at lying, me.'

Drake turned his coffee mug in circles as his mind went back. Lying had come easy, perhaps because he had been trying to imagine himself a different life for as long as he could remember.

'You have to be on all the time. Never let the mask slip. You have to believe you are who you are pretending to be.'

'Must get tricky,' she said. 'Emotionally.'

'The thing about trust is that it works both ways, no matter what you thought when you started out. Someone's trust means something to you.'

Marsh was watching him carefully. 'What are you saying, that your loyalties are divided?'

Drake remembered Zelda's eyes, how they would brighten. It didn't happen often, but there were moments, when she thought there was hope, a chance of a new life. The image of the half-lidded eyes flooded back. The head on the steel tray. It wasn't trust that undid you, it was being able to give someone hope.

'We needed her, but I wanted to help her get out.'

'And that was never a problem?'

'How do you mean?'

'Well, there's a conflict of interests right there. On the one hand you want to help the girl and at the same time you need her to testify.'

'The two things are not mutually exclusive.'

'Testifying against someone like Goran Malevich can get you killed.'

Drake sipped his coffee but said nothing. Marsh seemed to have grown, in confidence and experience.

'You felt it was your fault she was killed,' said Marsh.

'You're beginning to sound like Ray.'

'You don't need to be a shrink to see that you're in pain.'

'When did you get so wise?'

'Comes with the stripes.'

'I thought I was done with all this,' said Drake.

'Somebody obviously thinks different.'

'That's the bit I'm having trouble getting my head round.'

'You mean who would go to all that trouble of saving the head all this time?'

Drake stared out of the window. 'I keep going back over everyone I can remember, but there's nobody who was that close to her, nobody who would take it so . . . personally.'

'She had no family over here? What about friends? Lovers?'

There was nobody he could remember.

'What about you?' Marsh said. 'I mean, you and her?'

'No. I knew that would be a bad idea.'

'But . . .' Marsh set down her mug. 'You were stringing her along, right? I mean, you let her think that when all of this was over there was a chance?'

'She was unhappy, Kelly. She'd spent most of her life in a sewer. This was her chance to get out. She knew the risks. She'd seen what happened to people who snitched.'

'Look,' Marsh pushed a hand through her short hair, 'I'm just wondering. The more I hear about this, the more I worry that perhaps it's not such a great idea for you to be looking into this.'

'You're worried about Pryce? You think I won't be able to get past what he did to me?'

'You worked the case together. He filed corruption charges.'

'It was my word against his.'

'You were demoted, he was promoted. Where did they send you again?'

'Matlock.'

'Which most people couldn't find on a map.'

'Nowadays most people wouldn't know one end of a map from the other.'

'The point is, you would have been drummed out of the force if not for Wheeler.'

Drake was silent. He knew she was right.

'So?'

'So what?'

'So, can I ask?'

'Sounds like you already are.'

Kelly looked him in the eye. 'Were you taking money from anyone?'

'Do I really need to answer that?'

'Right now it would help. Right now anything would help.'

'Kelly, this is it. This is the moment to put it all to rest. There won't be a better time.'

'Maybe. Tell me about Pryce.'

'We worked the case together. He was on the outside, I was on the inside.'

'You trusted him?'

Drake tilted his head. 'I had doubts. But nothing's ever perfect, right? When you go undercover you have no choice. You have to hope that whoever is out there has got you covered.'

'Did you have any reason to suspect him of being on the take?'

Nothing solid was the answer to that. Hints, inconsistencies. Pryce has always had one eye on the career ladder, and bringing in Goran would have been a feather in both of their caps.

'There was a certain amount of rivalry between us. Nothing wrong with that. Look, Kelly, maybe you shouldn't be hearing all this. You have a career to think about.'

'Maybe I'm the best judge of that.'

'Pryce takes things personally. If he gets the idea you're siding with me could get nasty.'

en consider me duly warned. Now tell me why 'd hold on to her head for so long?'

question that had been going through Drake's

head since this thing first broke. He was still no closer to an answer.

'Whoever is behind this has been planning it for a long time.'

'But what for?'

'Could be for blackmail, or an insurance policy.'

'Meaning, maybe the people who killed her didn't trust each other?'

'Maybe we're not seeing the big picture. We're so focused on the idea that it's about Goran we can't see anything else.'

'You're saying someone else could have been involved back then? Someone nobody could see?'

'A third party.' Drake had considered the idea long and hard. 'The obvious candidate is Adonis Apostolis. He used Goran's death to move in on his operations. He did very well out of it.'

'You've never taken him down.'

'Donny is a tricky one. I've tried, but he moves around, keeps his nose clean.'

'You and him are tight.'

Drake glanced sharply at her. 'Where did you hear that?'

'I read Pryce's report. He claimed that Donny killed Goran. Lured him to Brighton, telling him that he had found his witness there, living in hiding.'

'Gunning down Goran in a car park in Brighton is not Donny's style.'

'Maybe it was the only chance he had.'

'It was a textbook killing, if your textbook was written by Hollywood mobsters.' Drake shook his head. 'Donny is a lot more subtle than that. He doesn't like to draw attention to himself. He's been trying to go straight for years.'

'So, what? Somebody was trying to make it look like Donny?'

'I don't know,' Drake admitted. 'But if you wanted to throw shade onto the obvious suspect, that's how you would do it. Even if that was the case, it still doesn't point to Donny killing Zelda.'

'Goran wouldn't have gone to Brighton if he'd known she was already dead.'

'Everything points to a third party.'

Marsh said, 'So we're talking about someone in the shadows. Someone nobody thought about at the time.'

'Someone who was on the inside but kept his head down. A lieutenant, or a foot soldier with ambitions.'

'No names spring to mind?'

'None, but we're making progress.'

Drake felt as though he had been going round and round on a funfair ride with no way of getting off, until now.

'How do you think Pryce fits into all this?'

Drake glanced round to be sure there was no one within earshot. 'I think DCI Pryce has a lot of secrets and he's probably shaken up by this. He'll try to sit on the case for as long as is humanly possible.'

Marsh tapped her fingernails on the rim of her mug. 'I get why you turned your back on us.'

'It wasn't about you,' he said, looking over at her. 'It was about me.'

'Sure.' Marsh sat back in her chair and contemplated him. 'Look, we're still catching up with last month. Break ins, assaults, burglaries, you name it. We're just treading water, and in this day and age that means the bad guys are way ahead of us. Especially when it comes to in-depth investigations, organised crime.'

'What are you saying?'

'I'm saying that if you want to run with it, this thing is yours, unofficially. Nobody's going to bother you. I can give you as much support as possible, mainly in the form of Milo dredging through the IT stuff.'

'Can you handle Pryce?'

'What he doesn't know can't hurt him. If he changes his mind and decides he wants to go for it then all bets are off. Until then, you're welcome to dig around. Unless you're too busy with all your wealthy clients.' She raised an eyebrow. 'That reminds me, the minicab you were interested in? Milo dug up a summary of his movements.' She reached into her jacket for a sheet of paper, which she handed over.

'Minicab? So, not Uber?'

'Puntland Private Cars.' Marsh spoke as Drake read. 'Driver's name given as Lal Ferit.'

Drake ran a finger down the list until he found what he was looking for: Kingsland Road to Pimlico. He looked up.

'Thanks for this, Kelly.'

'Just use it wisely.'

Drake folded the paper again and put it away. 'I let her down, Kelly. I promised I would keep her safe, and I didn't.'

'You couldn't.'

'Same thing, isn't it, at the end of the day?'

'Chief, I hate to break this to you, but you're a cop, private or otherwise. It's in your DNA. Your job was to get the bad guys, to use whatever means necessary to get the job done. Goran was the target. He did a lot of bad things, remember?'

'I remember.' Drake got to his feet. Kelly put out a hand to touch his arm.

'Cal, don't forget you're not alone on this.'

'Thanks, I won't. Just let me know if Pryce decides to change course.'

As she watched him through the window walking away, Kelly couldn't help wondering if she had made a mistake letting him get involved.

11

The big iron gate down at the road stood half open, which was not how Crane remembered things. In itself it was unremarkable, but it felt like a portent of what she could expect to find. Steering the bike through the gap, she twisted the throttle to send the Triumph shooting up the track that wound its way gently up the crest of the hill. To her left was a broad hillside dotted with trees. The grass a deep green. To her right a wall gave way to a high fence that ran alongside the unsurfaced track, separating empty fields from a more densely wooded area.

The sun broke through the indigo clouds as she reached the top and circled in front of the big house. Sunlight glinted off the high windows and painted the honey-coloured sandstone of the big house a rich amber. The driveway was empty but for a battered old white Range Rover that was parked over to one side. Crane climbed off the bike and looked up at the house. Her grandfather always used to tell the story that back in Cromwell's day a party of his Roundheads had commandeered the house as they headed north to do battle with the Royalists. Stories. This house was full of them. The last time she had been here was more than a decade ago, the day of her grandmother's funeral. Nothing else would have brought her back.

The front steps were worn and chipped. The original parts of the house were four hundred years old and it had received a few knocks in its time. The front door gave onto a wide vestibule with a chequered black-and-white tile floor. To her left light poured in through the high windows at the far end on the south side of the house. To her right a reception area and beyond that a dining room with views over the hillside down towards the hawthorns and yew trees that shrouded the river.

The only response to her shouted greeting was a heavy sigh that came from her left. She walked through into the drawing room, where a dappled grey mare was chomping contentedly on the stuffing coming out of an antique divan. The horse swung her head round to look at Crane and then carried on eating.

She wandered through the house, making a complete circuit of the ground floor and finding nothing but disorder. Overturned chairs and tables, the remains of what looked like weeks' worth of discarded food wrappings, empty bottles, whisky, gin and enough wine to sink a caravel. She lifted a bottle up to the light and saw sediment that had dried against the glass. She surprised two mice on the dining table.

A couple of geese were waddling along the upstairs landing. They paused here and there to tug free tufts of wool from the carpet. Her father was in what used to be called the library, although by the looks of it most of the books had been removed. Wearing a dressing gown, he was slumped over the big desk by the window, his long white hair in disarray. Her heart skipped a beat as it occurred to her that he might actually be dead. Then she saw his hand move, crawling across the polished teak towards a glass that had tipped its contents over the desk and onto the floor. Crane walked over and pushed open the windows to let some air in. Her father gave a shudder and sat up with a start.

'What are you trying to do?' he asked, squinting at her. 'Kill me?'

'If it was that easy, I'd have done it years ago,' she said, unzipping her jacket and throwing herself down in an armchair. He scrabbled around for his glasses and managed to put them on.

'What are you doing here?'

'I came to check whether you were still alive.'

'You always were the sentimental type.' He leaned back in his chair and yawned. 'What day is it?'

'Does it make a difference?'

'If you've come here to trade insults I'm not in the mood.'

'What's going on, Dad?'

'What do you mean?' He seemed baffled, as if he had no idea what she was talking about.

'I mean, look around you.'

'Look around? Don't you understand, I've been very busy.'

'I heard you were having problems.'

'What kind of problems? Look at me.' He thumped his chest. 'Sound of mind and body.'

'I'm not sure that qualifies as an expert opinion.'

Edmund Crane hung his head. 'You were always a contrary child. Never wanting to do anything you were told. You drove your mother mad.'

'Please. Don't bring my mother into it.'

The old man's lip trembled. 'Ungrateful and resentful, that's you. I mean, all of this will pass to you some day.'

Crane threw a glance about her. 'I hardly think so.'

'What are you going to do, give it to some socialist charity?'

'I can't think of a charity that would take it, other than an animal sanctuary. Are you expecting a flood or something?'

'Always so cynical. Why are you here anyway?'

'I heard you were in trouble.'

Edmund Crane was dismissive. 'Trouble? Nonsense. Where would you hear a thing like that?'

'Marco Foulkes.'

'Oh, that fool.' Edmund Crane's eyes sought refuge in the window. 'I tried to borrow money from him. He's got so much of it, I thought he wouldn't miss it. All those starry-eyed women buying his shoddy books. I mean, what has the world come to when you can peddle such rubbish as literature?'

'It's all gone downhill since Thomas Hardy.'

'Don't patronise me. I can't believe you're defending him.'

'I'm not. I certainly didn't come to talk about his writing. I want to know what he's been selling you.'

Edmund Crane groaned, putting his hands to his head. 'I asked him for a loan, just to tide me over. I have money coming in. It's just tied up in legal issues.'

'You mean the bank won't let you remortgage this place again?'

'When did you become a financial expert?'

'Why don't you get your old friends in the Foreign Office to help you? Oh, yes.' Crane smiled. 'That would be too humiliating. Asking for help.'

Edmund Crane grumbled to himself as he got to his feet. Stumbling across the room, he began pulling books off the shelves. Whole swathes of them tumbled to the floor until he found what he was looking for.

'Aha!' he said triumphantly, holding up a half bottle of Napoleon brandy.

With a sigh, Crane got to her feet and headed for the door, where she paused to look back.

'Why don't you get someone to help?'

'But I have someone.' The brandy had brought a smile to Edmund Crane's face. 'I have Hilda. You should say hello to her on the way out.'

Hilda? It took Crane a moment to remember Marco Foulkes' divorced mother's first name. She had been in pursuit of Edmund Crane for years. She vaguely recalled some story about them having been childhood sweethearts or something. The woman she found downstairs in the kitchen had mousey hair, the colour and texture of damp straw. She was wearing yellow rubber gloves and green wellies.

'He's not himself,' she confided.

'Clearly he can't manage. I mean, look at the place. He needs help.'

'Well, that's why I'm here.' Her smile was well meant, but shaky.

'All due respect, Mrs Foulkes, but you can't be expected to take care of him by yourself. You have your own life. He needs to hire somebody.'

'Well, he let them all go. The groundsmen, the housekeepers.' She lowered her voice. 'He doesn't like to talk about it, but it's his finances.'

'What's the matter with his finances?'

'Well, you didn't hear it from me, but . . .' Hilda's eyes lifted to the ceiling. 'I understand he made some unwise investments.'

Crane recalled Hilda Foulkes as eccentric and not particularly generous. A vain and rather self-absorbed woman with a fondness for wacky diets and health fads, all of which indicated a fragile grasp of reality. Perhaps Mrs Foulkes had finally taken leave of her senses.

'Marco explained it all to me. Most unfortunate. Your father put his money into a property company. Shares. Then the company was taken over by Russians, or something like that.' She paused to frown fiercely at the floor. 'Europeans in any case, or perhaps they weren't from Europe at all but somewhere in the east.'

Crane's patience was rapidly running out. It felt like a wasted trip.

'I can have a word with his solicitors, see if they can shed any light.'

'Yes, you should.' Hilda Foulkes' face lit up like a lantern. 'I understand you're helping Marco. He was always very fond of you.'

'That was a long time ago, Mrs Foulkes.'

'Hilda, please. We're practically family.'

Crane resisted the impulse to respond, deciding that compassion might be in order.

'Well, it's good he's got somebody to keep an eye on things.'

'I'm always here. I mean, I'm just across the way. You should come by some time.'

'I'll do that,' said Crane, with a smile so convincing she almost believed it herself.

12

Tuesday nights at Papa Zemba's could, generally speaking, be relied on to be quiet. They were playing Gregory Isaacs' 'Mr Cop'. On the elevated runway that ran down the central aisle within the U-shaped bar two women were gyrating around vertical poles, their skin glistening with oil and glitter. Behind the bar Zazie stood out like a shining beacon amongst all that darkness. She was standing in for her father. Usually she was a guarantee of a mellow mood. Her father came in early when the strippers were usually on, or later when trouble showed up. Tonight, however, Drake was surprised to find that things were a little more rowdy than normal.

'Private party.' As she spoke, Zazie rolled her eyes towards the far corner.

A group of about eight men were drinking hard. On the table at the centre of their booth they had a private dancer, who was doing her best to look as though she was enjoying herself while waving her behind at the men who were clapping and whistling like teenagers. They were young, in their twenties and thirties. One of the men stood up, took a swig of champagne from his glass and spat it all over the dancer. The woman didn't look too thrilled about this, but the men whooped, stamped their feet and showered her with twenty pound notes, which must have gone some way to easing her annoyance. The man holding the bottle of champagne took a bow.

'Who is that?' Drake asked.

'Zephyr. His friends call him Zef. He's Donny Apostolis' nephew.'

'I'm tempted to say he's grown up, but I'm not sure that's true.' Drake had a vague recollection of a spotty teenager from a few years back. 'Now he's partying with the big boys.'

'That one gets around.' Zazie leaned on the counter. 'One night it's the Russians, the next it's the Albanians. He's all over the place. I keep telling Papa he needs to get rid of these clowns and go for a better class of client. But what can you do? Money talks, right?'

'Talking your dad out of money would be like trying to persuade a leopard to change its spots.'

That brought him a laugh. Drake had a feeling that so long as Papa was calling the shots this was about as classy as it was ever going to get. He had been hoping for a quiet drink but the noise was a distraction so he drained his glass and was getting up to leave when somebody thumped into him from behind. He swung round to see a pale man swaying on his feet. He was in his early twenties. Dark hair, cut long at the front and combed back, the sides shaved to a bristle. A poster boy for the Hitler Youth, like something from another age.

'Sorry,' he muttered, before staggering away.

Drake didn't react. The man was clearly drunk. He watched him cut an unsteady path back towards the group in the corner.

'Who was that?' he asked Zazie. She had no idea. She looked over his shoulder and he turned to see Grayson Brodie walking towards him.

Brodie was small, compact and silent. His prematurely grey hair was shaved down to the length of metal filings. He walked casually, head down, hands hanging loosely by his sides. He gave the impression he wasn't paying attention, but Drake knew that he was registering every person in that room with every step that he took, evaluating the risk they posed.

'Cal.'

'How's it hanging, Brodie?'

'You know me, can't complain.' The two men shook hands. Brodie slipped onto the bar stool alongside Drake and ordered drinks for both of them.

'Are you babysitting tonight?'

'You could say that.' Brodie glanced over at the party and gave a weary shake of the head. 'Either they're getting younger or I'm getting older.'

'Who's the one in the middle, big feller?'

Brodie glanced across, turning his gaze on the large man who was wearing an open-necked black shirt that was tight around massive biceps.

'Khan.' Brodie sucked his teeth. 'Used to be a heavy for the Karachi mob, working for Hamid Balushi. As nasty as they come. Now I hear he's a free agent.'

'Is he working for Donny's family now?'

Brodie spread his hands wide. 'You know me, Cal. I don't ask questions.'

Which was true. The one thing Brodie was known for was his discretion. You could tell him anything and he would take it to the grave with him, so long as you had his loyalty. That was something that counted for him. Brodie would be loyal until the moment he wasn't; the moment he felt his trust had been betrayed.

Drake took another long look at Khan. His thick straight hair was cut into a foppish fringe that hung down over his face. The sides of his head were shaved clean. He was busy throwing money at the girl, who was bending over and shaking her hips at him. Drake knew he'd seen him before but couldn't remember the context. On his neck there was a dark tattoo of slashes and curves that looked like Arabic calligraphy, or in this case probably Urdu. Drake studied it, filing it away in his memory.

It was certainly an odd group of misfits. Difficult to say what they were doing together.

'So, how's the private eye thing working out for you?'

'Too early to say.'

Brodie was grinning. 'I'll give you six months, then you'll be begging to be reinstated.'

'You don't think I'll last.'

'Once a copper, always a copper.'

You might mistake Brodie for being slight, but it was all muscle and sinew. And he was a fast mover. Drake had known him since his days in the army, but since then Brodie had carved a career for himself as a hard man, a problem solver. You wanted something done and no questions asked, Brodie was your man.

'I guess it means I don't have to worry about having to take you in any more.'

Brodie lifted his glass in salute. 'Ah, you'd never have done it.'

'Now we'll never know.'

When he had first arrived in Iraq all those years ago, a complete rookie, trying to understand what he was doing patrolling a foreign country carrying an assault rifle, it was Brodie who had helped Drake to keep it together. 'There are moments in life, kid,' he told him, 'when the bigger picture can kill you. Focus on the details. The small things are what's going to save your life. Every time. The small things. Everything else is a distraction.'

How many times had Brodie saved his life? Hard to say. Directly, indirectly. His words would come back when you were under stress and they made you think it through, one more time. Often that meant the difference between life and death. Keep your eyes wide. Trust nobody. Double check everything. Sergeant Grayson Brodie, as he was then, was easily the most experienced man in the unit. None of the officers, with their Sandhurst training and their public school education, dared to make a move without his blessing. Brodie knew the terrain, but more than that he knew people. Didn't matter which side they were on or where they came from. It was an instinct for human nature. He knew who to trust and who to be wary of. Drake had seen him drinking with the men like there was no tomorrow, and going from that to stone cold sober in a matter of seconds when mortar shells started coming over the perimeter.

Like many others, Drake included, Brodie had lost his faith. He'd gone out there believing in the mission, in the existence of weapons of mass destruction and the moral duty to put an end to Saddam's reign of terror. What he saw told him there was a lot more at stake, things he could barely comprehend. He came back a broken man. It was only a matter of time before he drifted out of his marriage, his home, wandering from one job to another until he wound up living in the streets. After that there was a stint abroad, working as a military contractor.

The two men had finally come face to face again, years later, staring each other down across a darkened container park in Dagenham. They were on opposite sides. Drake was undercover and Brodie had become a hired hand for Goran Malevich. If either of them had acknowledged at that moment that they knew each other, both would probably have died, so they walked away without even a flicker of recognition passing between them. If it had been anyone else, Drake would have been worried, but with Brodie, somehow he knew he was safe.

Drake had spent six months posing as a small-time drug dealer eager to move up in the world. He had used the name Nash and was at that moment looking to unload a shipment of high-grade cocaine. It bought him a way in to the organisation.

Fitting into Goran's world wasn't all that hard. Drake had come back from Iraq feeling rage and anger at the people who had sent him out there. Not knowing what he wanted to do except that he didn't want to go back to his old life. He passed straight through police training without a hitch and soon gained himself something of a reputation. Running in when caution suggested otherwise. When the offer came that they were looking for someone to go undercover he was the first to volunteer. He was way more qualified than any of the other candidates. That much was plain. He had the right profile and the warnings about Goran only made him want it more. He was no longer afraid. It felt as though he'd been through fire. What could he possibly fear?

'You hear about the head they found on the Tube?'

'Yeah, it was on the news.' Brodie's eyes never left the stage, where a slim blonde was turning cartwheels in the spotlight. 'Makes you wonder what this country is coming to.'

'Remember Zelda?'

Brodie looked round sharply. 'Come on, man, that's water under the bridge.'

'I thought so too, until I saw it.'

Brodie swore under his breath. 'That's police business. I thought you were out of it.'

'You know how it is. Unfinished business. I thought I'd take a poke around.'

'Well, mind it doesn't turn around and poke you back.' Brodie took a long swig from his glass and wiped his mouth with the back of his hand. 'Are they sure it's her?'

'The pathologist is trying to match it to the corpse that washed up on the beach.'

'That was four years ago.'

'The case was unresolved, so they kept her in storage.'

Brodie swore again. 'Look, Cal, just take my advice and leave it alone.'

'She didn't deserve it, not like this.'

'Listen to me, she knew what she was doing. She had been in the game long enough. She knew what Goran was like.'

Drake slipped a sheet of paper onto the counter. It was his copy of the same newspaper clipping that had been found wrapped around the head.

'Someone is making this personal,' he said.

Brodie glanced at the clipping. 'Who?'

'Whoever is responsible for leaving her head on the train. It was wrapped in that.'

Brodie ran his eyes over the article. 'Might be a coincidence.'

'Doesn't feel like a coincidence.'

'Makes no sense. I mean, why hold on to her for all this time?'

'Maybe this is the first chance they've had.'

'Doesn't sound right. I mean, at the time, you went over all of this, right?'

'Right.'

'This isn't how Donny or any of the others would play it. You'd be hanging upside down in a warehouse somewhere with a welding torch to your head.'

'So how do you explain this?' Drake tapped the paper.

'How? It's a fucking psycho, is how.' Brodie threw up a hand and called for another round of drinks. 'Take my word for it.'

'I still keep coming back to the question of who killed her.'

'Well, obviously the wacko has been running around with her head for four years. What did he do with it, keep it in the freezer alongside the fish fingers?'

'It might not have been the same person.'

'So what?' Brodie frowned. 'Somebody came along and just cut her head off?'

'I don't know how it went down. I'm just asking questions.'

'Right. You keep doing that and it'll get you into trouble.'

'That's the point.' Drake indicated the clipping. 'I'm already in this. Someone clearly holds me responsible for her death.'

'You mean, they're coming after you? But why?' Brodie scratched the tip of his nose. 'Unless they think you killed her.'

Loud whooping brought their attention back to the party across the room. In the middle of the fray Zephyr, Donny's nephew, was surrounded by women. The kind that seemed to have been constructed out of male sexual fantasies. They all had straight, shiny hair and skimpy dresses. Over-inflated breasts, long legs and short attention spans. They had practised laughs that displayed a lot of even teeth and their English was barely good enough to order a drink. Despite this, or perhaps because of it, Zephyr was like a pig in muck. He was sitting back, arms around a pair of them, ordering more champagne. He didn't even seem to mind the disturbance.

'What happened to the rest of Goran's men after he died?'

'It's water under the bridge, Cal, let it go.'

'He left a lot of action behind and Donny scooped up a fair portion of it.'

'You know Donny, he hates to see opportunity go to waste.' Brodie licked his lips. He wasn't the kind of man you wanted to play poker with. He gave little away. But he did have a conscience. A rarity in his line of work.

'You were one of the few people who was there back then. You were on the inside.'

'It wasn't a good time. I was in a bad way. My head was messed up.'

'Brodie, help me out here. You're the only one from that time I can go to.'

'Look, we're mates, right? We've been through shit. We got through it because we had each other's backs. That counts for something, right?'

'Sure. I'm not trying to put this on you.'

'Goran's men were like a tribe. They stuck to themselves and didn't let us mere mortals close to the inside track.'

'If it wasn't Goran or Donny, then who?'

'It's over, Cal. Move on.'

There was a crash as one of the girls toppled off the table

into the lap of the big man, Khan. She spilled something onto his jeans. Angrily he tossed her onto the floor. Then all of a sudden it was turning nasty.

'Shit!' muttered Brodie. 'I'd better sort this out.' He rested a hand on Drake's shoulder. 'If I think of anything I'll give you a call.'

Drake watched him go, slipping back through the crowd. He wondered in passing how many men Brodie had killed. Under the quiet stillness of him there was the smell of death. He'd seen and done things that would give most people a breakdown. There was no doubt he'd been through some hard places. In Iraq, but also after he left the service. As a contractor, Brodie had seen action all over. Afghanistan, Syria, Mali. Drake only knew a few of the stories.

As he got up to leave, something made him turn around. Across the room, in the shadows, behind the melee, he caught a glimpse of the young man with the Hitler Youth haircut who had bumped into him earlier. He was staring right at Drake.

13

The shoe box full of old photographs was tucked into the back of a drawer at the bottom of the wardrobe. Crane sat down cross-legged on the floor and lifted the lid. She wasn't by nature a sentimental person. Her patience for that kind of poring over past events was limited, to say the least. She had always been so. There was nothing but the present. So perhaps she was changing as she was getting older. She would soon pass the forty mark and maybe that was significant. Birthdays were not something that she celebrated. They were as meaningless to her as Christmas.

She hadn't always felt that way. She still had fond memories of Ramadan in Tehran with her grandparents. The whole house would be full of relatives. So many aunts and uncles whose names she could barely remember. But they all knew who she was; the little girl who lived in England and whose Farsi was a clunky hash of misunderstandings topped with a bad accent. But she was one of them. They made that clear. She belonged. After the breaking of the fast the long nights were spent wandering the lighted avenues. She recalled squares full of people enjoying the cool night air, the endless rounds of greetings, the pastry shops and ice-cream parlours that buzzed with cheerful energy. It was like a month-long party and everyone was in on it.

The box contained a jumble of pictures, snapshots saved from her childhood along with prints from before the digital era struck. The earliest ones were colour faded, tinged now with a reddish orange hue. One showed her as a little girl with long black hair, standing next to the penguin enclosure in Regent's Park. That was always her favourite spot. She had even gone there a few times as an adult. The picture would have been taken by her father. She held it up, closer to the light to see better. Her mother looked younger than she remembered. How old would she have been then? Probably not much older than Ray was now.

The last time Crane saw her mother was in Tehran in 1995 when she was taken away by the Republican Guard. She was a few months shy of sixteen at the time. Her father was teaching at the university. Both of them were. What she didn't know then was that Edmund Crane was also an agent for British Intelligence.

Twelve years later found Crane in Iraq in 2007, working for the SIS herself, assisting Stewart Mason. She was assigned to a special investigations unit: Directorate for Operational Research and Intelligence Strategy (DORIS), which was a long-winded title for a unit that nobody really knew the purpose of. She found herself working alongside an international team from a range of different backgrounds. The idea being to bring their varied experience to bear on the way the war was going, to pinpoint weaknesses and, above all, to make predictions about what was to come. The war in Iraq was into its fourth year. The insurgency was changing up its tactics, metamorphosing into something that would eventually become Islamic State. Their job was to look under every rock, to talk to prisoners, soldiers, civilians, ex-Baath officials. All with the idea of building up a composite of the mental state of this nation which was unravelling under the pressure of the occupation. People no longer had jobs, they were frightened for their future, their children.

Another picture from around the same time showed all three of them. This was when they were visiting Tehran, staying in borrowed accommodation or with friends. These were her father's rebellious days, when he had turned his back on his family and refused to take their money. Her mother found work teaching at Tehran university and father was writing a novel instead of finishing his doctorate on Macaulay. He still dressed like a hippy in those days, his long blond hair already thinning to reveal the bald patch that would eventually take over the top of his head. Looking at the picture now, she imagined it was easy to see what her mother saw in him. You could see in his smile that he was still open, easy-going. All of that was to change. It must have been around then that he was recruited.

They were afraid of bombs, of kidnapping. These kinds of things could lead people into dangerous areas. DORIS's job was to identify what those areas were and who was being drawn to them.

The picture she held in her hand now showed a group of them. It was taken on one of their regular Friday barbecues. Their forward operating base was a handful of shipping containers set in the corner of a US military base outside Fallujah. They were close to the east-west highway that ran from Baghdad to Amman. The photograph was a print one of the others had made and sent to her. She was the only woman in the picture. They were all holding up bottles of beer and smiling. Her eye was drawn to the bearded man standing next to her. Orlando Araya. A Mexican American who had worked for the DEA before transferring to counter-terrorism. He was brought in as a specialist in urban warfare and indoctrination. For a time they had been close, although she had never really been sure whether he was completely honest with her about who he was working for. Orlando was smart. He played his cards close to his chest. They had a thing that, like everything out there, was built on the fact that all was temporary. He was transferred to Afghanistan and then disappeared below the surface. She had no idea where he was now.

She was rotated out, first to Dubai, which she hated, then to northern Iraq. It was there in 2013 that the event that really triggered the end of her time with the SIS and with Stewart Mason occurred. In February of that year she had been in a convoy heading east away from the Syrian border when they were ambushed and taken hostage by a small militia group. They were lucky in the sense that these were basically criminals hoping to cash her in for a fat prize from Islamic State. The disadvantage was that they were undisciplined. Crane was locked into a tiny space no bigger than a large closet. Her fear of confinement stemmed from there.

It was the longest six weeks of her life. Every day, every hour, felt like her last. She was convinced that she was going to be raped and murdered, dumped by the side of the road. They bought into her cover as an NGO trying to help women.

The fact that she spoke Arabic helped her. The men weren't sure what to make of her. She was lucky also that Islamic State couldn't make up their minds. Messengers went back and forth but there was always a problem of some kind. When she was finally liberated by a group of Kurdish women fighters she was literally hours away from being handed over.

It wasn't a time she talked about much, but seeing her father had brought it all back. She had decided long ago that the easiest way of dealing with him was just not to. Cut all ties and keep her distance. She had never forgiven him for abandoning her mother. She knew that she would never get over that, so the easiest thing was to let go of him. Which had worked fine until the moment Marco Foulkes walked into her office.

What should have been a straightforward job was proving to be anything but. Marco was using her, or trying to. She was pretty sure of that now. What intrigued her was how it tied in to Howeida's disappearance, and also to her father's financial situation.

Dropping the pictures back into the box, Crane slid the lid into place. Instead of rummaging around in her past she ought to have been out there with her partner, working on this investigation. And that was another problem. She was beginning to ask herself if Cal Drake really was a suitable partner. He seemed to have his own issues and by the looks of things would not be able to give his full attention to this case, or any other for that matter, until he had put to rest whatever it was in his past that was bothering him.

'What kind of a mess have I got myself into?' she asked herself aloud.

14

The sound of a helicopter rattled overhead, bringing Drake instantly awake. The sound always triggered a visceral memory that left him gasping for breath, his fingers clawing at the sheets, waiting for his mind to settle. As he stared at the ceiling he realised he had been dreaming about Zelda.

'Where did you find a name like that?'

'Zelda?' She looked surprised. 'You never heard of F. Scott Fitzgerald?'

Drake had to plead ignorance. He'd heard of him, of course, but never actually read anything by him. She looked at him as though she felt sorry for him. So much so that he went out and bought a copy of *The Great Gatsby* on his way home.

Zelda was fine. In his reports, that was the name he used. He didn't write down her real name anywhere. He told Pryce that she was a known criminal informant, without disclosing her identity. He was too worried about leaks. He was a detective inspector back then. Going undercover was a little below his paygrade, but he knew he was the best suited for the task and that nobody was going to stop him. Taking down Goran Malevich would have been a big feather in his cap.

But Pryce was leery. He wasn't happy that Drake refused to share his informant. Until he could prove she was valuable, that her information was good, Drake knew Pryce would never give him any credit. So he pressed her, and one day she came up with the goods: a flat in Camberwell. Pryce was pushing to undermine him. Drake knew that he needed to prove to him as well as to senior command that his work was good, that his informant was reliable. So he'd activated an immediate action raid based on Zelda's intelligence and they went in, not knowing what they would find.

The moment they broke open the front door the stink that

hit them was enough to make them retch. Inside, it was hard to see. The windows were taped over with newspaper, aluminium foil and glossy sheets ripped from porn magazines, alongside bikini-clad celebrities from the *Daily Mail*. His flash-light skimmed across, picking up headlines: 'Tali-ban-anas'; 'Panama Papers'; 'Hourglass Curves'. Like dipping a toe into the sewer of a confused state of mind. He didn't need it. What he needed was light, but he wasn't going to touch anything.

It still wasn't clear who was running this place. Zelda said it was Goran's but Drake wasn't sure how true that was. This was nothing like the kind of place he normally would have associated with the man. This was a glimpse into the black hole of his universe. Goran Malevich liked glamour, gambling and strip clubs, vodka and Cristal on ice. There were no bulbs in the light fittings. No water in the pipes. The uniforms crowded into the doorway behind him and Drake motioned for them to stay back. He held his breath as he edged past a toilet that looked as though something nasty had died and rotted.

'How many people are registered here?' he had asked the landlord just before they effected entry. The man was loitering in the doorway as if getting ready to do a runner, sucking nervously on a cigarette even though Drake had told him not to. He was unshaven. A grubby vest and sweat pants underneath an old gabardine raincoat. The man gave a useless shrug and started on a long rambling litany. Registered? Yeah, right. Nobody had any idea. Nobody cared. Now he was poking his head inside and going off on a noisy rant in what might have been Urdu. Drake suspected he was trying to warn whoever was in the flat.

'Quiet!' Drake could hear something. He held up a hand. One of the uniforms dragged the man back out onto the outside landing where he should have been in the first place. When things start to go pear-shaped it always seems to start in multiple places at the same time.

The silence was broken again. A faint scratching, squirming sound, like something wriggling about inside the walls. He went back to the front entrance and pushed everyone back.

Then he started inside again, down the hallway on the right. Past the toilet again. He stopped. Then back again. He shone the flashlight beam into a bath caked with what might have been mud, blood or shit. Beyond that was a small room. The last in the hallway. A bedroom. Posters of starlets in sequins and boy bands in hair gel. The sounds were coming from inside the wall. He pressed his ear to an Arsenal poster of the 2009 squad. Almunia, Nasri and Sol Campbell. He slid his way along until he reached the wardrobe. The sounds were stronger there. It was piled high with cardboard boxes, old trainers, a set of boxing gloves that a dog had chewed up. Junk you might find on a tip. He dragged it out of the way.

Someone had screwed a makeshift door into place. Hinges on one side and two metal hasps on the other, all held with outsize padlocks. Whatever was inside there was valuable to someone.

Drake poked through the boxes until he came up with a screwdriver. The bit had snapped off but there was still enough of the shaft to jam into the space between the clasp and the wall. He thumped on the door. The sounds from within became more frantic. Hysteria. Wailing, rising and falling.

Drake went out into the hall and called back to the uniforms.

'Get social services down here,' he yelled to no one in particular. He went back into the room and leaned on the handle until the nails slowly began to squeal. The wails from within turned into frantic screams. The second hinge proved more difficult. He was sweating by now. One of the uniforms came in with a crowbar. As he pulled the makeshift door open Cal caught a finger on a nail. He swore as it swung out then instantly reeled back from the stench.

The torch beam picked out ten, twelve of them in the tiny space, their eyes white against skin that was dark by nature, or grubby from lack of washing. Boys and girls, the oldest would have been about ten. They were crouched down in the far corner, huddled together, crying and clutching one another.

'Jesus wept!' muttered the uniform at his shoulder, who then began swearing and only stopped when Drake shook him. He snapped his fingers a couple of times in the man's face and he seemed to come out of his trance. Drake pushed him out of the way and waved a WPC forward.

'Let's get them down to the paramedics,' he said to her.

The children were weak. Some of them could barely stand, having been confined in that narrow space for so long. Turning back, he swept the torch about the little prison cell. It was the size of a bathroom in a cheap hotel. Just enough room to walk in and turn around. A bucket in the corner functioned as a toilet. The stench was thick enough to cut with a knife. Drake forced himself to swallow.

'It's all right,' he said, over the clamour. 'It's okay.' He didn't know if they understood English, perhaps he was trying to reassure himself as much as them. Finally he stepped aside as the paramedics arrived. The hallway was crowded with more uniforms. Looking big and clean, newly minted, all eager to see what they'd found.

'Let's back off here, give them some space. They're scared to death.'

One man was wiping tears from his eyes. Drake pushed past them all. He had to get out.

The grey light hit him with a jolt, as if he had forgotten that it was still daytime. As if such things could exist in broad daylight. He had to force himself to breathe evenly and deeply. He leaned on the concrete balustrade and waited for the dizziness to pass. Down below in the car park the cold blue light was dotted with the flash of more emergency vehicles arriving. A chorus of sirens was building in the distance.

Drake knew the risk he was taking, conducting a raid like this himself, that his cover might be blown, but he was convinced this was the beginning of the end. It was big, bigger than he had imagined. The only problem was linking it to Goran. Pryce made it clear that it wasn't enough. There wasn't enough to link the flat to Goran. Drake went back to Zelda, who could not understand.

'But why? I give you what you want.'

'It's not enough. I need more.'

'It's dangerous for me. I don't have more.'

Finally, after weeks of trying to calm her, Drake managed to convince her that the only other way was for her to testify. She shook her head.

'You don't know what they will do to me.'

'They'll never find you.'

'Goran finds anybody.'

Drake wasn't happy with it himself. He remembered that last meeting at an underpass in Brentwood. Zelda was standing close to the wall, half out of sight. The lighter in her hand clicked restlessly even though she had a lit cigarette in the other hand. She had a striking face that carried the trace of the long road that had brought her to this place. A sadness that seemed to be engrained in her soul. She was wearing a long grey faux fur coat that made her resemble a cat. Its colour matched her eyes.

'I give you so much and still it's not enough. It's never enough.'

'But we're close now. This is bigger than we imagined. Did you know they were trafficking children?'

Zelda shook her head. 'I hear things. I tell you what I know.'

'We need to pin down the whole network.'

'I can't. All over the country. They have people.'

'Goran knows about this?'

'Goran knows everything.'

'Where do they come from?'

'All over. Holding centres, shelters. Here, in Europe.' She was fluttering, like a skittish pony ready to take off. 'I have to go.'

'No, it's too late for that.' Drake caught her arm.

'I have to go back. They'll know it's me.'

Drake could see the panic in her eyes. She was tough, but this was something that scared her.

'You can't go back,' he said.

'Then what am I supposed to do?' She looked into his eyes.

'We have to end this, and you have to help me.'

'I can't.' Her voice was breaking. 'When they know I told you . . . You have no idea.'

'You have to disappear. Right now. Take nothing with you. Don't go back to your place.'

'I can't. I can't just go.'

'Zelda, listen to me. This is it.' He rested a hand on her shoulder. 'If we can pin this on Goran then he's finished. He'll go away for a long time.'

'I don't believe you. He has too many people in his pocket, even police.'

'Not me.' Drake reached into the inside pocket of his combat jacket and pulled out a burner. Brand new, straight out of the packet. 'Just you and me. Nobody else. There's only one number on there. You call me when you've found somewhere.'

Her eyes widened. 'This is crazy.'

'Think of those children. That's why you're doing this. Remember that.'

'I can't.' She wiped angrily at the tears running down her face. Then she looked at him. 'Come with me.'

He knew what she was asking. He'd known this question was coming, had dreaded it.

'Later, when it's safe.'

'You promise?'

'I promise. The main thing is to get you out of here.' He handed her an envelope stuffed with cash. 'That'll keep you going for now. I'll get more to you.'

She looked at the money. 'You protect me? You promise?'

'Yes, I promise. But you can't speak to anyone about this. Not even the girls at the club.' He watched Zelda run a painted thumbnail over the cash. 'You lay low. Somewhere you've never been before. You get there and sit tight. You understand? Tell me you understand?'

'Yes, yes, okay. I understand.' She wiped more tears away. She stuffed the envelope into the red bag slung over her shoulder. 'I can't do this alone.'

'You won't be alone, not for long.' Drake squeezed her shoulder. He felt the tremors running through her body. 'Go somewhere nice. Somewhere you've always wanted to go.'

'The sea. I like the sea.'

'Okay, good, then find a place by the sea.' Drake smiled. 'All of this will be over soon. We'll put the case together and go after Goran. Once that's done you'll be under protection. You won't have to fear him ever again.'

Her eyes held his. 'I need to know you're not going to just abandon me.'

'I won't abandon you.'

'When I'm gone. You won't forget me?'

'I won't forget you. I promise. Just do exactly what I say.'

Zelda gave a loud sniff and tossed her hair. 'I'm not idiot.'

Could he have saved her? If he had gone to Brighton sooner, perhaps? He should have gone. There had been no doubt in his mind, but he knew he had been playing long odds. It was his decision to hide her away unofficially. To keep her off the books, as it were. He told himself he had to be careful. But he knew that wasn't the only reason. Another part of him was afraid, afraid of leading her on, afraid that it might lead to something else. He needed to keep his distance.

In the inquiry they asked him why he had gone behind the backs of this superiors and fellow officers. His argument was simple. The reason Goran had managed to evade arrest for so long was the obvious one, that he had protection inside the police. He knew he was taking a risk. Going against standard procedure meant that if anything went wrong it would be his to own. He knew that time was of the essence. Drake was confident his cover hadn't been blown, but he knew he couldn't assume the same about Zelda. Goran would have all his people out looking for her in a matter of hours.

Then complications set in. The case became bogged down, tied up in legal matters. Convincing the CPS that there was a rock solid link between the children and Goran proved difficult. They seemed to be aware that if they were going to go up against someone like that they needed to be sure of what they were getting into. Drake found himself mired in paperwork, trying to put together an argument they would go for. In the end it came down to Zelda. There was also a lot of pressure to bring his key witness in. There was even a suggestion that she didn't exist, that he had simply invented her to cover himself and make the case more convincing. Some of this came from Vernon Pryce, who was milking the opportunity to make Drake look bad. Never one to miss a chance to promote himself. It was almost as if he cared more about getting himself ahead than he did about bringing Goran in.

Eventually, Drake caved. Zelda had been calling him non-stop, craving more and more attention. In the beginning it was practical things: she needed more money, or she was afraid someone was watching her. She wanted to find a better place to live. Later, these conversations evolved into what were almost therapy sessions. He would listen to her telling him about her life. How she was unhappy. She was scared. She didn't believe she would ever get out of this mess. These phone calls, invariably in the evenings, often late at night, would go on for hours. Drake began to worry that she was unravelling. By then she had settled in Brighton. He drove down and they spent the day together. They walked along the sea front. They sat in a café and stared at the sea.

'I can't go on like this,' she sobbed. 'I feel like I'm a prisoner.'

'It's not going to be much longer,' he told her. Not quite true under the circumstances, but he needed her to stay on board. She was his only chance in this.

'We need more.'

'Come on!' Zelda was incredulous. 'I've told you everything I know.'

'It's not me. The prosecution needs a stronger case. They need facts and figures, names and dates. Anything you can remember. Anything at all could be useful.'

'We've had this conversation before. How many times do I have to tell you. Give me a new identity. Give me a place to live. A real place, not a room in a boarding house where I can hear the neighbours fucking in the next room. I had a life. I want it back.'

'It doesn't work like that. I have to prove to them that you are worth it.'

'What about everything I've given you already?'

'I'm not the one who makes the rules. I just have to play by them.'

She leaned forward, resting a hand on his arm. 'I thought you believed in me. In us.'

The light from outside drew patterns on the ceiling. The rain had turned to hail. The little granules of ice clattered lightly against the glass.

How many times had Drake thought back to that day? It seemed to be in constant replay in his head. That was the moment when he knew he was losing her, that the CPS would never have enough and that he was going to have to find another way.

When she disappeared the following week he was not completely surprised. Deep down he had known that it could happen at any time. Whatever he saw in her eyes that day, she had seen in his. She had taken the only obvious course; she had taken her chances and gone on the run.

When the body washed up he knew in his heart that it was her. A woman in her early thirties. No identifying marks except the tattoo of a seahorse on her right thigh. He remembered driving down to the morgue in Brighton. He didn't need to look. She'd been in the water for days, but he knew it was Zelda. There was only one problem. The head was missing.

15

Walking in through the front door of the building on St James's Street, Crane had to step around a couple of builders who were struggling to put up a heavy brass plaque engraved with the names of the solicitors who worked in the firm. The hallway floor was covered by strips of cardboard and plastic sheeting. There were buckets of paint and men in overalls. Just inside the entrance a door on the right led into a reception area, where a woman wearing a headset was saying, 'Clayton Navarro, how can I help you?'

Her fingernails were long and curved and painted a shade of magenta with little gold nuggets stuck to them like dead insects. There was something out of place about her, which told Crane she was probably a temp. In between fielding calls she managed to take Crane's name and push a button on her console. She didn't have to wait long before she heard her name.

'Miss Crane?'

The man coming through the doorway from the hall was short with curly blond hair that had been parted and combed down with the use of some kind of wax. The grey-blue suit he wore was too tight. It made him look like an oversized doll come to life. His name, he said, was Dean Mitchell. He began by apologising. 'I'm sorry. As you can see, we're having the place redecorated.'

Crane wasn't interested in the decorating or the charm. She was, however, curious about why Mitchell was so nervous.

'I'm not exactly sure how I can help you.'

'It's simple. I have become a little concerned about my father's financial situation.'

'I see.'

'I understand that he's made some rather unwise investments recently.'

'I'm afraid I can't really help you,' said Mitchell.

'Look at it this way.' Crane smiled. 'If I find out that your firm misled my father in any way then your lack of cooperation at this point is not going to help your case in any lawsuit.'

There was a moment of silence. Even the receptionist stopped tapping her nails on the phone. Dean Mitchell swallowed.

'We seem to be at cross purposes. I would very much like to help you, but I am limited in what I can tell you.'

'Why don't we start with what you can tell me?'

Mitchell gestured towards the window alcove, where they were at least afforded some privacy. He tapped the file he was holding.

'I can tell you that your father has remortgaged the estate a couple of times.'

'That was at least ten years ago,' said Crane.

'Something like that.'

'I'm concerned with something more recent.'

'There I can't help you.'

'Why not?'

'Because your father is no longer a client at Clayton Navarro.'

'There must be some mistake. He's been here for years. His father was a client of yours.'

'As far as I know your father made it clear he was transferring his interests elsewhere.'

'Why would he do that?'

'I really can't say.'

Crane folded her arms. 'You don't actually know anything about this, do you?'

Mitchell's face took on a pained expression.

'It's all right, I'm not blaming you. I just want to get to the bottom of this. To be entirely frank with you, I don't honestly care whether he lives or dies. What I don't like, what makes me angry, is the idea that someone is taking advantage of him. Does that make sense?'

'Yes, of course,' Mitchell nodded. 'Perfectly.'

'So, let's try this again.'

Mitchell looked pained. He pushed a hand over his hair. 'There has been a lot of change recently.'

Crane nodded at the work going on in the hallway. 'New management?'

Mitchell glanced over at the receptionist and dropped his voice. 'The firm was taken over by a large holding company.'

'What's the name of this company?'

'The Kratos Corporation.'

'Kratos?'

'It's Greek. The name of a god, I think, but aren't they all?'

'Kratos was the son of Styx, the deity that guarded the river between the earth and the underworld.'

'Ah, well, there you are.' Mitchell nodded, as if this was another irrelevant fact he was eager to forget.

Crane was struggling to control her temper. It was like getting blood from a stone.

'I take it a lot of people have been fired?'

'Yes, that's about the size of it.'

'So who was it, the person who handled his affairs?'

'I think it was Barnaby Nathanson.' Mitchell frowned. 'I would have to check.'

'I take it he's no longer here. That's why I'm talking to you, right?'

'That would be correct.'

'Okay, now we're getting somewhere. So, tell me, Dean, how long ago did Nathanson leave Clayton Navarro?'

'That would be about a year ago.'

'Did this have anything to do with the new owners?'

'Mr Nathanson's leaving?' Mitchell's face darkened. 'I don't think so.'

'Do you know where I can find him, Nathanson?'

'I can find out.'

'That would be helpful.' Crane decided she had spent enough time on this. She only had one more question. 'My father's health is not good. If he were to pass away what would happen to the estate?'

'Oh, well, I couldn't say.'

'Humour me, just give me a general view based on what's in the file. You have read the file, at least?'

'Oh, yes.' Mitchell hesitated. 'As far as I can tell the value of the estate is already overstretched by bank loans and such. It's a big property so there's a substantial amount there. It all depends on what he has done this last year. You would have to speak to Mr Nathanson.'

'Let's say he's made some bad decisions.'

'Well, in the worst case scenario he could see the bank forcing him to sell in order to cover his losses incurred. But, like I said . . .'

'You don't want to speculate. Yes, I think I gathered that.'

On her way out, Crane had to step aside to make way as two painters traipsed by carrying rolls of wallpaper and pots and brushes. Her eye fell on the brass plaque that had been removed. Barnaby Nathanson was halfway down.

16

Drake replayed the footage from the CCTV camera in the train carriage on his laptop. He'd already been over it a dozen times. He knew the sequence by heart. Doors opening, people shuffling forwards, doors closing, train departing. New passengers moving, platform filling up, new train arriving. He went through every person, watched the flow of people coming in, jostling about, getting in each other's way. He watched them stepping aboard and stepping off. He saw young people and old. Carrying suitcases, rucksacks, shopping bags, children. People going about their daily routines. The counter in the top right-hand corner ticked off the minutes. In his email, Milo had conveniently added a timescale that ran down the left-hand side with the times that corresponded to each stop.

17:58 marked the moment when the head rolled out of the bag as the train began to slow, pulling into Clapham Common station. Suddenly everyone was moving at once and it was difficult to keep sight of what was happening, who was moving where. Centre stage was Ruby Brown, mother of Tyler, who appeared somewhat hysterical, understandable under the circumstances, one arm wrapped around her baby grabbing her son and trying to get off the train. Drake watched her actually kick one woman out of her way. The space around the IKEA bag cleared as people tripped over one another in their haste to get away from it and out of the carriage. Most passengers clearly had no idea what it was everyone was fleeing from. They couldn't see what was on the floor. They simply assumed the worst and fought their way out. A bomb was the most obvious thing running through their minds. The panic could be seen spreading like fire through the carriage and spilling out along the platform.

Drake moved on, scrolling through the files, going from station to station, trying to pin down the precise moment when the bag was brought on board. The train was so crowded at that time it was difficult to see. The spot where the bag had been placed also did not help. Being tucked into the corner behind the seats meant that even when it could be seen, only a triangle of the nylon bag was visible.

Drake rolled the tape back, moving the cursor at the bottom of the screen towards the left. Now he watched the scene at Euston, where there was a sudden surge in the number of people getting on board. Four Asian teenagers huddled together by the door. From their clothes Drake would have said Japanese. A large group of adolescents who looked like they were part of a school trip flooded the central part of the carriage. At that point Ruby Brown and her children were squashed into the corner. The pressure eased slightly at Leicester Square, and then thickened again at Charing Cross. The bag was already in place, just out of sight on the floor. The boy, Tyler, could be seen kicking his leg back and forth, his attention clearly drawn to something tucked into the corner in the luggage area.

Rolling the video back again, Drake tried to pick out individuals getting on and off the train. At a certain point it all began to blur and he was no longer sure what he was seeing. He decided to take a break and went down to the kitchen to make himself a coffee. While he waited for the water to boil he took a couple of swings at Ray's punchbag. He remembered being surprised when he'd first seen it hanging there. Who keeps a punchbag at the office? In time, he'd come to appreciate the way taking a few swings could help take the edge off. For a while he forgot all about the severed head and indeed the coffee.

Back upstairs he sat down behind the desk and resumed work. At Leicester Square, where the maybe Japanese women got off the train, another passenger close to the doors at the centre of the carriage got off to let other people out and then got on again just before the train departed. Drake moved the tape in increments, trying to get a better look at him. The pixellation made any close identification difficult. He guessed the man was in his twenties. He was wearing a lot of layers. Several jackets hanging off him. A sweatshirt with the hood up over a baseball cap, and still no bag in sight.

Drake worked backwards to the point when there was only a handful of people in the carriage. He went through them one by one. They made up an average assortment of the city's inhabitants. Middle-aged white woman with a terrier on her lap. The picture of respectability. Glasses, sensible shoes and clothes. He put her age around the sixty mark. No husband. Divorced? Widowed? Next to her was a young black woman. Late thirties. Wearing large spectacles that seemed to have been chosen, like the rest of her outfit, as a form of disguise. The polo neck, baggy trousers and heavy boots, all black. Around her waist she had tied a parka of some kind that flopped around like a dead animal. She had two or three shapeless bags hanging from her shoulders. She could almost have been a homeless person, but her clothes were too clean for that. Across from her was an old man. West Indian, was Drake's guess. In his sixties, fiddling on his phone with some kind of game, it looked like.

That left the man in the baseball cap. It was hard to see his face beneath the hood and cap, neither of which he ever removed. He shifted around a lot, from one end of the carriage to another. It wasn't even clear if it was actually a man. The person's hair was completely hidden. The logo on the cap was all he had to go on. Fender. As in the guitar? Judging by the layers of clothes the person wore they might have been sleeping rough. Baggy, dirty jumpers, a fleece jacket and grey gym pants without markings. Basically, the whole outfit might have been fished out of a charity bin.

Ruby Brown and her children had got onto the Tube at Finsbury Park. They took the Victoria Line to Euston, where they switched to the Northern Line. 'Fender', as Drake now dubbed this person, was the one closest to the spot in the carriage where the blue IKEA bag had been left. He or she got off the train at Warren Street. Platform footage showed that Fender remained on the platform, shuffling up and down, peering into bins, before boarding another southbound Northern Line train. This time the subject got off at Kennington, crossing through the connecting tunnel to another southbound train. This took him to Stockwell, one stop before Clapham Common, where southbound services were stopped. The head had by now been discovered.

On his tenth or eleventh sweep, Drake suddenly realised that the moment when the bag appeared, that is when the top corner came into view, might not be the actual time when the bag was brought onto the carriage. It might have been pushed into view by the crowds between Euston and Leicester Square. It could, in other words, have been brought onto the train much further back. But how far back?

Drake reached for his phone and called Milo.

'Are you busy?'

'Just tell me what you need.' Milo sounded half asleep, as if he welcomed anything that might be a distraction from the routine assignments he was dealing with.

'A couple of things. I'm just looking at footage from inside the carriage. I'm interested in one passenger in particular.'

'The guy in the Fender hat?'

'You spotted him too?'

'Well, he's the outlier.'

'He wasn't carrying the bag when he got on board at Walthamstow.'

'Hold on,' said Milo, as he pulled up the footage. There was a delay. Drake could picture him at his work station at Raven Hill. 'Okay, yes. I've got it. No bag.'

'Right. How about footage of that train before that moment?'

'Before Walthamstow?'

'It's an end station. The trains stop there for a while and then come back southbound.'

Milo took a moment. 'You think the bag was put on the train before it arrived in Walthamstow?'

'Why not?'

'Interesting. Then we're looking in the wrong place. Let me get hold of the footage and I'll get back to you.'

Drake put down the phone and sat back. The chair was a big, comfortable leather thing that rocked back. He put his hands behind his head and stared at the ceiling. How the bag got onto the train was one thing, but what really bothered him, the thing he was getting no closer to finding and answer to, was why?

Why would someone leave Zelda's head on the train? The more he thought about it, the more it seemed to him that it wasn't a random act. The perpetrator had not panicked and raced for the door. He, or she, had left the bag there on purpose; they had wanted her to be found.

Returning to the files Milo had sent him, Drake clicked through the ones of Walthamstow station. Interior and then exterior. He tried to look for the guy in the Fender hat but he seemed to have evaded the cameras as he entered the station.

Mib called back. 'I've sent you another file,' he said. 'Our man got on the Tube at Kennington.'

Drake clicked open the audio visual file that was sitting in his inbox and then spooled forwards through the new footage.

In the background a small-sized white van was parked. A traffic warden was busy writing out a ticket. In the foreground, passing through the ticket barrier was the man in the hat.

'You need to scroll back to the first reference I put in the mail.'

Drake found the counter number and moved the cursor back. It didn't take him long to spot Fender. Head down, he was shuffling along the platform. In his left hand was the blue IKEA bag. The only thing was that he was getting on the train going north. He got off the train at Walthamstow and disappeared from sight inside a connecting tunnel leading off the platform. This time he was not carrying the bag. Milo cleared his throat.

'There are no cameras in the link tunnel. And he does not appear in the ones in the main hall. That means he had to have concealed the bag on the train and then waited in the tunnel for it to depart, this time heading south.'

'He was watching the bag,' said Drake softly. 'He was standing in the tunnel watching the bag.'

'It's almost as if he's protecting her.'

'If anyone went near the bag, or tried to remove it, he would have intervened.'

'But why go to all that trouble?'

'So that when we see him getting onto the train, he doesn't have the bag with him.' Drake let the air out of his lungs slowly. 'Most people would have left it there.'

Milo was not satisfied. 'I still don't get why. Why does he go to all that trouble just to leave the bag on the train?'

Drake didn't have a ready answer to that. He had been struggling with the idea that the perpetrator had wanted the head to be found, but obviously not to be caught in actual possession of it. Meaning that he was smart enough to try not to implicate himself, but still determined for the head to come to light. Now, though, watching Fender moving back and forth from train to tunnel, he wondered if they were simply dealing with someone who was confused.

'He's not on the list of people interviewed at Clapham Common. Does that mean he just slipped out of the station in the confusion, or where did he go?'

'He switched to another southbound train and got off at Stockwell.' Milo sounded pleased with himself. Even though Drake was no longer his superior, he seemed to still feel a certain degree of pride in sharing the fruits of his work.

'Did you manage to follow him out of the station?'

'He didn't get out. He switched to the Victoria Line north-bound.'

'Where did he get off?'

'That's the problem. He exited in Victoria station, and you know how busy that can be.'

Silently, Drake swore at his luck. 'Any chance you can find him again?'

'I've been working on it.' Milo hesitated. 'But we're being told it's not a priority.' He lowered his voice to a whisper. 'Pryce is insisting that it's a waste of time and resources.'

'Well, he's probably got his reasons.' Drake suspected he knew exactly why Pryce wasn't going to pursue the case but appearing paranoid at this point probably wasn't helpful. 'One other thing. It might make sense to look up other similar cases.'

'You mean, headless cases?'

'Exactly. Missing heads, or heads minus bodies. That kind of thing. Modus operandi?'

'Modus operandi,' Milo repeated. 'You really think there are many people who've done this before?'

'I'm counting on that not being the case.'

Deciding he needed a break, Drake snapped the laptop shut and headed for the door. He stepped between two parked cars, intending to cross the street and buy a sandwich, when the doors of the car to his right opened and two men appeared. Both were in their twenties. The big one wore expensive-looking white trainers and tacky sunglasses. It took him a moment to recognise Donny's nephew, Zephyr. They didn't say much. The one with the Hitler Youth haircut nodded at the car.

'What is this?' Drake asked.

'Someone wants to see you,' said Zephyr.

'Tell them to make an appointment like everyone else.'

The other one nudged him from behind. There didn't seem to be much choice in the matter.

17

The Hercules was an upmarket restaurant on the seventeenth floor of a tower just down the road from Southwark station. They brought him up in the service lift and led him in through the back door. He wasn't sure why. The kitchen looked clean enough. The men and women in there glanced up and then away again, as though they had already learned that there was nothing unusual about people being bundled in through the back door.

It was only when he saw the name on the menu lying on the table in front of him that Drake knew where he was. He still didn't know why. The place was deserted. A sea of linen-covered tables stretched out in all directions. The walls were painted the deep blue of the Aegean Sea. Greek letters were dotted about in gold lettering. The Hercules had the kind of inspired mix of expensive and cheesy that Drake always associated with the man who entered through a door on the right.

Donny Apostolis clapped his hands.

'What do you think? Nice view, eh?'

'If you like that kind of thing.'

The view of London Bridge and the City across the river was impressive, but Drake wasn't feeling generous.

'You can even see the Shard if you stand close to the window.'

'You should charge.'

'Oh, I do. Believe me, I do.' Donny gestured at the table nearest them. 'What do I call you, now that you're no longer Officer Dibble?'

'Call me what you like, Donny. You can also just call me instead of sending the gorillas.'

Donny laughed. 'You know me, I like a little drama. It's the Greek in me.'

'Right.' Drake nodded at their surroundings. 'Who are you trying to impress?'

'I'm going upmarket.' Donny gave a nonchalant shrug. 'Life is like swimming. If you don't move, you sink.'

'I thought that only applied to sharks.'

Drake was never sure where Donny got his little philosophical sayings. He had a strong suspicion that he simply made them up. He was smartly turned out in a crisp shirt, open at the neck to reveal the tan along with the usual array of gold bracelets, necklaces, crosses, rosary beads and assorted amulets nestling in his chest hair. No matter how far up the ladder he went, Donny Apostolis never shook off his vanity or his old-fashioned superstitions.

'Sharks don't interest me. You, on the other hand, do.'

'Must be my lucky day.'

Donny sat with his back to the window. Something Drake had never seen him do before. Normally he had his back to the wall, 'so that when they come to kill me I can look them in the eye'. Who exactly he was expecting to kill him was unclear. Donny accumulated enemies the way most people collect bonus points at the supermarket. Up here, of course, the window was a safe bet.

'So, I hear you're a free agent now. No more working for queen and country. I approve, by the way. Government work is a mug's game. Thirty years' service and they toss you a pension that a dog couldn't live on.'

'A lot of dogs would be glad of it.'

'You should come work for me. I'm serious. I could use someone like you on my team.'

'It's a team now?'

'We all have to diversify. My nephew keeps telling me. Diversify!' He chuckled to himself. 'Now we are taking lessons from children.'

Drake assumed this nephew was the same one who had just brought him in. Zet, as he was known, seemed to be gaining importance in the uncle's little empire.

'What's all this about, Donny? If I didn't know you any better I'd say you were worried.'

'Worried, me?' Donny fluttered his fingers as a waiter appeared. 'I'm trying to lose weight. It's crazy, right? You own your own restaurant and you can't even eat there. One meal a day.'

'You're trying to lose weight?'

'I know, it's crazy. Just look at me.' He patted his stomach. 'Tight as a bell. I'm in great shape, better than ever, but I have to watch it. That's the first step.'

'Towards what?'

'Death, of course.' Donny rattled his bracelets as the waiter arrived with an ice bucket and a bottle of Moët & Chandon. He opened the champagne and poured them each a glass, before setting it back and disappearing. Two more waiters appeared with oysters and a large shell filled with caviar set in ice.

'You know you don't have to impress me, right?'

'I'm going upmarket.'

'So you say. But what exactly does that mean?' Drake surveyed the table and decided there was nothing he wanted.

'It means property. Basically that's where the money is these days. Do you have any idea how much money was invested last year?'

'Something obscene, would be my guess.'

Donny smiled. 'That's right, I forgot, you're not interested in money.'

'It's not that I'm not interested, I'm just not obsessed with the stuff the way most people seem to be these days.'

'I grew up poor. We lived on a farm in Macedonia. My father took care of the horses. I would watch the owners of the farm bring their daughters to ride every weekend. I promised myself that one day I would have everything they had.'

'And how's that working out for you?'

'I have a country house, land. I have horses, but my ex-wife won't let me take the children there.'

'Life is a bitch.'

'I didn't bring you here to talk about my ex-wife.' Donny reached for a cracker and pasted caviar over it. 'You hear the one about someone on a train with a head in an IKEA bag?'

Drake waited for the punchline.

'They was taking it back for a refund.' Donny sniggered at his own joke.

'That's why you wanted to see me?'

'You still have some pull.' Donny was pouring more champagne for himself. Drake hadn't touched his glass.

'Why the interest?'

'You know why.' Donny levelled a finger at him. 'You're thinking the same thing. That business down in Brighton.'

'You mean Zelda.'

'Who the fuck is Zelda?'

'That's her name, or that's what I called her.'

'We're talking about the same person, right? The woman who was going to blow Goran out of the water.'

'Zelda.'

'Is it her?'

'They're doing tests.'

'Tests, what the fuck do I care about tests?' Donny picked his teeth with a fingernail. 'Is it her?'

'It's possible.'

'There can't be that many cases like this. Headless body and now this.' Donny's face scrunched up. 'What was it doing on the Tube?'

'That's not clear.' Drake took a moment to examine the view. It was impressive. Maybe Donny was coming up in the world. 'Either it was being moved, or someone wanted it to be found.'

Donny nodded his agreement, as if he had been thinking the same thing. 'Now why would anyone do something like that?'

'Unfinished business.'

The finger came up again. 'Exactly.'

'Someone from back then who is trying to make a point.'

'More than a point, if you ask me.'

'Like I said, Donny, you sound worried.'

That brought a snort of derision as Donny dug the spoon back into the caviar and spread a generous dollop on another cracker.

'It takes more than that to worry me. What I don't get is that this happened years ago. Where's she been all this time, hiding in a bag?'

'It's strange, I agree.'

'Strange is the universe expanding so fast they can't keep track of it.' Donny lifted his hands. 'It was on the telly last night. Point is, this is more than fucking strange. It's sinister.'

'Let me ask you, why do you think this has something to do with you?'

'I didn't say that. Did I say that?' Donny was jerking back and forth, a vein throbbing in his forehead. 'I'm curious. I don't like surprises. Things popping up out of the past where they are supposed to remain.' He ran his tongue over his teeth. 'That's why I want to hire you.'

Drake sat back. 'That sounds like a bad idea.'

'What? You don't like my money, malaka? What do you say?'

'Like I said, I'm not sure it's such a good idea.'

'Because you think I might have done it?'

'Because three weeks after Goran was gunned down you were moving in on his business.'

Donny held his hands wide. 'I'm an entrepreneur. I see an opportunity, I'm obliged to take it.'

'But you're not saying you killed him?'

'I didn't say that.'

'If you want me to work for you, you'll have to level with me.'

'What's that, then, like talking to a lawyer? What I tell you stays between us?'

'Something like that.'

Donny lifted the bottle again. This time he didn't bother trying to top up Drake's glass.

'I'm not sure I believe you.'

'But you still want to hire me.'

'I want to find out what's going on. You have access to the forensics and all that. Police stuff. And besides, you're a good copper.' Donny gave Drake a long look. 'It's in both our interests to find out what's going on. Point is, you get paid for your time. Fair?'

'I'll have to think about it.'

'Right, and talk to that foxy partner of yours.' Donny grinned. 'Come on, you haven't touched your drink.' He held up his glass in a toast and Drake lifted his.

'I'll let you in on a secret. I would have taken that animal out for nothing.'

'What is this, some kind of speech about honour among thieves?'

'Call it what you like, I draw the line at certain things. All that stuff with children and women being brought in as slaves, that makes me sick.'

Drake wasn't entirely convinced he believed him. 'Let me ask you a question.'

'Fire away.'

'Back then, who else was trying to take over Goran's business?'

Donny threw up his hands. 'I don't know. I'd have to give that some thought. There was some smaller players. Most of them amounted to nothing.'

'Any of them still around?'

'Some.' Donny tapped his fingers on the table. 'So, straight up, you really think it's the same woman who was connected to Goran?'

'I'm pretty sure of it.'

'You think you can find the person who killed her?'

'I'm going to try.'

Donny tilted his head to look at Drake. 'She was a friend of yours, right?'

'She was trying to help me.'

'You owe her.'

'In a way, yes.'

Donny reached down for something on the seat next to him. He set a thick envelope on the table.

Drake looked at it. 'I told you I have to think about it.'

'I know what you told me. And I am telling you that when you have thought about it, you will agree to do this. Not for me, not for the money, but for you. You have to do this for yourself.'

'If I'm going to work for you, I need to know everything.'

'You're not my mother. I hire you to do a job, that's all.

'Who is it you're worried about?'

'If I pay a woman to fuck me I don't expect her to start asking questions.'

'Maybe that's the difference. I don't intend to get fucked, by you or anyone else.'

'Fair enough.' Donny leaned forwards to refill his glass. 'In my game you make enemies. People you never suspected one day grow a set of balls and decide to cut your head off.' Donny pushed the envelope across the table. 'You report to me and no one else. As soon as you have something, I want to know. Is that clear?'

'As mud.'

'We both need to do this,' said Donny. 'You'll see that as soon as you get off your high horse.'

18

The Imperio Romano had a touch of old-fashioned respectability about it. The kind of place your father-in-law might invite you to, assuming he liked Italian food and didn't mind spending money. Everything on the menu posted by the front door looked reassuringly familiar, while there was nothing reassuring about the prices. That didn't matter since Crane wasn't there to eat. It was mid-afternoon. Lunch was over and the place was dark and deserted as it collected itself for a few hours before the theatre crowds began to appear for a bite to eat before and then after the show.

The thickset woman behind the bar looked tired the way a centuries-old Roman wall looked tired. Dressed in black, she carried on polishing a glass while watching Crane approach. She listened as Crane went through her story, but was already shaking her head long before she'd reached the end.

'I can't do that.'

'I'm not asking you to do anything illegal.' Crane traced a fingernail across the marble counter.

The woman lifted her shoulders. 'I still can't do it.'

'Sure,' Crane said. 'Nice place you have here. I used to work somewhere just like this, over in Soho.'

The woman nodded but clearly this was not something that interested her. Still, Crane thought she detected something underneath that world-weary demeanour, so she pushed on.

'Have you had it long?'

'Oh, it's not my place.' The woman set the glass she was holding on the counter and reached for another.

'The thing is, if I don't sort this out my boss is going to kill me, and I know he's not joking.'

'Sorry to hear that, love.' The woman put down the glass and dishcloth. 'Look, if it was up to me . . .'

'It's just that this is my last chance. I promised I would take care of this, and he's not big on excuses. I could lose my job.'

'Like I said, I wish I could help, but . . .'

'We just need a copy of the receipt, for his taxes, otherwise he'll fire me. I'm sure of it.' Crane allowed her voice to spiral upwards. In the back of her head somewhere she was asking herself if she was capable of actually faking tears.

The woman rested her hands on the counter. They were swollen and red. 'Look, I've told you, I can't do anything. My own boss will kill me if he catches me chatting with you.'

Crane rested her hand next to the woman's. There was a rolled-up bundle of twenty pound notes underneath it. There was a moment's silence.

'Tell me again.'

'A table of three. About a month ago? Two of them ordered swordfish. The man had steak.'

'Do you have any idea how many receipts I would have to go through?'

'They ordered wine. A very special bottle. It had to come up from the cellar.'

The woman sniffed, her curiosity piqued. 'What kind of wine?'

'The expensive kind. Three hundred pounds a bottle.'

'Ohh . . .' The woman's chin lifted and stayed like that. Crane lifted her hand. There was a moment's hesitation before the money disappeared. 'Let me check.'

Someone who is willing to fork out absurd quantities of money for a bottle of wine is the kind of client nobody wants to lose. Crane enjoyed a glass of wine as much as the next person, but she was convinced that most people couldn't tell the difference between a fairly good bottle and a really expensive one. She was willing to bet that Howeida's uncle was among them. In all likelihood, he had been doing what people with money always do: judge the bottle by the price tag, which was fine if you could afford it. He was probably more concerned about making an impression on his niece and her American flatmate.

While she waited, Crane turned around to rest her elbows

on the counter and study the room. It was disappointing. There were stock photographs of the Coliseum, Sophia Loren and other statuesque figures. The kind of thing meant to entertain clients as they ate. To remind them that they were in the right place. It gave the impression they were dining with celebrities. They could tell themselves they were in a place that had some real connection to Italy. Even though anybody could hang a few pictures on the wall. Crane knew this was the way of the world. Everything was about the creation of illusion. Even the wine.

'A 2006 Sassicaia from Toscana?' The woman was thumbing back through the pages.

'What was the price?'

'Three hundred and sixty pounds.

'Sounds about right.'

'It doesn't happen every day, not even every week. Someone trying to impress a woman, you know?'

'That's the usual story.'

'I understand now. Your boss wants to put this on his expenses.' She excused herself and went into the back to make a copy. When she returned Crane asked her if she was on that night. The woman shrugged.

'To be honest, I'm on most nights. Between you and me, the manager is a bit handsy when it comes to the girls. Waitresses don't last, so we are always short-handed.'

'You don't have that kind of trouble?'

'Me?' The woman rolled her eyes. 'He's my husband, he stopped bothering me that way years ago. Thank god.'

'Do you remember this group?'

'Actually, I think I do. First of all, the man was older. Two women. One of them very pretty, the other, a lot of hair. Pelorosso.'

'A redhead? Were all of them drinking?'

'Yes,' the woman nodded. 'That's what surprised me, why I remember.'

'What surprised you?'

'The man was . . . well, I didn't expect him to order wine.'

Crane raised her eyebrows. 'Because of his looks?'

'Si. I was surprised that he ask for such expensive wine.' She gave a shrug. 'What can he know about wine from the Toscana, right? But today everything is upside down.'

'You can say that again.'

After she left the restaurant, Crane walked. It was raining lightly, but that didn't bother her. The chill helped to clear her head. What was Howeida's uncle up to? Was the wine some kind of a test? He takes his niece to a fancy restaurant and orders the most expensive bottle in the place. Was he trying to impress her, or Savannah? Perhaps it was all an act, trying to look sophisticated and worldly, a man who is at ease with the West and its ways. Comfortable ordering and drinking expensive wine.

Still, there was something not quite right about the whole picture. If Howeida's uncle was playing games, perhaps he was trying to convince the world that he was the last person to get all patriarchal and attempt to drag her back home. In which case all of this was part of an elaborate smokescreen.

The rain made the afternoon seem to evaporate. The light dimmed and Crane's face and hair were soon damp. Underneath her jacket she was dry and, for the moment at least, she was warm. She took a deep breath, enjoying the walk.

Crane had no direct training as an investigator, which was why the whole idea of starting up a bureau was contingent on joining forces with Drake. She had realised almost right away that her main problem was learning to trust him. Learning to trust anyone really. That had always been an issue. She was too much of a lone operator, which might have had something to do with being an only child, although she wasn't too bothered about digging into all of that.

Her experience came from the work she had done with the Met, but also before that, when she was working for Stewart Mason both at home and abroad. She had found herself in the company of some very good investigators in Iraq, Afghanistan and across Europe on Interpol cases. A missing persons case was, if anything, underwhelming after that. But this was no ordinary missing person. Marco Foulkes was no ordinary client. He knew her and that in and of itself made her uncomfortable. She felt vulnerable and that was affecting the way she was thinking.

The second thing was the connection to her father. Any link to him was disturbing and for him to be mixed up somehow in a case she was trying to run was also a distraction.

The Triumph was parked up on Long Acre. Ray walked up to the bike and carried on past it, deciding to circle the block rather than break the chain of her thoughts. She had been reluctant to accept Drake's initial response to Foulkes, partly because she had wanted to take the case. She was eager to make this partnership work. Now she found herself wondering. There were a lot of question marks hanging over Foulkes. Taking an interest in her father, for example, when so far as she knew they had never been close. It might have all been thanks to his mother, but Ray wasn't sure that was it. Foulkes was advising her father on how to handle his finances. Why would he do that? She was more concerned about his interest in Howeida, the person he was hiring them to find. The concern for her welfare might have been explained simply. Perhaps he really was smitten and, despite the voice of cynicism in the back of her head, this was a case of him being in love. Difficult to judge. She herself had never found Foulkes attractive. He was too full of himself, for starters. But she had never met Howeida, so anything was possible. Maybe she was being too harsh. Maybe she was listening too much to Drake.

Returning to the motorcycle, Crane pulled on her helmet and climbed onto it. Kicking down the stand she pushed the starter and listened to the engine come to life. Then she pushed the gear lever down and sped away.

19

The Moonstone was crowded with builders from nearby construction projects who were huddled around the bar. Drake emerged from within the scrum carrying drinks for both of them and then managed to find a small table in the back.

'How did it go with your father?'

Crane sighed. 'The thing you have to understand is that we're not close.'

'Yeah, I think I got that bit.'

'The point is, I haven't seen him for years. I disagree fundamentally with him.'

Drake sipped his lager. 'Because he's a lord, or whatever.'

'Whatever sounds about right. The estate is crumbling down about him and overrun by animals.'

'Sounds kind of sad.'

'Pathetic would be more accurate.'

'So, no love lost between you.' Drake was curious about where this harshness Crane felt towards her father came from, but he knew that she would only tell him when she felt she was ready. Until then, he would have to wait.

'There's something going on with his finances. He took his business away from the solicitors he has used all his life and put his faith in some snake oil salesman by the name of Nathanson.'

'Barnaby Nathanson? That's Foulkes' pal.'

'Foulkes was advising my father.' Crane raised a hand. 'And don't you dare say I told you so.'

'I wouldn't dream of it. But I have a question.'

'Shoot.'

'Why would a successful writer be peddling financial advice to your father?'

'Even successful writers don't make a lot of money. Not that kind of writer.'

'I thought they were all raking it in.'

'When was the last time you bought a novel?'

Drake had to nod. 'Point taken.'

'Marco is the kind of writer who is respectable, he wins prizes. People talk about his work. I'm not sure how many people actually read him.'

'But he has money. The family estate, the sports car.'

'He has expensive tastes.'

'So, Nathanson encourages him to start investing to cover his extravagant lifestyle.'

'Possibly Foulkes got a commission for bringing in new business.' Crane sipped her wine. 'The firm had just been taken over. What did you find out about Nathanson?'

'I tracked him to Dalston.' Drake reached into his pocket for the sheet of paper Milo had given him. He pointed to the underlined entry. 'This is the log from a minicab firm. Nathanson has an office in Kingsland Road and a home address in Pimlico.'

Crane frowned. 'That sounds a little off.'

'My feeling too.' Drake folded up the piece of paper. 'Seems a long step from St James's.'

'My father's problems are not the issue here. What we should focus on is Foulkes and his finances.'

'You think his financial troubles are connected to Howeida's disappearance?'

'It's a possibility, don't you think?'

'Only if we treat our client like a suspect,' said Drake. 'Did you learn anything about her uncle?'

'I spoke to her flatmate, the one from Virginia.'

'Ah, yes, the delectable Savannah. How did you get on with her?'

'She's touting the same story as Marco, highlights the uncle as an old-fashioned sleaze who wants to get his mitts on his niece before she's corrupted by bad old London ways.'

Drake raised his glass. 'The family honour and all that jazz.'

'He took both of them out to eat one night, at an Italian place nearby.' Crane handed him the receipt for their meal. 'He paid nearly four hundred pounds for a bottle of wine.'

'People pay that much for a bottle of wine?' Drake found it hard to believe.

'Some would consider that a snip.'

'Not in my neck of the woods.'

'Maybe you're moving in the wrong circles,' said Crane, taking back the receipt and putting it away. 'But you're missing the point. Why would a conservative, old-fashioned man worried about family honour be shelling out nearly four hundred pounds for a bottle of Tuscany red?'

'Maybe he likes to impress the girls.'

'Or maybe he's not as conservative as they would like us to think.'

'Also a possibility,' nodded Drake.

'I'll get Heather to start digging into Marco's financial history.' Heather was Crane's unlikely assistant. A matronly figure, she had been inherited along with the practice from Crane's former mentor, Julius Rosen. 'Then I'm going to try and meet this uncle.'

'What makes you think he'll agree to meet you?'

'If he's truly concerned about his niece, then he has no choice. He has to meet me. And if he's playing the innocent he'll do it too.'

'How do you know he hasn't left the country already?'

'I've already texted him. Savannah had his number. He's been in Germany on business, but should be back in London tomorrow. And he sounded keen to talk.'

Drake turned the rim of his glass. 'Just looking at this from an ethical point of view for a moment, are we in breach of contract by investigating our client?'

Crane gave a deep sigh. 'Marco came to us because he's worried about Howeida. We're still working on that. So far all we're doing is background research.'

'That works for me. I have another potential problem, or not.' Drake set the envelope of cash on the table. 'Donny Apostolis wants us to work for him.'

Crane reached for the envelope and peered inside. 'Are you pulling my leg?'

'I wish I was. The problem is that Donny isn't the kind of person who takes no for an answer.'

'That doesn't matter. We're not going to work for a gangster.'

'Technically, he assures me he's going legit. Actually, all he's asking is to be kept informed about anything I turn up on the Zelda case.'

'The woman whose head was found on the train?'

'There's a chance it might be Zelda.'

Crane frowned. 'Your old informant?'

Drake nodded. No further explanation was needed. The two of them had discussed the case enough times for Crane to know how important a role Zelda had played in Drake's life. She also knew that he had never given up the hope of one day solving her murder.

'I'm not working to help Donny. If I turn up anything about him, it gets handed to the Met.'

'So what does he get out of it?'

'He wouldn't say,' said Drake. 'My feeling is that he thinks it's tied in to a rival, someone who is coming after him.'

'I'm not sure I like the idea of taking his money.'

'We don't have to take it. We can hold on to it until such time as we feel we have to give it back, or accept it.'

Crane studied him for a moment. 'You're comfortable with that?'

'I'm fine with it. How Donny feels is another matter. On the other hand, I think his interest could tell us something about the case. I want to find out who killed her and why her head was left on that train.'

'I get it, but I'm not sure I like it.' Crane tossed the envelope down. 'This sounds less like a case and more like a personal obsession.'

Drake shrugged. 'Either way, I'm going to get to the bottom of it.'

'You said Donny was worried. What about?'

'Like I said, he wasn't particularly forthcoming, but I get the feeling he knows more than he lets on and that maybe he thinks whoever did this might be coming after him next.'

'So you're suggesting we might be getting ourselves into the middle of a gang war?'

Drake held up a hand. 'Not so fast. I'm suggesting we string him along, take his money and look into the case.'

'And where do we stand with the official investigation? You're no longer a detective, remember?'

'As I understand it, they have no objection to me looking into it. It's a cold case and they don't have the appetite or resources for it.'

'You're involved, Cal, front and centre. Zelda's murder, the whole thing with Goran, that's the reason you were demoted, remember, sent to the far north? The reason you're no longer a police officer.'

'You're asking if I can be objective?'

'I'm asking if there is a chance in hell of you being able to handle an investigation that you were so closely tied up in.'

'Whether we take Donny's money or not, nobody knows this case better than I do.'

'It's not your problem any more.'

'It's always going to be my problem.'

Crane rested her elbows on the table. 'Listen to me, Cal. We're trying to run a business here, not settle old scores.'

'I understand that. We're partners. We both have the right to veto a case. The moment you get the feeling it's getting out of hand, I'll pull the plug.'

'Fair enough.' Crane sat back. 'You should be careful, though.'

'Always. My feeling is that Donny wouldn't have done something quite so obvious as shooting Goran in broad daylight.'

'But he did move into a lot of Goran's businesses.'

'Yes. Clubs mostly, some of them places Donny had run years ago. He claimed them back, with interest. Property. That was his real thing. Goran owned a lot, mostly run-down buildings that he could claim housing benefit on. He wasn't interested in doing them up or selling them. Donny used them to move into the property market.'

'Nobody was ever charged with Zelda's murder, right?'

'Nope. Officially she was a missing persons case, and even then it took three weeks before the landlady started to get antsy about her rent. Zelda didn't know anyone in Brighton. Nobody missed her.'

'So the connection was only made when the body washed up?'

'Right.'

'I never understood why you were made to take the blame.'

'I broke the rules. I took a prime witness in a major case and hid her away without telling anyone. When you take a risk like that and it goes wrong, then you're the one left holding the can.'

'They threw the book at you.'

Drake nodded. 'The fact that I had kept it to myself suggested I didn't trust people in my own team. The Met doesn't like hanging out its dirty laundry in public. And I had offered no evidence.'

'So they drew the logical conclusion that it was you who was on the take.'

'Simpler and easier. They couldn't prove it, so they couldn't bring charges, but they could demote me and farm me out to the sticks.'

'Whose pocket did they think you were in?'

'They had no idea, but the suspicion was that it was either Goran or Donny.'

'There were no other players in the game?'

'I asked Donny that same question a few hours ago and he told me what I remembered. Small fry, nobody major.'

'You had a rough time of it,' she said. 'I mean, it must have felt like a betrayal.'

'It did.'

'Which explains why you're here now. And why you're interested in seeing this through.'

'I have to put this behind me, once and for all.'

Crane considered the situation before finally nodding her assent. 'Okay, just don't forget we're trying to run a business.'

'I'll try to bear that in mind.'

'And we need to keep an eye on Foulkes and Nathanson. There's something there that's not right.'

'I hear you.'

'Something tells me we're going to have our work cut out to pull this off,' said Crane, raising her glass. 'Where are you going to start?'

'With our mysterious man on the train. Fender.'

20

Drake spent the following morning in Victoria station, wandering in circles. He retraced the path from the Tube platform up to the main station. He walked round through the crowds, up and down the escalators. Then he moved to the main concourse and beyond in the surrounding streets. He stopped to look into coffee shops and supermarkets, pharmacies. His eye ran methodically over the people around him, dismissing them as soon as he got a handle on them. He saw the same thing everywhere: mostly commuters bored with their routine, tired, angry, fed up, clutching briefcases, rucksacks, handbags, newspapers and cups of coffee, and of course phones, praying to get home or to work without any delay. Then there were the tourists. He was good at spotting where they were from. Brash Americans, loud Spaniards, along with the French, Germans, Japanese, Chinese, Malaysians, Russians. It was all about clothes, luggage, language, hesitation, even types of confusion. Despite global fashion trends people still dressed and behaved in their own way. They carried themselves differently.

Then there were the misfits, the oddballs, the ones who had got off at the wrong station in life and never managed to get back on again. The ones who had no real idea what they were doing here or where they were going, let alone why. The ones who had lost their way and were simply dragging themselves along out of habit, refusing to give up without knowing why. They were down at heel, young and old, with torn, overloaded rucksacks, grubby hands and faces. Someone of them, the unbalanced ones, sought eye contact, but most of them didn't. They wanted to be invisible. They wandered through life in a daze, as if nothing around them mattered.

Gradually, Drake widened his circle. The rain had stopped and the sun came out, casting a strange light on the city. It seemed unnaturally bright and Drake had to squint as he walked. The striated red brick of Westminster Cathedral beckoned. Inside, he paused for a moment to look up at the gold inlay on the ceiling and the angels with their long, tapered wings.

As he turned to leave he spied a figure down at the far end. A man wearing a cap. Drake hurried left and worked his way down, staying close to the wall. When he reached the far end there was nobody there and no sign of where the man had gone. Had he imagined it?

Outside in the open air he sat down on the steps for a moment. People came and went across the square. He walked in a wide circle, chopping and changing direction at random, starting with the perimeter of the cathedral and working his way outwards, hoping for a glimpse of the figure he had seen.

He didn't even have a name for the man he had dubbed Fender. Right now someone would be going through missing person files compiling a list of possible matches. Procedure. The chances of him turning up as a MisPer or a convicted felon were slim. People moved through this city with the same fluidity as the river running through it. They came from every walk of life, high and low, and from all across the face of the earth. They changed their clothes, their hair, their names, their faces. They remade themselves. It was in the nature of this city. Its DNA. People could lay claim to it, but it belonged to no one. Not so much looking for a needle in a haystack as looking for an alibi, a shape-shifting shadow that could morph into someone else at any moment.

Drake got as far as the Embankment, turning the corner to find himself enveloped in the national madness. Flags and banners, people yelling through megaphones. Not so much democracy as a form of mob rule seeking respectability. As he dug his way through, a group of men burst into song. 'Rule Britannia' followed him to the corner.

On a bench beside two women eating their lunch a poster had come half unstuck and was flapping in the breeze. Drake walked over to take a look. It was an advert for a shelter; the Silver Linings Charity Shelter. It was a five-minute walk away. A non-descript doorway on a side street.

The entrance was brightly lit and decorated with pictures of trees and animals. It resembled some kind of amateur art project. A row of orange plastic chairs was bolted to the floor. Over a narrow window on the wall next to these was a sign that read 'Reception' and an arrow helpfully pointing down.

Drake leaned on the buzzer and waited. Through the frosted glass he could make out shadows moving about. Then the window was wrenched aside. A woman stood there. Broad faced and with her hair tied up in an untidy bun. She was talking to somebody else. When she finally turned his way, she took only a couple of seconds to appraise Drake and conclude that she didn't much like what she saw.

'Yes?'

'I'm looking for a friend of mine.'

'What's his name?'

'That's the thing, he has several.'

'Are you with the law?'

'No, this is personal.'

The woman's heavy sigh indicated that he was trying her patience.

'What do you mean by several names?'

'He has a tendency to give people different names. I know him as Fender.'

'Fender?'

'On account of the hat he wears.' Drake pointed helpfully at his head. The woman's eyes lifted and then dropped.

'Our policy is not to give out information about residents.'

'I understand. I wouldn't be here if I wasn't desperately trying to find him.'

'What is he, a relative of yours?'

'He's a friend.'

She considered that for a moment before deciding against it. 'Sorry, I can't help you.'

The window slammed shut and Drake stood for a moment staring at it. He hadn't expected to get much out of it, but the figure in the church, half glimpsed in the gloom and at a distance, had given him hope.

'Fender, you said?'

The man must have come in while Drake was speaking. He was sitting in the corner on one of the orange chairs, bowed forwards. Grizzled and old, he looked as though he'd spent years on the front line. Bird's nest hair and scruffy beard, stained nicotine yellow around the mouth, well-worn jeans and an old army parka, surrounded by a pack of bundles, plastic bags, stuff sacks. They sat around him like obedient dogs, resting before the next leg of their never-ending journey.

'Do you know him?' Drake moved closer. He dropped the concerned act. It might have worked on the carer, but not on a veteran like this. His gaze never met Drake's but he was watching him keenly.

'See a lot of things out there.'

'How about him?' Drake held out the still from the CCTV footage.

The man's eyes barely grazed the picture. 'You the filth, then?'

'No. Like I said, he's a friend.'

The man considered the answer and found it lacking.

'Well, you won't find him here,' the man sniffed. 'They wouldn't let him in.'

'You know that for a fact?'

'Might do.' The man scratched his beard.

'What are you doing for lunch?' Drake asked.

'Oh, I don't know, might stop by the Ritz.'

Drake was counting out a couple of tens. 'Will that do?'

'At the Ritz?' The man lifted his eyebrows. Drake added a couple more. The man smoothed the notes out as if they were made of silk.

'You said they wouldn't let him stay. Why was that?'

'I don't know, maybe he had a pet. Maybe they'd had trouble with him before. '

'But you're sure it was him.'

'The hat.' The man nodded. 'I seen him around a lot. He comes and goes. I'm not even sure he's really homeless.'

'How do you mean?'

'Well, you know, some people just get their kicks that way.'

'What way is that?'

'Hanging round with us. Gives them a thrill. Don't ask me.'

The man was running his thumb along the edge of the banknotes as if they were a blade. 'You suss people out. Learn who to trust, who to avoid. It's all about survival.'

'I could use less of the philosophy and more detail.'

The man looked up sharply. Not annoyed so much as concerned that he wasn't being taken seriously. 'I don't know his name. I don't know where he comes from, but I do know why he's out here.' The white eyebrows twitched. 'He's hiding from someone.'

21

The interior of the club in Frith Street had changed its style since Crane had last set foot in there. The woman behind the high reception desk wore a skin-tight dress that appeared to be made out of rubber and was decked out in shiny silver buckles. She wore bright red lipstick with black cat's ears in her hair. As she walked upstairs ahead of her, Crane saw that the woman's outfit had a tail to match the ears. So far, so kinky. The playful bondage theme darkened on the first floor, with heavy crimson drapes and black leather upholstery.

'Is this the new thing, or some kind of collective mid-life crisis?' she asked as she sat down.

'You're the expert,' said Stewart Mason. 'You tell me.' He looking round approvingly. 'I quite like it,' he said. 'Makes me feel warm, in a good way.'

'Maybe you should talk to someone about that.'

A waitress appeared, in PVC trousers with a safety pin through her nose.

'I'll have what he's having,' said Crane.

'It's a Tom Collins. Not bad.'

'Whatever.' Crane watched the waitress walk away. 'This is some kind of perverse schoolboy fantasy fulfilment.'

'Don't knock it if you haven't tried it. What's on your mind?'

'I need you to tell me about my father.'

Stewart Mason sat back. 'I didn't see that coming. I always understood you didn't want to talk about him.'

'Well, that's changed. I need to know.'

'Right.' Mason played with the swizzle stick in his glass. 'How's the new business venture working out?'

'Are you trying to change the subject?'

'Not at all, I'm genuinely curious.'

'Bad choice of words, Stewart. There isn't a genuine bone in your body.'

'That's not fair. Anyway, I meant it. How about your new partner?'

Crane considered her answer. She decided it was probably better not to tell Mason that their latest client was a high-profile leader of an organised-crime syndicate.

'Cal's a good investigator. He's smart and resourceful, and it beats trying to find someone to take Julius's place. The truth is I was getting bored with consultations and the odd contract work.' She fell silent as her drink arrived. As she was turning away the waitress flashed her a wink. No doubt all part of the service. 'Can we go back to my father now?'

'In a minute.' Mason smiled, that bland, bureaucratic smile that Crane always associated with Foreign Office mandarins and emissaries of the Diplomatic Service. Politicians and public servants. 'I wanted to float an idea by you. It's very simple really. I've been asked to put together a team of specialists.'

'What kind of specialists?'

'Investigators who would be able to travel at short notice. Look, the point is that the intelligence services are this big baggy monster. Too many people and too much information. When you introduce management and accountability into the mix you wind up with something whose primary purpose is sustaining itself.'

'Why are you telling me this?'

'Because yours was the first name that came to mind.'

'This would mean joining the National Crime Agency?'

'Well, not exactly.'

'You want this off the books?' Crane smiled. 'Let me guess. You want full deniability.'

'Partly, and partly it's just old-fashioned budgetary stuff. It's cheaper for us to outsource, like everything nowadays.' He rolled his eyes theatrically. 'This way we can get around a lot of corners.'

'But that would leave whoever did this quite exposed, wouldn't it?'

'Ahh.' Mason rocked his head from side to side. 'In theory, yes, but in practice of course you would be covered like any operative.'

'I'm not sure Cal is ready to go back to working for the

government just yet. I assume you're talking about both of us. And neither am I, for that matter, until I get a few things straightened out.'

'Such as?' Mason frowned.

'I need to know about my father.'

Mason studied the ice swirling in the bottom of his glass.

'What do you want to know?'

'Everything.'

Mason sighed. 'Okay. Well, he was recruited before my time. At Cambridge, which is where he met your mother, of course. You went there as well, didn't you?'

Crane gave a slight nod. 'He was doing PPE and she was doing a masters in Persian literature. This much I know.'

'Your father was a few years ahead of me. He fitted the bill perfectly. Public school education, good family background. I recall him as a stylish man, erudite, very charming.' Mason allowed himself a nostalgic smile. 'It seems like another world when you talk about it now.'

'It was.' Crane fought the tension she felt growing inside her. 'How was he recruited?'

'That I don't know. I assume it happened the same way it did with me. Someone approaches you. They mix in with the crowd. A friend of a friend, that sort of thing.'

'This was before he married my mother?'

'No, actually it was later. He was a reluctant convert, as I understand. Resisted first time around. Still fighting the system.' Mason broke off to wave his hand in the air and order another round of drinks. 'They take their time. They need to know if you will go the distance. There are a few courses, summer schools. It's all very gentle.' He broke off. 'Why are you putting yourself through all of this?'

'It's important to me.'

'Why? I mean, why now?'

'Why not? Is there ever a good time for these things?'

The waitress returned with the drinks. As she removed the glasses she discreetly slipped a card onto the table by Crane's elbow.

'Throughout all of this he stayed on course, finished his

degree, joined the Foreign Office and went into the Diplomatic Service.'

'And all the time he was actually working for the Intelligence Services?'

'You already know this. Why are you asking all these questions?'

'Maybe I just want to hear it confirmed. So, he wasn't working for the Intelligence Services the first time we moved to Tehran?'

'No, as I said, it was later. The first time you went there was back in the eighties, wasn't it?'

Crane knew that Mason was only feigning doubt. It was a little disconcerting that he knew every detail of her life. Some things, like her childhood, he knew better than she did.

'It was 1986. I was seven at the time.'

'He wasn't recruited until he went back to Cambridge to finish his doctorate.' Mason nodded. 'Two years later, in July 1988, the USS *Vincennes* shot down Ira Air Flight 655. An Airbus 300 carrying 290 people on board. There were no survivors.'

'I remember my mother was taken in for questioning and then released.'

'Because she was married to a Westerner. There was a crackdown.'

'But he was never touched.'

'Your parents were vulnerable. A mixed marriage. He was suspected of being a spook but they had nothing on him.'

'You think that's why he was recruited when he went back to Cambridge?'

'It's possible. People often need something like that, an event, a personal experience.'

'The second time we went there was later, in 1995.'

'She was never taken off the watch list. It was foolish of them to go back there.'

'My mother refused to be cowed by the mullahs in Tehran. She believed in continuing the struggle. My father used her to penetrate the dissident groups she had contact with.'

Mason shrugged. 'He believed in the cause.' He reached over

to cover her hand with his. 'That must have been difficult for you, seeing your mother taken away.'

Crane withdrew her hand. 'It was harder for her. She was tortured. We weren't allowed to visit her in prison.'

'You know how it works. He was trying to infiltrate the underground, to make contact with the resistance.'

'By using my mother's contacts.' Crane turned over the card the waitress had left. On the back she had scrawled a phone number. Over Mason's shoulder she could see the waitress laughing with another woman. They looked like models and were making a point of fawning over one another. As she watched, the waitress turned to look pointedly at her.

'Tell me what's on your mind,' said Mason. 'What's brought all this back?'

Crane thought about the question. The truth was that she knew now that this was the reason she had agreed to meet Mason. This whole business of her father was stirring up emotions she thought she had dealt with long ago.

'The case I'm working on seems to be connected to him. He made some bad investments.'

'Welcome to the club.'

'Does the name Barnaby Nathanson mean anything to you?'

'Who is he?'

'A solicitor who appears to have been advising my father.'

Mason looked pained. 'You know, Ray, I really liked your mother. I would never have willingly allowed anything to happen to her.'

'Except you did.'

'I wish I could have helped her.'

'But you didn't. Nobody did. '

'It was felt that it was best that way. The government didn't want to antagonise the authorities.'

'You mean it suited their purposes?'

'You can't go through life blaming people for things that happened a long time ago.'

'Try telling that to her, Stewart.' Crane got to her feet, tucking the card into her back pocket.

'What about the job offer?'

'I need time to think.' She paused as she made to turn away. 'If you want to atone for whatever you did, and I'm betting I don't even know the half of it, then get me what you can on Barnaby Nathanson.'

'Sure.' Mason sighed. 'I'll do what I can. You know,' he added, 'I think I understand now what it is that ties you and Drake together.'

Crane waited.

'You both blame this country for orphaning you. You have to learn to forgive. Move on, get over it.'

'This is funny. You're a psychoanalyst now? Look around you, Stewart. We're all orphaned, even you. You just haven't realised it yet.'

22

The message from Archie sounded a cryptic note on Drake's voicemail.

'You might want to drop by. Something's come up.'

Throwing himself down on the sofa, Drake stared through the window at the skyline. The long and fruitless day had exhausted him. He had come up with nothing in his search for Fender, even though he was more convinced than ever that he was key. He reached down to the floor for his drink, feeling warm anticipation in the gentle rattle of ice as he lifted the glass. He stared outwards as the rum swirled over his tongue. Love it or hate it, there was something mesmerising about this city. There were times when he had contemplated just cutting loose, heading out into the world, learning other languages. Metamorphosing. Turning himself into something else. Someone else. That thing Crane had, the ability to just melt in and out of places. One day maybe. Someday.

He picked up his phone again, replayed the message and then stared at the device for a long while, trying to decipher what might lie behind the coroner's words. Then he got to his feet and went through to the kitchen to get another drink.

Even back when he was in the Met, Archie generally never called him in person. He sent cryptic emails at best. Most of the time he just sent out his reports and waited, relying on the fact that Drake was generally more keen on getting information out of him than he was on giving it. This, then, suggested something different. Drake knew what it was. He also knew it couldn't wait. He set the glass down with a sigh and headed for the door, picking up keys and jacket along the way.

The chief pathologist was in his office when Drake arrived. It was still early evening, yet in front of him on the desk stood an open bottle of twelve-year-old Balvenie whisky. He held it up.

'Go on, then.'

'Don't tell me you've stopped drinking?' The pathologist arched an eyebrow as he leaned over to pour them both a glass. 'Perhaps it's this new life of yours? Good healthy living in the private sector?'

'It's a whole new world out there.' Drake sipped the whisky as he sat down. 'I have a serious feeling I know what you're about to tell me.'

'That's the problem with you investigator types, always guessing. I do actually have some news. Not sure if it's bad, or just interesting.'

'This is you being cryptic.'

'It's a condition. We call it being human, or trying anyway.' Archie sighed. 'Anyhow, we ran a DNA test on Mary Stuart and matched the head to the unidentified torso that turned up in Brighton four years ago.'

'So it is Zelda?'

'Everything seems to indicate that is the case.' Archie was shaking his head. 'One interesting fact. The DNA report matching the torso to items in her room has disappeared.'

'How can that be?'

'It happens. What can I say? As a result of that, the body was filed as a missing person. The pathologist filed her as an unidentified Jane Doe who had been in a collision with a boat. Not uncommon but still, any fool looking at that would know it wasn't made by a propeller. Luckily the body was kept in storage and we could do another test.'

'Will this change the circumstances of the investigation?'

'You mean, will they make it a priority? I doubt it. She's still a cold case from four years ago. An unknown foreign citizen who died under obscure circumstances. They're not going to be breaking the door down to find who did it.' Archie leaned forward to lock his fingers together on the desktop. Drake had never seen him quite this sober, despite the Scotch.

'Why so coy, doc? I mean, this is good, right?'

'What you hoped for, perhaps. You're looking for closure. I

understand that. Just beware of wishful thinking, trying to tie loose ends together.'

'Do I detect a note of cynicism?'

Archie studied the amber liquid in his glass. 'Forensics ran some other tests.'

'What other tests?'

'Well, they found dog hairs for a start.'

'Dog hairs?' Drake frowned.

'Yes, it's confusing the issue because there are extraneous tissue samples that look like they might be animal tissue.'

'Animal? You mean something had started to eat it?'

Archie looked at him like a man whose patience was not unlimited. 'What I'm trying to tell you is that it's not clear what the connection is between the hairs and the tissue. They might be unrelated.'

'So . . . you're not saying a dog was feeding on her?'

'Not exactly. There's no indication of that. The wound is remarkably smooth and clean, and the head is generally, as I said, well preserved.'

'You did say that, several times.'

'So these samples came from the area around the wound, which suggests that the knife, or possibly the head, came into contact with a surface that had contained animal matter.'

'Okay, so we're talking about a butcher's shop, something like that?' Drake still had the sense that this was not the whole story.

'That's not what immediately concerns me.'

Drake noted the change in the other man's tone. 'What does immediately concern you?' he asked slowly.

The coroner cleared his throat. 'Other items were located. The head was, you will recall, wrapped up in newspapers and old rags.'

'I do recall. In fact, if I'm not very much mistaken these items included a newspaper with an article in it all about me.'

'Which, I'm sure you'll agree, is interesting in its own right.'

'Depends on your definition of interesting. Look, I'm not trying to hurry you, but I would appreciate it if you would get to the point, Archie.'

'The fact that you were the subject of that article was not, I suggest now, an accident. It implies that the killer was trying to point the finger, at you.'

Drake shrugged. 'Sounds a fair conclusion. It could also be a coincidence.'

'We're men of science and deduction, Cal. We don't believe in fate. Things happen for a reason. Coincidence is trying to tell us something.' Archie refilled their glasses.

'And what exactly is that?'

Archie let out a long sigh and reached for his glass again. He was about to take a drink when he stopped himself. 'How long have we known each other?'

'Long enough to stop playing games.'

'I've always thought you were a good man, Cal. At heart, I mean. We all have our weaknesses, our indulgences, but at the end it comes down to whether someone is fundamentally, deep down, good or bad. I've always taken you for one of the good ones.'

'You say that as though you no longer believe it.'

'They found your blood on one of the rags.'

Drake sat up. 'My blood? That can't be right.'

'It's science, Cal, not the reading of tea leaves. Your DNA is on record for elimination purposes and it came up a match.'

Drake set down his glass, suddenly stone-cold sober. 'That makes no sense.'

'That's what I'm telling you. That's *why* I'm telling you.' Archie thumped a fist on the desk. 'I just want you to tell me that it's not true. You didn't kill that woman.'

'I didn't kill that woman.'

'Then how do you explain your blood being there?'

'I can't.'

'I hate to tell you this, Cal, but this is beginning to look like what used to be called an open-and-shut case. The blood samples are recent, but that doesn't clear you. Prisons are full of people denying what they did. I don't need to tell you that.'

By now Drake was on his feet, restlessly pacing from one side of the room to the other.

'Somebody got hold of my blood. A sample.'

'Did you give blood recently? Have a date with a vampire?'

Drake squinted at him. 'There's a funny side to this, Archie, but right now I'm not seeing it.'

'Well, you need to start thinking of one because I can't sit on this for long. Matches are time-logged. I can't change that. It'll only look like I'm doing you a favour.'

'You're sure there's no mistake?'

Archie inclined his head. 'Facts are facts. You need to find out how this happened.'

As he headed for the door, Drake paused once more. 'Let me ask you a question, doc. The condition of the head and the presence of animal tissue. That suggests a butcher's freezer to me.'

'Why not? A typical industrial freezer can go down to minus forty or more. At that temperature you can pretty much stop all deterioration processes in their tracks.' Archie reached for the bottle. Without bothering to offer, he poured himself a glass. 'There's also the line of the incision, which shows remarkable regularity, in dealing with bone, cartilage and flesh. To cut through material like that without deviation suggests a high-powered mechanical blade, possibly with small serrations.'

'Meaning an electric saw of some kind?'

'We're talking about an abattoir, a slaughterhouse, something along those lines. Once we get the measurements through to forensics for comparison we'll know more. Right now I would put my money on an abattoir tool. Long blade. Sturdy and powerful. This thing went through her spine like a knife through soft butter.'

Drake winced. 'Thanks, doc. Enlightening, as always.'

'All organic lifeforms are the same. Once they no longer carry the force of life in them, they become just that, inanimate matter.'

'I'm sure there's a more poetic version of that somewhere.'

Archie raised his glass in salute. 'If you want my advice, you need to move quickly. Someone's got it in for you, Cal. If you don't clear your name, you may not get a second chance.'

23

Drake arrived back home to find his way into the building blocked by a big man in a biker's leather jacket struggling with a child and shopping bags. It was only when Drake made to move past that he heard the child call his name.

'Cal!'

'Hey, Joe.'

João, or Joe, as he preferred to be called, was nearly nine now. His hair was growing out into a fuzzy afro of dark hair tipped with blond ringlets. He was still the skinny little kid that Drake remembered, although they hadn't seen each other for a while. The man ignored Drake. He picked up the shopping bags and shuffled over to enter the lift without anything more than a nod.

'See you later.'

'Later, alligator!' shouted Joe.

The doors slid shut and Drake turned towards the stairs. It was a long climb, but it was preferable to sharing the lift with Maritza's new friend. It was more than a year since Drake and his downstairs neighbour had brought their casual relationship to an end. Maritza was an artist, and she had the temperament to match. She'd disappeared for months without a word, but he felt that Joe shouldn't pay the price for the complicated way grown-ups lead their lives, so Drake hadn't wanted to press him. He could tell that the boy felt a little awkward about the situation.

Drake himself wasn't in the mood for small talk. Archie had given him a lot to think about. If it was possible that someone had gone to the trouble of trying to frame him for a murder that happened four years ago, then the question was why. Either someone was worried that an investigation might find the real killer, or they saw an opportunity to get Drake. There was something personal about that second prospect that disturbed him. This wasn't just business, this was someone with a grudge serious enough to hold on to Zelda's head for all this time. That someone had to be connected to Goran's murder too.

The name that kept popping into Drake's head was that of Pryce, even though he had nothing in the way of evidence that he was behind it. He knew only that Vernon Pryce had held a grudge against him for years and would have been more than happy to see Drake go down for Zelda's murder. He might even believe that he was responsible in some way. Pinning a murder on someone wouldn't have been all that alien to him either. Drake knew that Pryce wasn't beneath stooping to such methods to clear a case. There had been rumours about him for years.

Back on the sofa in the living room, Drake lay in the dark trying to think. He was curious about Fender. Who he was and where he fitted into the picture. Also, how he had managed to get hold of Zelda's head. It seemed clear now that he had staged the whole business on the Tube intentionally to draw the maximum amount of attention. He wanted Zelda and her killer to be exposed to the world. That seemed like an unlikely course for the actual killer, even if he thought he could throw the blame on Drake. Did that mean that whoever Fender was, he wasn't responsible for her death?

There were more questions than he had answers to and he was getting hungry. He'd been drinking on an empty stomach, he realised, having not thought about food all day. He sat up, reaching for his phone, and dialled in his usual order to a Balti place in Falcon Road. Then he flipped open his laptop and clicked through the audio-visual files Milo had sent him one more time. He wasn't sure what he was looking for any longer, but he was convinced that he must have missed something.

He stared at an image from the exterior of Clapham Common station for about ten minutes before he realised that he was looking at images from the day before the head was found. He was about to click away when something caught his eye. It took him a few moments to figure out how to move the image and zoom in on the top left-hand corner. A large white box truck was trying to park but was making a dog's dinner out of it. There was writing on the outside of the panelling. Green

Gardens Halal Meat Packing. Drake was staring at the image, trying to remember where he had seen it before, when the doorbell rang. He got up, expecting his food to have arrived. Instead, he opened the door to find Maritza standing there.

She took two steps back and wrapped her arms around herself. She wore a baggy brown cardigan over her usual paint-spattered overalls.

'Hey,' she smiled.

'Hi,' he replied. 'Wasn't expecting you.'

'Sorry, yes. I should have called.'

'No, no, it's fine. Come in.' He stepped aside, but she shook her head.

'Sorry, no, I can't. João said he saw you.'

It was Drake's turn to smile. 'Yeah, he's grown. You've been away.'

'We were in Rio for a couple of months to see my parents. My father was ill.'

'Sorry to hear that.'

'It's okay, you know me and family.' Her face broke into one of those great big grins that he had always loved and he felt his heart give an unfamiliar lurch. Then she was back on an even keel, all business-like. 'Look, I just wanted to say, João has been asking about you. I think he misses you. This whole thing . . .' Avoiding his gaze, her eyes fixed on a spot on the doorframe where the paint was flaking. 'What I'm trying to say is that, if you feel like it, some time, I'm sure he'd love to catch up.'

'Yeah, sure.'

'Great. I think he's looking for male role models.'

'What about . . .?'

'Shane?' She pulled a face. 'Kids are not really his thing. I think João can feel that.'

'Right.' Cal wondered when he had qualified as having kids as his thing, but he wasn't going to quibble. During their time together he and Joe had got along easily. They were comfortable in each other's company.

Maritza nodded. 'I think he just needs some sense of order.'

'Right, well, you know, sure. I'd be happy to.'

'Maybe just babysitting one evening? Not a school night.'

'Sure, pizza and television.'

'Sounds about right.' There was another long pause. The kind you could have fitted a coffin into lengthwise. 'You and me . . . I mean, we . . .' She left the sentence open ended. Drake knew what she meant. There were too many weird angles on this thing.

'It's complicated. Look, I'm happy to take care of Joe. You just tell me when.'

'You mean it?'

'I wouldn't say it if I didn't mean it.'

'I know, I just . . .'

'He's a great kid. Just, you know, give me notice.'

'Right. Thanks. You know . . .' she began as she turned away. They looked at one another. She waved the thought away with a swipe of her hand. 'Forget it.'

Drake shut the door and wandered back through the kitchen to the living room, fixing himself another drink on the way. He reached into the freezer compartment and winced. Withdrawing his hand he saw the narrow scar, almost healed. He took his drink into the other room and sat down on the sofa, holding his hand up to the light.

He remembered now. It was over a week since he'd cut himself. He'd fallen asleep on the sofa one evening. Maybe he'd had a few drinks too many, but he'd woken in the middle of the night thirsty and went into the kitchen to get some water. He'd knocked a glass over and then tried to catch it before it fell into the sink and broke. Throwing out his hand, he'd managed to punch the glass into the wall tiles. A shard of broken glass had cut him deeply. He remembered reaching for the closest thing to hand, a white T-shirt, and wrapped it around his hand. Then he lay down again. When he woke up the cloth was soaked in blood. The wound had clearly been deeper than he had thought. He washed it and poured iodine on it, then he patched it as best he could and hoped it would heal without stitches. The T-shirt had gone into the rubbish and was thrown out a day later.

Getting up now, he went over to the window and peered

down into the shadows around the base of the building. Had someone been watching him? Had they seen him buzzing himself into the yard behind the building where the bins were kept? Someone who had noticed the bandage on his hand? Someone who had been very lucky, or had spotted an opportunity. Or maybe luck had nothing to do with it. Maybe it was fate.

24

The club was in the basement of an old church. The word 'Cryptography' was spelled out in neon letters behind the bar. She wondered if that was the name of the place. Names seemed like the evening's theme. Her date introduced himself as Jindy, which she assumed was short for Jindal. The softer ending didn't suit him. It suggested he was trying to project a more female-friendly version of the macho guy that he really was underneath. She wasn't really in the mood for this, but they had arranged it days ago. So they danced and did shots and then danced some more. At a certain point, feeling sweaty and free, Ray decided that she would probably say yes if he invited her back.

His place turned out to be a huge penthouse in Canary Wharf, with floor-to-ceiling windows and nothing to block the view but an expensive leather sofa. The only other furniture on display was a bed up against the wall.

'I like the minimalism of it,' she said, as he handed her a drink.

'Oh, it's not intentional. All my stuff has been shipped over to Frankfurt. The firm is relocating.'

She remembered that he had told her what he did. Something immediately forgettable to do with finance and transferring funds in and out of various locations around the world. However you tried to dress it up, he was a glorified stockbroker. She sensed that if she allowed him to go on about his job her interest in him would wane pretty fast. Why was it that men who worked in finance thought they were geniuses, simply because they could move other people's money around in sufficient quantities to make a huge profit? It wasn't complicated, but since everything nowadays was judged in terms of monetary gain perhaps it wasn't surprising.

Things were moving along smoothly until she laughed at

some comment he made. Something related to the current political turmoil. He pulled back.

'It wasn't that funny.'

'No, it's just that it sounds like something my partner would say.'

'Partner?'

'Business partner, nothing more. Colleague.'

'Doesn't bother me.'

Either way, the damage had been done. She appeared to have hit a nerve. His manner had changed from one moment to the next. He was still smiling, but the warmth had gone from his eyes, replaced by a gnarly jealous flare.

'Believe me, there's nothing between us.'

'What's his name?'

'His name? Cal.'

'Cal? What is that, Irish?'

'No.' Crane sensed danger and started to get up. He put out a hand to grab her wrist.

'Where are you going?'

'I'm not sure this is working out.' She twisted her hand free and got to her feet.

He laughed. A cold, cynical cackle. 'So, one mention of the boyfriend and you're off.'

'I told you, he's not my boyfriend.' Ray located her jacket and pulled it on as she headed for the door. He blocked her way. The smile was back. Now she wondered what she had ever seen in him. The bad lighting in the club had done its magic.

'Come on,' he purred, reaching out to stroke her arm. 'I was joking. Let's just chill. Sit down, relax and have another drink.'

She placed the flat of her hand on his chest and held him in check.

'I don't think so,' she said.

She didn't see the blow coming. She was moving past him, half turned away, as his hand came up from down by his side. She wasn't expecting it. His fist hit the side of her head, just below her left ear. The force of the blow spun her sideways, away from him and into the door. The double impact left her dizzy. She felt herself being pulled backwards, folding to the floor.

There was a ringing in her ear and she couldn't quite understand what was happening. She was face down with the weight of him on top of her, his hands moving around over her body. She wriggled to get away from him but that only seemed to increase his efforts to subdue her.

'Come on, don't fight it.' His breath was hot in her ear. 'You know you want it.'

One hand held her down while the other was busy at her waist, reaching round to unfasten her jeans. She rocked from side to side, feeling that she had no strength and hearing his chuckle in response. His right hand was pulling, trying to get her jeans down over her hips. He had to raise himself up off her to do it and that gave her all the opportunity she needed.

As his weight lifted she bucked upwards and managed to twist round halfway. Pressing her elbow just under his chin, she pushed back, but her boots were slipping on the polished wooden floor and he was strong. His only response was to laugh.

'Feisty, eh?'

Then her foot touched the wall and suddenly she had purchase. She bent her knee, then thrust herself back, bringing her elbow up hard into his jaw. He cried out and tumbled off her. She rolled onto one knee, facing him. He had his hand to his mouth and there was blood coming through his fingers. He must have bitten his tongue.

'Bitch!'

He tried to get up, but she beat him to it. She ground her heel into the hand that rested on the floor. He swore and clutched it to him. That's when she hit him, the pointed toe of her right boot connecting neatly with his left temple. It was a nice, clean strike and flattened him nose down to the floor. He lay there for a minute and then began crawling away from her.

She fixed her clothes and ran a hand through her hair. Then she opened the door and stood there for a moment.

'Enjoy Frankfurt,' she said over her shoulder.

25

The view from the window was depressing. Couples going by with their ergonomically designed pushchairs and their carefully distressed clothing to downplay their obvious affluence. These new arrivals were transforming the neighbourhood. Beards and wholefood shops were proliferating like a bad rash, selling things he neither wanted nor could afford. Old places, familiar faces, it was all being displaced.

Maybe it was the weather that was getting him down. Dark clouds snapped by like ragged flags. They spat out their icy spume before flying on to parts unknown. It felt like it could turn to snow at any time. He watched an old couple struggling with an umbrella as they crossed the street, dodging buses and bicycle couriers. The umbrella whipped over their heads like a toy palm tree in a typhoon.

Drake was discovering that one of the advantages of private work was that you were unburdened of all the minor cases, the petty bureaucratic tasks, the accountability. You could devote all your energies to a particular investigation. Basically, it meant you had more time on your hands. Right now, he was thinking about Marco Foulkes and trying to get past his natural hatred of silk scarf-wearing pseudo-intellectuals driving expensive cars. Foulkes carried himself with an unapologetic sense of privilege. But Drake told himself that wasn't why he didn't trust him. It went beyond that. The whole story of why he came to Crane in the first place had struck him as odd. Not having faith in the police was fair enough, but it suggested that perhaps he had other reasons for not doing so. Quite what these reasons might be Drake couldn't say.

So far Foulkes had not stepped out of line. He had done nothing at all to indicate that he was worthy of such suspicion. On the contrary, he had gone out of his way to appear an upstanding, concerned friend. Perhaps it was this earnestness that made Drake wary.

Drake was aware that focusing on Foulkes was also a way of letting go of the matter that was really on his mind. The tangled details surrounding Zelda and the circumstances of her death. He still couldn't bring himself to think of her by her real name, Esma Danin. Somehow it was easier to think of her by her stage name, her working name, the alias she had adopted when she had wound up in this country trying to make a new life for herself. When they had first met, Drake had asked her about her name, but she had been coy.

'What difference does it make who I was? What matters is who I am now.'

'We all have a past. It's nothing to be ashamed of.'

'I'm not ashamed,' she told him, sternly. 'This is London. Here you can become anything or anyone you want, right?'

He couldn't argue with that. She had every right to believe it was possible to become whatever she wanted to. And perhaps she might have made it if she had managed to get away from Goran. Only someone had put a stop to all of that and Drake was going to find out who that someone was.

Across the street he watched Foulkes and the solicitor come out of the pub entrance. Today they were in Fitzrovia, a stone's throw from the writer's flat in Rathbone Square. The pub had flower pots hanging over the entrance and the two men shook hands under one of these before turning and walking in opposite directions.

Drake tailed Barnaby Nathanson north. He was walking slowly, his head bowed. In his left hand a battered leather briefcase thumped against his thigh. He seemed tired, weighed down by the world, unaware of his surroundings. He took the occasional misstep, which suggested that perhaps he'd had a couple of drinks too many. A woman in a business suit stepped smartly out of his way to avoid collision. Drake crossed the road to get a better look. He was watching Nathanson, but then something else caught his eye.

The sun had come out and the wind was whipping at the flags and standards hanging over an entrance. It took Drake a couple of seconds to realise that he remembered the place. It looked different. Like so many places in London, it had changed hands more than once. It had undergone some fundamental refurbishment. It had another name. One that he didn't recognise. But it was definitely the same place.

Nathanson was temporarily relegated to the back burner. Drake watched him reach the end of the street and turn in the direction of Russell Square tube station. He was pretty sure he was on his way to the office in Dalston Junction. He could catch him up later, either there or at his home address in Pimlico, which Drake was eager to take a closer look at. In the meantime, he found himself transported, momentarily, to a time four years previously.

Stepping down from the pavement, Drake crossed the street to walk through the wide entrance of the hotel. Everything in there had changed. He had a vague recollection of a low ceiling and corner lighting. Bland beige wallpaper and long flat sofas of varnished wood. Back then it had been crying out for a facelift and by the looks of things it had got one. A menacing-looking chandelier shaped like a killer drone floated over the centre of the lobby area. Guests wandered by oblivious. The furniture was now black leather and hard marble, which made Drake feel an odd fondness for the old days, a sentiment that was unusual for him.

Those were the days when Drake was inside Goran's operation. Like Zelda, he went by another name. He was Terry Nash. Not yet inside the inner circle. That was reserved for Goran's old pals from the White Knights, the Serbian militia he had been leader of back in the nineties. Nash was part of a loose network of new associates who connected Goran with the London set-up. Drake had lived in constant motion, never settling, cutting off all contact with his old life, afraid of his cover being blown at any moment. To protect his identity he had to stay away from places where he was known. It wasn't all that difficult, he found. Just a new pad across the water on the Isle of Dogs. Staying away from known acquaintances wasn't hard. Drake had always been a loner, so he didn't have a long list of family and friends who would wonder where he was.

Most people would have found it a little difficult to cut off all ties and slip into that twilight frame where he was what he wanted to appear to be: an ambitious and ruthless small-time drug dealer trying to move up in the world. He was smart and kept appointments, held up his end of the bargain, whatever that was. He made himself known as a reliable guy, someone you could trust to solve a problem whatever came up. Goran came to trust him, and he didn't trust a lot of people. Outside of work Nash kept his distance. It was important to respect how deep the bonds between Goran and his men were. Many were war veterans, fighters. They had lost mates and family back home and that brought its own loyalties. Push too hard and you hit a wall.

As Nash, Drake would allow himself to be followed, sticking to his assumed identity, never letting it slip, night and day. Contact with the team in the Met's Organised Crime Unit was old school: handwritten messages exchanged in plain sight; burner phones that were changed every three days. This wasn't standard procedure. This was the system Drake had insisted on with Vernon Pryce, who was supposed to be his outside contact, only Drake never trusted Pryce, not completely. Drake knew that it was only a matter of time before someone put two and two together, or they made a mistake, or some poor copper with a drug habit and a mortgage to pay fell into Goran's pocket.

They were trying to build a case against Goran and so far all they had was a list of gambling clubs, strip joints, protection rackets, prostitution. Nothing solid enough to convict him for anything like a substantial period of time. Goran was smart. He kept his organisation divided up into watertight compartments. Nobody knew what was going on right next to them. There was a maze of false trails, shell companies and smokescreens, empty flats, containers that brought in nothing but garden furniture or tyres. They switched up their communications regularly. There was nothing to tie Goran himself to the money that was flowing in. He never touched it personally.

Then Drake had a stroke of luck. He met Zelda and sensed in her a restlessness. She was unhappy with her lot and she had evidence that Goran was backing a trafficking ring. People were being brought in through ports on the south coast from Spain and Portugal. They were shipped in from Eastern Europe and North Africa. Mostly they were young women, who were passed through one club to another, picking up papers along the way. Increasingly, the people being brought in were getting younger – children, catering to a darker market. According to Zelda, Goran wasn't happy with the way this was going, but he was a businessman, and he wasn't going to turn a profit away. That's where he and Zelda parted ways.

According to her, Goran had a weak link. The other outfits he was working with were less disciplined, unreliable. The one thing that let Goran down was his temper. He was known to throw a hissy fit when someone didn't do what they were meant to, didn't get rid of telephones, bills of lading, or worse, tried to pressure him for more money or a bigger cut. According to Zelda this gang had tapes of Goran they intended to use as leverage.

Drake first met Zelda when he stepped in to do Goran a favour. One of the regular drivers didn't show. He was to take a girl from one of the clubs to a client who was waiting at a hotel. The client had paid specially and, though this wasn't what she did normally, Goran made sure that the money was so good she couldn't afford to refuse. That should have been the end of it. Someone else would pick her up. But Drake was curious. He wanted to know what was going on. So he parked the car and went inside after her. He spent the next hour circling the lobby. He picked up a newspaper and studied everyone in there. He sat at the bar and ordered a gimlet.

He was hoping for a chance to talk to her quietly, alone, away from the usual set-up, from the other girls, from Goran. But it was taking longer than he expected and he was starting to think that perhaps he was wasting his time. Then he looked up and saw her coming out of the lift. Immediately, he knew something was wrong. The way she was walking, in slow, awkward steps. He crossed the lobby to intercept her, putting out a hand to steady her as her knees buckled. 'I've got you,' he said, catching her before she fell. He spotted a trickle of blood running down the back of her left leg. Over her shoulder he saw the receptionist watching them. When their eyes met he returned to the ledger in front of him. No doubt he was also on the payroll. Drake led Zelda out through the front door and down a side street to where the car was parked. He helped her inside. There was a bruise on her cheek and her eye was swollen.

'You should see a doctor.'

'No doctor. Just drive.'

'Should I take you home?'

'Home?' The thought seemed to make her sadder. 'Not home. Just drive.'

They drove. Drake took his time, not sure which direction to take. In the end he let the traffic decide, taking the line of least resistance. They drove west, across the river.

'I live not far from here,' he said, watching her in the mirror. 'You could rest there for a while.'

'What is your name again?'

'Nash. I'm Terry Nash.'

'You're not the regular driver.'

'I'm not a driver at all. I'm just filling in, doing someone a favour.'

'Right.' He saw her nod. 'Everybody is doing someone a favour.' She gave a bitter laugh. 'I can't go home. If he reports me, Goran will do worse to me than this.'

'You mean the man in the hotel?' He watched her face in the mirror. 'Is he the one who did this to you?'

'He said he wanted to do it in the ass. I said no, I don't do that, so he forced me. It hurt. After, I said to him that he should pay extra. He spat on me. He say I have enough already. So I told him that men who want to do it that way is because they are gay.' She laughed quietly to herself. 'He didn't like that.'

Drake parked the car and helped her into the building. They got up to his flat and he drew a bath for her. He laid out a sweatshirt and tracksuit pants. She held the clothes in one hand. Her eye was swelling.

'You're very sweet, but I need to know, why are you doing this?'

'Does there have to be a reason?'

'With men, there's always a reason.' Then she fell silent, letting her question fall away. 'Do you have anything to drink?'

He went to the kitchen and fetched a bottle of dark rum and some ice. He poured her a glass and wrapped some of the ice in a handcloth.

'Hold that to your eye. It'll help with the swelling.'

He left her to it. Afterwards she came out in the baggy outfit and settled herself on one of the sofas. Drake sat opposite. He refilled their glasses. Zelda admired the view.

'Such a beautiful city, and so big. It feels as though you could just disappear into it and never come out again. But I can't.'

'Why do you want to disappear?'

She turned to look at him. One eye was swollen and her cheek was turning blue, but her gaze was steady.

'Are you serious? You think I like this life? I dance in a club, waving my ass at men whose heads are filled only with dirty thoughts. They think they own me because they throw money at me.' She was shaking her head. 'They don't own me. I own them.'

'I get it that you want to get away from this life.'

'I don't know you. I know nothing about you.' She reached for the bottle and refilled her own glass. 'From the look of this place you're in the same shit as me. In fact, I would say you are in a worse position. The difference is that you don't know you're being fucked.'

'I have plans. I'm in business.'

She laughed. 'You do business with Goran. Who do you think is going to come out on top? You and I are in same position. Only difference is I know when I'm being fucked.' She looked into her glass and revised her words. 'That's not what I do.'

'You're a dancer.'

'That's right, I'm a dancer.' She tilted her nose in the air. 'My mother was a dancer. My aunts. Everyone in my family dances. I don't ask people for favours. I only ask them to be fair.' She pointed a finger at him. 'Are you being fair?'

'I'm trying.'

She looked into her glass before taking a long drink. It seemed to settle her. 'There's no future in this business. Not for me, not for you, not for anybody. Sooner or later the police are going to kick down the door and take him away.'

'You think so?'

'Either that, or someone will kill him.' She formed her hand into a gun and pointed it. 'One day. I am sure. I will be the first to spit on him.'

She was younger than Drake in years, but in terms of experience Zelda was a million years older than him.

'Why don't you get out?'

Zelda was still. 'If Goran thought for one moment that I was trying to get out, he would kill me.'

'Who was he, the man who hurt you?'

'It doesn't matter. He's just a little prick. I don't care about him.'

'You don't want to get him back?'

Her eyes lifted to fix on his. 'Is that what this is about? You want to take revenge for me. Is this your game?'

'I don't have a game.'

'Everyone has a game,' said Zelda. She rattled the ice in her glass. 'Why are you doing this?'

'I'm just helping.'

'No,' she shook her head. 'Not helping. Nobody is just helping.'

'Supposing I said I could help you to get out.'

'Then I would say you are bigger fool than you look.' She got to her feet. 'I have to go now.'

26

It was mid-morning, and Heather was extolling the virtues of her raw carrot cake when Crane had a call from Dryden Wheeler. The superintendent sounded weary, as though he was having a hard day.

'This business at Clapham station, I take it you've heard about it.'

'The severed head?'

'Exactly. Well, we're trying to make sense of it, but the general feeling is that we don't have a lot to go on: no crime scene, no body.' Wheeler broke off, as if to contemplate his words in more detail. 'They are trying to kick this under the rug for the moment.'

'For political reasons?'

'That's how it is these days, I'm afraid. Everything is about appearance. The optics, as they put it. Budget considerations and, of course, results. You can't pour resources into a case if you don't think there's a reasonable chance of clearing it. We have to be seen to be acting.'

'Acting being the operative word.'

There was a faint, uncomfortable ripple of laughter down the line. Wheeler would forgive Crane anything, or almost anything.

'Perhaps we could discuss it further over lunch?'

Dryden Wheeler was an important ally. Crane knew she would need his help if she ever wanted to secure more work with the Met in future. More than that, she liked him. There was something honest about him. She also knew that he was not happy about the fact that she had withdrawn her name from the rostrum of active forensic psychologists. It was a temporary measure, but a necessary one. Crane was convinced that the future lay not in going through the motions of providing the Met with profiles and assessments, but in breaking away from routine and striking out in a new direction. It was more about her temperament. In that respect she wasn't all that different from Drake. She preferred to be free, to be her own boss. Now, she found herself trying to break this news to Wheeler in as gentle a manner as was possible. As it happened he made it easier for her.

Wheeler chose a place he knew in Wimbledon. It was a bit of a hike for her but she didn't mind. A gastropub with a view of the common. You could almost believe you were in a picturesque English village.

'Your father, of course, was a great asset to the country in his time.'

'You know my father?' She could hear the steel creeping into her voice, but there was nothing she could do about it.

'Not well. We met a couple of times, but I meant more by reputation.'

'Of course.'

Wheeler leaned back, relaxed. Crane, on the other hand, was feeling decidedly itchy. Places like this, with their cut flowers and dark wood, did that to her. The walls were covered in paintings of trees and horses. It was like a three-dimensional still life. Like being trapped beneath a glass bell jar.

'I genuinely believe in your contribution. We're old-fashioned by nature. Breaking the mould is not easy, but we have to change things.'

Crane's smile was as generous as she could spare. 'I'm always happy to help, and I feel an obligation to live up to Julius's legacy. He was always very committed to our forensic work.'

Mention of her former partner and mentor brought an emotional gulp from Wheeler.

'He was a fine man, and sorely missed.'

'Yes, he was.'

'And how's it working out with Cal?'

'We're getting there.'

'He's a fine officer and a first-rate detective. I'm still hoping that we'll get him back one day.'

Don't hold your breath, was Crane's first thought, but she kept it to herself. The next few minutes were spent studying menus and deciding what to order. Wheeler was a traditionalist at heart and went for shepherd's pie, while she chose a Waldorf salad. The waitress was a nervous woman with bad skin who spilled sparkling water on the tablecloth. When she finally left them alone, Wheeler cleared his throat as he turned to the subject he had come to discuss.

'It's a delicate matter. I'm not sure how much you know about the case, but I am concerned about the repercussions.' Wheeler's face took on a pained expression. 'DCI Pryce is in charge of the Murder and Serious Crimes Unit these days and right now they have their hands full with current cases. No time to start looking back. We are in the midst of an epidemic of knife crime. Kids as young as twelve stabbing each other. It's a terrible thing.' He shook his head at the state of the world. 'We simply can't allocate the resources to something like this.'

'It's getting a lot of attention in the press.'

'Well, exactly. A severed head on the Tube. It's the stuff of nightmares. Pryce is right in the sense that clearing a case like this is not easy. The chances of success are low. But that is not the only consideration.' Wheeler was silent for the moment. 'If this is connected to that business with Goran Malevich, then we could end up dragging that whole case back into the spotlight.'

'You're uncomfortable with that?'

'It's not a matter of being uncomfortable. The point is that we don't need more stories about corruption in the Met.'

'You're thinking about Cal.'

'Among other things.' Wheeler began spreading a thick layer of butter onto a piece of bread. 'He got a rough deal out of that whole business. It was all I could do to stop him being dismissed from the force completely. He did his penance, but, if you ask me, he never really recovered. Dropping out of his own accord.' Wheeler folded his hands together, bread and butter now forgotten.

'You blame yourself?'

'To some extent, yes, of course I do. I was his senior officer. I should have protected him better. But these undercover operations are always tricky. Too many unknowns.'

'Cal knew what he was getting himself into.'

'The problem with Cal is that you never know what he's going to do. I used to say to him, Cal, if only you would commit, you could go as far as you like.' He brought his gaze back to rest on Crane. 'But I honestly never knew from one day to the next if he was going to show up.'

'He has his own ways.'

'Oh, I'm not saying he was unreliable. Once he got his teeth into a case he stuck with it, come hell or high water. But he's an individualist, likes to beat his own track.'

'I had noticed.' Crane fell silent as the food arrived. The salad was a disappointment, although Wheeler appeared delighted with his pie.

'So, tell me, how can I help?' she said, after a while.

'I've managed to convince the commissioners that what we should do is build up a case, without sacrificing manpower. Can you do a breakdown for us of the perpetrator?'

'That sounds as if you are taking the case seriously.'

'Well, I'm old-fashioned that way. I don't want to upset Pryce, but I do want to have something in hand if this thing goes pear-shaped. These are strange times.'

'You can say that again. Send over everything you've got and I'll get cracking.'

'Thank you.'

As they were getting ready to leave she turned to him. 'Can I ask you one question?'

'Of course, anything.'

'You said you'd met my father. How would you describe him?'

'Well,' Wheeler shifted his weight from one foot to the other. 'I remember him as a complex character. But also a man of great sadness. A very lonely man, I thought.'

Lonely was not how Crane would ever have described her father, but it gave her food for thought on the ride home. Back at the office she found Heather feeding the fish.

'They always look a little grey around the gills this time of year.'

'I feel the same way,' said Crane, going behind her desk and sifting quickly through the pile of mail lying there. 'Did you manage to get anything more on Foulkes?'

'Ah, the mysterious Mr Foulkes.' Heather set down the pot of fish food on Crane's desk and picked up a notepad and pencil. 'I have to come clean and confess that I was a bit star-struck when I heard he was coming in. I mean, there's something rather debonair about him, don't you think?'

'Debonair?'

'Not that I'm a big fan of his books.' Heather's expression soured. 'I did some checking and it seems it's a few years since he had a real success. Doesn't really surprise me. I tried a couple of them. Too clever for me. I prefer a good old yarn.'

'I'm afraid I've never read him either.'

Heather did a theatrical double take. 'That's a surprise. I thought with you and him being old sweethearts . . .'

Crane rolled her eyes. 'We played together as children a couple of times, when I was very small. That's as far as it went. He stole my tortoise and painted on its shell with his mother's lipstick.'

'Oh.' Heather looked askance. 'Sounds like a bit of a creep when you put it like that. Still, boys will be boys.'

'So' – Crane dropped into her chair, suddenly weary – 'tell me what you found.'

Glancing down at her notepad, Heather said, 'I did the usual background checks, credit ratings and so forth. More importantly, I managed to speak to a couple of people. One at his old bank. Not easy finding people who still work in banks. I mean, they've closed down all the branches. It's all online now. Remember when you used to queue to deposit a cheque? Those days are long gone. Not that I miss them. Anyhow, according to her, and she wouldn't give me a lot of detail, Mr Foulkes' finances are in something of a precarious state.' Heather looked over the top of her reading glasses. 'Which is not what you expect with a bestselling author, is it?'

Crane disagreed but she wanted Heather to get to the point, so said nothing.

'His outgoings are well over his incomings. In short, he's in debt. Has an overdraft arranged and manages to stay just above water, as it were.' She removed her glasses this time. 'Of course, the reason they are so generous with overdrafts and suchlike is that he stands to inherit the family pile. Bit like you in that respect.'

Again, Crane let it go, even though she bristled inwardly at the comparison. She remembered the barn at the Foulkes estate, the old Rolls-Royce in mint condition and the dogs. Something about that scene stuck in her mind. The air of menace she had felt in that barn was palpable. It made the hair on the back of her neck stand up just remembering it. She would never have admitted it, but Cal's instinct towards Foulkes was proving persistent.

'Who's your second source?'

'A girl who used to captain our old lacrosse team at school.'

'Lacrosse?' It took effort to visualise Heather on a playing field of any kind, but Crane managed to summon a rather terrifying picture of a large, bony, hefty figure wielding a stick.

'She's a bigwig at one of those big financial services companies.' Heather rolled her eyes. 'Hard to believe. I mean she was never voted person most likely to succeed. Far from it. We used to call her Whinging Wendy. Always moaning about one thing or another. Now she's very glamorous. I think she's had some work, you know?' Heather indicated cheeks and lips. 'Anyway, she was very helpful. She says Foulkes has a lot of tricks up his sleeve, including offshore accounts.'

'How does she know that?'

'Well, she doesn't, not really, but she can read profiles. She recognises the pattern. All of this was off the record, of course.'

'Did you ask about Barnaby Nathanson?'

'I did. She actually groaned when I mentioned the name. Mr Nathanson has something of a disreputable record. He has been involved in a lot of very underhand dealings with some very dodgy clients. We're talking about second-rate oligarchs, so not the top rank but the sleazier crud that bubbles just under the surface. Nathanson has helped lots of these characters to invest in a number of hedge funds, shell companies, property consortiums and, of course, overseas tax havens.'

'And he's close to Marco Foulkes?'

'They went to school together apparently. Old Carthusians.'

'That's Charterhouse School, right?'

'Oh, well done,' Heather beamed. 'I didn't know that until she told me.'

'Okay, so they're old school chums and they are doing each other favours. So far, so normal.'

'Yes, except that it's not.' Heather raised a finger. 'It seems that there is something of a cloud hanging over Nathanson. Wendy mentioned some rather unsavoury friends.'

'Anything more specific?'

Heather tapped her pencil on the notepad she was holding. 'When I pressed her, she got all vague and said these were just rumours. So, cold feet. She did mention one name, an offshore investment company called Novo Elysium.'

'Okay. Well done, Heather.'

Heather was wringing her hands. 'I have to confess, I'm a little confused. I thought he was our client. Why are we investigating him?'

'Good question.' Crane leaned back in her chair. 'So far it's just a feeling.'

'Yours, or Mr Drake's?'

'Shouldn't make a difference, Heather. We're partners now.'

'Yes, I know, but . . .'

'What's the problem, Heather?'

'I don't know, I just find it difficult. I find him difficult.'

'Just give him time.'

'If you say so.' Heather didn't sound entirely convinced. 'What I suppose I'm saying is that I don't see how investigating our client will help that poor girl.'

'I understand that. But hopefully it will all come together.'

'That's the kind of thing he would say.'

Crane glanced up at Heather and wondered if she had a

point. Maybe Cal's influence was beginning to rub off. She ran an eye over the inbox on her phone and saw a message that had just come in. 'There you go. Her uncle has confirmed that he's happy to meet.'

'So, onwards and upwards, as they say,' said Heather heavily, as she headed for the door.

27

The sign over the narrow doorway spelled out Wet Wax Wonderama in twisted red and yellow neon letters. Lighted arrows on the staircase drew Drake down into a basement so low he had to duck his head. It was a long room with a short bar at the far end. There were booths with low tables and fake white leather upholstery. The kind of place you wouldn't want to touch anything. There were lava lamps set in little niches and on the tables. Most of them were switched off. Congealed globs of wax in vials of coloured liquid took on the shape of alien lifeforms.

It was deserted if you disregarded the cobwebs. Drake stood for a moment to take stock of the place. He recalled it from the old days. Age hadn't mellowed the sleazy feel. A door in the back squeaked open and shut to admit a man coming down the narrow corridor beside the bar. Thin, balding and doing up his pants, he wore an Arsenal shirt and a moustache so out of date it matched the wax lamps.

'How can I help you?' he asked, wiping his hands on his trousers.

'Nice touch with the lamps,' Drake gestured.

'Yeah, nice.' The man reached under the counter for a packet of cigarettes and a lighter. He blew smoke over Drake's head. 'You looking for something special?'

'Just looking.'

The man said nothing, just stared, unable to decide what to make of him. Drake thought he could have been Arab, North African probably, Algerian possibly.

'It's early. Things don't usually start to get busy until later. How about a drink?'

'No, you're fine.'

The man sniffed, clearly unhappy. He turned as a woman appeared out of the same rear door. Drake put her around her early forties. She wore a lot of make-up and a platinum blonde wig that wasn't quite straight. The red satin dress might have fit her a couple of years ago but now it was less flattering than pleading for mercy. The slit up the side went as far as it could go in decent company. She fixed a smile on her face as she slid round to his side of the bar.

'Hello there. What's your name?'

'Nash.'

Drake watched her face for any trace of recognition, but she turned away to lift a foot on the bar rail and reveal a little more thigh.

'I'm Sonja,' she said. The man did his part by producing a bottle of champagne.

'A glass, on the house, what do you say?'

He shook water off a glass he'd fished out of a sink somewhere out of sight. Drake said nothing. He watched the man pour, aware that the woman's eyes were on him.

'You like champagne?'

'Not particularly.'

'Ah, more of a beer man.' Her eyes lit up with feigned empathy. Drake remembered her now. He'd seen her back in the old days when her drug habit had been worse. From the smell of her breath it looked like drink was her choice of poison these days. Drake made no move to touch the glass that was set in front of him. The man watched him out of the corner of his eye as he wiped down the bar with a dirty rag. He'd played his part. Now it was up to her.

'Why don't we make ourselves comfortable?' The woman nodded in the direction of one of the booths. 'Maybe you can pay for the drinks first.'

'Pay?' asked Drake. 'I didn't ask for it and I haven't touched it, why would I pay for it?'

'You got to pay,' said the man. 'Everybody pay.'

'I'm not everybody.'

'Forget it, Sal. He's a copper, innit?'

The man's face froze. 'Says who?'

'Says me.'

He looked Drake up and down. 'I never seen him before. How you know he's a copper?'

'Just look at him.'

The man didn't seem convinced.

'Sal? Is that short for Salah?' Drake asked.

'Huh?' He was wagging a finger now. 'No pay, no talk.'

'Just leave it, Sal,' the woman said. She leaned over the counter for the cigarettes and lit one, throwing the pack back down on the counter. But Sal was offended. A vein throbbed in the centre of his forehead.

'You can't talk to him,' he said, grabbing for her wrist. 'He hasn't paid.'

'Fuck off.' She shook herself free. 'I don't work for you. And besides, I'm not talking to him.'

Sal stood for a moment before tossing the rag into the sink and stalking back down the narrow hallway where he had come from. Sonja turned to Drake.

'I remember you.'

'You knew Zelda.'

Sonja held his gaze while taking a long, slow drag of her cigarette. She jerked her chin in the direction of the back.

'He's calling them, you know. You don't want to be here when they get here.'

'Who gets here?'

'The ones who own the place.'

'Who are they?'

'What difference does it make? They change the name, the paint, the lighting, but it's still the same shit on the inside.' She looked him up and down, not in a good way. 'I remember you. You were bad news back then.'

'I was trying to help Zelda.'

'She went back home.' An emptiness came into her eyes. 'You have to go.'

'I'd like to talk to you,' said Drake. 'Not here.'

'You shouldn't have come here.' She turned away and stubbed her cigarette out in the ashtray on the counter. 'If you know what's good for you, you'll leave now.'

Drake could see he wasn't going to get any more out of her. He climbed the dark narrow staircase and emerged into the light, surprised to see ordinary people going about their lives.

As if a part of him had expected the world to have been replaced with brimstone and fire.

The car was parked around the corner in Bridle Lane. He waited there, tapping his hand on the wheel. It didn't take long. They drove up at high speed in a large silver Transit van that screeched to a halt outside the club entrance. He made a note of the number plate. The side door slid open and four of them jumped out of the back and went in down the stairs. They were big men wearing turtlenecks and leather jackets. One of them carried a cricket bat. It seemed a little over the top, old school. Nothing too sophisticated. They would have leaned on him until he paid. If he refused they would have dragged him out and given him a kicking before emptying his pockets and dumping him by the side of road somewhere that it would take hours to walk back from. Drake recognised one of the men as Khan, the heavy with the tattoo he had seen at Papa Zemba's place with Donny's nephew.

How much could they make in a place like that? When it was run by Goran Malevich it was small time, a place to break the women in gently. It stayed open all day and into the early hours. Men walked in off the street. It was random. They were invited to order champagne for themselves and the hostesses. There was a list of services ranging from private lap dances and hand jobs, occasionally going all the way up to full sex with one, two or more women. The local vice mob took a slice of the action. For a little cash and free access to the girls they stayed out of their hair. But business was uneven. The punters irregular. Men on their lunch breaks, or on their way home from work. Groups of drunken youngsters. The odd tourist looking for a little variation before heading home to the wife and kids. It was a sideline. Goran had other things going on, but this was a prime location and he wanted to hold on to it. He made more money on drugs and gambling than on this, but it was all part of the territoriality of it; holding on to your piece of turf.

'Places like this don't fall into your hands every day,' he would say, with that stupid gap-toothed grin and a hint of gold eyeteeth. He'd had that done early on, when he wanted to look like a rapper. A white rapper from the Balkans. 'I own a little bit of London. You know how that feels?'

'How does it feel, Goran?'

'It feels like I'm the fucking king of England.' He threw back his head and laughed.

Drake settled himself back in his seat, as he watched the men disappear through the narrow doorway and down into the club. They stayed there for a while, maybe fifteen minutes. Sal would have been telling them the whole story. Then he would have poured them all a drink so that they left in a slightly better mood, despite not having had a chance to break someone's legs. The van came back around, the driver hooted and the goons piled up the stairs and into the back. The door slid shut and away they went.

The afternoon was fading now, as the pale winter light gave way to an angry neon that fizzed like sparklers in the wet pools in the road. It was around six o'clock when Drake finally spotted Sonja emerging. No longer recognisable as the hostess in the red dress. The platinum wig was gone and she wore a long sheepskin coat over jeans and a hoodie. She was holding something wrapped in a handkerchief pressed to the side of her face. Ice. So they had taken out some of their frustration on her after all.

Leaving the car where it was, Drake decided to follow her on foot. She walked down to the Tube station at Piccadilly Circus. He let her get a little way ahead of him, even though she wasn't paying much attention to her surroundings. To all intents and purposes, she was just another commuter eager to get home in the rush. It was so busy he wasn't really worried about being spotted by her. Nevertheless, he stayed back just out of sight in case she turned.

There was a moment of panic when he thought he had lost her on the eastbound platform. He rushed through to the westbound platform, which was deserted, and then back again in time to spot her stepping onto a train. He jumped into the next carriage and watched her exit at Caledonian Road. He followed her down the main road to a nondescript grey terraced house. Along the way she had stopped at Salwar's Supermarket.

Through the window of the minimart he watched her take a bag of ice cubes from the freezer, along with a bottle of vodka and a packet of frozen hamburgers. He stood across the street beside the unlit front of the Chiang Mai Thai Massage Centre and watched Sonja disappear through the front door of the grey house. Through a glass panel over the door a naked lightbulb could be seen as it came on. A few minutes later a light came on in a window on the third floor. A low sash window that was half open and in urgent need of paint. Drake turned and made his way back towards the station. He would have liked to call it a day, but he knew the night was far from being over.

28

Drake got back to the car in Soho only to find a fine waiting for him on the windscreen. It was to be expected. He did what he should have done earlier and drove around the corner to the NCP car park in Brewer Street. He backed into a space and then changed into the old set of clothes he had brought with him.

The evening got off to a bad start. Coming round the corner onto Trafalgar Square he bumped into a group of men wearing yellow hi-vis jackets and waving union flags. As he tried to make his way through he found his path blocked. The men surrounded him, closing in as he turned in a circle trying to find a way out. As they jostled him, they began chanting, blowing beery breath into his face.

'We are the people! We are the people!'

Drake was already sizing them up, trying to work out a tactic, quickly picking out the biggest of them as the first one to go for. The odds were bad and he didn't want a confrontation, but he knew he had to be ready if it came to that. There were ten or fifteen of them. His only hope was that taking two or three of them down might cause the others to reconsider their actions, or scarper.

One of them reared up into his face. 'What's the matter, don't you speak English?'

'Traitor!' Spitting and shouting in his face, they pushed by. 'Go back to where you came from!'

He watched them move on, blocking the traffic and shoving their placards in the faces of anyone they came across. Drake picked up his belongings, the carrier bags stuffed with old sweaters and socks. Anything, really, that wasn't of any value. Stuff he'd been meaning to throw out but never got around to. He was a walking jumble sale. A couple of them had been kicked across the pavement. Not that they contained anything.

'Crazy, what this country is coming to.'

Drake looked up to see a young man. In his late twenties, his tattered clothes and unlaced boots told their own story. He stepped forwards to hand Drake the fat purple caterpillar that was his sleeping bag.

'They're angry,' muttered Drake.

'Yes, but not at us. I mean, we didn't do this.'

'You've got a point there.'

There was something about his manner that was slightly off, as if he was trying to remember something. He stuck out his hand.

'Spike.'

'Nash.' For some reason, Drake was sticking to the alias he had used four years ago when he was undercover. It was easy to remember. Perhaps that was it, or maybe it was the sense that this whole episode was leading him back into his past. Spike told him that he was ex-service too.

'Never settled down,' the man said, shaking his head. 'I know blokes who came home and fitted right back in, as if they had never left. I mean, they were working, taking care of their families. I don't know how they do it. Me, I wasn't the same person.' He cast an eye over his shoulder. 'I never expected to wind up here. It's getting more dangerous. People don't care. They'll give you a kicking just for the hell of it.'

'How long have you been back?'

'Home, you mean?' The man lifted his head in wonder. 'I'm still trying to get there, mate.'

Spike, who was something of an old hand, led the way across Trafalgar Square. 'Come on, we can get a cup of tea around this time.'

Drake didn't have to try to make conversation. Spike simply laid it all out. 'I had problems. I admit it. But I never asked anyone to take care of me. I mean, I can take care of myself. I just need, like . . .' He cast around for the word he was looking for. 'The basics. That's all I ask. A roof over my head, food. I mean, they took me off the medication, said it was for my own good. What do they know, right? I mean, I'm on the inside, dealing with this stuff, not them.'

The two men walked to an old church off the Strand. In a large hall they were served tomato soup in Styrofoam cups. All around them people moved, surging round, back and forth, looking for somewhere to lodge themselves for a time. Everyone was lugging things with them: carrier bags, black plastic sacks, torn backpacks that looked as though they had been trampled by horses, and maybe they had. Where they came from was impossible to say. Drake picked up a smattering of accents, some familiar, others not. There was every race, colour, shape and size, young and old, mostly male.

'Ever run into a guy wearing a Fender hat?'

Spike's back stiffened. 'Friend of yours?'

'Kind of. Did me a favour once.'

'You mean like a favour, favour?' Spike's eyes darted up and down, from side to side, as if following a particularly vexed fly.

'Just a favour.'

'Right. I don't judge other people. That's all I ask, right, not to be judged? Not too much to ask, is it?'

'Sounds fair.'

'I don't pay much attention to what people are wearing.'

There was a change in tone, suggesting Spike was having second thoughts about his new-found friend. Drake's questions were unwelcome. Some unspoken rule about minding your own business. Maybe not so unspoken. Spike got to his feet and slipped away to speak to someone else before vanishing beneath the surface of grubby faces.

Left alone, Drake scanned the crowds. Some faces were so caked in dirt their own mothers would have had trouble recognising them. Others were wrapped in layers of hoodies and scarves, woollen hats and so forth, as if expecting an ice storm. Sunglasses, bandannas, even an airline sleep mask in one case. There was something medieval about the scene, as if they were all part of some ancient exodus. It seemed like an appropriate parallel, since these people were clearly suffering the aftermath of real social catastrophe. Talk about floods, or plagues of locusts, here was a society on the edge of collapse. Aren't we judged by how well we take care of our most vulnerable?

Across the room he glimpsed an unexpected figure and felt

an instinctive recognition. He looked older and the long grey dreadlocks were unfamiliar, but still . . . Drake crossed the room, clumsily pushing his way through until he could stretch out a hand.

'Dad?'

The word was out of his mouth before he realised his mistake. The man sniffed, staring at him, ready to fight or flee. Drake lifted his hands in apology. 'Sorry.'

What had made him think of his father? Something about this place. Something he had always feared. Coming across an older version of himself shuffling around the streets. One of those things that woke him in the middle of the night with a shudder. He wasn't afraid for his father. He was afraid for how much of his father he might carry inside him.

Cal's father had been absent for most of his childhood, and when he had been around it had not been for the better. Between his father, who was always trying to find some way of scrounging a living, and his mother's addictions and fragile mental state, there hadn't been much of a childhood to salvage. What was left of it had been spent in foster homes and institutions. But it never left you. Although there had been no contact between them for years, it wouldn't have surprised him to find his father out here among the legions of the lost.

After that, he wandered aimlessly around the hall, latching onto conversations, drifting on when he got the leery eye. Nobody he spoke to had seen the man in the Fender hat, although sometimes he got the impression that people would say no to anything you asked them, simply because they were beyond wanting to comply with anyone. After a time he'd had enough and felt it was time to move on.

Lugging his bags back out into the rain, Drake soon discovered that he was hopelessly unprepared for a night out. Even when the rain eased off, it left a bitter chill to the air. The sleeping bag he had with him might have been fine for summer camping but at this time of year it was cheap, thin and ineffective. It was getting late and the warmth drained from his body into the cold ground. He sat upright with his back to the wall, arms hugging his knees. He'd managed to scrape up some sheets of cardboard, old boxes that had been tucked behind a rubbish container at the back of a fast-food place that smelled of burnt oil and piss, but he was so cold he was beyond caring. Sleep was impossible. After an hour in the doorway of a shuttered bank, he moved on, picking up his bundles and heading down the street.

Walking seemed the best way of passing the time. It was the most efficient way to cover the most ground and it also kept him warm. He arrived eventually, several hours later, with aching feet, at a bench outside a homeless shelter in Victoria, where a large man was eating his way through a huge pile of macaroni cheese without saying a word.

Drake began to wonder if perhaps the man he was looking for was not homeless at all. He recalled the grizzled old man at the hostel. Like Drake, perhaps Fender was just faking it. Still, he was committed to his plan and spent the next few hours walking. Not quite aimlessly, but determined to cover as much ground as possible. The rain came and went. He met a group of women who'd set up tents on the Embankment.

At one point Drake became convinced that he was being followed. By then he was beginning to grow tired of walking in circles. It occurred to him that he might be imagining it. He was weary and cold. His feet hurt and he contemplated packing it in and going back to the car. He longed to just go home and crawl into bed. But now, as the clock ticked steadily into the early hours, the field grew thinner. Here was a sign that perhaps his plan was working. A couple of times he circled round to see if he could spot anyone, but either he was losing his touch or his quarry was too nimble for him. Or perhaps it was all in his head.

At the bottom of Villiers Street he met Bekri, a Moroccan man who had set up an all-night mobile kitchen to hand out harira soup and pastries to those who were sleeping rough. When Drake asked him why, he was treated to a lecture on the virtues of charity.

'We have zakat, which is one of the five pillars of Islam. You must give to the poor, to those who have less than you. It is our religion.'

Inspired by this, perhaps, Drake went over to a young boy, who couldn't have been more than fourteen and handed him his sleeping bag. The boy was reluctant at first. Drake held up his hands, not sure the boy understood him.

'It's okay, I don't want anything in return.'

When the boy still wouldn't take it, Drake placed it on the ground next to him and turned away. When he looked round the boy had disappeared, taking the purple sleeping bag with him.

The city felt darker somehow and more deserted. Drunks jostled one another as they waited for the night bus to take them home. Sirens flashed by. Police, ambulances, all heading for one crisis or another. There seemed to be an almost permanent state of emergency.

Still no sign of Fender. It was almost four in the morning by then. The rain had stopped again and Drake found a bench in the park on The Mall, where he curled up to sleep for an hour or so.

It was there, exhausted, cold and in a dazed state, that he fell into an uncomfortable sleep. He was beginning to feel as though this whole excursion might not have been such a great idea. As a boy, Drake had run away from home more times than he cared to remember. Homes, would be more accurate. He had run away from countless foster homes. Before that from his mother and father in the early days, when they would be trying to stab each other in the kitchen. Both of them out of their minds on something. On one of the early occasions he had spent the whole night sleeping under a bench on Tooting Common. He was woken in the morning by the sound of people playing tennis. He was eight at the time. Somebody eventually spotted him and led him home. His father was out cold and hadn't even noticed he was missing. His mother, to her credit, was frantic.

Just being out here like this was unsettling. It brought back the feeling of not belonging anywhere. The way he'd felt most of his life. What was scary was the sense that he could easily slip back into this. Let go and fall through the net, away from the order that kept him in line. When he'd come back from the war, he had almost lost himself this way. Questioning what it was that had made him go out to Iraq in the first place. What had he been hoping to find? He'd found something out there, but he wasn't sure he could explain what it was.

At some point between waking and sleeping, Cal became aware of someone approaching him. He was lying half asleep. Somebody was standing in the dark, off to one side, watching him. He struggled upright, feeling so tired that it almost felt as if he was drugged. When he looked back, he saw only shadows and trees. He heard the wind strumming through the thin branches overhead. There was nobody there. He wondered if he had imagined it.

Then he realised he was cold. Not just cold, but shivering, freezing. The rain had returned, light but relentless. It had soaked through his clothes, which now felt stiff and uncomfortable. It wouldn't make any sense if he caught pneumonia, so he decided that enough was enough. Unlike most of the people he had seen and spoken to that evening he was in the luxurious position of having a home to go to, and that was exactly what he intended doing.

He started to walk back towards the all-night parking to get his car. He was crossing under Admiralty Arch when he saw the flashing blue lights of emergency vehicles and made his way over. The commotion was on the north side. The early hour meant that there were not many onlookers. Drake caught sight of a familiar face on one of the officers putting up crime scene tape.

'What happened?'

'Kid was stabbed. Looks like he was sleeping rough. That's the second this week.'

For his part, the uniform didn't recognise Drake. The Scene of Crime Officers had still not arrived. Looking towards the crowd of police officers and paramedics gathered around the figure on the floor, Drake noticed the sleeping bag the victim was covered by.

'Hey, mate. Sir, you can't walk over there.'

But Drake was already past him. He was almost there when he was intercepted by a burly WPC in an anti-stab vest who put a hand up to block him.

'Step back, please, sir.'

Drake allowed himself to be led back to the line. He had already seen enough; the wind flipped up the edge of the white sheet laid over the victim. The soft purple shape underneath told him that the victim was the young boy he had given his sleeping bag to only a few hours ago.

He stood there for a time, feeling the pulse of blue light against his face, then he turned to look at the people in the small, huddled crowd behind him. There weren't many of them, and some were clearly sleeping rough. He wondered if the killer was amongst them.

29

The call from Heather came in as Crane was pulling up the arched drive in front of the Gothic red-brick hotel building above St Pancras station. She clicked on her earpiece as she walked through the majestic entrance.

'I did some more digging on Howeida's uncle.'

Crane smiled at the uniformed doorman as he tipped his hat to her.

'Anything interesting?'

'Well, I thought it might be an idea to look more closely at the type of places he was investing his money.'

'Okay.'

The front lobby had the feel of a cathedral and Crane had a vague recollection that Gilbert Scott, the architect of this place, had been well known for his work on churches before he turned to buildings of the Industrial Revolution.

'The interesting thing is that it does link to our friend Nathanson.'

'Okay, explain.'

'Did you know that London has been dubbed the "Death Star" of global kleptocracy? I was shocked, I have to admit. This is public money. It's being stolen, pushed through an array of accounts and then invested here. We've got all kinds of evil people living in this city on their ill-gotten gains. Isn't that terrible?

'Shocking.' Crane worried that Heather was about to launch into one of her rants, which were often endless and hard to make sense of.

'Okay, so I told you about Novo Elysium, didn't I?'

'This is the offshore company that Nathanson and Foulkes are tied to?'

'Oh, it's much more complicated than that. They tuck one firm inside another. It's like boxes, or those Russian dolls, which makes sense since much of the cash is coming out of there. Russia, I mean.'

'But not just Russia, right?' Crane gazed up at the elegant staircase. The weave of white stairs and black iron bannisters created a kind of domino effect, as if the whole thing might just tumble and fall.

'Oh, no. There's money coming from all over the place. That's what makes it so hard to pin down. All of your Kazakhstans and Azkabans and what have you.'

'I'm not sure Azkaban is actually a real place.'

'Well, you know what I mean. Their regulatory systems are non-existent. The point of these offshore havens is that they are not covered by respectable banking authorities.'

'So there's nobody ruling the movement of the money?'

'Exactly. It all gets mixed up. The only thing we can be sure of is that some of it is very dodgy. But the point is . . .' Heather paused to compose her thoughts. 'The money comes back and is then funnelled into London property. It's estimated there's nearly a hundred thousand properties owned that way. It runs into the billions.'

'So the London property market is a money-laundering merry-go-round?'

'You said it.' Crane could hear crunching coming down the line and knew that Heather was tapping into her biscuit supply. 'Novo Elysium has an impressive portfolio of clients from around the world – Kuwait, Russia, Ukraine, China, the oil rich states of Central Asia. You name it.'

'All of them investing in property here in London?'

'Exactly.'

Crane changed the subject. 'I'm about to meet Howeida's uncle, Heather, so I need to know what you've got on him.'

'Ah, well. Mr Almanara is also a property owner, of course. I found this out through a friend who works at an estate agent. They know all the tricks. You should see where she lives. I mean, it's like walking into a film. I'm always really careful. You can't really sit down anywhere because you're afraid of disturbing the tone.'

'Doesn't sound very practical.'

'I know. I couldn't live like that, but it is gorgeous.'

'Howeida's uncle?' Crane tried to nudge Heather back on track.

'Right, well, Mr Almanara owns quite a number of properties, mainly in the Knightsbridge and Edgeware Road areas, as well as in the Shard. He has a place up there apparently. I have to say it would make me feel a little queasy to live in a place like that. It looks as though it could fall down if the wind blew too hard.'

Crane closed her eyes to try not to lose track. 'So, he owns these through a company?'

'Yes, absolutely, didn't I say that?'

'No, you didn't.'

'Well, I meant to. The thing is that my friend Ilsa, that's the one who works for the posh estate agent, she called this company. I mean, she knows everybody. Anyway, she heard an interesting story. Apparently, Mr Almanara was about to invest in a firm called YDH. Ypres Development Holdings. I haven't been able to find out much about them.'

'Okay, and what happened?'

'Well, he pulled out at the last minute.'

'Did she say why?'

'No. That was all she could get out of them.'

'Okay, we need more on that. Also on this other company, YDH.'

'I'll get on to her. She loves this kind of thing. Actually, she's a bit of a gossip, if truth be told.'

'Well, ask her to be discreet.'

'I shall instruct her to remain clam-like.'

'Gotta go. Sorry, Heather. Speak later.'

Crane clicked off and tucked her phone away.

Abdelhadi Almanara was waiting for her in the Gilbert Scott bar above the station. The stone arches, brass rails and old railway lamps gave it a timeless feel. He was younger than Crane had expected. Dressed in a dapper grey suit and open-necked white shirt with tan leather shoes. Casual, but clearly classy. He rose to his feet to meet her. His hand in hers was as soft as a bird.

'So delighted you could make it.'

'I couldn't afford to let the opportunity slip away,' she smiled.

He had chosen a seat close to the high windows.

'I hope you don't mind meeting here. It's the most convenient place for me, as I have just flown in and I am due to catch a train up north to see my horses.'

'Sounds very nice.'

'Yes. I have three of them at stables outside Doncaster. I love travelling by train, especially in this country.'

'Some would view that as a special kind of masochism.'

He laughed at that. 'Of course, I understand, but for me it is a novelty. I rarely travel by train. I go from one airport to another and they are all the same. But this . . .' He gestured at the splendour of the room they were in. 'Such magnificence is rare to come by.'

'So, how did an Emirati prince become a fan of the architecture of the Industrial Revolution?'

'Good question, although I would have to correct you on one point. I am not a prince.'

'I thought you were all princes, one way or another.'

He bowed gracefully. 'Tell me, your background is Persian?'

'On my mother's side.'

Almanara beamed. 'The beauty of Persian women is legendary. You have no idea how many poems were written about it.'

'I have some idea. My mother specialised in poetry.'

'Ah.' He nodded appreciatively. 'Hafiz, Saadi Shirazi.' The waiter came over and took their order. Almanara suggested Manhattans and Crane agreed, partly to go along with him. She was interested to see how far he would take this liberal portrayal of himself.

'Perhaps you could tell me why you agreed to meet me.'

'As you know, I am very concerned about Howeida. It is now ten days since she was last seen.'

'Is it true that you are cousins?'

'We are first cousins, directly. My mother and her mother are half-sisters. They have the same father but different mothers.'

'Okay. I'm not sure that qualifies as first cousins, but let's say it does. Why did you want to see her in London?'

'Howeida and I were due to be married. It was a family thing. I understood that she wanted to come here to complete her studies and I applauded this.' Almanara's face darkened slightly. 'There were unkind tongues at home saying this was wrong, for an unmarried woman to come here to London alone. I disagreed.'

'You weren't trying to take her home?'

'No, not at all.' The frown deepened. 'If you knew her, you would never make such a suggestion. The women in her family are very strong-willed. Howeida is no exception.'

Crane sat back. She was having a hard time reconciling this story with what she had heard from Howeida's flatmate, Savannah.

'So how do you explain her disappearance?'

'I can't, and frankly that is why I am so concerned.' He tapped a finger on the table's dark varnish. He cleared his throat. 'I realise, of course, that there are certain parties interested in painting me as some kind of monster.'

'By certain parties, you mean my client Marco Foulkes?'

'Also his accomplice, the lady from Virginia.'

'Accomplice?' Crane sipped her drink. 'You think they are working together against you?'

'Isn't that obvious?'

'What makes you think they would do that?'

He exhaled slowly. 'That is an interesting question. There are obvious reasons, and there are the more general . . . shall we say, assumptions.'

'You're saying they have a biased opinion of you.'

'We live in an age of ignorance and prejudice.' Almanara gave a half-smile. 'To some people, I can appear as a threat.'

'And you're here to convince me that you are not?'

'I am not a monster.'

Crane smiled. 'Isn't that what all monsters say?'

'Perhaps,' he said, and left it at that.

He certainly didn't look like a monster. The corners of his eyes crinkled when he smiled, which was often. Clearly Abdelhadi Almanara had rather a fond view of himself. A bit of a ladies' man, if you like. Old-fashioned, too. Like the carefully trimmed moustache, which added a touch of Omar Sharif.

'I didn't come here to accuse you,' said Crane. 'Or to confirm the beliefs, right or wrong, of my client. I'm here because I am concerned about the welfare of your cousin, Howeida.'

'Then,' he said, lifting his chin, 'we are on the same side. I share your concerns. Why else would I be here, meeting you like this, if I had something to do with her disappearance?'

'Because you are rich and powerful and this is the best way to save face?'

'I don't need to save face. I am a wealthy man. I love horses and trains, but if you told me that I must leave this country and never come back, I would not shed a tear.'

'So, not the emotional type?'

'I deal in facts. I am concerned that what is happening here is not what it appears.'

Crane swirled the ice in the bottom of her glass and Almanara waved a hand for the waiter to bring them another round.

'Tell me about Howeida.'

Almanara's expression lifted. 'She was always the most outspoken, the most spirited and the most intelligent person in the family, male or female. Also the most amusing.' Almanara laughed. 'She is younger than me by about fifteen years.' He held up a hand. 'I know, perfect marriage material because in my part of the world we are all paedophiles by nature, right?'

'I didn't say that.'

'You didn't have to.' He drew a sketch with his finger. 'It's written in the air.'

'I'm not here to condemn you.'

'Fair enough,' said Almanara. 'Let us begin again. Tell me what I can do to help you.'

'First, I'd like to ask about your connection to Marco Foulkes.'

'Well, it's very simple really. I had never heard of him until I contacted my cousin. I was over here on business, so naturally I called her. She told me she had met the most amazing man. A writer. Naturally, I was intrigued.'

'Not jealous?'

'Perhaps a little bit.' Almanara squinted at her. 'Our families wanted us to marry, but I was not prepared to marry her against her will. With a woman like that it would never work, whatever our families wished. I knew that I needed to give her space.' He heaved a deep breath. 'I thought, if I give her freedom then perhaps she might come to me.'

'A bit of a risk, isn't it? Letting her come here?'

'We don't live in a medieval age, no matter how much we like to pretend we do. People see what is going on in the world. They watch films and television, they connect. In short, I had no choice.'

'So you must have expected that someone like Marco might turn up.'

'Not exactly. A fellow student perhaps. I was prepared for that. Someone her own age. Marco is older. He is famous. He can show her another side to life, one that I can't.'

'So you were jealous, at least a little bit.'

'When I heard about him I felt I had to re-establish myself in her life.'

'Hence the restaurant and the expensive wine?'

'Ah, of course. That is why you agreed to meet me.' Almanara nodded to himself. 'Am I a liberal, or did I simply order expensive wine to give that impression? This is the question you have been asking yourself. And now, what is your conclusion?'

'I'm not sure I'm ready to draw one yet.'

'Ms Crane, I agreed to meet for the simple reason that I am concerned about Howeida. This is a foreign country. I would be happy to hire your services, but I suspect that since you are already working for Mr Foulkes you would perceive that as a conflict of interests.'

The fresh drinks arrived. Crane knew that many men from the Gulf were regular drinkers, not in public but at home, or abroad. There was nothing too remarkable about Almanara drinking.

'As you say, working for Mr Foulkes puts me in a difficult position.'

'I understand,' he said.

'Perhaps we should try to assume we are on the same side.'

'I would appreciate that.' Almanara raised his glass. 'But first I have a confession to make. I do not drink alcohol as a rule. When I am abroad, I find it is useful when dealing with clients.

They expect it. More than that, they do not trust a man who does not drink. But my choice at the restaurant was pure guesswork.'

'Fair enough,' she said. 'Tell me what you make of Foulkes?'

'I have to admit that my instincts when I met this man were not encouraging.'

'Tell me about it.' She was thinking about Drake. 'I think that's a male thing.'

'I felt there was something insincere about him. I did not trust him. However, it was clear that Howeida was stuck on him.'

'Supposing for a moment it was serious. Would that be problematic? I mean, in terms of family approval and so forth.'

'Up to a certain point.' The smile was gentle and persuasive. 'We are a liberal family.'

'So if Howeida decided to marry Foulkes, say, there wouldn't be opposition within the family?'

'It's not going to happen.'

'You sound pretty sure of that.'

'I am.' Almanara gave a short nod. 'I know her. I know how she thinks. How she feels.'

That was the kind of explanation Crane had expected from him, but even though she had anticipated it, it sounded odd, slightly off beat. Something here didn't match up.

Almanara set down his glass. 'I would urge you not to take anything for granted and certainly not to jump to the obvious conclusions.'

'I think I'm capable to making my own mind up about what to believe.'

'Of course. I did not mean to imply otherwise.' Almanara bowed his head slightly in deference. 'Can I ask, have you ever read *The Arabian Nights*, what we call *Alf Layla wa Layla*?'

'Of course.'

'In English translation?'

'Also in Arabic.'

That lifted his eyebrows. 'My point is that most people would be surprised to learn there are no camels in *The Arabian Nights*. Only horses.'

'I'm not sure I follow.'

'I am trying to tell you that things are not always as they appear.'

'I'll bear that in mind.' Crane had to fight her natural response to being lectured.

'Allow me to ask one more question. Did you expect me to offer you a bribe to drop the case?'

'I try to keep an open mind.'

'I have the same impulse, but Marco Foulkes hired you to find what happened to Howeida. He suggested to you that I was the patriarchal uncle who was trying to spirit her back to where she belongs. How am I doing?'

Crane said nothing. Almanara smiled.

'Very well. I have tried to hire your services and we have agreed that is problematic. Therefore, I have a suggestion. If you find her, I shall give you a bonus. Call it an incentive.'

'It's a generous offer, Mr Almanara, but I can't agree to that either. I'm afraid we just have to play this out and see where it leads.'

He leaned across the table towards her. 'The reason I agreed to meet you was twofold. Firstly, to convince you not to waste any more time considering me as the prime suspect. I would never hurt Howeida, or do anything against her will. Secondly, I came to urge you to find her, quickly. I have a feeling she is in great danger.'

'That's precisely what I intend to do.'

30

The Golden Scales was the name of a Chinese place on Wandsworth Road. Close enough to Drake's old station at Raven Hill to be reached in a few minutes by car, and far enough away to be sure you weren't going to run into a lot of other cops. It wasn't much more than a takeaway, though they had high stools and a long bar running across the window so clients could eat on the premises if they wanted to. Decoration was pared down to a minimum. The walls were a grubby off-white, with the only addition of colour being provided by the red tassels over the counter and an out-of-date calendar celebrating the Year of the Dog. On the other wall were a couple of faded posters for films in Cantonese. Drake studied the images, trying to work out what they were about, while the woman behind the counter muttered to herself as she fussed over something out of sight before looking up to take his order. She was so tiny you couldn't actually see her without leaning over the top of the Formica counter. Drake chose king prawn curry and fried rice for no reason other than it was what he always ordered. Why break the habits of a lifetime? She scribbled characters on a small chit of paper and asked him to pay in cash. When that was settled she slapped a packet of chopsticks, a napkin and a plastic spoon onto the counter and disappeared through a bead curtain behind her.

A bell jangled as the door opened behind him and Drake turned to see Kelly Marsh shaking the rain off her anorak. She took in the place with a loud sniff.

'Classy,' she said.

'It's an old favourite.'

'Not sure I see why. What did you order?'

Drake told her. 'It's spicy,' he warned.

'Just what I need in my life.'

'You want order?' The diminutive woman was back behind the counter, watching them.

Kelly pointed. 'I'll have what he's having.'

'You trust him?' The woman frowned at her, as if this was patently a bad idea. Marsh looked at Drake, who shrugged.

'That's a moot question,' said Marsh. 'Let's give him the benefit of the doubt.'

The woman ducked back through the bead curtain into the kitchen, where raised voices could be heard in heated discussion.

'So, there's a reason we're meeting here, right?' Marsh asked, as they climbed onto the high stools in the window. 'Aside from the wonderful food?'

'Don't knock it till you've tried it.'

'I always heard dubious accounts of this place.' Marsh glanced around her. 'What have you been up to?'

'Mainly looking for our mystery man from the Tube. Fender.'

'On account of the hat?'

'We don't have anything else to go by. I got close to him in Victoria.'

'That's where he left the Tube.'

'Exactly.' Drake recalled the figure in the cathedral. 'The thing is, I think he saw me.'

'How would he know who you are?'

'Well, that's another thing. Anyway, there's a shelter down there run by something called the Silver Linings Charity.'

'So, he's homeless?'

'I'm not sure,' Drake mused. 'It looks that way, but he's hard to get a fix on. The people running the shelter are protective. They don't like to give out information on their clients.'

'You think it's worth going in with a warrant?'

'I'm not sure that will bring results.'

'But still, you got the idea he'd been there.'

'I spoke to someone there, a fellow traveller. I couldn't get a name, but he seemed to recognise the picture.'

'People like that, they don't like questions.'

Drake heard the inflection in her voice. 'You speak from experience?'

Marsh was turned towards the street. He studied her as she

stared straight out through the window. The slightly flat profile and the upturned nose made it easy to imagine her as a precocious child.

'My father had mental health issues. Used to go missing on a regular basis.'

'Sorry to hear that.'

'Water under the bridge. Used to take off all his clothes on the train. A regular showman.'

Drake wondered if it was the fact that he was no longer her superior officer that made Marsh feel she could tell him these things. Or maybe it was that, with time, she was beginning to trust him.

'A kid was murdered last night,' said Drake. 'He was sleeping rough.'

'I heard about that. He was stabbed. That's another case nobody's going to bust a gut trying to solve.' She stopped herself to look over. 'Wait a minute, you're saying there's a connection to this?'

'He was inside my sleeping bag when it happened.'

Marsh was silent for a long moment. 'Okay, you've got my attention. How close were you?'

Drake explained the sequence of events.

'Did you see the killer?'

'I was across the way, in the park.'

Marsh frowned. 'Don't tell me you were sleeping rough.'

'Seemed like a good way of finding our man.'

Marsh was staring at him in wonder. 'You can get seriously hurt out there, you know.'

'I know.' Drake broke off as the woman appeared. She came round from behind the high counter and handed him a plastic bag.

'King prawn curry, fried rice.'

'Thanks. You have some of that chilli oil?'

The woman reared back, offended. 'It's already hot. You know?' She dismissed her own objection. 'Forget it. You all think you know hot sauce. You don't know it.' She slammed a bowl of dark black bean chilli oil on the counter before disappearing again.

'Must be the way you tell 'em,' murmured Marsh. 'Anyway, tell me about the sleeping bag.'

'Nothing to tell. I didn't know him. He was just a kid.' Even as he began to unpack his food, Drake realised this was not quite true. The kid had done nothing wrong. He felt responsible. He just didn't know how to say it. 'It was cold. I felt sorry for him. I gave him the bag, then I moved on. I should have thought.' Drake lifted a prawn out of the viscous sauce and examined it before putting the chopsticks down again. 'If I hadn't tried to help him he would still be alive.'

'You can't blame yourself. You couldn't know that they might target you.'

Drake looked at her. 'I should have known.'

'Why? I mean, why would you think he'd come after you?'

'Because he's been watching me.' Drake told her about the DNA that Archie had found.

'Your blood?' Marsh stared at him in disbelief. 'How could that have happened?'

Drake explained about the shirt and the cut on his hand. He picked up the chopsticks again and started pushing the prawns around. It was no good. He'd lost his appetite.

'Whoever this guy is, he's been planning this for a while.'

'This is personal. He's making it personal.' Marsh shook her head. 'We're talking about someone with an obsession, a personal fixation. The question is why.'

'I don't know.'

'We're talking psycho here, you realise that.'

'Maybe it's not as cut and dried as that.'

'You think he picked up on it when you were trying to find him?'

'It's possible.' Drake nodded. 'I was doing the rounds close to Victoria, asking a lot of questions, trying to track his movements. He may have caught wind of that.'

'And you never spotted him that evening? Did you get a look at him?'

'Nothing. I thought I was wasting my time. There's a lot of people moving around, plus everyone is covered up. Hoodies, rain jackets, headgear.'

'And you're convinced that this man, Fender, is responsible for leaving the head on the train and murdering that kid last night.'

'It looks that way.'

'I have to say, Cal, this is beginning to look a lot bigger than we thought.'

They both looked round as Marsh's food appeared.

'You too skinny,' the woman said to her. 'You eat.'

'I'm beginning to see why you like this place,' said Marsh.

'It grows on you.'

She began to unpack the foil dishes inside the bag and set them out in a row. There was a packet of spring rolls. Marsh held them up.

'I didn't order these.'

'She's taken a shine to you. Don't even think about taking them back.'

'You might have a point.' Marsh glanced over her shoulder. The rather terrifying little woman was nowhere to be seen. 'That's how William Holden died, by the way.'

'What are we talking about now?'

'The actor, you know? Hollywood, in the old days. He fell down drunk in his living room and cut his head. Put a towel on, lay down and bled to death.'

'Anyone ever tell you you're a mine of useless information?'

'Not quite as bluntly as that. You're not worried about this guy watching your flat? He's going to a lot of trouble on your behalf.'

'Tell me about it.'

'He wants to frame you. He wants you to take the blame for Zelda's death.'

'To cover his own tracks?'

Marsh's fork wagged at him. 'That's assuming he did it.'

'What other conclusion is there?'

'Maybe he's not the one who killed her. What if he's trying to get our attention?'

'Why point the finger at me?'

'He believes you are complicit, one way or another.'

'It's possible.' Right now anything was possible.

'Either way,' said Marsh, dabbing at her mouth with a napkin, 'Somebody thought this out.'

'You don't like?'

They both turned. The woman from behind the counter was standing there. She jabbed a finger at Drake and repeated her question.

'I'm just not that hungry.'

'You don't like!' she declared triumphantly.

'I'll take it with me and eat it later.'

'Later cold. No good.'

She stalked away. Her angry voice could be heard taking her wrath out on someone in the kitchen.

'You've really hurt her feelings,' said Marsh. 'How long were you and Archie planning to keep this DNA story to yourselves?'

'Archie's not happy. He can sit on it for a day or so, after that he's obliged to inform Pryce.'

'Pryce will be in seventh heaven when he gets wind of this. I have to say I was surprised he wanted to kick this thing into the long grass. I mean, it's not every day something as spectacular as a severed head comes your way.'

'Pryce doesn't do anything without a reason,' said Drake.

'Meaning?'

'Meaning, maybe Pryce knows more about this than he is letting on.'

Marsh stared at him. 'Did you ever consider the possibility that maybe you're getting a little paranoid in your retirement?'

'A case like this draws attention. Either he doesn't want to wind up with egg on his face, or he just wants it to go away.'

'Are you seriously not going to eat that?'

Drake slid the foil tray across and Marsh went to work on it. 'Really good,' she said between mouthfuls.

'Maybe we'll get out of here alive yet.' Drake glanced over his shoulder, but there was no sign of the diminutive woman.

'Maybe next time we could try that ramen place down the road.'

'Why not?'

'It's what civilised people do, isn't it?'

'What is?'

'Working lunches.'

'If you say so. I'm not that familiar with civilised people.'

'If Pryce does come after you, you'll need to sort this one out double quick.'

Drake stared out of the window. It felt as if Pryce had been after him for as long as he could remember. Maybe it was time to sort that out. One thing he knew for sure, if Pryce thought he could nail him for Zelda he would do so without hesitation.

'Hang in there,' said Marsh, as she got up to leave. 'We've got your back.'

'Good to know,' said Drake. And he meant it. As he watched her walk away, he had a feeling he was going to need all the help he could get.

31

Kelly Marsh arrived back at Raven Hill to find Milo looking worried.

'Wheeler's on the war path.'

Marsh rolled her eyes. 'Why do I get the feeling you spend your free time watching re-runs of 1970s sitcoms?'

'I can't deal with the present reality.'

'Makes about as much sense as anything, I suppose.' Marsh threw herself down in her chair only to be rewarded with an alarming groan of protest from the springs. Milo slid his chair towards her, the wheels squeaking over the linoleum. He looked around and lowered his voice.

'Well, what did he say?'

Marsh swung round to face him. 'You'll never guess where he was last night. That stabbing up in town.'

Milo reeled back. 'What was he doing up there?'

'He was undercover, trying to find our missing man from the Tube.'

'Full marks for initiative.'

'The point is he's convinced the killer was after him.'

'Ah, paranoia? Delusions of grandeur?'

'You have to stop reading so many long books.' Marsh reached for a well-chewed pencil on her desk and twirled it round her fingers deftly.

'Everything seems to point to the fact that the appearance of this head is aimed at him.'

'Someone's trying to frame him?'

'There's the newspaper cutting and the bloody rag. Both tie him to the crime scene.'

'Both?' Milo did a double take. 'How did that happen?'

Marsh filled him in.

'So somebody broke into his place?'

'Somebody has been watching him.' Marsh tossed the pencil

down with a sigh. 'To be honest, I don't know what to make of all this.'

Milo frowned. 'You mean, you don't believe him?'

'Back then, when it went down, and Cal was suspended, the suspicion was that he was on the take. Why hide away the key witness without telling anyone and then she disappears?'

'There was no conclusive proof,' Milo pointed out. 'That's why he was suspended. There was an internal inquiry that turned up nothing. So they banished him to the far north.'

'Matlock,' murmured Marsh. 'Hardly the Arctic.'

'Anything north of Watford Gap . . .'

'The point is that we don't really know if he's out there trying to find the killer, or setting up a watertight alibi for himself.'

'Wait a second.' Milo's face was a picture of bewilderment. 'You're not saying you don't trust him?'

'Don't look so shocked. We have to try to be as objective as possible because that's the way Pryce is going to look at it.'

That made sense to Milo. 'What about Wheeler?'

'I don't know, but we need to think fast.'

'Shit!' muttered Milo. 'Talk of the devil.'

Over the top of the office unit dividers they could see the superintendent coming through the door.

'Ah, there you are,' said Wheeler, as he reached their corner of the room. 'I was looking for you earlier.'

'Just popped out for lunch, sir.'

'Right, well, bring me up to speed. Where are you on the Tube murder?'

'Officially, we're not involved.' Marsh sifted through the paperwork on her desk. 'Right now we've got a stabbing in King George's Park. A couple of serious assaults. A joyriding incident that ended in tears and a domestic battery charge in Freetown.'

'Good, sounds good.' Wheeler cleared his throat. 'Am I right in thinking that you are . . . er, in contact with Cal?'

'Well . . .' Marsh glanced at Milo. Wheeler raised a hand.

'I'm not looking for someone to blame, DS Marsh.'

'I have been in touch with him, yes.'

'Is he making any progress? With the case, I mean.'

'Hard to say, sir.'

'Okay, well, try to keep up with developments.'

'Will do, sir.' Marsh paused. 'Do you think DCI Pryce will change his mind about the case?'

'Stranger things have happened at sea.'

'Yes, sir.'

'Carry on, Detective Sergeant. Just carry on.'

As Wheeler walked out of the room, Milo turned to Kelly. 'Do you ever get the feeling you don't really know what's going on around here?'

'Tell me about it.'

32

Puntland Private Cars was run by a Somali by the name of Lal Ferit, a rotund man in a brown checkered shirt with a receding hairline. His office was a hole in a wall in Union Street in Southwark. A medium-sized kitten could have swung happily in that confined space, but not much more. Ferit sat behind a window plastered with lists of rates and destinations, along with a blizzard of notes advertising everything from rooms for rent to Kerry's Curried Goat and the Taipan Massage Service (discreet).

'Mr Ferit?'

The jaundiced eyes ran up and down. 'Salesman?' he asked wearily.

'No.'

'Journalist?'

'Wrong again.' Drake placed a business card on the narrow counter. Ferit turned his head to read what was written there without lifting it.

'Crane & Drake Investigations.' He gave a half laugh and reached for a drumstick inside a box of 'halal' fried chicken. 'What's this, some kind of insurance pitch?'

'I'm interested in one of your clients.'

'Yeah? Well, we're running a cab service not a gossip column.'

'Can I explain how this works?'

'Don't mind me.' He chewed steadily.

'Well, as you may know, like everything else nowadays, the government no longer has the resources to keep on a staff of their own investigators, so when, say, the Inland Revenue wants to conduct an enquiry into a business they call in an outside agency to do the legwork.'

'I knew it.' Ferit's jaws stopped moving. 'You're asking for money.'

'I'm not here for money.'

Ferit tossed the half-finished chicken leg back into the box and dragged a greasy napkin across his mouth.

'All my books is in order, innit.'

'Well, that's good start. But I'm afraid I can't just take your word for it.'

The man looked at him for a moment, then he spoke in a language Drake didn't understand. There was movement inside the room and Drake saw there was someone else in there with Ferit. A much darker man sitting against the wall in the shadows. He got to his feet, opened the door of the office and looked Drake over before stepping out into the street and disappearing. Ferit sniffed.

'Must be another way of dealing with this.'

'Maybe there is.'

Ferit reached under the counter for a packet of cigarettes and lit one, blowing a stream of smoke over his shoulder.

'Who you interested in?'

'A solicitor by the name of Nathanson.'

'I know who it is. He's a regular.' Ferit studied Drake. 'I start talking about my customers and their affairs . . . I mean, where does that leave me?'

'That's not really my concern.'

Ferit considered his position. 'We don't have nothing to do with his business.'

'Once a person comes under scrutiny we have to look at everyone connected to him.' He glanced round at the office behind Ferit. 'You understand that, right?'

'You're saying this could come back on me?'

'I'm saying when it comes to financial misconduct we have to look under every stone.'

'Come on, we just drive the man.'

Drake gave a shrug. 'It's how it works.'

'Okay, so back up a bit, right? I can't tell you more than I know.'

'Well, then, let's start there.'

Ferit tapped the keys on the grubby computer next to him. 'Most of the time it's a regular late-night job. Dalston Junction to Pimlico. Kingsland Road to Alderney Street.'

'That's quite a good ride. You must make some money out of a regular customer like that.'

'We offer a reliable service.'

'I'll bet you do. How does Mr Nathanson pay you?'

Ferit's eyes were wary. He looked at Drake as a man might look at a con artist who you know is trying to pull a fast one, you just haven't figured out how yet.

'He doesn't.'

'How so?'

Ferit shrugged. 'Company account.'

'Who runs the account?'

Ferit pulled a face.

'Look, we've just been through all this, remember? We're on the same side. I'm the human face of the system. If I'm happy, everyone's happy. End of story. If not, then I file a report and things take their own course. I can't help you after that.'

Ferit mulled over that one for a while, before reaching down to dig out a box file from under the counter. He flipped it open and licked his index finger. While he searched through his accounts, Drake let his eye roam over the office behind the man. It was furnished with odds and ends: tubular chairs with torn covers, filing cabinets, a tan sofa covered in PVC, an acrylic rug on the floor like a dirty zebra. On the wall was a calendar. The picture was an image of the faithful gathered in Mecca, circling the strange black cube of the Ka'aba. Across the top of the picture was the name Green Gardens Halal Meat Packing, Southall.

'There you go.' Ferit passed over a strip of paper. 'Just keep me out of it, yeah?'

'I'll do my best.' Drake hesitated. 'Let me ask you one last question. If I wanted to transfer money to somewhere in the world, could you do that for me?'

'Why don't you try Western Union?'

'I don't like Western Union. They charge too much in fees.'

'I hear you.' Ferit tapped the counter in front of him, still unsure what he was dealing with. 'Come back in a few days, maybe I can help.'

'I'll do that,' said Drake.

33

When Jindy looked up from his telephone, he didn't quite believe his eyes. He was sitting on a bench outside the synagogue in Bevis Marks. The little yard was quiet. His lunch was arranged alongside him. A large plastic cup held what looked like a raspberry smoothie while on his lap was a Styrofoam container and a mound of pasta out of which a plastic fork protruded.

'You look surprised to see me,' said Crane as she sat down.

'I . . . I didn't expect to see you again.'

She leaned over and lifted his *Top Gun* shades. The bruise under the left eye was now an array of colours.

'That's coming up nicely. What did you tell people at work?'

'That I'd walked into a door.'

She gave a snort of laughter. 'Not very original. Did they believe you?'

'I don't know.'

'When are you going to Germany?'

'In about a week.'

'I need you to do something for me.'

Jindy shifted in his seat. 'Something? What kind of something?'

'There's a company I need to find out about.'

Jindy began to relax. He realised that he was not in immediate danger, that she had come to him for help.

'That's what you do, isn't it? Financial advice?'

'Among other things.' He reached for the smoothie and took a slurp.

'I want to know if there is a connection between two companies. Can you do that?'

'I don't know. I mean, I'm really busy these days with the move and everything.'

Crane looked at him but said nothing. Jindy put down his cup.

'I mean, I'll see what I can do.'

'That's not going to be good enough, I'm afraid.'

Jindy gave a half shrug. 'I can't promise.'

Crane slid along the bench towards him. Jindy instinctively drew back.

'What do you think will happen if you don't help me?'

'I don't know.'

'You don't?'

'No, I don't.'

'What kind of a person are you?'

Jindy frowned. 'I'm sorry? I don't know what you mean.'

'I mean, you have a job. A nice job. You make a lot of money. You're about to transfer to Germany. That's all fine. But what if someone was to start digging?'

'Digging?' His expression froze.

'Looking into your past, say. The kind of people who know you for who you really are.'

'What do you mean?' he asked slowly.

She slid closer, until they were almost touching. 'How many women have you hurt? The other night wasn't the first time, was it?'

Jindy decided enough was enough. He made to get up. Crane took his hand and twisted it until he sat down again. The smoothie toppled to the ground and rolled, painting a crimson smear across the paving stones. A woman walking by glanced over at them.

'You're hurting me,' he whined.

'You have no idea.' She kept the pressure on, turning his hand over across his wrist. 'You don't like taking no for an answer, do you.' It wasn't a question. 'I have the names of two women who lodged complaints and then withdrew them. You like intimidating women, making them do what you want.'

Jindy stiffened. 'I don't know what you're talking about.'

'You've never had any trouble with your employers. It's never come up, or if it has it was never considered a problem. That's about to change. Do you know the name of your new boss in Frankfurt?'

'What's that's got to do with anything?'

'I'll tell you. It's Schact. H.L. Schact, to be exact. Or Frau Hilda Schact. She takes a different view.'

'What?'

'She takes a dim view of men who enjoy hurting women. She was herself a victim of domestic violence and she will not tolerate any form of chauvinism under her command.'

'Why are you doing this?'

'Why? I thought you of all people would understand that. Because I can.'

Jindy stared down at the floor. 'Okay,' he said finally. 'Tell me what you want.'

34

The name of the accounting firm turned up little of interest. Drake sat at home on his sofa with his laptop and dug up as much as was available to the public online. He made a couple of calls but by the end of it couldn't really say that he had much more than what he already knew.

Barnaby Nathanson's expenses were paid by an accounting firm that, by coincidence or not, also happened to do the accounts of one Marco Foulkes. So far, so unremarkable. Foulkes was there on their company website. No doubt someone had decided that there was value in advertising the fact that they were taking care of a celebrity writer's tax returns. Drake made a note of the firms that were listed. He would try and get Milo to do a little more digging, assuming he and Kelly were still willing to play.

Drake went to the kitchen and reached for the bottle of Jamaican rum. He squeezed the last drops out of half a lime before dropping the shell into the glass for good measure. Then he stood for a moment staring out of the window, his eye following the flashing lights of a helicopter that buzzed across the night sky. Some wealthy crook on his way home from the City to his pile in Surrey. The skyline was like an upturned crystal ball in which the fortunes of the obscenely rich showered sparks of light down over the ordinary lives of mere mortals.

Drake took a long sip from his drink and turned his attention to the other thing that had been nagging him all afternoon. The calendar on the wall of Lal Ferit's office. He typed in the words Green Gardens Halal Meat Packing and a link came up to a website that was both rudimentary and unhelpful. It showed a picture of a warehouse and an address in Southall. Parked alongside the loading bays were half a dozen vans ranging from compact vehicles to large white box trucks. There was something about that picture that was familiar. He just couldn't place it.

That night he slept badly. He woke in the middle of the night and rolled over to stare at the liquid digits that read 03:36 and knew he wasn't going to sleep again.

The turmoil in his head kept leading him in circles and all of them led back to the inquiry. He hadn't thought about it for ages. Or rather, he had tried not to think about it, which was a different thing altogether. It had been the source of countless nights like this, tossing and turning, unable to rest. Now that demon was back to haunt him again.

He could still picture the conference room on the third floor of the Curtis Green Building. The newly refurbished Scotland Yard appeared to be made of glass. The entrance, the tables, the walls and the long windows overlooking the Thames. Transparency. The catchphrase of a new era. Drake had put on his best suit for the occasion. Shiny around the knees and elbows, with a couple of threads waving loose on one lapel. He'd even managed to find a clean shirt and a tie. None of that was enough to lift the feeling of a caveman being brought out of the darkness to be scrutinised. Generally, he was uncomfortable in such places, a reminder that when it came down to it he was a small and ill-fitting cog in a very large machine.

From his left came the nasal hissing of his union rep. A sandy-haired man with nicotine stains on his fingers and what sounded like a bad case of asthma. He spoke in monosyllables, none of which added up to much. So far he hadn't said anything worth repeating. Opposite Drake sat Superintendent Marshall. A tall man with an egg-like dome of a head. He lifted his eyes from the pages in front of him only to make sure that Drake was still there and hadn't nodded off.

'For the record, this is the closing session of the hearing into the shooting of Goran Malevich. Present are Detective Sergeant Patel and myself representing the DPS. Also present are Detective Inspector Drake and his representative, Mr Stoughton, along with Detective Inspector Pryce, who is here in observer capacity only.'

Drake recalled pointedly not looking in the direction of Pryce. He knew that there was something else going on here and that Pryce was the driving force. If not for him, this whole matter would have been laid to rest months ago. To say he blamed Drake would be an understatement. Pryce appeared to have decided to make this his life's mission, to see Drake taken down for this.

'Let us quickly summarise the details of the case,' Marshall went on. 'DS Patel?'

The junior WPC shuffled her papers and made the appropriate bleating sounds. Clearly she was present to stamp out any possible accusations of racial bias. Drake had deliberately not made any such claims. He'd also kept out of the report and all of his subsequent accounts any reference to Pryce's behaviour. He didn't want to give him an excuse to keep going with this one. Keep it clean, for the moment at least. If the case went against him, he was going to need everything he could get his hands on to launch an appeal.

While Patel outlined the facts of the case Marshall was staring at the ceiling. They were all familiar with the details by now. Drake had given in and glanced up casually to find Pryce glaring at him. He found himself thinking back over his time on the inside of the organisation.

Goran Malevich was a beast who had crawled from the mud of another age, or so it had seemed to Drake the first time they crossed paths. The White Knights had emerged from the Serbian militias in the Balkans in the 1990s conflict during the breakdown of the old Yugoslavia. To Goran and his people, the war was nothing less than the last crusade, defending Europe against an encroaching Islam. He once pulled a gun on Drake: a gold-plated Colt .32 automatic with mother-of-pearl grips. It had been the proud possession of a young Saudi prince who had gone to Bosnia seeking glorious martyrdom. Goran made that particular wish come true and confiscated his toy in the process.

This too provided motivation for Drake. He knew from his dealings with Goran and his men that they regarded him as a necessary evil. They dealt with him because they needed to, despite the fact that he was part of the racial degeneration, as they saw it, that was London. They never left him in any doubt that they viewed him as inferior. There were comments, jokes, laughter, insults that did not require an understanding of the language to grasp the gist.

For eighteen months Drake and his team had done everything they could to track Goran's operations and there was a lot of it. Illegal gambling, prostitution rings, human trafficking and drugs. Over a year or so they built up contacts within his organisation, but it was hard to find anyone willing to speak out openly against the man, or even inform on him. Goran was incredibly secretive. The slightest suspicion of disloyalty was enough for him to take someone out. Whether the person in question was actually guilty or not didn't bother him. Goran felt it showed weakness not to act on mere suspicion. That was the ultimate concern; you couldn't have people thinking you were weak. People disappeared, those who remained lived in terror, but still nobody was willing to speak up. Then they had a stroke of good luck. Drake managed to find one person who was willing to help.

Zelda was in her late thirties when he first met her. She had been passed from one man to another for over twenty years. She was fourteen when she ran away from home. The way she told it she had been sold off by her family after having been abused by her stepfather and his friends. Her father was killed in the war. Her mother was weak. When the opportunity arose to move to London, Zelda didn't hesitate. It was a chance to make more money, to break free. She was intelligent and resourceful. Smart enough to know that one day her looks would not be enough to make her a valuable asset, so she hatched a reckless and very dangerous plan, one that would have got her killed if Goran had ever caught wind of it. Over time, she had collected evidence, memorising names, places, documents, transport routes, police and customs officers on the take all over Europe. Over a two-year period she had kept track of everything she heard and saw, the people she met, the telephone numbers. She wrote it all down in a notebook that she hid behind a vent grille in the kitchen of the flat she shared with four other girls.

Drake had no idea when he came to pick her up that afternoon from the hotel in Russell Square that within a matter of weeks she would become the keystone, the star witness in their case against Goran. Drake passed the word. But somewhere inside the machinations within Operation Hemlock the cogs ground to a halt and Drake found himself out there on his own, no longer able to trust his partner on the inside, Detective Inspector Vernon Pryce, who made no secret of the fact that he didn't like Drake. He kept demanding more evidence and each time Zelda was terrified that whatever she showed them would be traced back to her.

Pryce's stalling made Drake wonder if Zelda was right when she said that Goran had the police in his pocket. Could Pryce be on Goran's payroll? It was this more than anything that convinced him to take matters into his own hands. He took Zelda off the radar of his own accord, without even telling his own team, and without informing Pryce.

'DI Drake circumvented the chain of command,' WPC Patel was saying.

Marshall cleared his voice. 'This is an important point. In your statement you claim that you felt it was necessary for the security of the witness. Can you tell this inquiry if there was any other reason for this course of action?'

'No, sir. I just thought it was the right call.'

'I see.' Marshall sounded unconvinced.

It would have been fine, if only things had gone according to plan. Drake needed to keep Zelda safe for long enough to get her to trust him with the written evidence and get a proper statement. She was unwilling to do either of these things until she was sure she was safe. So he got a couple of burner phones, gave her some cash to tide her over and told her to disappear.

'Nobody else, as far as you are aware, was in contact with the witness?'

'No, sir.'

'Then how do you explain her disappearance?'

'I can't . . . sir.'

'If I may,' Pryce intervened. 'DI Drake has always had problems with authority. His record shows a history of insubordination and recklessness, both within the Metropolitan Police force and, prior to that, during his time in the army.'

'I understood that he had a distinguished military record.'

Marshall looked up from his files at Drake. 'You were decorated for your service.'

'That is correct, sir. The Distinguished Service Medal.'

Marshall shot Pryce a wary look. 'Hardly chimes with insubordination.'

Not quite true. Drake had been sanctioned enough times for insubordination to know that he would never have a career in the military. It wasn't that he was bad at his job. He'd proved himself a good soldier. What he had problems with was obeying orders when they made no sense, which kind of rubbed up badly against the whole idea of the chain of command. In the army you do what you're told, no questions asked.

Drake knew that some of the resentment he experienced was due to those who were convinced that he was being favoured because he fitted nicely into the group picture of a racially diverse police force. He didn't care about any of that and did his best to ignore it. The world was full of people looking for someone to blame. And besides, Drake hadn't exactly made it difficult for them. He was often a little too reckless, a little unconventional in his methods.

The elephant in the room and the root of this DPI investigation was the accusation that it was Drake who had been bought off, that he might have given up Zelda to Goran Malevich.

'DI Drake?'

'Sir?'

'I was asking about your witness.' Marshall peered over the rim of his reading glasses. 'I believe her name was Zelda.'

'That was an alias she used. Her real name was Esma Danin.'

'You maintain that while she was in your care she disappeared without trace.'

'We had worked on finding someone to testify against Goran for over a year.' Drake glanced at Pryce, who stared back at him. 'Zelda was the best opportunity we had. I couldn't risk losing her.'

Marshall's face scrunched up as if he had accidentally bitten into a lemon. 'I find it hard to accept that your justification for keeping all of this under wraps is that you believed you could not trust your own team.'

'It was a risk I felt I couldn't take.'

'Was there anyone in particular within your team who gave rise to this suspicion of yours?'

That afternoon, Drake knew that Pryce was watching his every move, waiting for an opportunity. 'Nothing I could put my finger on.'

'So, this was all mere speculation on your part.'

'Every time we came close to getting something on Goran he would change up the system. Deliveries, routes, storage facilities. It was as if he knew where we were looking.'

'But you had no solid evidence of there being an informer in your team.' Marshall pressed the point home.

'That is correct,' Drake conceded, ignoring the snort of derision coming from Pryce.

'But you had confidence that the material she was offering was genuine.'

'I knew it was. Everything she showed me was solid.'

'If I may, sir.' Pryce could no longer restrain himself. Marshall conceded with a nod, not lifting his eyes from the documentation in front of him. 'We've been over this before. DI Drake provided no solid proof that his witness had reliable evidence that would have been sufficient. That was the reason I had my doubts. I believed that DI Drake was emotionally involved with the witness and that this had affected his judgement.'

'Any truth to that, DI Drake?'

'None, sir.'

'So, you were not involved with this witness in a personal way?' Marshall's voice dropped to a whisper. 'You did not lead her on?'

Did he lead her on? It was the question that had tugged him awake on countless nights just like this one, left him wandering the house in the dark. No, he had been careful not to step over the line. To have done that would have been to jeopardise the whole case. That would have been a catastrophe. But he knew, deep down in his soul, that he could not truthfully claim not to have led her on. The look in her eyes was seared into the back of his mind.

It may have been desperation, but Drake knew that Zelda

saw him as her saviour, the man who would deliver her from the suffering she had experienced all her life. When you promised someone something like that you went beyond the professional, you were making a personal commitment.

'Thank you, DI Pryce, your point has been duly noted for the record.' Marshall sounded weary. 'I'd like to turn back to the issue of your witness, Zelda. Are you saying, DI Drake, that you had no way of tracing her once she had gone off the radar, as it were?'

'That's correct, sir.'

'A little reckless, don't you think, letting a witness disappear?'

'I thought it was for the best.' He would have added that Zelda herself refused to cooperate under any other conditions. She trusted nobody, not even Drake. Not fully anyway.

'And you chose to take this decision yourself, without even consulting your direct superiors. You thought it was worth it. Can you explain why?'

'Zelda knew everything there was to know about Goran Malevich's operations, in particular his child-smuggling ring. We had never come anywhere close to anything as good as this. The implications were far reaching. Goran was connected to a ring that extended across Europe. But she was in fear of her life. I needed her to trust me.'

'You are aware, I take it, that the torso of an unidentified female was discovered along the coast from Brighton around the time of her disappearance?'

'It was three weeks after she disappeared.' Drake glanced at Pryce. 'At the time there was no firm evidence to connect the torso with my informant.'

'But the possibility that this was her must have crossed your mind.'

'It did, of course, but by then the whole thing was over. Goran himself was dead.'

'Malevich was gunned down in a multistorey car park in Brighton, so your case was effectively useless.'

'That is correct, sir.'

'Your witness was no longer of any use to you.'

'She still had valuable information. Information that could

have been used to dismantle Malevich's operations and prevent them from being taken over by someone else.'

'But that didn't happen.'

'No, sir.'

Marshall leaned back, dropping his pen on the stack of papers in front of him to regard Drake.

'Can you tell us why that didn't happen?'

'Operation Hemlock was closed. I was suspended, pending this investigation.' Drake lifted his chin. 'Everything stopped.'

'And who benefitted from that?'

'Certainly not me.'

'Am I correct in assuming that you believe Malevich was responsible for the disappearance and death of your witness?'

'Everything would indicate that.'

'Can you explain how he could have managed to find her?'

'No, sir, I cannot.'

'You can see how this looks, can't you? You were the only person who was in contact with her. How could anyone have found her?'

'I don't know.' Drake studied the backs of his hands. 'I can only speculate that she used the phone I gave her to call someone other than myself and she paid for that mistake with her life.'

'But you have no idea who that person she rang might be?'

'No, sir.'

Marshall gave a deep sigh and closed the folder in front of him, then carefully replaced the cap on his fountain pen and lay it alongside it.

'There are many aspects of this case that I find deeply troubling. All I can say with certainty is that there is clear evidence of breaches of procedure, none of which has an adequate explanation.'

Marshall leaned back and folded his arms. Pryce cleared his throat.

'DI Pryce, you have something to add?'

'Sir, I believe it is important to note that Goran Malevich was gunned down by unknown assailants using assault rifles. It had all the hallmarks of a gangland assassination.'

'I am aware of the facts, DI Pryce. What is your point?'

'Simply that the story did not end with Malevich. Removing him left the field open to a number of his rivals. Several of whom continue to thrive today. A number of them are known to DI Drake personally.'

'That is a serious accusation. Do you have any evidence?'

'No, sir.'

'Can you shed any light on the subject, Detective Inspector?' Marshall returned his gaze to Drake.

'None, sir, no . . .' He cleared his throat. 'If I may, sir. All of this is pure speculation on the part of DI Pryce. I'd be happy to respond to any evidence put before me, but so far I haven't seen any.'

'DI Pryce?'

'There is no hard evidence yet. I believe the matter warrants further investigation.'

'I would agree.' Marshall nodded. 'Your statement to that effect is now on record. DI Drake, do you have anything to add?'

'No, sir.'

'Very well.' Marshall heaved a breath and folded his glasses. 'So, we're just about done here. Anyone wish to add any closing statement?'

'If I may, Superintendent?'

'Let the record show that DI Pryce would like to make a statement.'

'In my opinion, DI Drake has conducted himself in a way that is incompatible with the behaviour of an officer of the Metropolitan Police. He has consistently shown a lack of respect for his commanding officer and his seniors in rank. This insubordination sets a bad example for the service as a whole. On top of that there is the impact on our efficiency and professionalism.'

Pryce had been practising. It was a good speech, Drake had to admit, but he'd heard the same crap before. Countless times, in fact. But Marshall had had enough. You could see that in his eyes. The inquiry had run its course. Everybody wanted to move on. Drake more than anyone. There was just that nagging voice at the back of his head that prevented him feeling any satisfaction.

'We shall withdraw to consider the facts once more and decide on our recommendations.'

On the way out, Pryce cornered Drake.

'Don't go blowing champagne corks just yet, Drake. This isn't over.'

Even now, nearly four years later, Drake wondered whether it would ever be over.

35

This time she was greeted by a monkey. Crane was no expert, but she was pretty sure she was looking at a chimpanzee. It was perched on the staircase as she came in through the front door. No horses or geese this time. Where had it come from? The chimp stared at her for a while and then looked around. It was big enough to seem a little intimidating and she stood her ground for a moment without saying a word. Unimpressed, the ape hauled itself quite effortlessly onto the handrail and walked up this on all fours, to disappear somewhere on the upper floor.

Crane wandered down the hall below the staircase that led through to the rear of the house. The kitchen was empty this time. She went from room to room until she found her father sitting on the terrace outside. He appeared to be oblivious to the light rain that had turned the blanket around his shoulders damp. Droplets of water clung in a spidery web to the lank hair that hung down over his face.

'You shouldn't be out here in this weather.'

'It helps to clear the mind.'

'Well, you'll catch your death,' she said, helping him to his feet.

'Don't pretend that you care about me.' He tried to shake her off, but he was weaker than her. Nevertheless, she stepped out of his way. Let him fall on his face. Perhaps that would teach him to appreciate the effort she was making.

'I suppose you've come to gloat.'

'I came to ask you about your dealings with Marco Foulkes.'

'Oh, not that again. It's so boring. Why don't you settle down and start a family? You'd feel much better. Or don't you like men?'

'He's taking advantage of you.'

'Nonsense.' Edmund Crane paused, his finger trembling in

the air. 'You're worried about your inheritance. That's what all this is about.'

'I hate to disappoint you, but this isn't about you, or your money.'

'Just as well, because there's bugger all left of it.'

'Marco used your name to set up a shell company. Novo Elysium.'

'I have no idea what you're talking about.' He weaved across the room to pick up a cut glass decanter from the sideboard and hold it up to the light. 'They always forget to refill the damn thing. You simply can't find the help.'

'You don't have any help, remember? You sent them all packing.'

Edmund Crane turned to survey his daughter, who remained standing in the doorway, silhouetted against the light.

'God, you remind me of your mother.'

'You almost make it sound like you cared.' Crane walked past him to throw open the French windows, hoping to lose the animal smell that filled the room. Something had been in there and left its droppings behind. Her father carried on talking.

'I didn't hate her, you know. We were happy once.'

'You left her in prison. You let her die.'

'She knew the risks. She was prepared.'

'Nobody is prepared to rot in an Iranian jail.'

'It was a difficult time. There was a lot at stake.'

'Sounds like the same old excuses to me.'

'I know you see me as the enemy, but we're not as different as you like to think.' He gestured at the house around them. 'You're a part of all this. That's what you can't accept. That's why you hate yourself.'

She looked at him and pulled a face. 'Do me a favour, don't try to analyse me.'

'I thought you were a psychologist.'

'Exactly, and you're not. Tell me about Marco Foulkes.'

Her father turned away, got down on his knees and started rifling through the contents of a cabinet until he found what he was looking for. 'Aha.' He held up a bottle of crème de menthe. 'Care to join me?'

Ray didn't answer. Edmund Crane shrugged off the rejection and found himself a glass, which he wiped on the tail of his shirt before pouring himself a generous shot.

'He sat there, right there.' He pointed at the divan, whose stuffing was erupting from one corner. 'Told me all about how he would make us both rich.'

'And you believed him?'

'I've never been good with money. My father was even worse. Runs in the family.' He sipped his drink and smoothed a hand over his remaining hair. 'Why are you really here?'

'What exactly happened to Foulkes' father?'

'Killed himself. He was a coward and a fool. Cheating on his wife. Nobody missed him.'

'Yet you welcome his son with open arms?'

'I felt sorry for him. And besides, I always had a soft spot for his mother, Hilda.'

The liqueur seemed to mellow the old man. He was dressed in a paisley dressing gown, out of which the collar of a shirt poked.

'She deserved better than me,' he mused. 'Your mother, I mean.'

'For God's sake!'

He looked up. 'Where are you going?'

'I'm not listening to this. All this self-pity. You know you don't mean it.'

'How can you say that?'

'If you had cared about her, you would have done something back then, but you didn't.'

'I did what I could.'

'Keep telling yourself that. Maybe one day you'll actually believe it.'

In the front entrance she caught a glimpse of a shadow swinging through the plane trees beside the house, but when she turned to look up there was nothing there. She climbed onto the Triumph, kicked the side stand up and pressed the ignition. It felt like a waste of time coming here. She told herself she shouldn't be too disappointed, she had expected something like this. The rear wheel spun on the gravel as she took off.

There was something reassuring about being back on the motorcycle and moving, putting as much distance between herself and the madness behind her.

At the bottom of the track she skidded to a halt. She should have swung right onto the lane and headed downhill towards the main road. Ahead of her stood the open gate to the Foulkes estate. She hesitated for a moment and then aimed the bike straight through the gates and twisted the throttle, speeding up along the tree-lined drive.

36

In contrast to her father's place across the valley, the Foulkes' manor was well maintained. The house and grounds were clearly well cared for. The lawns around the main house were neatly trimmed and rollered, hemmed in by little islands of roses and fuchsias. Thick banks of green ivy fluttered up the walls around the front entrance.

Crane climbed off the Triumph and hung her helmet over the wing mirror before walking up the front steps. A big brass knocker shaped like a cherub's face beckoned, but before she could lift it the gleaming black door opened to reveal Mrs Foulkes, bearing a pair of pruning shears and a basket over one arm.

'Ah, what perfect timing!'

'Mrs Foulkes.'

'Oh,' she squealed, waving the secateurs in the air. 'Please, I insist call me Hilda. Mrs Foulkes makes me sound so old.'

She spoke over her shoulder as Crane followed her round the side of the house, where she set about pruning a large rose bush.

'It's good to see you. I'm glad you're taking an interest in your father. He scares everyone off. They all arrive with good intentions and then he gets into one of his moods, ranting and raving. And all those animals.'

'I was wondering about that.'

'Somebody talked him into hiring out some land to an animal sanctuary. Something like that. He's harmless of course, but people are more sensitive than they used to be, don't you find?'

'He's rude and manipulative. He enjoys insulting people. You'd have to pay someone pretty well to ask them to endure that.'

'Oh, come now. Underneath that scaly exterior there is a heart of gold.' The corners of Hilda Foulkes' mouth wrinkled in a thin smile. 'I genuinely believe that.'

'Well, then he's lucky to have neighbours like yourself who take an interest in his welfare.'

'It's the least I can do. Our families have been neighbours for centuries, after all.' As Crane met her gaze Mrs Foulkes turned away.

'I actually came up here to ask you about Marco.'

'Oh, dear, it's all so worrying, this whole business of this young lady friend.'

'You met her, Howeida?'

'Yes, that was her name. I was trying to remember. Well, of course I only met her once or twice. She seemed nice, considering.'

'Considering?'

'Well, I mean, her background, the circumstances under which she was brought up. Imagine? It must have been horrific.' Mrs Foulkes moved on, turning her attention to the next rose bush. She paused her pruning to survey the garden. 'It's going to be much better with the new greenhouse.'

'New greenhouse?'

Mrs Foulkes pointed to a rectangular section that had been dug up at the far end of the lawn. Then went back to the subject of her son's love interest.

'She must have suffered, growing up over there. The way they treat women. I mean, it's positively medieval.'

'Did she ever talk about her uncle?'

'No, not that I recall. It was Marco who told me her uncle was planning to take her back any way he could. It's like that princess, you know, the one who was trying to escape on a yacht? I watched a documentary. Terrible. I mean, in this day and age. Apparently, it's quite common. They never let their women go.' She was shaking her head now, snapping at the stems in front of her with quick, angry snips so that Crane was actually worried about the plant. 'If it had been up to me, I would have warned Marco against getting involved.'

'You didn't approve?'

'Of the girl?' Mrs Foulkes suddenly seemed aware of a need

to tread carefully, as though remembering who she was addressing. 'I tried to warn Marco, but you know how it is. Love is blind, they say. You can never protect your children.' Mrs Foulkes ran an eye over Crane, taking in her slim figure, along with the leather jacket and boots. 'I suppose you don't have any yourself. Children, I mean?'

'Too busy, I'm afraid.'

'Everybody is,' said Hilda Foulkes. 'He used to be very fond of you, you know, when you were children.'

'That was a long time ago.'

'Well, feelings like that don't change. Why else would he come to you?'

'I'm sorry?'

'The investigation. I mean, you're hardly likely to be impartial.'

'I'm not sure I follow.'

Hilda Foulkes chose not to spell it out. Instead, she changed her tack. 'Why are you here, when you should be looking for the uncle?'

'That's actually why I am here. I spoke to him and feel I need a fuller picture.'

'You spoke to her uncle? How extraordinary!' Hilda Foulkes seemed taken aback. 'Did he tell you what he did with that poor girl?'

'He assured me that he had nothing to do with it.'

'And you believed him?' She gave a derisive laugh. 'What did you expect, a full confession?' Mrs Foulkes lifted the secateurs as if she was thinking of throwing them at something. 'I mean, they're all like that.'

'I'm not quite sure I follow.'

'Oh, for goodness sake! I've never heard such nonsense. Why are you here?'

Crane pushed her hands into the pockets of her jacket. 'To be honest, after speaking to Howeida's uncle I began to wonder if there could be another explanation.'

'Such as what?' Mrs Foulkes turned to face Crane.

'Well, if we assume for the sake of argument that Howeida's uncle didn't kidnap her with the intention of spiriting her back to the Gulf, then perhaps there's something we're not seeing.'

The hand holding the secateurs dropped to her side. 'I'm afraid I don't follow.'

'I understand that Marco was advising my father on financial matters. Do you know if he was doing the same for Howeida?'

'How would I know something like that?' Mrs Foulkes' face darkened. 'What are you saying?'

'I'm just doing my job, exploring all the avenues.' Crane ventured a smile, which came out awkwardly. Mrs Foulkes wasn't buying it.

'You know, when Marco told me he was going to hire you, I assumed it was for sentimental reasons. I said to him that I had no idea you were trained as an investigator. Frankly, this is what I was afraid of.'

'What is?'

'Clearly, you don't have the experience.'

'Well, I appreciate your concern, Mrs Foulkes, but that doesn't change my question.'

'Marco trusted you. He thought you would be able to get to the bottom of it, because of, you know, your background.'

'My background?'

'Of course. I mean, why else would he come to you?'

Crane had no answer to that question. Certainly not the one Mrs Foulkes was expecting. She pulled off her gloves and dropped them into the basket, along with the secateurs.

'I'm afraid I've got aphids.'

'I'm sorry?'

'Greenfly.' Mrs Foulkes gestured at the plants. 'They need to be sprayed.' With that, she spun on her heels and headed off across the lawn.

Crane followed her over to a privet hedge that ran perpendicular to the main house. Behind it lay a garage. Mrs Foulkes led the way through a gap in the hedge to a side door that brought them inside. They were greeted by the barking of dogs. One side of the building was taken up with a large fenced-off cage in which half a dozen rather beautiful creatures jostled one another. They had bright, fluffy dark pelts. When Crane drew close to the wire they snarled and bared their teeth.

'Don't get too close,' said Mrs Foulkes over her shoulder. 'They have been known to take off the odd finger.'

'Charming.' Crane kept her distance. 'Greenland Dogs?'

'Siberian Huskies.'

'What is that they are eating?'

In the middle of the cage was a bloody mass of flesh and bone. Mrs Foulkes chuckled.

'The remains of a sheep. They'll eat the whole thing, bones and all. Nothing left.'

She carried on and Crane followed, the familiar smell of engine oil and damp earth reaching her nostrils and carrying her immediately home. Her love of machinery, cars, motorcycles, any kind of vehicle really, brought a sense of calm to her that she found difficult to explain. It was sensory memory, laid down early on in her childhood. When they were in Iran, one of her mother's brothers, Uncle Bijan, ran a workshop. After her mother was taken away, Ray found herself being taken care of by her family. Her father had to travel a lot and she would often go straight from school to wait at her uncle's workshop. Bijan was an exception. The rest of the family were academics. Poets, painters, they belonged to an old line of cultured intellectuals who were quite dismissive of someone like Bijan, who had chosen an entirely different line. Of course, Bijan was really the most political of all of them. He was a die-hard communist, who refused to write poetry but would always find time to speak fondly of Marx and Lenin. He had been imprisoned in the early years of the revolution, but had miraculously survived. Now, as she stood in the garage and inhaled the oil-soaked air, Ray remembered him.

While Mrs Foulkes rummaged around on a row of metal shelves along the wall, Crane turned her attention to the car that was parked over by the opposite wall. It was half covered with a tarpaulin and appeared to be abandoned. The rust-coloured tarp was slightly askew, affording a tantalising glimpse of metallic peacock blue panels. Crane tugged the cover off to reveal the shining Rolls-Royce Silver Shadow. Mrs Foulkes let out a sigh.

'I don't know why we keep it. Nobody has driven it since Harold died. Marco keeps promising to get rid of it, but he never does.'

'Maybe he just can't bring himself to do it.'

'Boys will have their toys, eh?'

'Yes, I suppose so,' said Crane, examining the car. She leaned over to peer inside. 'Looks nice.'

'Well, it's just taking up space. I must get Marco to get rid of it. The problem is, nowadays, everyone wants something that's environmentally friendly, don't they?' She wore the same lopsided smile Crane had seen earlier.

37

The massage parlour on the Caledonian Road was being refurbished by the looks of things. A gang of overweight men were carrying furniture in and out of the building. Drake distanced himself from the action and took up a position in the next doorway, shielded by their van.

It was mid-morning before the front door opened across the street and Sonja, wearing the old sheepskin coat, appeared pulling a child's stroller behind her. Two Bangladeshi women passed him and Drake fell in alongside them, walking at the same pace as they chattered away, clearly oblivious to his presence. He stayed with them until they reached the corner, where he saw Sonja turn away from him and disappear down the road to her right. Drake crossed the street at a fast pace and stayed close to the wall as he followed behind her at a comfortable distance.

At the end of the street he watched them disappear through the gates of Paradise Park. A few moments later he stepped through in time to see Sonja settling herself on a wooden bench while the little boy ran over to the adventure playground. Drake watched her light a cigarette and tilt her face back to allow the sun's rays to play over her, closing her eyes to absorb the warmth.

'Hello Sonja.'

She glanced up, saw him and swore, several times, some of it in English but most of it incomprehensible.

'I'm here with my kid. You have no right.'

'I'm sorry about the other day,' he said, sitting down alongside her. 'Walking in like that.'

She turned her face towards him so that he could see the swelling under her eye. 'I can't work like this. Who is going to pay the bills, you?'

'Look, I just need to ask you a few questions.'

'Questions?' she frowned. 'About what?'

'About the old days, about Esma.'

'Since when you care about her? That was nearly four years ago. My best friend. Fours years she is dead because of you.'

'I came here because I want to find out who killed her.'

'Who killed her?' Sonja was incredulous. 'What do you care who killed her? She gave you what you wanted, right?' She tossed her head. 'Typical! Like all men, you take and you leave. Well, you'll get nothing from me.'

Perhaps sensing something was amiss, the little boy came running back from the playground to throw himself into his mother's lap. He twisted sideways to look at Drake.

'Who's this, Mummy?'

'Nobody, baby. He was just leaving.'

The boy didn't look convinced. He stood and stared. Drake tried smiling at him, but the look of suspicion did not go away. Finally, he turned and ran back to play.

'Nice kid.'

'Don't!' She jabbed a finger at him. 'He doesn't exist for you, okay?'

Drake raised both hands in defence. 'Hey, I'm not here to hurt you.'

'I don't know what you came here for, you got her killed.'

'I only want to do what's right by her.'

Sonja gave a bitter laugh. 'I told her not to talk to you, but she wouldn't listen. Esma trusted you.' She took the cigarette from her mouth with a sigh. 'She thought you would save her.'

'It didn't work out that way.'

'No, you don't hear what I am saying. She was smart, you understand? She was careful.'

Rather than placating her, Drake seemed only to stir her animosity. There was anger in the tone of her voice that hadn't been there a few moments ago.

'She would never have put her trust in anyone. But in you, she did. Why is that?'

Drake said nothing. He had the feeling his part in this conversation was to be silent and listen.

'You men are so stupid sometimes.' Sonja was shaking her head in disbelief at her own words. 'She was in love with you.

It's as simple as that. And you led her on.' She held up a hand to stay any objections. 'Just let me finish.' She dropped the cigarette and ground it into the dirt with the toe of her boot. 'Esma never knew happiness. No man had ever made her happy. They fucked her, they beat her, they used her. But love, this was not something she ever expected from a man.'

Drake stared into the distance. 'I never touched her.'

Sonja shook her head. 'She didn't want that from you. She believed in you. She saw you as a kind of saint, someone who could get her out of the mess she was in.' She fell silent.

'Is it true she had a child?'

Sonja stared grimly into the distance. 'She was raped when she was fourteen, by her uncle. Her parents were gone by then. When her aunt discovered she was pregnant she blamed Esma. She ran away after she gave birth.'

'What happened to the child?'

'She had to leave it behind.' Sonja looked down at the ground. 'The way she told it she had some kind of depression. The boy was something dirty that came from inside her. She didn't want it.'

'What happened then?'

'She wandered for a while, moved to the city, fell in with the wrong crowd. She took drugs and then did what she had to do to pay for them.' There was a lost feeling in her gaze that told him this was a familiar story. She knew a thousand like it. She knew it as she knew her own story. It was all part and parcel of the same cruel tale. 'She was young and pretty, so there were opportunities, and men. Always there were men. Eventually she found Goran, or he found her.'

'This was in Serbia?'

'In Belgrade. He used her, for a time, like he used all women, and then he moved on to someone else, someone younger.'

'He took care of her?'

A nod.

'So if he found out that she was about to betray him.'

Her eyes found his. 'He would have cut her to pieces.'

'Tell me about the club.'

'What's to tell?' She lifted her shoulders.

'Now. The people who run it now.'

'It changes,' she shrugged. 'Always it changes.'

'The man I saw this afternoon. Khan.'

'He's a bad man.' Her fingers trembled as she reached for a cigarette. 'A bad man.'

'Are they part of the Karachi mob?'

'I don't know what they are. They're Pakis.' Another shrug. 'Men. They're all the same.'

'The ones who hurt you, who do they work for?'

'What difference does it make?' She blew smoke. 'Nobody uses their real name. Never. No.' She sighed. 'They are not important.'

'Was he around in the old days, Khan?'

'You don't give up, do you?' Sonja stared at him. 'That was a long time ago. It's all changed since then.'

'Khan works for Hamid Balushi, right? Or he used to. Was he running that racket in those days?'

'I don't know. I hate all of them. I just want to die. If it wasn't for him . . .' She nodded towards the boy standing at the top of the slide. 'I would just end it now.'

'You can always get out.'

'Oh, you're going to save me now?' She snorted smoke. 'That didn't work out too well for Esma, remember? Do you have any idea what they would do to me if they saw me talking to police?'

'I'm not police. Not any more.'

'Same difference.'

Neither of them spoke and for a time the air was filled only with the sounds of the playground. Children screaming in delight and parents calling to their offspring.

'Did she ever try to contact you while she was away?'

'Esma? Never. All she told me about you was that you were going to help her. She would smile. A stupid smile, like she'd found religion or something. This one is real, Sonja, she would say. You'll see.' In the distance, the boy began running towards them. She got to her feet, turning her back on him. 'Don't come back here, and don't come to the club. I never want to see you again.'

38

There was no answer at the flat near Drury Lane. Crane stood on the doorstep and peered through the glass until a voice behind her said, 'Can I help you?'

Crane turned to find a woman in her forties with mousy hair that needed combing. Under one arm she held a pile of purple binders and in her other a set of keys.

'I was looking for the young lady in the first-floor flat.' Crane noted the logo on the binders. 'Are you from the lease company?'

'Yes. I'm afraid she's already gone.'

'Gone, as in moved out?'

'Yes, that's why I'm here. I only got the news last night. Something to do with her family. She was called home urgently. I was just going to check on the place.' She brought her chatter to a close. 'I'm sorry, are you a friend?'

'I'm an investigator. I'm looking for the other woman, the flatmate.'

'Oh, I don't know anything about that. These places are very much in demand, as you can imagine. We need to get it tidied up as soon as possible.'

By now she had managed to get the front door open and was trying to wrestle the key out of the lock while holding the door with her foot. The folders threatened to escape her grasp, so Crane stepped in and held the door for her.

'Would it be all right if I came up with you, just for a moment?'

'You said you were an investigator?'

'That's correct.' Crane handed the woman a business card.

'There's nothing criminal involved here, is there?'

'Not so far. All I'm concerned with is the welfare of the young lady who used to live here.'

The woman considered the situation. 'Well, I suppose there's no harm in it.'

The flat was neat and tidy. It looked as though the cleaners had been by. While the estate agent checked that none of the appliances was missing, Crane took a look in the bedrooms. Savannah's was empty. The wardrobe was bare of everything, including hangers. In the opposite room Howeida's clothes were still in place and the big silver case was there behind the door. Crane stared at it for a long time before she realised what she had missed the first time around.

Crane thanked the estate agent and left her to her inventory. It took her ten minutes to walk across the Kingsway to the London School of Economics. She had managed to reach only one of Howeida's friends, the round-faced Adela, who was waiting for her in the café behind the main building.

'Did you know Savannah was going away?'

Adela looked surprised, but not shocked. 'No. She never said anything.'

'Apparently it was something to do with her family.'

'Oh.' Adela looked askance. 'Right.'

Crane leaned forwards so that the young woman was forced to look at her. 'You don't like her, do you?'

'It's not that.' She dipped a forefinger into the froth on top of her coffee and drew circles. 'The thing is, Howeida was our friend.'

'You and the other girl, Meena?'

'Exactly. The three of us just got on very well, right from the start. Then Savannah comes along and just sort of . . . inserts herself. I mean, they were just such opposites.'

'Savannah and Howeida?'

Adela nodded. 'They came from totally different worlds.'

'They must have had something in common.'

'Ambition. They both just wanted to be successful. I don't know, they thought they would rule the world or something.' She hesitated. 'They had money. Meena and I were always a little shocked at how much they spent. They didn't care. I mean, the flat they were staying in. Did you see that?'

'In Drury Lane, yes.'

'Meena lives with her family and I am in a miserable place out in Bethnal Green. Takes me an hour to get in here.'

'Howeida had money from her family. How about Savannah?'

'That's the thing. It was always a mystery with her. I mean, you said she went home because of something in her family?'

'That's what the estate agent told me.'

'The thing is, she changed her story so many times. I mean, she would tell you some long story about her father walking out on them, and the next time it would be her mother. I mean, it was like she wanted to be the poster girl for a dysfunctional family.'

'What about money?'

'She had some kind of trust fund that was set up for her. I think she had wealthy grandparents or something. They left her some money. The thing is . . .' Again, Adela hesitated. 'I got the impression it was all a front, that she wasn't really wealthy, she just wanted to look that way.'

'What made you think that?'

'Like I said, that was just the impression I got. Meena had the same feeling. She was always trying to get Howeida to invest her money in some scheme she had. I didn't understand it.'

'An investment? What kind?'

'I don't know the details. Sorry. Anything to do with money and I just switch off. That was the whole thing with Howeida's uncle. When he came here, they were going to talk to him about it.'

'About her investments? So she trusted him?'

'Sure,' Adela nodded.

Crane sipped her coffee. It tasted a lot better than the coffee she remembered from her student days. 'One thing I noticed. Maybe it's not important, but when I looked at Howeida's room I didn't see a rucksack or a small bag of any kind. Do you remember anything like that?'

'Oh, yes,' Adela nodded. 'She had a really cool backpack that was, like, leather?'

'Okay, so not vegan?'

The young woman laughed. 'No, Howeida was a little behind on stuff like that. That was really a sign of her background, where she came from.'

'How about an overnight bag? Did you ever see anything like that?'

'Yeah, sure. We went to Paris for a weekend, all of us, on the Eurostar. That was fun. We drank way too much wine.' She put up a hand to cover her teeth as she giggled.

'And she had a small bag, not a big suitcase?'

'No, I mean this was like Louis Vuitton or something. Really expensive design? Tan coloured, also leather. I remember holding it for her. It was really soft.' Adela's face had grown sombre again. 'This is not good, is it? I mean, her being away for so long.'

'No,' said Crane. 'It's not good.'

39

Drake headed across to Shepherd's Bush market, where he found Gebelawi busy trying to flog a bright yellow trolley case to a woman in a black abaya.

'Sister, I swear by the prophet, peace be upon him, this is the real thing. Samsonite. You know, it's a mark of quality.'

'I'm not stupid, you know. That says Sansomite.'

Gebelawi squinted. 'It's all the same. Someone in Guangdong make a mistake, right? So what're you gonna do? Destroy it? No, instead they come to Gebelawi. They say, help us out mate.' He beamed as he came to the end of his story. The woman swayed, caught between the silver-tongued salesman and the attractive price tag.

'I must speak to my husband.'

'Sister, please, take your time.'

She disappeared out the door and Gebelawi sighed. 'I swear, they drive me crazy. They come in here and flirt like mad. Then, just before they say yes, they get hit by a dose of guilt. It's the thrill, innit? Married Muslim women, man. I swear, there's a sexual revolution just waiting to happen.'

'Dream on.'

'Seriously, they cook, they clean, they give birth to half a dozen little monsters, while their husbands slowly lose interest. The only vice they're allowed is food and fizzy drinks, which is why they turn into blimps. That one,' Gebelawi nodded at the door, 'she's not interested in food, no sir.'

'They have a special place in Hell for people like you.'

Drake had known the Egyptian for years. He'd been flogging his wares from one market to another and saw himself as a world-class businessman. He had a wife and five children at home, but that never stopped his womanising. He had a certain rakish charm and eyes that twinkled with mischief.

The narrow space was cluttered with cheap suitcases, mixers, ironing boards, used washing machines, stoves, refrigerators. You name it and he would give you a price. He also ran a little side line in electronic devices.

'Step into my office,' Gebelawi said, moving aside.

Office was a glorified term for a fenced-off area behind a glass-topped counter whose interior was stuffed with a range of battered mobile phones. They lent an air of hopelessness to the place. The class of clientele who came in here were not primarily concerned with such matters. Needs overcame their resistance. It was all about the price tag and at Gebelawi's there was always room for bargaining.

'What can I do you for?'

'Surveillance equipment.'

Magical words. You had to look closely to spot it, but a little flicker crossed Gebelawi's eyes. He selected a key from the ring on his belt and slid open a cabinet to reveal an array of surprisingly sophisticated devices. Not exactly what you might expect to find in Shepherd's Bush market.

'Best thing you ever did, by the way.'

'What's that?'

'Leaving the force, going private. Believe me, you will not regret it. Who believes in all that stuff anyway, for Queen and country? James Bond? You think he'd last five minutes in Beirut? Big sign on his back saying I'm a khawaja, right? You know what I'm talking about?'

'I was a police officer in London, not James Bond in Kabul.'

'Same thing now, innit?'

Following Gebelawi's reasoning was not always easy.

'Believe me,' he went on, 'from now on you're gonna be up to your neck in it. Take my word, man, more pussy than you can handle. It's going to be brutal. Okay, so, what have we got here?' Gebelawi laid out a selection of devices on the counter. 'These are Czech made. Very good quality at an affordable price.'

'Czech?'

'Don't look at me like that, bro. In the old days they was busy spying on everybody. I'm telling you. Just have a look.'

Gebelawi found a packet of Marlboro and lit one while Drake took a closer look at the device.

'Wireless, okay? You can pick up the signal up to two hundred metres away. But even better. I throw in something so you can tap it straight into the telephone network. You can listen from the comfort of your own home. How does that sound?'

'Expensive.'

The other man rolled his eyes. 'My friend, listen to me, you come to Gebelawi to solve your problems, don't think about money. Don't pay me anything. I just want to help you. That's all.'

It was late afternoon by the time Drake drove onto the North Circular Road and skirted east round the city towards Dalston and the solicitor's office on Kingsland Road. He sat there for half an hour before there was a knock on the window and the side door opened.

A wiry figure eased himself in to the passenger seat; in his forties, wearing a red beanie hat over greasy, shoulder-length hair. Drake knew Jerry 'Spider' Moffat from his early days as a PC in uniform. Spider was a repeat offender. His speciality was breaking and entering and he spread his net wide, working all across London. Small and agile – he was still no bigger than your average teenager – Spider could climb drainpipes and walls with remarkable ease. He could crawl through tiny openings, bathroom windows, even a chimney once. Despite this, he had an odd sense of moral principles – never touched drugs or had anything to do with the seamier side of crime. He had one area of speciality. The rest he steered clear of.

'How's tricks, Spider?'

'Ah, things are getting more complicated.'

'How so?'

Spider shifted nervously. 'I mean, these modern alarm systems. You need a degree in electronics to get through some of them.'

'I thought you were on the straight and narrow?'

'Yeah,' Spider sniffed. 'I mean, I'm just being speculative, like.'

'Right. Maybe it's time to consider an education.'

'Never going to happen, mate. No good with institutions,

me. Self-taught. Have been all my life. No point in changing me spots now.' He nodded ahead of them. 'So, this is it then?'

'This is it.'

Spider turned his head to look at Drake. 'How legit is this, then?'

'Well, it's like everything.'

'Meaning, not at all.'

Drake shrugged. 'It's low risk. You get in and out, you leave things as they are.'

'And if anything goes wrong?'

'Then you've never heard of me.'

'Sounds about right.' Spider rubbed his nose. 'Okay, well, I've had quick shufty and it looks doable. Old-school alarm system, so shouldn't be a problem. There's a toilet facing onto the back. They leave the window open. I can get through there.'

Drake reached over into the backseat for the holdall with the items he had picked up a few hours earlier in Shepherd's Bush. Spider zipped it open and went through it with a meticulous eye.

'Nice.'

'You know how to set these up?'

Spider cocked an eye at Drake. 'Give me a break. You want microphones in the main office?'

'The boss's office is at the back.'

'Leave it with me.'

Drake watched Spider cross the street and disappear into the shadows between two buildings. He hadn't told Ray about this little plan of his. He was pretty sure she would not approve, so better to wait and see what the outcome was before crossing that particular bridge. It took less time than he thought. Twenty minutes later Spider could be seen cutting over the road again.

'Did you manage to get in?'

'Sure, no problem.' Spider peeled the latex gloves off his hands. 'The microphone is voice activated. You'll be able to pick up the signal remotely on your smart phone once I install the app.'

Drake was impressed. 'Are you sure you didn't go to college for this?'

'I told you, man, I'm against institutions. Matter of principle.'

'If you say so.' Drake leaned over to start the engine. 'One more job and then you're free to go.'

'So long as you're paying I'll go where you like.'

They drove across town, more or less following the route taken by the minicab the other night. The traffic was heavy and it took them more than forty minutes before they were parked in a side street looking at the red-brick building in Pimlico where Barnaby Nathanson lived. The lights were off in his flat on the second floor.

'Funny, him living all the way over here and his office in Dalston. You'd think it would be the other way around.'

'You'd think.'

Spider spent a couple of minutes selecting and packing everything he needed into a neat little black bag that he slung over his shoulder and strapped into place.

'Might take a little longer with the locks and all.'

'I'll call if he shows.'

Drake watched Spider as he crossed the street. He pressed a number of buttons on the door panel until someone buzzed him in. Then he disappeared from sight. Drake kept his eye on the windows of the flat on the left-hand side of the building, watching for any sign of light. The minutes went by. Spider would be picking the Yale lock on Nathanson's door. Then he would have to attend to the alarm system, for which he had his own tried and tested method. Although it was hard to believe, Spider had spent a couple of years working for a burglar alarm company. He knew everything there was to know and still kept in touch with some of his old mates, who were happy to give him updates. One thing you had to say about Spider, he was resourceful.

Drake looked at his watch again. He was beginning to worry. This part of the job should have gone smoothly. No alarms had sounded and no sirens or flashing lights were going on. So there might have been a problem with the locks, or Spider might have been challenged by someone inside the building. Drake resisted the temptation to go over there and take a look.

Then, just when he was about to get seriously worried, he saw the front door of the building open and Spider appeared. He looked left and right, and then without a sign to Drake or a word of explanation he turned and took off running.

Drake sat up. 'Now what . . .'

40

The entry phone on the wall beside the front entrance displayed some forty-odd numbers. Drake ran a finger down one side, pressing all of them until he heard a voice. An elderly lady who sounded surprised, as if she didn't get a lot of visitors.

'British Gas, we have a report of a leak. Would you mind letting us in?'

'Oh my goodness, what happened?'

'Nothing to worry about, love, but better safe than sorry.'

'Yes, of course. Of course.'

The buzzer sounded and Drake stepped into the vestibule. It was carpeted and brightly lit, with gilded stucco around the ceiling and mirrors on the walls. Altogether a very respectable kind of place to live. Avoiding the lift, Drake climbed the stairs carefully. He hadn't gone far before he heard a chain being removed, a lock turned and a door opening somewhere high up. The same wavering voice called down.

'Hello, hello?'

'Nothing to worry about,' Drake sang out. There was a muttering and then a shuffling of feet, followed eventually by a closing door.

By the time he reached the second floor he had his tool kit out and was getting ready to pick the lock. Then his eye fell on the door and saw it was ajar. He listened, his ear to the opening, but he could hear nothing from within. Nudging the door gently with his toe, Drake stepped into the gloom of an unlit hallway.

A faint light hummed from a small table light by the door. A coat rack along the wall displayed a couple of raincoats and an expensive oilskin jacket. The light shone on the varnished floorboards. He paused for a moment to pull on the pair of disposable latex gloves he had brought with him. Then he walked to the end of the short entrance hall. The living room facing the street was lit partially by the glow coming from outside. Drake felt glass crunching beneath his boot and stopped. There was a smell of alcohol in the air. He crouched down. A bottle had smashed on the ground. A heavy bottle. If he were to have hazarded a guess, he would have said Scotch, single malt, the expensive kind. Drake stepped onto the rug and moved to the windows ahead of him. There were two of them, high and wide French windows that gave onto a narrow balcony. Drake lifted the curtains aside cautiously. The street was quiet. He could see his car. Staying out of sight, he looked left and right, tried the doors on both sides and stepped away again.

Turning his back to the windows, he looked around him. He switched on his flashlight. On his right an old fold-up bureau was pushed up against the wall. Above it hung a large oil painting of a rather stern-looking woman in white. A family heirloom of some kind, no doubt. The flat had been modernised, with a kitchenette installed beside the entrance hall. This was neat and simple, with wooden cupboards and a large refrigerator that hummed to itself contentedly. Low backlighting along the wall illuminated a counter of black stone that glistened with chips of mica. It looked clean and untouched, the kind of space you used to eat breakfast and unpack your takeaways. A plastic carrier bag sat on the counter. Water was dripping onto the floor. The bag was leaking. Drake went over to take a look. Inside were gently melting packages of lasagne, Black Forest gateau and burnt cinnamon ice cream. A bottle of wine had smashed. Glass splinters glittered darkly in a ruby red stain on the white tiles. The rest of the bottle lay on the floor. A small trickle of wine led towards the edge of the counter and drops fell to the floor.

Drake was beginning to get a bad feeling. Moving away from the kitchen he went right, crossing the entrance hall and passing from the living room to a darkened dining area with a long table made of glass and steel. The chairs were some kind of modern design. Behind the dining area two wide steps led up to an office. Sliding glass doors stood open. He saw heavy bookcases and a shiny, antique desk. A window looked out onto the side street. Everything had been turned upside down. The drawers had been pulled out of the desk, books and papers littered the floor.

Retracing his steps, Drake found a bedroom at the end of a hallway. It was empty. The drawers had been tipped onto the floor. Bedclothes lay strewn about and someone had taken a knife to the mattress, cutting deep slashes and digging around inside. Nathanson was in the adjoining bathroom.

It looked as though the solicitor had tried to barricade himself inside. The doorframe was splintered around the lock. There were grubby marks left by the rubber soles of a large boot. Drake was careful not to touch anything. He leaned in through the doorway to take a closer look. There was a lot of blood on the walls and floor. A bloody smear on the mirror. The solicitor was in the bathtub. Crimson water had slopped over the sides, leaving a sticky mess on the floor. Nathanson was underneath the surface. His eyes were open and he was still dressed. One of his legs hung over the side. Drake estimated that he had been dead for at least a few hours.

Backing away, Drake followed the trail of blood spots that led towards the far end of the flat. Over the years, Drake had learned to pick up on the essentials of what a murder scene could tell you. There were stupid killers, there were killers who were numbed by what they had just done, still high on the thrill, on the horror of what they were capable of, and there were panicky killers. Murderers were caught because they made mistakes, and the reasons for those mistakes varied. Despite the commonly held belief in the prevalence of serial killers, most murderers were amateurs, experiencing their own capacity for homicide for the first and usually last time. Repeat offenders also made mistakes but that was often down to stupidity, or overconfidence, which was a form of stupidity. Here there was a certain arrogance to the way in which the killer had wiped their hands along the wall, smearing blood over the paisley motifs. As if they didn't care to be identified, daring the police to find them.

Someone had come here looking for something. They had confronted Nathanson, tried to get the information out of him, dunked him underwater and eventually drowned him. Drake guessed that they had not been successful. Which explained why they had then turned over the office and the bathroom.

He found a partial bloody footprint on the wooden floor in the hall, leading back towards the office. In a few hours, every inch of this place would be under the scrutiny of a team of SOCOs, with all their boxes of tricks. He stood for a moment in the doorway and surveyed the scene. Facing the bookshelves on the left-hand wall was another large painting, this time a still life, showing a table on which there lay a brace of dead pheasants, a withered vine with grapes on it and a glass of wine in which the light gleamed, even in the dimly lit room.

Now he saw that the painting was slightly off kilter. It stood at an angle to the wall. Moving round it, Drake could see that the frame was hinged. There was something that prevented it from closing properly. He pulled it gently open to find a safe embedded in the wall. It was the old-fashioned kind, with a circular dial. The reason the picture wouldn't fit against the wall was that there was a broken drill bit sticking out of the safe door. Somebody had tried to drill a hole just under the dial, rather clumsily by the look of things, and then abandoned the job. Amateurs. A killer trying his hand at safe cracking? Or a safe cracker who was hard at work and then surprised by the owner coming home? Drake stared at the safe for a long time and realised that neither of these things offered a full explanation.

He went back through the house, searching for Nathanson's phone but found no trace of it. It was gone. Presumably that meant the killers hadn't found the combination on the phone. He went through the desk, running his hands around the insides of the drawers. Bending down, he examined the underside of each one. He moved aside the blotter, turning it over. Nothing. In his experience safe dials were a nice idea but most people had trouble remembering a combination that was ten or more numbers in a sequence that had to be loaded precisely, moving left and right. Usually they kept a note somewhere handy, nowadays on a telephone but failing that somewhere obvious.

In the kitchen Drake opened every door he could see.

Eventually he found what he was looking for. A yellowed sheet of paper taped to the inside of a cupboard, with a long list of telephone numbers. The kind of thing nobody kept any more, all the details you needed being stored inside your phone. Although there was an old socket on the wall from the days when there was a landline here, this list still served another function. Drake went through it slowly. It looked legitimate, with contacts for plumbers and sisters and parents, a GP. Then he spotted it. Hidden close to the bottom was a number with several angle brackets inserted between the digits. The brackets indicated which way to turn the dial, left and right. Drake stripped the paper off and went back to the safe.

It still took him three tries, not being familiar with a lot of safes, but eventually he heard a satisfying click. When he turned the handle the door opened. He waited for a moment, listening for an alarm. That he couldn't hear anything didn't, of course, mean there wasn't one. It could be a silent alert sent to a security company. Either way, he'd already overstayed his welcome.

It was a small safe. The contents could all have fitted easily into a normal briefcase. Only there were no contents. It was completely empty.

He closed the safe again and spun the dial, leaving the broken drill bit in place. He returned the paper to the kitchen cupboard. In the distance he picked up the sound of a police siren that was getting closer. The woman upstairs must have decided it was better to be safe than sorry. It was time to move. He walked softly down the hall and pulled open the front door. Then he stopped in his tracks.

'Either you're moonlighting as a burglar or you've been holding out on me,' said Crane. 'I think you owe me an explanation.'

41

Crane's motorcycle was parked behind Drake's car. They were on the side street facing the building, far enough back from the corner to be shielded by the row of cars ahead of them. They had only just made it out in time. Through the windscreen they watched the action unfolding ahead of them. First there was a lone patrol car, but soon squad cars were coming in fast and furious from both sides.

'The full five-star parade,' murmured Drake.

'Sounds like you miss it.'

'Nah, truth is I was never really comfortable being inside a uniform.'

'You don't need to tell me that. You're uncomfortable with authority.'

'You read me like a book.'

Ahead of them the flashing lights played across the walls of the building. There were uniformed officers going in and out. Drake hunched down in his seat. A van from the coroner's office drove past them to park alongside a forensic unit crime scene van. A SOCO team could be seen suiting up and getting their equipment ready. Curtains were twitching up above and faces could be seen peering out, as the neighbours tried to gauge what was going on.

'I have a bad feeling about this,' said Drake.

'How come?'

He felt an odd craving for a cigarette. It had been months since he had last given up, but this time the craving was strong.

'Whoever did this was trying to tidy up loose ends.'

'You're saying that the answer was in the safe?'

'That's my feeling.'

'And this guy . . .'

'Spider? Yes, I'll have to have words with him.'

Drake spotted Kelly and Pryce talking outside the front of

the building. The familiar lanky figure of the chief forensics officer, Fast Eddie, was there too, walking purposefully with long, slow strides.

'I'm having trouble seeing the big picture here,' said Crane. 'Why would anyone kill Nathanson?'

'The way I see it,' Drake began, 'Barnaby Nathanson was up to his neck in some scheme involving clearing money through property deals and the shell companies he was managing.'

Crane nodded. 'One in particular. They all trace back to Novo Elysium.'

Drake glanced over at her. 'And you got this from?'

'Guy I met. He's something in the City. Finance.'

'Interesting. Is it serious?'

Crane sighed deeply. 'It's a long story.'

'You can give me the details later. Okay. So, as I see it, Nathanson's office in Dalston was a front.'

Crane agreed. 'Wealthy clients get tossed into the mix with poor unknowns, people in genuine need of legal help. I wouldn't be surprised if he was receiving subsidies for providing legal aid.'

'Whoever killed him wanted what was in that safe.'

'Which brings us to why we are here.'

'Why are we here?'

'The reason we took an interest in Nathanson was his relationship with Foulkes.'

'Agreed, only I think this goes a lot deeper than we thought.'

'It would help if we had whatever was in that safe.'

'Agreed. Leave that to me,' said Drake. 'Explain how you got here.'

'Howeida's flatmate. Our Southern belle from Virginia. She's gone. Taken all her things and flown home. One of the other girls said it was connected with her family, but I think she got cold feet.'

'You think she was in on all of this?'

Crane leaned her head back. 'Let me think out loud here for a moment.'

'Let it rip.'

'Okay.' Crane closed her eyes. 'Let's say Foulkes is in trouble financially. The books brought him up to a certain lifestyle, but he's been having trouble lately. So he talks to an old friend and starts to go into some rather dodgy investments.'

'All of this is speculation.'

Crane opened her eyes and looked over at him. 'It's imaginative thinking.'

'Funny you should say that. They have a term for it now.'

'Do you mind?'

'Sorry, please, go ahead. Where does Howeida fit into this?'

'I think Foulkes was after her to invest in one of the schemes he was running with Nathanson. I'm willing to bet that his interest in her was not entirely disconnected from the fact she has a family with oil wells in their back garden. I wanted to see what Nathanson had to say for himself.' Crane sat up. 'Okay, your turn. What made you come up with the surveillance tactics?'

'I thought about approaching Nathanson, but I was afraid that might scare him off. I thought this might give us some leverage.'

'It might have done at that.' Crane was silent for a moment. 'What did you mean, when you said this goes a lot deeper?'

'Something I saw a long time ago,' said Drake quietly. 'Something I thought I had completely forgotten, until I saw it again.'

'What was it?' Crane asked.

'A tattoo.' Drake shifted in his seat. 'Years ago, I drove Zelda to a hotel to meet a private client. She didn't do that kind of work often, but sometimes a man saw her in one of the clubs and took a shine to her. So she went. She didn't have much choice. This man abused her. She wouldn't tell me the details, but it was bad. I could see that.'

'Who was the client?'

'I never saw him. What I did see was his minder, waiting, like me, in the lobby of the hotel.'

'The one with the tattoo,' said Crane.

'Khan.'

'Can you describe it?'

Drake reached into his pocket for the sketch he had made. 'Something like that.'

Crane held the paper up to the glow coming from the streetlamp behind them. 'Could be Khan-e-Qalat. A tattoo is unusual on a Muslim but common in gangsters. They don't care too much for tradition. This is calligraphy. It's the name of the old rulers of Balochistan.'

'That's western Pakistan, where Hamid Balushi comes from.'

'Who is Hamid Balushi?'

'Small-time Karachi gangster,' said Drake. 'Violent, and ambitious.'

'And you think he was the client who abused Zelda?'

'I think it's possible.' Drake's phone began to buzz. 'It's Kelly.'

Through the windscreen he could see her standing outside the building. She was looking up and down the street. 'Hey, Kelly, what's up?'

'What's up indeed. Where are you exactly?'

'Right now?'

'Right now.'

'Babysitting.' Drake and Crane exchanged glances. 'My neighbour. It's a long story. Why?'

'You'll have to tell me sometime. The lawyer you were asking about, Nathanson?'

'What about him?'

'He's just turned up dead. Drowned in a bathtub.'

'Accident or intent?'

'Looks like a break-in that went sour.' Marsh was walking up and down, out burning off nervous energy. 'I've got Pryce breathing down my neck. I'm going to have to tell him everything I know, Cal.'

'Do what you have to do, Kelly.'

'I'm warning you. This is going to get his juices running. Nice neighbourhood. Lawyer with money. It's right up his street. If he finds out you're involved he's going to tie it to Zelda.'

'I hear you.'

'Just tell me you didn't have anything to do with this.'

'You think I had something to do with Nathanson's death? Why?'

'I don't know, maybe because you didn't ask where this happened, or when.' Marsh paused.

'Sometimes I'm a little slow off the mark.'

'Plus you have your hands full.'

'Sorry?'

'Babysitting, remember?'

'Listen, Kelly, while I've got you, I wonder if you could run a check on something.'

He saw her cover the mouthpiece of her phone and swear. She came back on the line. 'Last time I checked, we're not part of your private enterprise.'

'It could be important. Zelda had a child. A boy, I think. Is it possible we can check with immigration if they have anything on that?'

'You think he might be in this country?'

'I think it's worth checking. The only thing we have to go on is his mother's surname, Danin.'

'That's really not a lot.'

'He would be in his twenties now.'

Marsh was silent for a moment. 'I'll think about it.'

The line went dead. Through the windscreen, Drake saw her staring at her phone for a moment. She tucked it away as a uniform came up to her. She followed him back into the building.

'Are they going to find you were in there?'

'I was careful,' said Drake. 'But you never know. Hopefully it won't matter.'

'How do you work that out?'

'By the time the lab gets through with its work, this thing will be over.'

'There's something else that's bothering me. This doesn't look good for Howeida. If she was involved in whatever killed Nathanson, she could be in danger too.'

Drake agreed. 'Perhaps it's time to have a talk with our client.'

They both fell silent as they watched the body being brought out from the building opposite. Upstairs, the scene of crime officers were visible moving around behind the windows on the second floor. They had set up powerful lights in the flat and intermittent flashes indicated they were still busy taking pictures.

Drake's phone began to buzz once more. He saw the name on the screen and swore.

'Sorry, I have to take this.'

'Don't mind me.'

'You haven't forgotten, right?' Maritza asked. 'Only it's coming up to half seven and we're not going to make it if we don't leave soon.'

'No, of course. I was delayed. I should have called.'

'But you're still on?'

'Yeah, sure. I'll be right there. Five minutes, I promise.' He rang off and caught the look on Crane's face. 'What? I promised to babysit. No big deal, so don't say a word.'

'I wouldn't dream of it. I'm impressed. I thought you were joking. This is very enlightened.'

'Enlightened? Now there's a word I don't often associate with myself.'

42

Maritza was waiting for him. The door opened almost before he had knocked. All dressed up and ready to go. She looked remarkably good. Beside her, Joe was jumping up and down with excitement.

'Cal! Cal!'

She had instructions. He was to make sure João brushed his teeth before he went to sleep, which she repeated to both of them. Joe nodded as she spoke. Clearly he had heard all of this before. He was wearing his pyjamas underneath his parka. He took Drake's hand and allowed himself to be led up the stairs.

'Sure you'll be okay?'

'We'll be fine. Don't worry about it. Have a great time.'

'Enjoy yourself, amorzinho,' she called as they moved away.

'You look great, by the way,' Drake said over his shoulder.

She waved him off, but not before he saw that she didn't mind the compliment. Upstairs, they soon settled down to a game of chess. To his surprise, Drake lost the first game and had to work hard to win the second.

'You've been practising.'

'I go to a club now. They teach us how to play properly.'

'I can see that.'

After that they watched part of a film that Joe had brought with him. He had a whole bag full of things to keep him entertained. If they had gone through the lot it would have kept them busy for a week. But the film soon had him yawning and so they cut it short. Then Drake waited in the hall outside the bathroom while the boy went to the toilet and brushed his teeth. He seemed to have grown so much in the past year. Cal still remembered him crawling into bed with them when he stayed over with Maritza. Then Joe had seemed like a very small child. In another year he would be on his way to adolescence. It all happened very quickly.

Once Joe had settled down in the spare room, Drake read to him from a book about space travel and eventually the boy fell asleep. Drake tucked him in and closed the door halfway, leaving the hall light on. Then he poured himself a drink and sat down. His phone began to buzz and vibrate on the coffee table. He reached for it to find that it was Brodie, who had something on his mind.

'After we were talking the other night, I started thinking about the old days.'

'About Zelda, you mean?'

Brodie exhaled slowly. 'Yeah, right, about Zelda. What can I say, mate? She didn't deserve to die the way she did.' There was a long pause. 'I get why you feel this.'

Drake reached for his glass. 'If I hadn't convinced her to turn against Goran, she'd still be alive.'

'That's a cross you have to bear. Just make sure it doesn't take you down with it.'

'I just need to clear it. If I can find out who killed her—'

Brodie cut him off. 'You know as well as I do that revenge is a mug's game. Even if you find the person who gave the order, you're never going to make a case of it, not now.'

'That's not enough reason not to try.' Drake knew Brodie was right. He also knew he couldn't stop until he cleared this.

'Walk away, Cal,' Brodie urged. 'Let it go. Move on.'

'I wish I could. Somebody cut her to pieces.'

'Yeah, I know. That's some weird shit, as they used to say.'

'Why would someone do that?'

'Take the head? I don't know, as a trophy maybe?'

'Or as proof.'

'Right, but why keep it all this time?' Brodie asked.

It was a question Drake had been struggling with. It made no sense, and yet to someone it did.

'Somebody has been trying to lay this on me.'

'That's what this is all about?'

'It looks that way. My DNA was all over the bag.'

'Why would they do that?'

'You see, the fact that it's taken this long seems to suggest that, whoever it is, they actually believe I'm responsible.' Drake rattled the ice in his glass. He wished he could think more clearly.

'Which means it's someone who doesn't know you.'

'I should hope so.' Drake was so tired he was slurring his words.

'It's almost as if they were taunting you with your own guilt.'

That was how it felt. 'You know, the other night, at the club . . .'

'What about it?'

'You were babysitting Donny's nephew, right?'

'Zef? Sure, he's a real live wire. Tends to get a little excitable.'

'I thought it was an odd group. You know, Zephyr and Khan and that weird little one with the Hitler Youth haircut.'

'Oh, that's Vuk.'

'Vuk? What kind of a name is that?'

'Serbian,' said Brodie. 'He's a kid in Goran's old crew.'

'And now he's working for Donny?'

'He's just a friend of Zef's. They all hang around together. What has this to do with anything?'

'Goran was set up. I think he went to Brighton on a tip-off and walked into a trap.'

'You mean he was set up by his own people?'

'I mean somebody close to him saw an opportunity to get rid of him.'

'That's a bold move. You don't go against someone like Goran unless you're ready.'

'Right.'

Brodie was silent for a moment. 'If you're accusing me of something, Cal, you might as well come out and say it.'

'You're the only person in Goran's crew who knew that I was undercover.'

'What does that have to do with anything?'

'If I took him down, it would all be gone. The money, the drugs, the girls.'

'I find it insulting that you would even think that.'

Drake wasn't sure what he was thinking. Brodie had been working for Goran. He was the only one who knew who he really was. But they'd come through Iraq together. Drake trusted him with his life. A bunch of Serbian mobsters weren't going to come between them.

'Forget it, Brodie. I'm not accusing anyone. I'm just trying to piece this thing together.'

'Maybe you should be looking somewhere else.'

'Like where?'

'I don't know. What did she give you?'

Drake could still recall the stench in the little crawl space hidden behind the wardrobe. It was as if the smell had taken up residence inside his body. It came back to him at the oddest moments.

'The flat Zelda took me to, they were trafficking in kids.'

'That wasn't Goran's business,' said Brodie.

'You're sure about that? Why would she take me there?'

'It's an easy mistake to make. Goran had his fingers in a lot of pies. When his mob moved into London they wanted it all. They pushed money and drugs on anyone they thought could win them influence. It took them into some pretty strange alliances.'

'Who are we talking about?'

'Hard to say. Goran made deals with everyone. He lied. He strung them along. He did what he had to do to keep the competition sweet. Sometimes he found himself in with something he didn't like.'

'Sounds like you're trying to make out he was an angel.'

'No. All I'm saying is because he was involved doesn't mean he was close. I'm willing to wager you would never have traced that operation back to him.'

'Zelda knew I was after Goran.'

'She was never on the inside. She didn't know who he was working with. She was like everyone else. She heard stories.'

'She sounded pretty sure that it was Goran's operation. She wouldn't have taken the risk for less.'

'You could turn it around and say maybe that's exactly why. She wanted to keep you sweet without too much risk of it coming back on her. Ever think of that? Limited damage. You get the score, but nothing really gets traced back to Goran.'

'You're saying she was playing me?'

'You were her ticket to freedom.' Brodie sighed. 'Look, all I'm saying is it's a consideration. Look at it from her point of view. You were asking her to trust you, a cop she doesn't know, against a vile gangster she does know. If it worked fine, then she was free, but if it didn't . . .'

'Then it wouldn't harm Goran.'

It made sense in a crazy kind of way. He remembered his excitement when she told him about the flat. Trafficking was a powerful charge. It made people sit up and pay attention. The flat was a turnaround. They brought the kids in and shipped them out in a few days. Drake was familiar with the set-up. He knew how hard it was to track them down. They broke into empty flats, changing the locks and then boarding up windows and doors. They stayed for a few weeks and then moved on somewhere else. Had he been blinded by the fact that he was hoping this was the one, that this would lead to Goran, that it would be enough to bring him down?

'Who were the kids for?'

'All kinds. It was big. Business people, high-grade politicians. The kind of people whose names you read in the paper over breakfast.'

Drake leaned his head against the window. The glass felt cool against his skin. 'You're saying she didn't really know what was going on?'

'She knew bits of it. Like I did. But nobody had the full picture.'

Drake heard Brodie's dry chuckle. 'You wouldn't be the first person she'd strung along.'

It still didn't sound right. 'I keep asking myself how they found her.'

'Cal, do yourself a favour, put this behind you. Forget about it. Get on with your life.'

'I'd like to do that, Brodie, truly I would, but there's a severed head lying in the morgue and I'm a prime suspect. This isn't going to go away anytime soon.'

'Okay,' Brodie sighed. 'So run it by me again and see if that stirs anything.'

'When Zelda disappeared, the finger pointed at Goran. He

was the one with the most to gain. The case against him dropped through the floor and our star witness was gone, literally. That made Donny suspect number one.'

'Because he was the one who made the most out of it?'

'Right. But Donny's too smart to do something like that. Leaving himself exposed.'

'Anyone can make a mistake.' Drake listened to Brodie sucking air into his lungs. A long rasping sound. 'You need to be careful where you go with this.'

'Meaning?'

'Meaning Donny has spent the last couple of years trying to straighten out his business. He won't take kindly to you trying to pull him back into the past.'

'I have to go where the story takes me.'

'Be that as it may, you should be careful.'

'This is beginning to sound like a warning.'

'Look, Cal, it's late, we're both tired. Maybe we should take this up another time.'

'The other night at the club, the big guy with a tattoo on his neck.'

'Khan. Sure, we talked about him.'

'He and Donny's nephew are tight.'

'I told you, they're all kids. They like to hang out together.' There followed another lengthy pause. 'Look, mate, I know how you feel. You were the fall guy. They hung you out to dry. But that's no reason to go after anything that moves.'

Drake had gone from leading a major undercover operation to being a pariah. The assumption being that he had compromised the operation to protect Donny Apostolis. The Met's internal inquiry had been inconclusive. All they could do was point at irregularities in his actions: hiding a witness away without clearing it with his superiors, keeping information from the acting head of the unit, Vernon Pryce. Pryce, for his part, had never hidden the fact that he believed Drake was dirty. The inquiry drew its own conclusions. There was no mention of Adonis Apostolis in the final statement, but everyone knew who they had in mind. Superintendent Marshal had been clear in his closing comments: 'Although we have no evidence to support the claim, it seems plain to this board of inquiry that there is more than enough circumstantial evidence to leave an indelible stain on your name. We therefore recommend that you be suspended from your present duties until such time as we can establish your trustworthiness.'

They didn't want to kick up a fuss. The Met didn't need more bad publicity. Nobody wanted to see headlines about police corruption on the front pages of the tabloids. Drake had been a rising star, the kind of detective who gave diversity in policing a good name. They just wanted this to go away quietly.

'Nobody could prove I was on the take.'

'Sometimes they don't have to.'

Drake thought about pouring himself another. Then he thought about Joe, sleeping in the spare room, and he decided it probably wasn't a good idea. For some reason he wanted to impress Maritza that he could be responsible. Where did that come from, he wondered.

'Tell me about Khan.'

'What about him?'

'I'm sure I remember him from the old days.'

'He used to work for Hamid Balushi.'

'Used to?'

'Balushi is getting old. Khan is a new generation, more at home here than in the old country. Take my advice, you don't want to mess with them.'

'He used to be a driver. He used to drive Balushi around.'

Brodie sighed again. 'Come on, Cal, it's getting late. I just wanted to hear how you were doing.'

'How do I find him, Khan?'

'Christ, you are persistent. I'll give you that.' There was a long pause. 'The Green Gardens Halal Meat Packing. Just don't ask me any favours for a while, Cal.'

The line went dead. Drake stood there for a long time, staring at the window. Thinking about the past was never helpful. It brought back feelings of loss and failure. Now, however, he suddenly felt he had something. Nothing more than a spark, but it was enough. His instincts told him he was on the right track.

Deciding one more drink was in order, he wandered back

through to the kitchen. The only form of decoration on the walls was a black-and-white photograph of a group of jazz musicians from back in the 1950s. It had been resting against the wall of the flat when he had moved in and somehow he'd taken a liking to it. Now it was a part of him. He lifted his glass in salute to Dizzy Gillespie, one of the few faces he recognised. Then he went back to the living room and lay down on the sofa. His favourite spot for thinking.

The conversation with Brodie had stirred a lot. Some of it he didn't want to unpack just yet. He sat up and reached for his laptop. He spent the next fifteen minutes digging through the material Milo had sent him until he found what he was looking for. The van parked outside Clapham Common station. He took a screenshot of the vehicle as it was being towed away that included the time in the corner of the picture. He then emailed it to Milo and asked him if he could trace the movements of the van that day. After that he lay back again and closed his eyes. The next thing he knew the doorbell was ringing and his phone was buzzing. He opened the door to find Maritza standing there looking frantic.

'Cal, where have you been?'

'I was here. I just fell asleep.'

She frowned. 'Have you been drinking?'

'No. I mean, yes. I was asleep. Joe's fine. He's in bed.'

She didn't wait for him to finish but rushed past him into the flat and down the hall to the spare room. Drake remained where he was, by the front door.

'Look, I . . .'

She went straight past him without a word, tugging the child along with her. The door swung shut behind her.

43

Breakfast time and the Ithaka was crowded with builders from multiple construction projects in the surrounding area. Eleni was complaining loudly about their muddy boots while Kostas was trying to convince her that they needed the customers.

'Would you mind if I joined you?' said Crane.

Donny Apostolis looked up from his newspaper and broke into a smile.

'Ah, what a pleasant surprise. Please, sit.' He snapped his fingers and folded his paper. The chair opposite him was immediately vacated by the goon who'd been sitting there chewing his nails.

'I'm surprised to see you still come here.'

'Ah well, you know how it is.' Donny beamed. 'It's important to remember your roots.'

The waitress appeared to be indifferent to their presence. She was new and seemed confused as she went rushing by from table to table without any real sense of purpose. She was also having trouble understanding what the builders wanted. The conversation was at cross purposes since neither side appeared to speak English properly.

'Eleni's niece,' Kostas explained after stepping in to clear up the confusion. 'She arrived from Athens. She came here to get over a divorce. Her mind is not on the job.'

Crane ordered coffee and one of Eleni's spinach pastries.

'I assume this is not a coincidence,' Donny said. 'You want to talk to me about the money I gave your partner.'

'Among other things.'

'You are not happy working for someone like me. Why? Am I not respectable enough for you?'

'It's not so much that as the fact that your interest in this case is not clear.'

'Do you treat all your clients with such suspicion? You assume I am trying to use you.'

'All I am saying is that this is a tricky case. Cal's involvement already puts us in a difficult position.'

Donny stroked his pointed beard. It was a gesture Crane had seen him use before. He seemed to think it made him look wise.

'You're not saying you won't take my money?'

'Not in so many words.'

Crane's coffee arrived, or rather landed on the table. She looked up, but the waitress was already gone.

'I just need to be sure that there are no conflicts of interest.'

'I'm a businessman. Actually, all of this is behind me. I am interested only in clearing the cloud that hangs over my name. You can understand that.'

'Of course. I understand perfectly, and believe me I'm not here to judge.'

Donny mulled this over and appeared to find nothing he objected to. 'So, what can I tell you?'

'I'd like to talk about your investments.'

Donny frowned. '*Éla re,* what investments?'

Crane reached into the bag she had slung over her shoulder. 'Well, let's start with the Kratos Corporation. Was that your idea – the name, I mean?' She flashed a broad smile. 'I really like the reference to the old god.'

A knowing smile formed on Donny's face. Nothing improved his mood more than being recognised as a sophisticated man of learning.

'Thank you. I feel it's important to remember these things. You know, all of that stuff, the old gods, these are what made the world we live in possible.'

'Of course. I see that.'

Donny was enjoying himself. 'So, what else do you need to know?'

'Well, according to this, you have been investing in property through a number of firms, including the construction company YDH. Ypres Development Holdings.' She offered him another smile. 'Not Greek this time. It's a nice reference to the Ypresian formation.'

Donny's expression suggested the name wasn't his idea, but he wasn't going to pass up the opportunity to claim it as such.

'It's just a name.'

'I meant, since it's part of the London Clay sequence that runs underneath this city.'

'Sure.'

'So, have you heard the news about your lawyer, Barnaby Nathanson?'

'What about him?'

'He's dead. Someone murdered him last night in his flat in Pimlico.'

'Dead? I don't . . .'

Donny's response seemed genuine.

'Let's get back to the business at hand. YDH was connected to Magnolia Quays and Howard Thwaite. His wife was murdered on the site and the company's shares subsequently dropped. At which point you bought a controlling share.'

'That's not a crime. It was an opportunity. I would have been a fool not to.'

The new waitress sailed past their table three times without noticing Donny snapping his fingers. The bodyguard was equally useless, sitting by the door playing a game on his phone. Donny's irritation began to show.

'Why are you so interested in my business affairs?'

'We need to know that our clients are not trying to use us for some kind of illegal activity.'

'Illegal what? I'm legit. Didn't he tell you? I've gone straight.'

'Come on, Donny. You don't expect me to believe that, do you? Completely legit?'

Donny looked pained. 'Well, we're getting there. I mean, it's not for want of trying, right? With all these regulations and what have you. I blame the EU.'

'Sure you do. Let's get back to your investments.'

'*Gamoto!*' muttered Donny. 'Okay, what do you want to know?'

'You have money invested in a firm called Novo Elysium.'

'I've never heard of that.'

Crane tilted her head. 'It's the offshore company Nathanson put your money into. He specialised in moving money around.'

'If you say so.'

'Donny, what I'm trying to get at is that there's too much smoke here for there not to be a fire.'

'I get that. I hear what you're saying.' Donny waved his goon over and told him to fetch him a brandy. Then he leaned over and tapped his finger on the table in front of Crane. 'I've done nothing wrong. Whatever this Nathanson was doing for me, it was legal. That's what he did.'

'I'm not disputing that. What I'm saying is that somebody killed him for a reason, and if it wasn't you then you could be in danger.'

That amused Donny. He threw his head back and laughed at the ceiling. A cartoon laugh.

'You are priceless, you know that? Your idiot partner is lucky to have you. Speaking of which, shouldn't he be here with you for this interrogation?'

'He's busy, and besides, I don't need him to hold my hand.'

'Right, right.' Donny reached for the bottle of Metaxa that had arrived on the table and poured them both a glass without asking. He drained his and refilled it. 'Okay, what more have you got?'

'You're involved in something you don't really understand, Donny. Nathanson is dead, probably because he was blackmailing somebody.'

'I appreciate your concern, darling, but you don't have to worry about me. Let's talk about why you don't want to work for me.'

'Okay, let's talk about that. You asked Cal to keep you informed, basically of anything he found out relating to the murder of a woman who used to work for Goran Malevich. Why does that concern you?'

'It concerns me because I was suspected of having something to do with Goran's death. I don't like suspicions hanging over me.'

'And you think finding out who killed the girl will vindicate you?'

'Isn't it obvious? I am an innocent man. I want the world to know.'

'Right.' Crane sipped her coffee.

'Look,' said Donny. 'Let me ask you a question. Why is this a problem? The police don't care who killed that girl. Your boy has an interest and I'm paying him to find out.'

'You see, that's the bit that interests me. Of all the people still around you're the one person I would think had a pretty good chance of knowing who did it. You were there, on the inside. You knew who was in the game, who had something to gain, who could have found her.'

Donny held his hands wide. 'What can I say? I don't know everything.'

Crane looked at him. She wasn't sure she believed him. Hell, she wasn't even sure Donny believed himself.

44

The message from Doc Wyatt came in while he was sleeping. Drake listened, yawning while waiting for the kettle to boil.

'You might want to stop by. Somebody dropped something off for you.'

Kelly called as he was driving over.

'So we managed to get the safe open at Nathanson's place and guess what we found?'

'You're asking me?'

'That's another question,' said Marsh. 'You need to get your act together.'

'No doubt. What did you find?'

'The answer is nothing. Safe was bare. And according to the people at his office he kept a lot of cash in there.'

'How much?'

'Anywhere between fifty to a hundred grand.'

Which explained, at least in part, why Spider had taken off. 'That's a lot of money to keep at home.'

'Nathanson was the nervous type, by all accounts. He would disappear every now and then.'

'The money was in case he needed to make a quick getaway.'

'That's what I would say. The point is that it's gone now.'

'The killer took it.'

'That would be the logical conclusion,' agreed Marsh. 'Except they left a drill bit embedded in the safe door. We found the combination inside a cupboard in the kitchen.'

'So either they found that before they finished drilling . . .'

'Or somebody else found it afterwards. We spoke to a neighbour who recalled a visit by a gas man around the time. Only British Gas has no record of a leak being reported or one of their engineers being called out. Where were you at the time?'

'Me? I told you, I was babysitting.'

'As an alibi that sounds just far-fetched enough to be true.'

'You know Maritza, don't you? It's her son, Joe. You can check with her. I'm sure she'll be happy to confirm.'

'I'm sure she would. Sounds like you have it all covered. You do realise that removing evidence from the scene of a crime is an offence.'

'I remember something about that. What makes you think I had anything to do with this?'

'Call it my sixth sense.'

'I've always felt that was overrated. What did you find on Nathanson?'

'I'm not sure I'm authorised to share that with you.'

'Kelly, I've been trying to do you a favour, remember?'

'That's exactly it. I'm not sure any longer who's doing who a favour.' Marsh sighed, realising that resistance was hopeless. 'The fraud squad were building a case against him. Nathanson was running a string of investment funds that were transferring finances out to the Gulf and back. Dubai seems to have been a favourite destination. They've been through his offices but the feeling is that we're missing a stack of documents.'

'Which you think were in the safe.'

'I'm just saying. If you know anything about this, you need to come clean now.'

'Where is Pryce on this?'

'He's not a happy camper. He keeps asking for the forensic lab report and Archie keeps stalling.'

'When he gets it, he'll come after me.'

'I think that's a safe assumption.'

'Great,' said Drake. 'Look, I appreciate you sticking your neck out on this one, Kelly.'

'No problem. I'm just waiting for you to return the favour.'

'I'm working on it.'

Drake clicked off the call. He was still puzzled about Nathanson. Whoever had killed him was after something he was holding on them. Was he running some kind of extortion racket on top of everything else?

The Mad King George had finally changed its name officially

to the one most people knew it by. The Alamo. Doc Wyatt was behind the counter, looking pleased with himself, still his usual cheery self. He wore red and black tartan trousers and a yellow Hawaiian shirt covered in blue parrots.

'So, the stranger returns.'

'How are things, Doc?'

'You know me.' The tall man shrugged the dreadlocks over his shoulders. 'Never one to complain.'

'Things are changing.'

'You saw what they done?' Doc Wyatt nodded his head.

On his way into the Freetown estate Drake had been surprised to notice how much was going on here. The old swimming baths, which had been the scene of the end of his last case as a police detective, were now shrouded in scaffolding and green netting. It was about to be turned into a shopping mall named, obviously, the Bathhouse.

'Whole neighbourhood's changing, man.'

Not for the worse, Drake might have ventured, but he knew how sentimental Doc was about the old days, when the two had grown up running wild over the estate. One of the differences between them. Drake was not the sentimental type, generally speaking, and he wasn't interested in nostalgia. Nevertheless, he had noticed that the row of run-down shops that stretched along the east side of the square had undergone some visible renovation. There was now a health-food shop and some kind of Italian trattoria promising stuffed artichokes and *coniglio al forno*, whatever that was. Doc rested an elbow on the counter.

'Had to change up the whole menu. Now we got tapas and I don't know what. Can't pronounce half of it. But what can you do, right? Progress, innit?'

'If you say so.'

'Yeah, that's right. I forgot. As if you could give a fuck.'

'I'm here, aren't I?'

'You are at that. You had a visitor.'

'Don't tell me, Spider?'

'You're clairvoyant. I tell you, I've known him for longer than I care to admit, but that boy was hopping up and down like a cat in a burning car.' Doc Wyatt wagged a finger. 'What kind of trouble has he got himself into?'

'He was doing me a favour. He got cold feet.'

'I heard you'd chucked in the Old Bill.'

'This is different. Private security firm.' Drake was never sure exactly how to explain what he was doing these days. 'Spider left something for me, you said?'

Doc Wyatt levered himself off the counter and disappeared through a doorway into the office. He came back out carrying a mauve carrier bag from a fancy supermarket and a wide grin.

'Don't see many of those round here,' he said. 'Well, not yet at any rate.'

'Give it time.'

Drake took the bag over to a table in the corner and laid out the contents. There was a large accounts ledger and a series of card document folders. Drake leafed through the ledger and saw lists of acronyms, none of which made immediate sense to him.

'There was no cash in here?' he asked when Doc Wyatt arrived with a couple of beers.

'Do I look like the kind of person who would try something like that on?' Doc looked offended.

'Course not. I had to ask.'

'Fair enough. How much are you missing?'

'A lot. How did Spider look?'

'Well, he wasn't driving a Ferrari, if that's what you're asking.'

'So, his usual nervous self. Say where he was staying, how I could get in touch?'

'Nothing like that. I mean, he hasn't been around here for ages. He probably thought this was a good spot for a drop-off. If there was money in there he'll be long gone. He moves like a rat up a drainpipe. Disappears like a ninja, that one.'

Drake knew it was true. The money in Nathanson's safe wasn't really his concern. Spider was welcome to it. He would have liked to have heard his side of the story, but Doc Wyatt was right. He was probably on his way to Thailand or somewhere. He'd be back when the money ran out.

'You win some, you lose some, is what I always say.' Doc Wyatt smiled as he got to his feet and went over to serve a customer.

Drake turned back to the folders and began pulling out sheets of paper, trying to make sense of them.

45

Drake was driving west when he became aware of the siren coming up behind him. In the mirror he spotted a dark Mercedes saloon with blue hazard lights. He pulled to the kerb, expecting it to go by. To his surprise, it slowed. When the window slid down he saw the man in the driving seat was Vernon Pryce.

'Follow me.' Pryce pointed ahead and then took off. Drake swore to himself as he put the car in gear. The lights and siren cut out. They drove for about ten minutes, west in the direction of Battersea Park, and then north towards the river.

Without taking his eyes off the road, Drake reached for the bag lying next to him and leaned down to tuck it out of sight under the seat. He followed along behind the Mercedes, thinking about possible outcomes. If Pryce had something solid enough he wouldn't have wasted time with all of this. He would have stormed in and slammed the cuffs on Drake with as much fanfare as he could muster. But that wasn't what was happening.

It wasn't long before he saw the indicator light on the Mercedes start flashing as the car ahead turned down a narrow street. Then they were pulling up alongside the brick walls of St Mary's Church. The Mercedes rolled down the low ramp towards the river before coming to a halt. Pryce switched off the engine and got out of his car. Drake followed suit. The sun was shining and the gleam off the river carried a hint of warmer days to come.

Pryce leaned against the front of his car and lit a cigarette. Drake didn't ask for one and none was offered, which was just as well, as he didn't want to have to accept.

'Okay, so what's this all about?'

Pryce had a slick grin on his face. 'I've got the missing link. The piece to tie it all together.'

'That would explain why you're looking so pleased with yourself.'

'Last night someone broke into the flat of the solicitor Barnaby Nathanson.' Pryce blew smoke at the sky. 'This is where you tell me that name means nothing to you.'

Drake stared at the river but said nothing.

'Nathanson was tortured and killed. They were trying to get into his safe.'

'Any idea what they were after?'

'As far as we can tell there was cash in there, a fair amount, but that's not what they were looking for. Nathanson had a cocaine problem. Feeding that habit led him into some dark places. He made a lot of unsavoury friends, and a few famous ones too.'

'Why are you telling me this?'

Pryce held up a hand to stop Drake interrupting. 'I think he was blackmailing someone and they got tired of it.'

'So they killed him. Took the evidence away with them.'

'It looks that way.'

'What does any of this have to do with me?'

A thin smile carved itself into Pryce's narrow face. The kind of smile that is devoid of emotion.

'Turns out one of Nathanson's clients was your old friend Donny Apostolis.'

'He's not my friend.'

'Whatever.' Pryce jabbed a finger. 'The point is that my feeling is this is the missing link. Once we start going through Nathanson's records we'll find it.'

'Find what?' Drake stared at the other man. There was something inherently primitive about the set of his jaw, the closeness of his eyes.

'The silver bullet. The head found at Clapham Common station was wrapped in a bloody rag. The DNA analysis of that blood doesn't match the victim's. If it matches yours, then I'm going to be a very happy man.'

'Even you have to admit that would be a little too convenient, don't you think?'

That brought a laugh. 'Poor old Cal. The whole world is against you, right?'

'I had nothing to do with that woman's murder.'

'Listen to yourself. Do you really believe that? I mean, whichever way you cut it, you're in the mix somewhere. She was your witness. You wouldn't share her with anyone and then all of a sudden she's gone. Three weeks later she's dead, cut into pieces by some savage butcher. Well, now she's back. Risen from the dead, if you like. Come to ask for justice.'

'Very poetic, but about as credible as little green men in spacecraft.'

'That's where you're wrong. I'm all about the facts. You know why, because I go by the book. It's called police work, Cal. Or have you already forgotten?'

'Then why are we standing here talking?'

'Because this is your chance to set the record straight. Forget all that other stuff. We can work it out, just the two of us.'

'Sure,' nodded Drake. 'That would make your job a lot easier.'

Pryce tossed his cigarette aside and stuck his hands into his coat pockets. 'You wouldn't be the first undercover officer to get his emotions tangled up with a witness. Maybe you were jealous. Maybe there was another man. Who knows? The point is that she vanished on your watch. That's down to you and you alone.'

'The only reason you've taken an interest in this is because you think you can tie me to this lawyer of yours.'

'Nathanson.'

'Right, Nathanson. In other words, you've got nothing. I was trying to help her. I had no reason to kill her. More importantly, even if I had, why would I keep her head for all this time and then leave it on a train?'

'It's human nature. People make mistakes. We see it all the time.'

'It makes no sense and the CPS will throw it out. She was my witness. I kept her location secret because I didn't trust anyone on the case and that includes you.'

'Tell it to the judge. I could never prove that it was Donny who paid you off, but I will.' Pryce crossed one foot over the other and folded his arms. 'I always assumed it was Goran who was paying you off. Then Goran died and your pal Donny stepped into the picture. Suddenly Goran is lying in a pool of blood and Donny is taking over his operation. That tells us everything.'

'That tells us nothing. There was an official inquiry, remember? You couldn't get any of it to stick.'

Drake watched a black cormorant sweep down in a low arc across the water. It was remarkably peaceful here, considering there were a million kinds of mayhem happening on either side of the river.

'I still don't see why you're telling me all this.'

'I'm giving you an opportunity. We've been going at this for so long it's hard to think straight. But maybe now's the time.'

'Yeah, well, maybe it would help if you stopped trying to implicate me in Zelda's death.'

'Don't overrate your importance. I have evidence, and I admit I will get a certain degree of personal satisfaction watching you go down for this, but the truth is you're nobody. I'm more interested in your pal, Donny Apostolis.'

Drake laughed. 'That's what this is all about? Even if I had evidence on Donny, what makes you think I would share it with you?'

'I don't know. How about civic responsibility? You know, the problem with you is no one ever knows if you're on our side or on theirs. I think you hate us so much you're happy to see the whole thing go up in flames.'

'Maybe that's always been your problem.'

'What is?'

'Not trusting me.'

'Believe me, you want to get out from underneath this thing while you still have a chance.' Pryce turned to go back to his car. 'Your choice, Cal.'

When he was gone, Drake stood for a while. He breathed in the air and wished he was far away. But wishing wasn't going to change anything. After a time he went back to his car and sat. Actually, he thought, it wasn't so much that the river was a peaceful place, more like it was too damn quiet.

46

The sun was doing its best to shine over Borough Market. Drake wasn't quite sure why Crane had suggested meeting here. To his mind, it was a place to be avoided at all costs. Too many people. Most of them wandering about in that mindless zombie state of all tourists. The rest were urban professionals, rushing from one latté fix to another, eyes glued to their phones. Hard to decide which was worse.

Crane was seated on a bench in the middle of a square at the back. She had her shades propped on the top of her head and her eyes closed, her face tilted back to absorb as much as possible of the sun's faint rays. She squinted out of one eye as he sat down.

'I got us duck sandwiches.'

'The more time I spend with you the classier I get.'

'It's just a sandwich,' she said, handing him the brown paper bag and a cup of coffee.

'I always had you tagged as the sushi and beanshoots type.'

'Is there such a thing?' she frowned.

'I'm really not the person to ask,' he said, sinking his teeth into the sandwich and chewing away. He hadn't realised he was hungry.

Crane sat up and reached for her own lunch. 'I've always had a healthy appetite and not much patience for dietary fads. I basically eat anything.'

'Amen to that.'

The wind whipped her sleek hair across her face and she pushed the strands away from her mouth as she ate.

'So, where do we stand?'

'I just had an interesting conversation with DCI Pryce.'

'Interesting, as in he threatened to throw you in prison?'

'Interesting, as in he wants me to help him land Donny Apostolis.'

'And this means he's no longer interested in you?'

'In my dreams. No, he thinks he's got me bang to rights.' Drake explained the bloody T-shirt.

'You've been keeping that to yourself.'

'I didn't see a reason to start panicking.'

'And now you do?'

'It looks like Archie is still covering for me. It'll be game over when Pryce discovers that my blood matches a sample from the crime scene. Until then, everything is in play.'

'So what is he proposing?'

Drake sighed. 'He wants me to help him land Donny.'

'Then he'll let you off the hook? You don't believe that?'

'Not for a second, I'm just running out of options.'

'I hear you.' Crane nodded to herself, trying to let everything settle. 'I talked to Donny.'

'Really?' It was news to Drake. 'When was this?'

Crane explained meeting Donny at the Ithaka. 'He's hiding something, but I believe him when he says he's trying to clean up his act.'

'Donny has two sides to him. On the one hand, he's smart enough to know that he's never going to get away forever.'

'And on the other?'

'He has a reckless side to him. Crazy Donny. The one who doesn't care what happens or how much it hurts. He just has to do it.'

'You think that's the side that killed Zelda?'

'It's possible. She was an inconvenience. Once she revealed all she knew about Goran's operations, Donny would be compromised.' Drake had lost interest in lunch. He set his sandwich on the bench beside him. A pigeon paced up and down in front of him, watching with a beady eye. 'I've been doing some reading.'

Crane sat up. 'You got the files from Nathanson's place?'

'My man, Spider, did a runner with the money but he was kind enough to leave behind the rest of what he took from the safe.' Drake set the Waitrose carrier bag on the bench. 'According to this, Nathanson had a shitload of dodgy clients. I mean, I've just been skimming through but these are a real mixed bag.

Small businesses, drug dealers – Nathanson had a habit – and some bigger clients. It's hard to follow. A lot of the names look like fakes.'

'Cleverly Dixon, Maid Merrione, Eddie Smurfy . . .' Crane ran a finger down the list of account holders. 'Very imaginative, in a spotty teenage boy kind of way. My father must be in here somewhere. Anonymous drug dealers, Russian oligarchs, property tycoons. Howard Thwaite is here too.'

'The mix helps to muddy the waters. So where does Donny Apostolis come into this?'

'He's in there somewhere, no doubt under a number of names.'

'So, Nathanson was running a money-laundering scheme with some very dubious clients.'

'And that gave someone a reason to kill him. You think that could be Donny?'

Drake shook his head. He still wasn't entirely convinced. 'I think Donny's in trouble. He thinks someone's making a move on him.'

'The same person who killed Zelda?'

'It all goes back to Zelda.'

Crane was still working her way through the files. 'So, through Nathanson, Donny's pumping his dirty money into construction projects all over London, as well as abroad in places like Dubai. He's shifting it about, turning it around from all kinds of sources.'

'A lot of cash flow in the building industry.'

'It's very fluid. People are paid off in cash, no questions asked. And then there are overheads, expenses, dodgy-looking receipts.' Crane tapped her hand on the pile of folders. 'Money is funnelled out of the country through a string of shell companies and then pumped back into this country as property investments under the control of a company called Novo Elysium.'

'So the money goes to Dubai and comes back clean.'

Crane nodded. 'Ready to be invested in property here. All over England, the South East and London mostly. The key is a handful of companies in the construction business.'

Drake stretched out his legs. 'Okay, but how does this relate to Marco Foulkes?'

'I'm willing to bet that once we dig through this more thoroughly we'll find plenty to tie him to all this. Foulkes was working with Nathanson. Finding him clients and taking a cut of the profits.'

'You think that's why he was interested in Howeida?'

Crane nodded. 'It's beginning to sound more reasonable by the minute.'

'And how does that connect to her disappearance?'

'That's the part that worries me.' Crane recalled her visit to the Foulkes' family home. 'His mother said something that struck me. She said, why else would he come to you?'

'You think he was using you. A cover story?'

'It had crossed my mind.'

Drake picked up his sandwich again. The duck was tasty, if hard-going. 'He made it sound as though he was doing us a favour, remember?'

'That was your gut reaction.'

'Never fails. Or maybe I just don't like writers.'

'You're a philistine. Admit it.'

'You say that as though it's a bad thing.'

'I'll get Heather to do some more digging on Donny. Maybe we'll find out who's after him.'

'And Howeida's flatmate, Savannah?'

'Not as wealthy as she made out. I think Foulkes tried to bring her in and she freaked out.'

'How about your father, how's he taking it?'

'I don't care about him.' Crane crushed up the napkin she was holding. 'When you're a kid you want your parents to be perfect.'

'I wouldn't know.'

Crane glanced at him and nodded. 'They never are.'

'So, if you don't mind me asking, what actually happened to your mother?'

'They were both working at the university in Tehran. Or so it seemed. In actual fact, I now know my father was an intelligence agent.'

'He was spying on your mother?'

'She wasn't a spy, she was just opinionated. Everything was political. Anyone opposed to the Islamist revolution was routed out. She loved the country, but she hated what it had become.'

'She was arrested?'

'More than once. She managed for several years to carry on the deception. Outside the home she behaved herself, wore the chador and all the rest of it. They couldn't prove she was against the revolution but many people knew of her opinions. Eventually she was told she could no longer carry on teaching. After that she was at home. Students would gather at the house, where they could talk openly about the things they cared about – literature, art, things that were forbidden.' Crane crouched forwards, her hands cupped around the coffee she was holding. 'Eventually, the inevitable happened and someone denounced her to the Gashte Ershad, the morality police. She was taken away.'

'That must have been hard for you.'

Crane slumped back on the bench. 'It was devastating. Like the whole world had caved in on top of me. Things were never the same after that.'

'When did you realise your father was a spy?'

'Not until years later. The whole marriage was a front. He used her to contact dissidents.'

'You mean he used her to infiltrate opposition groups?'

'He was a spy. All the time I thought they were this perfect couple.'

'She never got out?'

Crane shook her head. 'She died in prison. We had left by then. My father brought me back here. He said it was for my own good. Later, I realised it was to save his own neck. She died alone.' Crane stared into her coffee cup. 'I never believed it. I always used to dream of her struggling across the mountains in thick snow, trying to get to me.'

'Must have been tough.'

'It's what it is.' Crane snapped her shades back into place. 'Do you ever wonder why someone is trying to frame you for Zelda's murder?'

Drake understood that the subject of her family was closed. 'Someone has a personal thing for me.'

'Someone from the old days. Someone you knew.'

'That's my thinking.'

'But you have no idea who it could be?'

'I keep going back over it, trying to fill in the blanks. Somebody who was there back then, someone who wanted me out of the way.'

'A rival for her affections?'

'I don't know. One thing I did find out is that Zelda might have had a child.'

'When was this?'

'Before she came here,' said Drake. 'She was abused by an uncle apparently.'

'How old was she at the time?'

'Young. A teenager.'

'So the child could be in their twenties by now.'

'I asked Kelly to see if she can find any trace. He could be the missing link,' said Drake. 'He could be off the grid.'

'The way a homeless person might be?'

'Exactly the way a homeless person might be. They could have used him to get to her.'

'He could have led them to her unwittingly.'

The two of them fell silent as they followed through this scenario in their heads. Both seemed to arrive at the same conclusion.

'Could he have killed her?' Drake asked finally, speaking their thoughts aloud.

'If he did it knowingly, that would imply a hugely disturbed person.'

'If Fender is the son, then he left his mother's head on a train. Could that possibly be interpreted as some kind of act of love?'

'There have been cases. People living with the body of a loved one. Traumatised mothers in Germany during the war holding on to a dead baby, for example. Or a son keeping his mother's body in the house for years.'

'And there was me thinking *Psycho* was just a film.'

'It's not so bizarre. We try to hold on to the dead. It's quite common to keep the ashes of a parent who has passed away.

You could even argue that cemeteries are ways of preserving the remains of loved ones.'

'Remind me to make my own funeral arrangements.'

'A small minority doesn't see the distinction.'

Another thought occurred to Drake. 'Would she even have known about the boy? I mean, she hadn't seen him since he was born.'

'Maybe he just turned up out of the blue.'

'Or maybe he came here to find her.'

'Either way, I still need to find our mystery man from the Tube. I have a feeling I need to try another approach.' Drake watched a group of tourists going by. A man holding up a Korean flag on an umbrella was speaking into a microphone. The people behind him all had headphones. They looked left and right in unison. 'What's your next move?'

'Marco's mother. I think she knows something.'

'Zelda is the wild card in all of this.' Drake scratched his chin and realised he had not shaved for two days. 'Whoever killed her was sending a message. He kept the head for a reason.'

'Something must have changed. In this person's circumstances, or his surroundings, which have made it imperative to act now,' Crane said. 'Whoever it is, they have decided that the time has come for you to pay for your part in Zelda's death. They want to confront you with the evidence.'

'Zelda never told me everything.'

'How do you mean?'

'I mean, supposing someone else offered her something, something I could never give her.'

'Such as her son back?'

'That,' nodded Drake. 'And maybe enough money to live happily ever after.'

'Is there such a person?'

'All I have is a vague impression. A memory of someone Zelda was meeting. A man who was willing to hurt her.' Drake threw up his hands. 'I need to get into her mind, to see what she saw. It feels like I'm asking for a miracle.'

'That's how miracles work, isn't it?'

'I wouldn't know.'

47

The address for Green Gardens Halal Meat Packing was a warehouse off Garrett Lane in Southall. Drake could read the sign along the front through the chain link fence. It was an unremarkable shed of white aluminium siding that was in need of a new coat of paint. The green letters across it were faded.

'Is this it?' asked Crane.

They were in Drake's Astra, which was unusual. Crane normally would not consent to getting into the car. In fact, she had complained so often that Drake was seriously thinking that perhaps it might be time to trade it in.

'Looks like it.' Drake pointed to the row of vans.

The place looked run-down. The front gate was open and unmanned, so there was nothing to prevent them driving straight onto the forecourt of broken concrete. As they drew nearer they could make out the little logo at the end of the lettering. A faded green crescent within which was a square black cube that looked like a blurred version of the Ka'aba in Mecca. The same logo could be seen on the side of the vehicles parked to one side: vans and box trucks similar to the one Drake had seen on tape being towed away from Clapham Common station.

Drake pulled up to the loading bay and parked the car. There was a rumble of traffic in the distance. A train screeching across rails. The slow howl of rising jet engines from an airliner leaving nearby Heathrow. Somewhere in the midst of all that a bird could be heard singing. It sounded like a tiny miracle.

'How do you want to play this?' asked Crane.

'My plan was to improvise. How does that sound?'

'Works for me.'

Climbing up onto the concrete ramp running along the front of the building, Drake pushed his way through a curtain of rubber strips and shivered. He was inside a refrigerated storage area. A man in a white coat was dragging a pallet jack stacked with boxes across the floor.

'Where do I find the manager?'

The man stared at them blankly for a moment and then pointed wordlessly in the direction of a battered red door. It opened onto a narrow corridor that ran down one side of the building. The walls were scuffed and the air was fetid and stale. They walked along until they reached an open plan office with about six desks ranged about it. Only two of these were occupied, both by women who chattered into headsets while their fingers moved across keyboards. At the far end was another office that was closed off from the main area. A sign on the door read 'Manager'. Through the glass window a plump man with sweat stains on his shirt was shouting and gesticulating wildly at a slender young woman who stood facing his desk, looking down at the floor. Then, without hesitation, he struck her with the back of his hand, hitting her so hard she spun away and careened into the glass window. Crane muttered something and started forward. Drake put out his hand to stop her.

'Maybe give it a second before you break both his arms,' he said. Turning, he smiled to the woman sitting behind the nearest desk. 'Excuse me, is that . . .?'

The woman's flat stare did not waver. 'That is Mr Farooki.'

Drake stepped neatly through a gap in the counter and walked towards the office. Crane was right behind him.

'Sir? Excuse me, sir, you can't just go in . . .'

They both ignored her. Drake knocked and opened the door without waiting.

'Mr Farooki? I hope I'm not interrupting . . .'

The man was still yelling in what might have been Urdu. When he caught sight of Drake, he switched to heavily accented English.

'What the bloody hell do you think you are doing?'

The slender woman took advantage of the distraction to duck past Drake and out through the door. She ran down the office and disappeared. Crane went after her.

'I'm sorry,' Drake said. 'I have another appointment after this and I was just wondering . . .'

'What?' The man stared at Drake as if he were mad. 'Maderchod!'

'If this is a bad time . . .'

He was an ugly man, and anger made him uglier. There was a vein throbbing in the middle of his forehead. His face was painted with a patina of sweat. He waved a finger at Drake.

'Who are you, and what do you want from me?'

'I'm sorry. I was told we could do business.'

'Business? You want to buy meat?'

'Not meat,' said Drake.

'Not meat,' repeated the man. He took a moment, rocking his head from left to right. 'Who told you to come here?'

'A man named Khan. Maybe you know him?'

'Khan?' Mr Farooki frowned.

'Big guy. Has a tattoo here.' Drake put a hand to his neck.

Mr Farooki's eyes narrowed. 'You know this man?'

Drake shrugged. 'He said we could do business.'

'We are meat processing plant. We pack . . . meat. Wait here.' Mr Farooki pushed past Drake into the outer office. He went over to the second woman, who was still at her desk. The two of them conferred in low voices.

Crane followed the young woman from Mr Farooki's office down the corridor and out into the main area of the warehouse. She watched her crossing the floor of the front storage space, where two electric forklifts were busy shuttling pallets out to the loading bay. The pallets came from an interior area, closed off by plastic strip curtains. Crane watched the woman slip through these and out of sight. The temperature dropped on the other side. This section was refrigerated and the pallets, wrapped in plastic, stood waiting to be loaded. A small door led into the processing area, where cuts of meat were being sorted on long steel tables. There were about fifteen people in there, all of them men. They were dressed in bloodstained white overalls, hairnets and rubber boots. A good number of them wielded very sharp-looking knives. Crane felt their gaze following her as she moved down the production line. Signs overhead divided the areas into chicken left, lamb and beef right.

The noise grew worse the further in she went. Through another barrier, and suddenly there were high-pressure hoses delivering bursts of steam and water. A shrill electric whine filled the air. Carcasses hung from hooks in the ceiling. Men operated handheld power saws. The sound of steel ripping into bone set her teeth on edge. The floor was slick with moisture and drenched in red. Unidentifiable bits and pieces of flesh and cartilage slithered about under her boots. The woman leaned close to one man and spoke to him. He pointed down to the far end. Crane hurried after her, wondering where she was going. All she wanted to do was talk to her. She saw her duck behind a row of carcasses swinging round on an overhead rail. Here the men were covered from head to toe in white. Their faces were shielded by goggles and masks. They moved through the maze of dead animals like ghosts in a macabre forest. The floor was wet and the air was icy damp. Plastic trays filled with carcasses trundled along a conveyor belt. It was enough to put you off meat for life.

A big man pushed by her carrying a large carcass slung over his shoulder. Crane felt him brush against her. Something wet on her shoulder. When she put her hand to her jacket it came away red. She looked around for something to wipe it on but there wasn't time. Ahead of her the woman disappeared through a large set of steel doors.

Crane stepped through behind her and felt the blood in her veins cool instantly. It was difficult to see. There was white mist swirling over everything. She could make out long rows of metal shelves going deeper inside. Careful not to touch anything, she walked along the passage between these. At this temperature her skin would stick to the metal instantly.

'Hello!' she called out. There was no reply. The hum of the machinery and the grumble of chain links behind her was punctuated by the high-pitched whine of the saws.

The shelves were stacked with Styrofoam boxes. Inside some of them were large cuts of meat packed in thick plastic bags. It was almost impossible to see what they actually contained. She found herself staring at a bag full of frozen sheep's heads.

Something made her turn.

He was standing right behind her. A big man. Broad shoulders. Ninety-five kilos maybe. It wasn't his size so much as his expression, or lack of one. He stared dully at her and didn't say a word. There was no doubt in Crane's mind that he intended to harm her. She was already calculating her chances and trying to work out a strategy. In this confined space she was limited. She needed to get past him to reach the door. She started with a smile.

'Hi there, I seem to be lost. I was looking for someone.'

There was no response. Not a word, not a flicker of recognition.

That was when she saw the tattoo on his neck. It was exactly as Drake had described it. Khan.

48

'What do you mean, she left?'

Drake was having trouble understanding what the woman was talking about. He was pretty sure she spoke English perfectly, but right now she was pulling a theatrical number, shaking her head, shrugging, clasping her hands in supplication, imploring him to believe her.

'She wouldn't leave here without telling me.'

The woman held thumb and little finger to her ear. 'Phone call, sir. Most urgent.'

Drake still didn't believe that Crane would go off without him. On the other hand, being impulsive was not exactly out of character. He pulled his own phone out and tried calling her but only got her voicemail. Either she had it switched off or her battery was dead, or she was out of range of a signal. He might have done something more about it, except at that precise moment his phone began ringing. It was Kelly Marsh.

'You've had words with Pryce.'

'Well, he's getting ready to pounce. He's talking to the CPS about whether there's enough to issue a warrant for your arrest.'

'Pryce is nothing if not predictable.'

'Anyway, he believes we are dealing with a cell of radical jihadists.'

'Of course he does.'

'The van left outside the Tube station on Clapham Common. Green Gardens Halal Meat Packing. Possible link to Islamic State sympathisers. Decapitation being one of their hallmarks.'

Drake groaned. 'Never a man to let logic get in his way. Is that why you called?'

'Hold on, Milo wants a word.' There was a scratching noise and then Milo came on.

'Chief? I haven't had much time. They've been pushing us pretty hard.'

'I know, Milo, but I'd appreciate anything you can give me.'

'Well, I managed to trace it back to Castelnau.'

'What is that again?'

'Castelnau? It's a road in Barnes. Named after a French baron, I think. It's Occitan for New Castle.'

'Of course it is.' There would come a day when Milo wouldn't be able to surprise him any more, but Drake was pretty sure that day was still a long way off.

Marsh came back on the line abruptly. 'Sorry, but we don't have time for this now.'

'What's up, Kelly?'

'We've had a report of an abduction. It's a boy of nine.' Another long pause. 'It's at your home address, Cal, and you've been named as a possible suspect.'

'Wait a second. What child?' He knew the answer. It came to him even as he spoke.

'The boy's name is João. His mother is Maritza Pereira.'

Drake was already running for the door. He jumped into the Astra which, to his amazement, started first time. He swung it round and went straight through the gates, feeling the bottom of the car scraping on the ramp. He was trying to find Maritza's number on his phone while changing gears and turning a corner. The phone slipped from his hand to the floor. He seemed to have forgotten that he was no longer a member of the Metropolitan Police, that his vehicle was not fitted with flashing lights and a siren. The fact was that he no longer cared. Instead, he leaned on the horn and put his foot down. His rational side overruled. Putting his own life and that of others at risk, he cut through red lights and charged across intersections with reckless intent.

There were already a number of emergency vehicles stacked up around the entrance to the building by the time he arrived. Red and blue lights flashed, reflecting back off the surrounding walls. Drake pushed his way through the crowd until he found himself barred at the front door.

'I need to speak to the officer in charge,' he told the uniform blocking his way.

'And I just need you to stand back, sir.'

'No, you don't understand, I live here.'

'Let him through!'

One of the uniforms had recognised him. A burly Mancunian by the name of Collins. 'You're like a bad penny, Drake, always turning up when nobody wants you.'

'I live here. I need to know what happened.'

'Yeah, well, take a number and wait.'

'Just let me talk to the mother.'

'Know her, do you?'

'Yeah, and I think I know why they took the boy.'

'Hold on, I need to check.'

As he turned away to speak into his radio, Drake ducked past him and went through the open door. He had no choice. As soon as Collins mentioned his name he would no doubt he ordered to hold him, which would mean more delay. Behind him he heard shouting, but by then he was already on the stairs.

The door to Maritza's flat stood open. The boyfriend, whose name Drake could not remember, was standing outside with a couple of officers. Drake recognised one of them as DS Bishop.

'There he is!' The boyfriend launched himself at Drake. 'What have you done with him, you sick bastard!' he yelled.

The second officer stepped in front to block him. DS Bishop rolled his eyes.

'Should have known you'd be mixed up in this, Cal.'

'What's the story here?'

'Arrest him. Why don't you arrest him?' The boyfriend was still gesticulating wildly as he was pressed back across the hallway.

Bishop said, 'The boy went outside to play early this afternoon. He never came back.'

'That's all you've got?'

Bishop jerked a thumb at the boyfriend. 'That and his claim that it was you who took him.'

'You're jealous!' The boyfriend was yelling. 'You can't accept that she chose me over you.'

'Why would I abduct Joe to get her back?'

'Because you're a sick fuck!'

'Shane!' Maritza appeared in the doorway. Her eyes were red as they fell on Drake. 'Cal, what's going on?'

'You need to tell me everything.'

Bishop didn't like that. 'Hold on a minute. You're no longer on the force, remember? And besides, you're suspect number one.'

Drake ignored him and stepped towards Maritza. 'Did Joe mention anyone? Someone he was going to meet?'

'He mentioned you,' Shane thrust his finger at Drake.

'What do you mean, me?'

'That's what he said. He was going down to the playground to meet you.'

'That's it.' Bishop pulled a phone from his pocket. 'I'm calling DCI Pryce.' He pointed a finger at Drake. 'You stay right here.'

Drake addressed Maritza. 'Why did Joe think he was meeting me?'

'You must have told him.'

Drake shook his head.

'Your mate,' Shane said. 'Your friend spoke to Joe.'

'What friend?'

Maritza was shaking her head from side to side. 'Perdão, perdão meu amor,' she murmured to herself in Portugese.

'I'm going to get him back,' Drake said quietly.

Her eyes came up to meet his. 'You promise?'

'I promise.' Drake turned to Shane. 'This man you saw, can you describe him?'

'Come on, you sent him.'

'I didn't send anyone. Describe him.'

'Look, this has gone far enough,' said Bishop, taking Drake aside. 'I have orders to keep you here until Pryce gets here. He wants to take charge personally.'

Drake kept his voice low. 'If that happens we'll have no chance of finding the boy. If I'm right, then this person is after me. He's not interested in the boy. He wants me. We can't afford the delay.'

Bishop was shaking his head. 'What are you talking about? You don't even know who this person is.'

'That's the thing. I have a feeling he's linked to the Clapham Common head.'

'Oh shit!' Bishop wiped a hand over his mouth. He looked nervous, like a man who just realised he was holding a time bomb in his hands.

'Tell us what you can,' Drake said, turning back to Shane. 'What did he look like?'

Shane was wagging his head and backing away. 'No. I'm not happy talking to him.'

'For god's sake!' Maritza begged. 'Tell him what you know!'

'You can't trust him,' he insisted.

'We have no choice.'

He wasn't happy about it, but even he could see there was no point in protesting further. He kept his eyes on Drake.

'I saw him a couple of times,' he began. 'He was hanging around outside when I brought Joe home from school. He would smile and wave. I thought Joe knew him. He thought I did. One day he said that he was waiting for a friend and did we know you.'

'He mentioned me by name?'

'I think so. He knew you were a policeman. Joe knew immediately who he meant.'

'How often did this happen?'

'Like I said, a couple of times. I didn't pay him any attention.'

'Did you ever see him inside the building?'

Shane thought for a moment, then nodded. 'Yes, he was in the lift once. He went up with us. Always smiling.'

'Can you describe him?'

'Young, maybe in his twenties. Very dark eyes.'

'Did he have a hat? Like a baseball cap with a logo on it?'

'Yeah, I remember that. A name.'

'Fender?' asked Drake. Shane gave a shrug.

'You know this man?' Maritza was frantic. 'How do you know him? What does he want with João?'

'I don't think he means to harm Joe. I think he wants me.'

'By why?' Maritza began to cry. 'Why my boy?' Shane put his arm around her and turned to lead her back inside the flat.

'I have to go,' Drake said.

Bishop shook his head. 'You're not going anywhere.'

'This is not on you.' Drake leaned closer. 'I promise you, once Pryce starts stamping around with those oversized boots of his, we'll have no chance.'

Bishop looked Drake in the eye. He wasn't the only one who had little faith in Pryce's abilities.

'Go. Get out of here.'

49

Crane realised she was freezing to death. She couldn't at first remember where she was or how she had got there. It came back to her slowly. The man she knew as Khan. The tattoo on his neck. He hadn't said a word and she'd realised that her options were limited. She couldn't fight him in there. It was too small a space, and he was too big to begin with, maybe forty kilos more than her in body weight and most of that was muscle.

Still, when he put his hand out to grab her throat instinct kicked in. She knew she had to make it to the door and to do that she was going to have to go around him. Using the nearest shelf as leverage she jumped high and twisted round on him. It was a good move and took him by surprise. She managed to bend his wrist back and dropped her weight down on his elbow. That brought a cry of surprise and pain from the big man. It gave her a couple of seconds to get past him.

She almost made it.

He threw out a hand and managed to grab the back of her jacket. She felt herself being hauled up and swung round. She slammed into the wall and thumped her head, hard enough to stun her. Khan was massaging his wrist. Her knees buckled underneath her and she was trying to rise when he hit her. It was a wide, swinging backhand blow. His knuckles connected with her temple and everything went black.

When she opened her eyes she knew she was going to die. The temperature was dropping. The thermostat was on the outside. She'd seen it on the way in. Khan would have turned it down after locking her in. She managed to stand. Her hand rested for a moment on the frame of the shelving and the skin immediately stuck to the metal. When she ripped it away she felt a searing pain that made her cry out. Her breathing was slowing down. Soon she knew that her mind would start to slow too and then she would be finished. As the system began to shut down she would start to feel tired, then the desire to sleep would become irresistible. It would be a sleep from which she would never awake.

She reached the door and began hammering on it, being careful to pull the sleeves of her jacket down to protect her hands.

'Help! Open up!'

She could see the safety handle on the inside had been removed. All that remained was a square spindle. She looked around for some kind of tool to use, but there was nothing. She thumped on the door again. The steel was so heavy and thick she couldn't even feel her blows reverberating, meaning there wasn't much chance of them being heard outside.

She slid down to the floor and began to feel despair rising inside her. She pulled her telephone from her jacket and checked for a signal. There wasn't one. She'd expected as much. She thought about sending a message to Cal. Maybe her last. He would get it when they dragged her lifeless body out of here. That thought filled her with anger and she hauled herself up from the ground and began hammering wildly again. Deciding she needed something more solid to use she went back through the room, looking, until she settled on a shelf. She kicked it free of its mooring and dragged in over to begin swinging it at the door. At least now she was making some noise.

But there was no response. Either everyone had gone home or they simply couldn't hear her. Finally, exhausted, she slumped down to the floor again. What a stupid way to go, she thought to herself. She rested her head against the wall behind her and felt her eyes closing.

How long she was out she couldn't say.

There was a sound like a tomb being opened as the vacuum seal was broken and air rushed in. Crane felt herself being lifted up. Someone was leaning over her.

The woman was screaming at her to wake up.

'You have to wake up!'

'It's okay.' Crane fought the woman off, defending herself as she was slapped in the face. 'You can stop now.'

Eventually, the woman stood back. Crane allowed herself to

be helped up from the floor and led out of the freezer. The outer room was not warm but compared to inside the freezer it felt tropical. Crane collapsed to the floor again, her teeth now chattering uncontrollably.

'No, no,' the woman urged her. 'You can't stay here. They will be back.'

'Khan,' Crane gasped. 'Where is he?'

'He's gone. They've all gone to eat. But they will be back. You have to go. They can't find us here.'

'I understand.' Crane struggled to her feet. The woman tucked herself under her arm for support.

'You disappeared,' Crane said. 'And then you came back.'

'Yes, yes.'

They were staggering along, out through the plastic strips into the main hall. The place was dark and deserted, closed down for the night. Crane tried to focus on putting one foot in front of the other. She could feel the warmth coming back to her body as she moved.

They reached the loading bay and Crane once more collapsed to the floor. The air felt warm and she could hear the sounds of the city, trains shuttling by, planes taking off.

'You must go!' the slender woman urged.

Crane smiled as she reached for her phone. 'Don't worry, I'm going. Just give me a moment.'

50

Drake had no real idea where to begin. All he had to go on was the tiny fragment of information Milo had given him, that the earliest CCTV sighting he had picked up of the white van from Green Gardens was in the Hammersmith area. He also had an email from Wheeler that had just come in. It was the information from Interpol on Zelda's boy. He was swiping through the documents on his on his phone when it began to buzz. He put it on speaker.

'Where are you?' Kelly Marsh asked. When Drake told her, she gave an exasperated sigh. 'Pryce has put out an arrest warrant for you.'

'I'll have to live with that.'

'Seriously, when he heard you'd been named in a kidnapping case he even called off SO19 and the counter-terrorism raid.'

'Kelly, I asked you to look up whether Zelda might have had a son.'

'Yeah, sorry about that.'

'Wheeler found out about it.'

'How did you know?'

'He sent me an email. Seems there is a possible candidate.'

'Darius Danin. He's the right age. According to Interpol he's a real charmer. You think he could be Fender?'

'He's a strong contender. I think he's got Joe.'

'Joe? You mean Maritza's kid?'

'I think he took the boy because he wants me to come after him.'

'Which is exactly what you're going to do.'

'I don't have a choice, Kelly. I can't let him hurt Joe.'

'It doesn't make sense. If he's Zelda's son, why would he be holding on to her head, or leaving it on a train?'

'People do strange things.'

'Still doesn't make a lot of sense.'

But Drake thought he was beginning to see it. 'I think Darius has been on the track of his mother's killers for the last few years. Somehow he found out about her, about her death. I think he found her head.'

'How would he do that?'

'I think he traced it to the meat-packing plant.'

'You mean, he found out the people who killed her were connected to the place?'

'He might even have been working there.' Drake was thinking aloud. 'That would explain the van. Maybe he was a driver there. You could check that.'

'Sure, but let me ask you this. Why would the killers keep her head?'

That was something Drake couldn't explain. 'I'm not sure,' he said. 'But there has to be a reason.' Kelly had put her hand over the phone and Drake could hear her talking to someone else. When she came back she was excited.

'Okay, so the Boy Wonder has done it again. Milo has traced three parking fines for the same van all in the same area. Do you think that could be him?'

'It's the best we've got at this point.'

'I'll text you the details.'

'Give Milo a big kiss from me.'

'Not sure about that,' said Marsh. 'Maybe I could just thank him.'

'Much appreciated.'

'Listen, Cal. Pryce is going to have us jumping through hoops to try and pin this on you, so I can't promise we're going to be there for you.'

'I just need a little time.'

'That's what I'm trying to say. You don't have to go all Lone Ranger on us. As soon as you have something I can act on, you call me, all right?'

'Deal. And, Kelly, I'm a little worried about Ray. She might still be at the Green Gardens plant. Can you send a car over to take a look?'

'I'm on it.'

Drake clicked off the call and then tried Crane again. It went straight through to voicemail. He was more than a little worried about her, but right now he knew Joe had to be his first priority.

Turning off the A4, Drake drove slowly in the direction of the river and parked the car under the Hammersmith Bridge to proceed on foot. He wasn't sure why, but he had a feeling that he was on the right track. The whole homeless routine had been designed to throw them off the scent. Darius had had a place all along.

In the dwindling wisps of daylight Drake stared out over the river and saw nothing but shadows layered one over the other. He stared at it for so long they seemed to lose form, becoming a swirl of greys. The light played tricks, every tiny flicker igniting a beacon of hope that was extinguished almost instantly. There was nothing. Only mud, and water that had flowed here for thousands of years. Unchanged and changing at the same time.

He made his way carefully along the path. He'd already located the street where the van had been parked. It seemed plausible that Darius had used the company van to drive himself back and forth to Garratt Lane and didn't much care about fines. Maybe he didn't much care about anything.

There was a third and final possibility, which was the one Drake settled on now. Out of the corner of his eye his peripheral vision picked up something and he knew instantly what it was. He was moving already, before the thought had really formulated itself. Running west along the towpath he kept his eyes focused on the spot in the distance where he had seen the movement.

On this stretch of the river there were a number of vessels moored alongside one another, two or three deep. They were mostly converted steel-hulled barges, with a smattering of lighter craft dotted here and there. Drake climbed over the railing and stepped onto the highest vessel he could see. Edging along, he moved round the back of the housing. The wind blowing in off the river was cold and bitter. Two gulls tangled overhead, black scars against the sky. Their cawing blocking out other sounds. Drake peered around the side, looking towards the spot where he had seen movement. He ducked down and hopped over the gunwales to the adjacent vessel, a stately wooden sailing barge. The mast looked largely decorative now. Staying low, Drake slipped across to the other side of the deck.

The next houseboat along was a flat-bodied structure that lay several metres away on the grey mud flats. Climbing over the side, Drake lowered himself until his arms were fully extended before letting go and dropping. He landed awkwardly, letting out a cry as his right foot sank into a soft spot. When he had extricated himself, he was daubed in mud up to his knees but there seemed to be no serious damage done. His ankle hurt but it still worked. He moved with an awkward limp towards the round keel of the next ship. The steel hull was painted black. Rust scars showed here and there where water trickled down from the deck above. He listened, pressing his ear to the metal. He thought he could hear a faint shuffling from within. Then a short, distinctive sound, something that might have been a little boy crying out, only to be quickly silenced.

Drake made his way over towards where a rope ladder hung down. The wooden slats were worn but the heavy rope looked as though it would hold his weight. Scrambling onto it and up wasn't easy. Every tiny noise he made was amplified to his ears. He might just as well have announced his arrival with a brass fanfare.

He stood for a moment on the deck before moving towards the housing and the hatchway. He peered inside and listened for a long time. Then he stepped through and crept slowly down the steps. He was descending into darkness. It smelled of stale water and rusty metal. There was a creaking that might have come from somewhere down in the hull.

Off in the distance he could hear the faint sound of a church bell chiming. The short flight of stairs brought him down into a long living area. To the right of the stairs there was a seating arrangement, with a rounded couch and a long wooden table with a raised border. To the left was a kitchen area with a gas stove, a sink and draining board. Drake took a moment to examine this for signs of life. He saw plates drying on the rack. A loaf of sliced bread toppling from a plastic bag. A jar of peanut butter, a packet of Frosties on its side beside a pizza box, a cap with the word Fender on it next to the sink. Drake moved deeper into the vessel. He listened every time he placed a foot down. He wondered why he couldn't hear the child any longer, whether he had just imagined it.

Halfway along the deck was a bulkhead with another hatchway and a set of steps leading further down into the boat. Keeping to one side, he peered into the gloom and saw the edge of a wide bed. He still didn't know if he was in the right place, but his instincts told him he was. He was also aware that Darius might be armed and that he had nothing to defend himself with. Still, that didn't really help him at this point. He had no option but to press on. Stepping over the lintel, he descended into the darkened cabin.

The bed took up most of the space down there. A narrow doorway straight ahead led deeper into the longboat. Drake could see light coming in from a porthole further down. It was so quiet in there he could hear someone up on the towpath calling their dog.

Drake reached the doorway and stopped, realising suddenly that he had missed something. He had a sense that he was not alone. As he began to turn, he heard the snick of a spring-loaded knife flicking open.

51

Crane was slumped in the back of an Uber when the call from Wheeler came in. She stared at her phone dully for a moment before swiping the screen.

'I went through your profile. It makes for very interesting reading.'

Crane glanced through the side window. She was still shaking from her ordeal in the freezer. The car was taking her back to where her bike was parked in Southwark. Drake had picked her up there on the way out to Southall earlier that afternoon. Her mind was trying to focus on other things, but Wheeler was still talking.

'You conclude that we are dealing with a very disturbed person who has suffered a history of consistent abuse and may as a result be unable to form social bonds.'

'We're talking about someone who is capable of storing the severed head of another human being. In this case, even more disturbing is the fact that it might be the head of his own mother.'

'Well, exactly.' Wheeler gave a kind of half-laugh. 'I was a little taken aback by that bit. For the simple reason that it seems to be stretching the facts.'

'You don't believe someone would be capable of that?'

'Well, the discovery of the head would obviously prove that case. No, I was thinking more of the idea that the perpetrator might be the child of the victim.'

'I wasn't suggesting that the child killed and decapitated the mother, although there are plenty of examples of such cases, generally in war zones. Cambodia in the 1970s springs to mind, also Rwanda and the Congo. In this case, I was thinking of Sierra Leone.'

As she climbed out of the car, Crane was shivering. She had documented atrocities carried out by children forced to prove their loyalty to war lords. Brainwashed, drugged, coerced into committing sickening acts of mutilation – to kill their parents, to cut out their hearts. Crane had studied so many of such cases and each one left their mark on her. She reached the Triumph and bent over, lowering her head until the nausea passed.

'It's possible that Zelda's son actually tracked down his mother's killers. He found the head and took it when he decided to put his plan in action. If I'm right, then we are looking for a very disturbed individual. Someone who has been traumatised, possibly since childhood.'

'Good god!' muttered Wheeler. 'I've seen a few things in my time, but this is worse. Where are you?'

'Southwark.'

'I was hoping we could talk about this.'

'I'm a little pressed for time right at this moment.'

'Did you know that Cal asked Kelly to check into the possibility that Zelda had a child?'

'He might have mentioned something.'

'Well, it's the first I'd heard of it. Anyway, DS Marsh ran the name through immigration and came up with nothing. So I took it to Interpol and they just got back to me. It seems that they have come up with a match.' There was a pause, and Crane could hear him shuffling papers or reaching for his reading glasses. 'Darius Danin, born April 1992, which would make him twenty-seven years old right now.'

It was a strong enough match to fit with what Sonja had told Drake.

'Do they have any idea of his current whereabouts?'

'His fingerprints surfaced in Vienna five years ago during a battle between Turkish migrants and Far Right supporters. Apparently it was rather bloody. Danin's prints were found on a butcher's knife.'

'Nothing after that?'

'No, and our records show no sign of his entering the country.' Wheeler sounded tired. 'Of course, that doesn't mean anything. He could have come in with false documents, or been smuggled in. Both are possible.'

'So we have no evidence that he is in this country. That's what you are saying.'

'Not exactly. Forensics lifted a partial print from the Tube station that seems to match Danin's. We're waiting for confirmation from Interpol, but as usual they're taking their sweet time.'

'So it's possible that it's him?'

'It seems that way. I tried calling Cal but he's not answering. I've sent him the information by email.'

'I'm sure he'll get back to you when he has a moment. This is all extremely helpful.'

'Cal needs to know that this man is extremely dangerous.'

'I'm sure Cal can take care of himself.'

Crane clicked off the call and pulled on her helmet. She pressed the starter button and sped off, bending low as the machine catapulted forward. She focused on the road ahead of her, wondering if the jitteriness she felt was due to her ordeal over the last couple of hours. There were still questions in her mind, about Khan and why he had tried to kill her. Leaving her inside the freezer was a smart move. It would look like an accident; someone straying where they shouldn't be. Perhaps he had intended it only to scare her.

Her mind turned to the information Wheeler had just given her. It really wasn't clear to her that Darius Danin was the one responsible for Zelda's death. Khan and his boss, Hamid Balushi, somehow played a part. It seemed more plausible that her son tracked them down with the intention of avenging his mother. If so, why had he used Cal's shirt to try and put the blame on him? Did that mean he thought Cal was working with Balushi? That still left the question of whether Darius had hidden the head in the freezer, or if he had found it there.

The answers would have to wait. Right now, she had other things to deal with. Oddly, when she had thought she was freezing to death, she had suddenly understood what had happened to Howeida.

The gates to the Foulkes estate stood open. The same battered white Range Rover that she had first seen parked outside her father's house now stood in front of the stately building. Ray climbed off the bike and waved her arms about to shake the cold out of her limbs.

She walked up the front steps and rang the bell. When there was no answer she tried the door, only to find it locked. She walked around the side of the building, expecting to find Mrs Foulkes busy working in the garden, but she was nowhere to be seen.

Then Crane turned her attention to the barn. She could hear the dogs keening and yapping at one another. The big wooden doors stood open. As she came in, the excitement inside the dog cage increased. They were bouncing over one another and throwing themselves at the chain link fence in their eagerness to escape. She walked alongside the cage. Close up, the dogs were formidable. Once you looked beyond the cute fur you could see they were powerful animals, with strong jaws and very sharp teeth. The floor of the cage was strewn with straw to soften the concrete and take up some of the waste.

There was one dog in particular that drew her attention. A large black male, heavier than most of the others. His fur looked mangy and uncared for. There was something disturbing about the way he loped back and forth along the wall. The others gave him a wide berth. They scrabbled out of his way whenever he approached.

The way this dog moved reminded her of a caged leopard she had once seen as a child in a zoo in Tehran. Its movements were repetitive and gave the sense of a disturbed mind running back and forth over the same thought, unable to move on.

She stood for a time and watched it, ignoring the other dogs, who were clamouring around the fence close to her, perhaps thinking that feeding time had arrived.

As she looked, Crane caught a glimpse of something winking in the straw. It was hard to get a closer look. When she moved to one side or the other, the pack of dogs trailed behind, blocking her view. She saw the object move, dislodged by the paw of the black dog. The animal stopped for a moment, digging its snout into the straw, moving the thing around before its restlessness took over again and it jogged away along the wall.

Crane moved on, deeper into the gloom. She spent a while nosing around, looking in cupboards, behind wheelbarrows, farm machinery of one sort or another, a motorised lawnmower, some kind of hoe attachment. She wasn't sure what she was looking for. Something, anything that might confirm her suspicions.

Finally, she turned towards the largest object in that space, the covered Rolls-Royce. Lifting up the tarpaulin on one side, she peered into car. It looked clean. Slightly worn, as if age was slowly encroaching. The white leather upholstery was yellowed and had a wrinkled feel to it, like weathered skin. Pulling the tarp further back, she opened the door and slid into the driver's seat. She ran a hand over the smooth wooden texture of the steering wheel and panelling. It was a nice car, but she imagined driving it would be like trying to control an elephant.

Out of idle curiosity, Crane leaned over and opened the glove compartment. There was nothing in there but the usual insurance documents, maintenance records and a lapsed Royal Automobile Club membership card. She snapped the little panel shut and sat for a moment. It felt almost as though she was hidden from the world, here inside this huge old car, half buried under the heavy tarp. She glanced up at the mirror and then a thought occurred. Climbing out, she closed the door carefully and went round to the rear. The boot was not locked. She popped it open. There was nothing much in there. A large green oilskin lay to one side. She reached down and pulled it. Underneath there was a bag. A tan-coloured leather holdall. Crane zipped it open to find it contained clothes. Women's clothes. A couple of blouses, a dress and a pair of slacks, underwear. There was even a pair of high-heeled shoes. They all looked expensive. Designer brands. They were also new.

In a side pocket she found a make-up bag and a zipped jewellery case; inside were several sets of earrings, expensive ones. A pair of silver ones caught her eye. They were large and looked like they might be antique Bedouin silver. She zipped the case up and put it back where she had found it.

Closing the boot, Crane started back across the barn to the dog cage. In the corner nearby was a large blue plastic barrel filled with dog food. Using the big scoop buried in the top, she proceeded to spread a line of dog food across the far side of the barn. Behind her she could hear the excitement in the cage. When she had put enough out she went over to the cage. By now the dogs were hopping up and down frantically. Hesitating only for a second, she pulled back the latch and stepped out of the way.

The dogs poured out, leaping over one another in their eagerness to get to the food. All but one. The big black husky refused to move. He remained back there against the wall. As she stepped through the gate, the dog bared its teeth at her. His eyes were small, dark discs. His whole body was twitching; his paws scratched at the ground.

Crane didn't have a weapon. She was still holding the plastic scoop. It wouldn't really be much help, but it was all she had. She held it out ahead of her, as she edged around the side of the cage trying to keep as much distance as possible between her and the animal. The dog was clearly disturbed. Over on the far side of the barn the other dogs were busy feasting on the food that was spread out on the floor. Some of them had rushed out into the open air, basking in the sunlight, hopping and jumping. Their barking would soon bring attention and Crane knew she didn't have long.

She scraped the straw aside with her boot, trying to find the spot where she had seen the glint of metal. The dog bounded forward two big steps and then stopped. Crane stared it down. There was more growling. It pawed the ground, snarled, bared its teeth. Crane continued her search. As the straw moved aside her eye was caught by a number of white fragments. They might have been wood chips, but they were sharp, as if something had been shattered. She went down on one knee and swept a few of these up in her hand, slipping them into her pocket. As she did so, the dog went for her. She heard it, and saw it out of the corner of her eye. She straightened up again, stepping back and bringing up her arm, the hand holding the scoop. The dog went for it, digging its teeth into the hard plastic. She held on, knowing that she needed to keep its jaws occupied. She dragged it left and right. The dog held on. It felt as if her shoulder was being torn out of its socket. She pushed and then swung, using the dog's own momentum to propel it and send it skidding across the hard floor into the wall. It howled and retreated.

That was when she saw the object she had been looking for. It was right in front of her. She picked it up and headed for the gate. She managed to get through and slam it shut, pulling back, but not before the dog's teeth sank into her finger. She yelled out in pain as she stumbled back. Two of her fingers were bleeding but she was grateful not to have lost them. Pressing her hand under her arm to try and stem the flow, she headed for the door. The dogs had lost interest in her. Either they were eating or they were out chasing each other around the grounds.

Crane leaned against the door of the barn and looked at the object glittering in the palm of her hand. It had been damaged, twisted and bent by powerful jaws, but it was recognisable all the same. It was an earring, made of old silver. Similar, in fact, to the pair she had seen in Howeida's bag. She could still make out the whorls that had been inscribed in the metal. Crane felt her blood run cold. Then she heard the change in the noise the dogs were making. They were growing more agitated. She turned to look at them and saw Marco Foulkes coming towards her. In his hands was a shotgun and it was pointed at Crane.

52

Darius had been crouched out of sight inside a cupboard in the corner of the room. He had waited for Drake to go by before coming out. Drake kicked himself for not having seen him, but at the same time he was impressed that the other man had managed to stay so still.

The knife in his hand was a short steel blade. He made no attempt to move. Drake turned until he had his back to the doorway.

'You found me.'

'You left a trail for me.'

It was the first real opportunity Drake had to study him. He was unkempt and looked as though he hadn't washed for weeks. His sweatshirt and jeans were grubby. He gave off a bad smell. His face was long and narrow, covered by a light dusting of soft downy hair that wouldn't grow into a beard.

'You're Darius.'

'Correct.' His accent was softened by years of living in this country. 'You're Cal Drake.'

'That's right. I'm here for Joe. Where is he?'

'He's safe.' Darius gestured at the corridor. 'Look for yourself.'

Drake turned his head cautiously. Through the doorway he could see two sets of bunkbeds built into the woodwork. Joe was lying on the nearest one. He was on his side and appeared to be sleeping.

'What did you do to him?'

'He's fine. Don't worry. He was making noise so I give him hot chocolate with a sleeping tablet. He'll be fine for the next few hours.' Darius smiled. 'When he wakes up this will all be a dream.'

Drake reached over to feel the boy's pulse. It felt regular.

'You don't need him. It's me you want.'

'True.' Darius felt the tip of the knife with his thumb. 'You are the one I want.'

'Well, here I am.' Drake moved a step closer. Darius pulled back. Drake held up his hands. 'Easy. Do you mind if I sit?' He gestured at the bed. The young man looked at him for a moment and then nodded his consent. Drake perched himself on the edge.

'You're Zelda's son.'

'Esma. Her name was Esma.'

'A name is just a name.' Drake shrugged. 'She chose the name Zelda.'

'When you kill someone you should remember their names, no?'

'I didn't kill her.'

'You might as well have. If it wasn't for you, she would still be alive.'

Drake rested a hand on his knee, where he could see his wristwatch. 'Look, why don't we take the boy back to his mother and then you and I can talk?'

Darius laughed at that. 'You think I'm stupid? Stupid Darius. I don't believe you.'

'Then what, what do you want?'

'I want you to confess. She was trying to help you. Why did you have her killed?'

'I told you already. I didn't do it. I was her friend. I cared about her.'

'You fucked her.'

'No.' Drake shook his head. Darius brandished the knife.

'Liar! Everyone fucked her.'

'That's not true. She wasn't like that.' Drake realised that he was dealing with a very disturbed man. 'How did you find her?'

'I saw her.' Darius grinned. 'Just like that, I saw her. It was like a vision, you know.'

'Where was this?'

'I was working in a car wash.' Darius frowned at the memory. 'Such places. They are full of lost souls. Men and women who have no papers, no rights. They are slaves. All day you wash cars. Your eyes sting from the soap. In the cold your hands are so painful.' He closed his eyes at the memory.

'Where was this?'

'The car wash? East London. Dagenham.' Darius busied himself locating cigarettes and lighter in his jeans. He managed to light one. Drake remembered a car wash belonging to Goran. Not so much of a coincidence, then. Mother and child both happened to be working for the same man.

'You saw her at the car wash?'

Darius smoked his cigarette in silence for a moment. 'It was like a miracle. The cars that came there were ordinary people. They want to save money because we are cheap. Slave labour is always cheap. But the boss also sent people round. One day a fine big car comes by. A big Merc, with a driver in front and one passenger, a woman.'

The memory seemed to give him pause for thought.

'I never knew her as my mother, you understand. I was brought up by my aunt, but I saw pictures of her. She sent money and from time to time a photograph would arrive. They always made her look glamorous.' He reached into his back pocket for a creased and torn snapshot. He handed it over. Drake looked at the picture. The colours were faded, but it showed Zelda smiling. She was wearing a denim jacket and waving. It looked like a market somewhere. A sunny day. Happier times.

'That was my mother. That was who I had come to find.'

'That's why you came to London, to find her?'

'I had no choice. I had to find her. She was the only thing I had in the world.' Darius dug the point of the knife into the wooden panel next to his head and began grinding away at it. 'Nobody wanted me. When I was a child. Ashamed. All of them. They wanted me to disappear. When I was fourteen I was sent to a home in Banja Luka. Do you know what that's like, to live in a home?'

'Actually,' said Drake, 'yes I do.'

Darius sniffed, studying Drake for a moment, unable to make up his mind.

'In those days, there were many orphans.'

'After the war.'

'After war,' nodded Darius. 'I had to get out. I didn't care what it cost. I just wanted to get out.'

Drake recalled Zelda telling a similar story. She too had fled from home at a young age. Everybody running away.

'I lived on the streets. I learned to fight for what I wanted. I was in Belgrade, then Vienna, then Germany. You know Essen?'

Drake shook his head.

'It doesn't matter. One thing led to another. But all the time I am coming here. That's all I have in my head. London, London.'

'So, you got here finally.'

'I couldn't believe it. All my life I've heard London this, London that. Now I am here. But London is big. Very big.' Darius stubbed his cigarette out on the panelling and lit another. His fingers were grubby and his nails long and stained.

'I don't know if it was really London or some kind of fantasy world. A nowhere land. An in-between place. The rich in their fine clothes and big cars. I saw sports cars and beautiful houses. I also saw misery. People living in the streets like animals.'

'You mean like the kid who was in my sleeping bag?'

Darius straightened up slowly. 'That was a mistake. I only wanted to scare him, but he screamed. I was scared. I didn't mean to kill him.'

'He was just a kid, he had nothing to do with any of this.'

'You don't understand, what happens to you when you're out there, when you have nothing.' Darius was growing flustered, trying to find words that weren't coming, his voice cracking with emotion. 'I was stuck. I couldn't move, up or down. It wasn't heaven and it wasn't hell. It was nowhere. I was afraid. I was numb. I couldn't breathe.'

'Limbo, it's called.' Drake had the sense that what Darius really wanted was for Drake to hear his story. This was about his claim on his mother, a woman he didn't even know.

'You saw her in the car and you knew it was her?'

Darius thumped a hand to his chest. 'I could feel it. Here, inside me. I knew it was her, but I couldn't say anything.'

'So, what did you do?'

'I asked around. I found out that it belonged to an important man. This man owned a piece of everything, including the car wash.'

'Goran Malevich.'

Darius nodded. 'I decided to go and work for him. It was written.'

'Written?'

'God, fate, call it what you will.'

Darius grinned. It wasn't a good look for him.

'I had contacts. People who could recommend me. I made some calls.'

'Did you tell anyone who you were?'

'No, of course not.' He was shaking his head. 'These people are animals. You don't tell them anything.'

'But you did speak to her?'

Darius nodded. 'I went to the club. I paid for her.' He studied the end of his cigarette. 'She didn't know who I was. She thought I was just some young man looking for fun.'

'What happened when you told her?'

'At first she was angry. She said I should have stayed home and never tried to find her. I told her I hate home, that now London is my home. Then she told me she was going away.'

'But you followed her, to Brighton?'

'Yes, of course. I wanted to know she was all right.'

Drake glanced down at his watch. He wondered how much time they had.

'How did she react when she saw you?'

'She was afraid. She told me to stay away from her, that it was dangerous. But then she changed her mind. She was happy to see me.' Darius paused. 'It was the happiest day of my life, I think, even though she was very sad.'

'Why was she sad?'

'She was lonely. She told me about you, how you had promised to save her, to help her out of the mess she was in.' Darius let the words sink in. 'You lied to her.'

'I didn't lie. I was trying to help her.'

'No.' He shook his head. 'You used her, like everyone used her.'

'She was a witness in an important case.'

Darius laughed again. 'You think you can catch a man like Goran with the law? You're crazy. She should never have listened to you. She would still be alive.'

Drake didn't answer at first. What could he say, after all? He knew, of course, that there was a chance she might have made it if she hadn't listened to him.

'She wanted to see Goran brought to justice,' he said at last.

'No. She wanted to believe you.' The smile returned. 'She was like me, caught in the middle, unable to move.'

'I've always wondered how they found her,' said Drake. 'Now I wonder if they followed you down there.'

The phone in Drake's pocket began to vibrate. He held up a hand to silence Darius. It was Pryce.

53

Crane opened her eyes. Night had fallen and the dogs were settling down for the night. She could smell them, nosing around the cage, pushing their snouts through, trying to reach her.

She was seated on the ground. Her hands and feet were tied. One thing about country folk is they certainly know how to tie a knot. Thick blue nylon twine that dug into her skin. Her hands were bound to one of the corner posts of the cage. She wondered what time it was. She had heard nothing for hours and after struggling to get herself free she had decided to do the sensible thing and close her eyes.

She need to think.

She knew now that Howeida was dead. At least, she was pretty sure of it. The white bone fragments she had collected from the floor of the cage could have come from a sheep, but she was willing to bet that tests would reveal them to be human. The dogs could eat their way through anything. She had seen evidence of that. They crunched up the bones with their teeth and powerful jaws. They sucked the marrow out. Not pleasant. Though it was still unclear exactly how Howeida had lost her life.

The only evidence she had was, she hoped, still in her pocket. The earring that had been twisted and bitten but then miraculously spat out as unpalatable by the dogs. A silver earring. Along with the bag and personal effects in the boot of the Rolls. That should be enough to prove that Howeida had been here and never left.

She could hear footsteps coming across the open ground from the house. A shadow appeared in the doorway of the barn, silhouetted against the outside light that came on above the door when a sensor was tripped.

Marco Foulkes was wearing an oilskin jacket and wellington

boots. He drew closer and squatted down in front of her, shaking his head in dismay.

'Extraordinary, the degree to which you are incapable of following simple instructions.'

'I've never been good at taking orders.'

'Naturally.' He smiled, pushing his hair back. 'Part of your charm. Only now you present a problem that needs to be resolved.'

'How did it happen?'

Foulkes fell silent. He looked down at the floor. 'I don't know if you'll believe me, but it was an accident.'

'You're right. I don't.'

'As you wish, it makes no difference. But it is the truth.'

She struggled upright and held up her hands. 'No chance you could undo these while we talk?'

Foulkes shook his head. 'Sorry. That would be unwise.' He breathed deeply. 'I find myself in a difficult situation. I never intended to harm her, just as I have no wish to harm you.'

'Right, you just keep finding yourself in these situations.'

That brought a slight smile to his face. 'Trust you to be able to read into this your own little interpretation.'

'Fine. Convince me otherwise.'

'You must believe me when I tell you that I was very fond of her. I wanted us to be together. Sometimes wishing for something is not enough.'

'She came up here with you, to stay with your mother?'

Foulkes nodded. 'Mother was a little reluctant at first, but she took to her. Howeida is a very easy person to like.'

'Was.'

'Sorry?'

'You said she is.' Crane shook her head. 'Past tense. Was.'

Foulkes did not respond. When he spoke again his voice was deeper and slower than before.

'I thought we understood each other. I thought we were on the same wavelength. But then she kept asking all these questions.'

'What kind of questions?'

'About me, about my work, about stuff that really shouldn't concern her.'

'Like what? Personal stuff?'

'No. About my business affairs, my investments.'

'You mean the things that Barnaby Nathanson did for you?'

Foulkes looked genuinely surprised. 'You know about that?'

'I know that he was running a complex series of offshore firms and that you helped to drum up business for him. You split the profits.'

'Well, what of it? It's all above board.'

'Perhaps. We'll find out when the investigation runs its course.'

'What investigation?'

'You haven't heard?' Crane watched Foulkes' eyes. She wondered if she could tell if he was lying. 'He's dead.'

'Dead? How?'

'Someone killed him in his flat in Pimlico. The police will be going through his finances as we speak, looking for a motive.'

Foulkes turned away from her, resting a hand on the door-frame. Maybe he was good at faking it, but he looked genuinely shocked by the news. Crane decided to press on.

'You were trying to get Howeida to invest some of her family's money.'

Foulkes waved a dismissive hand. 'They have so much, they have no idea what to do with it.'

'So you thought you would help them with that, but Howeida wasn't too thrilled. She didn't like it when she found out you had been stringing her along. Not so much the glamourous author as the grubby-handed letch.'

'Please.' Marco Foulkes gave her a disgusted look. 'I don't know why I ever thought you would be of use. You're so full of resentment.'

'You said it was an accident. Tell me what happened.'

He was silent for a moment, looking down at his hands.

'I tried to make amends. I told her the money didn't matter. That's why I brought her up here. I thought if we could just spend some time together, but she wouldn't let it go. She kept asking why, why would a man in my position care so much about money? I had all of this. She had some romantic notion about writers.'

'Poor her. What happened then?'

'Well . . .' Foulkes sighed. 'I suppose I lost my temper.'

'You hit her?'

'She'd been holding out on me. I mean, we hadn't actually slept together. I accused her of using all of this money talk to avoid sex.'

'Maybe she wasn't comfortable with the idea.' Crane's mind inevitably went back to Jindy. Men with fragile egos. What could you do? 'But you couldn't deal with that.'

'I got carried away. I mean, she'd been leading me on for months and nothing.' He looked into the distance. 'Afterwards, I was ashamed. She was furious, said she wanted to leave. It was the middle of the night. I was afraid she was going to wake my mother and I knew everything was going to come out. I thought about the humiliation of it all. I . . . I just lost it.'

'That's when you killed her.'

'Like I said, it was an accident. I was just trying to . . . restrain her. To stop her.' Foulkes fell silent. 'It just happened. I panicked and knew I had to finish it.'

'You strangled her?'

Foulkes was talking slowly, his eyes fixed on a spot on the ground ahead of him. 'Suddenly it came to me. This force inside me. I was no longer alone, I was an instrument of fate.' There was an odd look on his face now. 'This was bigger than me.'

Crane had to swallow her disgust. She knew it was important to keep him talking.

'What did you do when you realised she was dead?'

'At first I thought she was just unconscious. I left her there to sleep it off. My mother had heard the commotion and came running over. I led her back across to the house. She was distraught. When I came back I realised that Howie was cold.'

Crane swore under her breath. 'Let me out, now, Marco. This can end here.'

It took a while for Foulkes to return to the present. He looked round at her and slowly shook his head from side to side.

'You don't understand. The scandal. Something like this would be the ruin of us. Not just me, but all of us. The family name.'

'Nobody gives a fuck about the family name, Marco. You have to do the right thing.'

He straightened up. 'No. I can't. My mother . . . It would kill her.'

Outside, through the trees, Crane could make out a full moon rising in a clear sky. Foulkes turned towards her with a start.

'I don't want to do this. You understand that, don't you? I've always been fond of you, Ray.' Foulkes was watching her with a look that was a cross between desire and irritation. She wasn't sure which one she preferred to deal with. 'Why do you care anyway? I mean, we can just agree a price, leave it at that.'

'That how you've dealt with everything in life, is it, Marco?'

'Principles come and go. It makes no difference. The world moves on. I never understood that about you. You were set up. A respected forensic psychologist with a good practice. Why branch out into something as sordid as private investigation?'

It was a question Crane had asked herself but there really wasn't a clear answer.

'I don't know how to explain it. At the end of the day it has something to do with the urgency of our age. It's about caring. About wanting to hold on to something good. To make a difference.'

'You know how ridiculous that sounds?' The half-smile was a glimpse of the old Marco Foulkes. The rakish man about town.

'To you? Yes, I suppose it does sound pretty pointless.' Crane's eye was drawn to the black dog at the back of the cage. It was gnawing on something and glaring at her. 'Where did you bury what was left of her? Out there under the new greenhouse, I'm guessing.'

'Maybe you're not so bad at this as you appear. Too late, I'm afraid.' Foulkes looked at his watch. 'Much as I've enjoyed this, I'm afraid I have to leave.'

'Ah, yes, your American tour. Your chance to get out of here and lie low until things sort themselves out.'

'Call it what you will,' said Foulkes. 'But I really don't have time for this.' He reached for the shotgun, which was leaning against the door. 'For what it's worth, I am truly sorry.'

'You're going to feed me to the dogs too?'

'You were right about the greenhouse. Whatever's left will be laid underneath the foundations. You arrived just in time. Not a bad place to wind up.'

He leaned down to release her from the cage. Her hands and feet were still tied.

'You need to stand up.'

Crane got to her feet. She tried to assess her chances of overcoming Foulkes and decided they were low, but better than nothing. As she stood, she appeared to lose her balance and stumbled into him. He stepped back and gave her a shove, sending her sprawling to the floor again.

'No tricks, please. I know how strong you are. You were always the tomboy. I thought you'd turn out to be a dyke.'

'Dream on.' Crane had drawn her knees in, ready to kick his feet out from under him, when a voice spoke from behind Foulkes.

'I think that's enough for now, Mr Foulkes.'

The man standing in the doorway was wearing an expensive leather jacket and holding an automatic pistol.

'You?' said Foulkes in disbelief.

The man held up an identity wallet. 'Lieutenant Colonel Almanara. I have half a dozen Interpol agents with me, so you need to consider your position.'

'What the fuck does that mean? Interpol?' Foulkes was incredulous, even as two more men entered the barn and proceeded to disarm and handcuff him. 'You're her uncle!'

Abdelhadi Almanara knelt beside Crane and cut her free.

'Thank you,' said Crane. 'I think you just saved my life.'

'My pleasure,' Almanara said, helping her to sit up.

'Aren't you supposed to be playing nice with your horses?'

'Apologies. I couldn't let you know. But thanks to you we now have enough on tape to be able to get a lot more on him.'

'So you're not Howeida's uncle?'

'I am, or was, but I was also her boss. She was working for me as an agent of the Abu Dhabi Police Special Unit. We've been investigating allegations of fraud connected to Mr Nathanson and Mr Foulkes for two years now. Howeida herself volunteered.'

'She was very brave.'

'Yes, she was. Unfortunately I was too late to save her.'

'What happens now?'

'He will stand trial for the murder of a law enforcement officer and Howeida . . .' Almanara sighed. 'I will make sure she gets a medal for her service.'

'Well, that's something at least.'

Almanara looked up sharply. 'Believe me, I do not take the sacrifice she made lightly. The commendation is more for her family. It means something to them, to know their daughter's work was appreciated.'

'I'm sure.' Crane was rubbing her wrists.

'How did you know what had happened to her?'

'I didn't, until I found this.' She reached into her pocket for the mangled earring. 'They'll crush bones but they draw the line at jewellery.' She held it out. Almanara took it gently, as if he were holding something very delicate and valuable.

54

'I need to take this,' said Drake. Darius shook his head. 'If I don't, they'll get suspicious.'

'Put it on speaker.'

Drake did so, placing the phone on the bed beside him.

'Where are you, Cal?'

'I need more time, Vernon.'

'We're out of time, Cal. You have to bring yourself in. Just come in and we can sort it all out.' There was a pause. Drake imagined he could hear others in the room. He wondered who else was there. Marsh? Wheeler? Possibly a whole team of negotiators.

'Is he there with you?'

'Yes.'

'Can I speak to him?'

Drake saw Darius shake his head.

'That's not going to work,' said Drake. There was a long pause.

'How's the boy?'

'He's fine.'

'You've got him, then?'

'He's here,' Drake said. 'I need more time.'

'Listen to me, Cal. The time for games is over. I don't know what you're playing at, but either you come in now or I'm going to bury you so deep you won't see the light of day. Make no mistake, I'm going to crucify you.'

'Let me get back to you in five minutes.' Drake swiped the screen before Pryce had a chance to answer. He looked at Darius. 'That won't buy us much time.'

'We don't need much time,' said the young man, getting to his feet.

'What is it you want from me?'

'Me? Nothing. I have everything right here.' He walked over

and began to climb the stairs. With a glance back in the direction of the doorway and the sleeping Joe, Drake decided to follow.

Upstairs in the main living area, Darius stood in the kitchen. He poured himself a glass of water and drank it in long slow gulps, wiping his mouth with the back of his hand. He stared out through the window, smiling, unseeing.

'We can still end this, Darius. You didn't kill her. Help us find who did and they'll be more lenient.'

'I don't know who killed her.'

'Tell me what you do know,' Drake said quietly. 'Tell me what happened that day.'

Darius was playing with another cigarette, flicking the lighter, unable to bring himself to light it. After what felt like an age, he began to talk.

'She was staying in this house on a hill, overlooking the sea. A beautiful place. A house with a pink door and flowers on the window. The kind of place she had always dreamed of. That's what she said. We went for a walk along the seafront. It was a sunny day. She looked beautiful. It was perfect.'

Drake remembered the day he had visited Zelda. The little house with the room at the top of the stairs that had a view down a hill to the sea.

'What happened then?'

'She didn't want me to stay. She said I had to wait until things were clear, until it was safe.'

'What did you do?'

'I said goodbye to her. I didn't want to. I said I would go back to London, but I promised I would be back. Then I watched her walk into the house. That was the last time I saw her.'

'They were waiting for her,' said Drake.

Darius nodded. 'I didn't leave right away. I waited. I felt, I don't know what. I felt I wanted this day to last forever. For as long as I can remember, I dreamed of finding my mother. Now finally it had come true. We were going to have a great life together. I wanted to remember that.'

'So you waited outside and you saw the men who killed her.'

Darius slumped back against the counter. His eyes were fixed, staring at the floor. His voice sounded dead. 'It was dark by then. I saw a man come out. I didn't know who he was. I realised later that he was the one who killed her.'

'Can you describe him?'

'Nothing special. He was like the men I had known as a child. Fighters. Killers. A small man with silver hair. One of Goran's men.'

Drake stiffened. 'You'd seen him before?'

'Yes.'

'How did he know about you and Zelda?'

'I don't know. I . . . Maybe I told someone, one of the others at the car wash.' Darius's voice was breaking again.

'What happened then?' Drake said, his voice low, almost unrecognisable.

'He stood outside in the street and soon a van came with more men. They went into the house. They were in there a long time. When they came out they were carrying her with them. At first, I didn't know what it was. It was wrapped in plastic. You couldn't see.'

'You followed them.'

'I knew she was dead. I had borrowed a small motorcycle from a friend. I followed them back down to the sea. They drove a long way. I followed with my lights off.' His eyes lifted to meet Drake's. 'I watched them throw her into the sea.'

'Then what?'

'I've seen death before. I grew up around it. I knew what I had to do. I had to find them and make them pay.'

'So you followed them back to London?'

'I followed them to a place in Southall, a meat factory.'

'You got a job there.'

Darius lifted his chin. 'That was later. That was when I found her.'

'You mean, you found her head?'

'They had kept it. I don't know why.'

Drake had an idea. 'They wanted it because they were planning to use it against Goran.'

'I don't understand. He was one of Goran's men.'

'There's a group of them,' said Drake. 'They had decided to take him out, to take control of his operation. In the end they got rid of him.'

'Then why keep her?'

'Who knows? Maybe it was forgotten, maybe it was a war trophy.'

Darius was quiet for a long time, then he looked up. 'None of this would have happened if not for you.' He pointed a finger. 'You're the reason she was there. The reason she betrayed Goran. The reason she was killed.'

'I told you, she wanted out. I was helping her.'

Darius gave a cynical laugh. 'Yeah, right. Tell yourself that. Maybe it helps you to sleep.'

His voice had become slow, leaden, heavy with gravity. Drake realised he was looking at a man who had driven over the cliff edge of his own sanity. He had stopped making sense of the world a long time ago.

'If you know who killed her, then help me bring him to justice.'

'Justice?' Darius laughed. His eyes flashed. Drake saw his hand tighten around the knife. 'What is justice? I don't care about them. They are animals. The world is full of people like that. But you? She trusted you, remember? You betrayed her. Loyalty, now that is something we can all agree on. It's the worst kind of betrayal.'

'She wanted to help.' Drake started to explain again. Darius wasn't having it. He grabbed Drake by the collar and pressed the knife to his throat.

'What do you care about in this world? That little boy? What if I was to cut his throat in front of you? Would you know how I feel then?'

'Look, Darius. I know how you feel, but hurting that boy is not going to help.'

'You care about the boy? Why? He's not your son.'

'He's done nothing wrong. He's just a boy, like you were, like I was. You want to hurt me, I understand, but let him go.'

'I know what this world is like.' Darius broke off to wipe the tears from his face. 'You're right, he's like me. All the pain, all the suffering. I wish someone had put me out of my misery all those years ago.'

'You don't mean that.'

'Yes,' hissed Darius. 'It's better for him to die now.'

Drake didn't like the way his tone had changed. In the distance he caught the chop of helicopter rotors chugging up the river. An executive heading home at the end of a long day, or something else?

'Listen? You hear that? They're tracking my phone. We don't have much time.'

'We don't need time.' Darius thrust Drake back and reached under the kitchen sink for a small rucksack. With his eyes on Drake he unzipped it and reached inside to withdraw a hand grenade. With a gesture he threw the bag at Drake, who had to catch it. He looked inside. There were about a dozen of them, enough to blow this whole ship to pieces and all of them with it. Darius held up the grenade.

'You were in the army. You know how these things work.' He gestured. 'Go and fetch the boy. Leave the bag there.'

Drake turned to go back down the stairs to the lower deck and then stopped.

'You know, you don't have to do this. Together we could go after the man who killed her.'

Darius sniffed, wiped the back of his hand across his eyes again. 'That will never happen and you know it. They have protection. They always have protection.'

'You don't know that.'

'I know it.' Darius studied the grenade in his hand. 'I've been living with this pain for years, for as long as I can remember. I just want it to be over.'

Drake reached the hatchway and stepped through. He turned around to look back at Darius. In the glass of the window behind him he caught the glimpse of a narrow pencil beam of red light. A laser sight. Darius took his hesitation as delay.

'Get a move on!' He raised the grenade high.

'No, don't do that!' Drake yelled, but he was too late.

Three shots shattered the glass, sending Darius flying forwards. Staying low, Drake crawled over to him. He was still alive. The front of his sweatshirt was soaked in blood. He was gasping for air and not getting any. His lungs were punctured.

'Hold on,' Drake said, pressing a hand on the largest of the wounds.

There was blood on his face. His lips moved. Drake leaned in close but no words came. Then he felt the life go out of him and it was all over.

55

The Moonstone was quiet at that hour. It was mid-morning when Drake pushed open the stained-glass door and surveyed the calm interior. He didn't see Crane at first. She was sitting over in the far corner, concealed behind the high wooden panels of a booth with her sunglasses on.

'Mind if I join you?' he asked, slipping round the other side of the table.

'How are you doing?' she asked.

'I've had better days. You look as though you haven't slept.'

'I haven't.' Crane slipped off the sunglasses. 'It was a long night. By the time the police got out there and everything was processed. Yeah,' she sighed. 'A long night.'

'So Howeida was an undercover agent?'

'Who knew? Apparently they had been trying to make a case against Novo Elysium for years. This was Abdelhadi's pet project.'

'And he used his cousin as bait?'

'I'm guessing he didn't have much of a choice. They're part of a ruling class. Everyone's related. The fact that she was his cousin is almost coincidental. The point is she believed in what she was doing.'

'So the meeting with Foulkes was planned?'

'They went to a number of readings before she caught his attention.' Crane gave a deep sigh. 'She was determined. I'll give her that.'

'And she paid the price.'

'The way he tells it, he was torn between hanging back or moving in. He didn't want to blow it for her.'

Drake was looking around for someone behind the bar. 'So Foulkes really thought we would fall for the idea that she had been abducted and whisked back home?'

'He took us for a soft touch.'

'That'll teach him. She was already dead by then. He knew that sooner or later someone would come looking for her. But why not go straight to the police?'

'I don't think he wanted to risk it. It was too soon,' said Crane. 'He was buying time. The whole story about them not being interested. In the end he would have gone to them, I suppose, when she was safely under the concrete floor of the greenhouse and he could tout us as an example of how concerned he was.'

Finally, Drake spotted a woman behind the bar. Just as he was about to go over a group of tourists stumbled in, their large rucksacks thumping against the door. He slumped back down.

'How about you?' Crane asked.

'I'm only sorry I couldn't save Darius. After all he'd been through.'

'That's your emotional response. You're still trying to save Zelda.' Crane saw the look on Drake's face and raised a hand in apology. 'Sorry, but he did kill that young man, remember? He was no angel.'

'There are no angels or demons,' said Drake. 'Just a lot of people struggling between good and evil.'

'Amen to that.'

'There are still a few loose ends.' Drake traced a fingernail over the scarred surface of the table. 'Darius wanted to avenge his mother, I get that. He followed them back to London, to Southall. He took his time, got a job at the meat plant and then found out where the head was being kept.'

'Why was it being stored? I mean, wasn't that risky?'

'I'm guessing it was insurance. The men who got rid of the body didn't trust their partner.'

'The one who killed her.'

'She had to know her killer. It was someone she trusted.'

'Darius thought it was you. That's why he put the head on the train with your blood and the newspaper article. But why. Why did he think it was you?'

Drake lifted his eyes from the table. 'Because he'd seen me with the killer.'

Crane leaned back. 'You know who it is?'

Drake nodded. 'If it's who I think it is, then there's a problem.'

'Why?'

'Well, for starters, he saved my life.'

Crane took a moment. 'You're talking about the war now.'

In his heart Drake knew it. He'd known it the moment Darius had described the man he'd seen outside Zelda's place in Brighton.

'So what about Khan and Hamid Balushi?'

'They're all part of it. I think it goes even further. Some kind of internal coup that involved taking out Goran. Zelda just got caught up in the middle.'

'Why her?'

'I'm guessing that some of what she knew would have hurt not only Goran but some of his rivals.'

'So where is he now, this person?'

'Brodie? I don't know. He's disappeared.' Drake sighed. 'I've known him for years, Ray.'

'He's a hit man. A hired gun.'

Drake nodded. 'He's been around the world. Africa, the Middle East, South America.'

'Jesus.'

'Yeah, I wouldn't put that past him either.'

'So now what?'

Drake looked at her. 'This is bigger than a case. I mean, this is personal.'

'I'm not sure that's a good thing.'

'I'm still not sure how this relates to Donny. If Brodie was working for him, or for someone else. Despite all his pleas of innocence, at the end of the day it might come back to him.'

'So we go after Donny.'

'You don't just go after someone like Donny. You have to make sure you're three steps ahead of him, always.'

'Okay.'

Drake looked at her. He still wasn't really sure he understood what made her tick. But right now he wouldn't have picked anyone else to have by his side.

'Okay,' he repeated, coming out of his reverie. 'Okay.'

Then he looked back towards the bar. 'What do you have to do to get a drink around here?'

Acknowledgements

By some strange coincidence or constellation of fate this intermediate book in what I think of as the opening Crane and Drake trilogy (written under the sign of Dante's Purgatory), turned out to mark my own transition from one publishing house to another.

So, in order to acknowledge the old and the new, I would like to start by thanking Susie Nicklin at The Indigo Press, along with Alex Spears, Sue Amaradivakara, and Becke Parker.

At my new home, my thanks go to Jamie Byng and everyone I have had the pleasure of working with at Canongate and Severn House: Kate Lyall Grant along with Vicki Rutherford, Leila Cruickshank, Debs Warner, Sara Porter and Aa'Ishah Hawton.

Thanks also to Euan Thorneycroft and his team at A.M. Heath including Jessica Sinyor, Vickie Dillon, Prema Raj and Alexandra McNicoll.

Thanks to everyone for their support and hard work, and apologies to anyone I've managed to leave out.

Finally, a debt is owed to Ellah Wakatama Allfrey, the mystic empress guiding these planetary motions: gratitude and respect.

Acknowledgements

[illegible]